P9-AQD-781

DIAMOND IN THE ROUGH

Patricia Waddell

ZEBRA BOOKS
KENSINGTON PUBLISHING CORP.

http://www.kensingtonbooks.com

To Joan Hammond.
A Friend, a mentor, and
a fan of romance.

One

Cape Town, South Africa
October 1883

"Remember the favor you owe me," Sidney Falk said to the man sitting across the desk.

It was early in the morning and Matthew Quinlan, Quinn to anyone who had known him for more than ten minutes, looked as if he had just crawled out of bed, or hadn't taken the time to go to bed, at least not to sleep. His dark hair was disheveled, his shirt wrinkled, and his jacket completely forgotten. Piercing blue eyes stared over the rim of the coffee mug he was holding in his right hand.

"No," Quinn replied, although he remembered very well. The fact that his friend was reminding him meant the good-mannered solicitor was about to collect the debt. It also meant Quinn wasn't going to like it.

Sidney leaned back in his chair, crossed his hands over

his plump middle, and smiled. "I have a client who's in need of an escort. Since you'll be leaving for Kimberley in a few days, I thought—"

"No." Quinn shook his head. "I don't escort people through bush country. Try the Dutchman—he enjoys traipsing around with a herd of nobles at his heels."

The Dutchman, Hans Van Mier, considered himself a hunter and guide. He made a living taking wealthy aristocrats on safaris, making sure they got their money's worth even if he had to shoot the game himself.

"One Englishwoman doesn't make a herd," Sidney replied casually.

"In that case, it's hell no!" Quinn pushed back his chair and stood up. "I deliver diamonds. Not women."

"That's why you're the perfect escort. You don't have to worry about anyone attacking you, because everyone knows diamonds move from Kimberley to Cape Town, not the other way around. Miss St. John won't be in any danger." Sidney leaned forward, placing his hands on the black blotter covering the top of his desk. "No ones knows the country better than you do. I can't trust someone like Van Mier to see to her welfare. The man isn't reliable. While on the other hand, everyone knows that you're impeccably honest and extremely trustworthy."

"Flattery won't get you anywhere."

Quinn walked to the window overlooking Queen Victoria Boulevard with its impressive homes and elite shops. He'd come to Cape Town when he was fifteen after hearing about the twenty-one-carat diamond that had been found in a dry creek bed. Hell, the whole world had heard the news. The mines were just opening, and everyone thought they could scoop up a fortune with their bare hands, including Quinn. He'd been a rawboned kid from the East End looking for fame and fortune. Within weeks, he'd found it, working on a jackal crew. Jackal was the local term for the men who guarded the diamonds once they'd been taken out of the mines.

His first trek through the barren bush country that separated Cape Town from the Kimberley mines had been an eye-opening experience. Halfway between the rough mining town and the port city where the diamonds would be transferred into the hands of a broker before being shipped north to Europe, they'd walked into an ambush. Quinn had survived, but only because life in the East End had taught him to run as well as fight. When he'd finally stopped running, he was still carrying a bag of diamonds. Suddenly as rich as Midas, and knowing the mine owners would be after him with bloodhounds if he tried to cash in the loot, he'd decided to deliver the gems to the broker instead. That miraculous moment of maturity had established his still-sterling reputation. He was a man who could be trusted. A man who kept his word.

Now Quinn worked as a jackal for De Beers Consolidated Mines. If Cecil John Rhodes, the self-appointed monarch of the industry, could trust a hellion from the East End, anyone could.

But even an honest man had his faults, and Quinn had more than his share. He might live in a lavish home and mix with the crème de la crème of Cape Town society, but underneath the expensive veneer of tailored suits and exclusive club memberships, he was still a hard-knuckled street kid. He lived on the edge, loving the danger as much as he'd come to love the wildness of Africa itself. He enjoyed whiskey, any time of the day or night, and there was nothing more rousing than a good game of cards when the stakes were high. Women were a lusty pleasure he enjoyed whenever the opportunity presented itself. Whatever respectability he had came from his association with De Beers's diamonds.

Beyond the civilized walls of Cape Town, he was known for being a man who did his job too well for most thieves to consider pilfering a pouch of diamonds. If they were foolish enough to underestimate him, they usually paid with their lives.

Quinn had prospered in South Africa, not because fate had favored him, but because the slums of London had taught him how to fight and win.

"What business does this client of yours have in Kimberley?" Quinn asked, knowing how relentless Sidney could be when he wanted something.

"She's inherited some property."

"A mine?"

"A boardinghouse."

"There aren't any boardinghouses in Kimberley fit to inherit."

"Since I haven't seen the prospering town for several years, I'll take your word for it," Sidney responded. "However, Miss St. John has come into property and she intends to claim it."

Quinn went from looking skeptical to looking downright hostile. "You want me to *escort* an English *lady* through the middle of bush country to claim a boardinghouse that's probably a whorehouse."

Sidney shrugged his shoulders. "Her uncle, a former client, willed her the land and buildings. She's determined to take possession of her inheritance and assume her rightful place as the new proprietor." A short sigh escaped him. "I did my best to explain that it would probably be more profitable for her to sell the business, but my advice wasn't heeded. Instead of responding to my letter, she sailed from Portsmouth to Cape Town, arriving yesterday. She's a very insistent lady. I fear she's going to Kimberley with or without an escort."

After diamonds were discovered, Kimberley had literally sprung up overnight. The rough and tumble shantytown was constructed from corrugated iron and whatever building products the influx of miners could find in the barren countryside that surrounded the settlement. Better now that Cecil John Rhodes and Barney Barnato had organized the mines, the town was still a raw settlement compared to the cities that flourished along the Atlantic coastline.

Fortune seekers had rushed to the diggings. Even now, crooks and scoundrels mixed with thousands of honest men, each hoping for a big find, a diamond the size of a fist that would keep them in luxury for their rest of the lives. The men worked hard, gambled hard, and drank hard. Whores, and the brothels that housed them, were commonplace. The upper crust of Kimberley society, the elite few who controlled the mines, lived in grand houses on the outskirts of town with walled gardens to keep their privileged world intact.

Quinn hated walls. It didn't matter if they were built of wood, brick, or whitewashed sandstone like the ones that surrounded the luxurious homes of Cecil Rhodes and Barney Barnato, he still hated them.

He'd grown up with walls, towering alleyways where he'd hidden after stealing a loaf of bread off a vendor's wagon, narrow muck-filled passages that never saw the light of day because even the brilliance of a summer sun couldn't penetrate the smoky, stench-ridden lanes of the East End.

He supposed that's why he loved Africa, or at least the bush country. He could breathe free in the untamed country that was so wide, so spacious, a man could look from horizon to horizon and never see anything but shrub grass and endless blue sky.

"Since, Olivia St. John is now my client, I can't in all good conscience allow her to travel alone," Sidney explained. "The railroad will only take her as far as Calvinia, after that—"

"There's nothing but wilderness until she reaches Prieska and the railroad picks up again," Quinn said for him. "Between the two she's liable to end up dead."

"Exactly," Sidney said, letting his friend's conscience take over.

There was a long silence while Quinn stared out the window, knowing damn well that Sidney wasn't going to let him off the hook.

"Tell me about the insistent Miss St. John," he finally said.

Sidney's smile went from ear to ear. "She resigned from her position as a governess to come to Cape Town. The uncle, a gentleman by the name of Benjamin St. John, insisted she was the only member of his family worth leaving anything to. Seems the lady corresponded with him at least twice a year, mailing the letters so they arrived on or near his birthday and Boxing Day. I wrote the will myself, at his insistence. He bequeathed her all his worldly goods."

Quinn wondered just how worldly those goods were. He doubted if there was anything in Kimberley a spinster governess would consider valuable once she'd seen it. He could easily imagine a pale hand moving to the prim and proper bodice of her high-necked dress just before she fainted dead away. Kimberley had that affect on women, especially women who didn't have the slightest idea what a mining town was really like once the glitter of diamonds evaporated and reality took its place.

He turned around, glaring at the solicitor. "I bet she balks the minute we get to Calvinia. After a look at what's in front of her, she'll gather up her skirts and put her bustle back on the train faster than I can uncork a bottle of whiskey."

Knowing Quinn's fondness for Irish spirits, Sidney was

tempted to accept the wager. But having met the resolute Miss St. John, he hesitated. The odds were fifty-fifty. Either way, his client would reach her destination with more surety than any other man in South Africa could offer her. Quinn wasn't just the best jackal in the business, he was the best bushman to be found, excluding the San natives who had inhabited the Cape Peninsula for countless generations.

Whether or not Miss St. John reversed her path when she reached Calvinia or went on to Kimberley, Sidney had done his best to guarantee the lady's safety.

"Where is she?" Quinn asked, clearly irritated that he hadn't found a way out of the corner his friend had so skillfully painted.

"At the Krotter Hotel."

Quinn looked down at scuffed boots. He'd spent the night gambling in one of the city's best establishments. Before he met a lady, any lady, he needed a hot meal, a bath, and a good stiff drink, not necessarily in that order. "Send a note," he said. "I'll meet her in the lobby at eight this evening. If I can't talk her out of going to Kimberley, and I can be *very* persuasive when it comes to women, we'll leave the day after tomorrow."

"Excellent," Sidney said, standing up and offering his hand.

Quinn shook it, then stomped toward the door. He hesitated as his lean fingers wrapped around the brass knob. He glanced over his shoulder, giving the solicitor a lethal stare. "Once I get her to Kimberley, she stops being *my* problem. Agreed?"

"Of course," his friend concurred.

With that, Quinn opened the door and stepped outside into the tranquil sunshine of a South African morning. Being at the bottom of the world meant the seasons were topsy-turvy. England was preparing for winter, but here in Cape Town, summer was just beginning to blossom.

On his way to the house on Waterkant Street, a stylish residence he'd purchased three years earlier, Quinn questioned his sanity at letting Sidney Falk trick him into taking a white woman into the bush. Africa wasn't for the faint of heart. There were things in the Great Karoo, the name given to the uninhabited stretch of land that had to be crossed before reaching Kimberley, that could make a grown man wish he'd stayed tucked up nice and tight at home.

Standing on the balcony of the Krotter Hotel, a fashionable establishment near St. George's Mall, Olivia St. John looked toward the aquamarine waters of Table Bay. The city of Cape Town clutched the coastline, curving around the bay to the north and south. Behind it the exhilarating sandstone sentinel, Table Mountain, loomed tall and barren and majestically foreboding.

She'd read about the city and the sprawling province of South Africa, but nothing had prepared her for what lay before her eyes. The calm waters of the bay mixed with the colder currents of the Atlantic while seagulls soared overhead, chattering before they swooped down to pluck a fish from the majestic waters. Awed by the natural beauty of the rugged landscape, Olivia let her gaze move slowly along the shoreline where rivulets of tiny waves washed onto white sandy beaches. The harbor was filled with ships, ocean steamers from England and France and Germany. Flags from all over the world fluttered in the brisk breeze, while the smoke from the ships' tall stacks drifted south toward the lighthouse at Sea Point.

The perfume of exotic flowers mixed with the earthy odor of jungle foliage and the scent of salt air. The streets were a musical buzz of foreign tongues, the people a blaze of color. Some were dressed in European fashions, either purchased in the local shops or imported from London and Paris, while others wore lighter linen suits, better suited to the climate. The dark-skinned natives wore almost nothing at all, especially the men. They walked along the streets in loose-fitting trousers gathered about the waist with a drawstring, their ebony chests gleaming with sweat as they loaded and unloaded luggage in front of the hotel. The native women wore material draped around their bodies, covering one shoulder before it wrapped around them like a large towel, ending midway between their knees and ankles. Very few of them wore shoes.

Olivia studied the strange mixture of people and European architecture, the towering steeples of the Dutch Reformed Church, the gothic silhouettes of English cathedrals, and the clapboard buildings that fronted the harbor. Closer to the hotel, she could see the tiled rooftops of the prestigious government buildings along Parliament Street.

She could scarce believe that the adventure of the ocean voyage had ended only to have another, more daring exploit, begin. When she'd received word that her uncle had died, leaving her his South African property, she'd been stunned. Her family had thought her impulsive in her decision to abandon her post as a governess, pleading that she reconsider before purchasing the ticket that would take her so far away from the comforts of Portsmouth. Her older sister, Meredith, had recently married and had advised her sibling against making a hasty decision that would in all probability be laced with regret. But Olivia hadn't heeded the advise of her well-meaning family and friends. Instead, she'd purchased the steamer ticket, packed her belongings, and said her farewells. Teary-eyed, but determined, she'd left Portsmouth behind.

She had survived her twenty-sixth birthday dinner, a boring event attended by half a dozen people, to realize that she dreaded the next one. As much as she loved her family, and teaching, she hated falling asleep at night with nothing more than the tales of a notorious novel to fuel her dreams. She wasn't classically beautiful, and she certainly wasn't rich enough to encourage a marriage proposal on her financial merits, but she did have a quick mind and a deep yearning to experience life.

It was that yearning, that indefinable craving for something Portsmouth couldn't offer, that had prompted her to come to South Africa to claim her inheritance. Reaching into the pocket of her gray skirt, she withdrew a token of her uncle Benjamin's affection. The small wooden lion had become the symbol of her dreams. Holding the tiny teakwood animal in the palm of her hand, she looked with hopeful eyes toward the horizon.

She might not find the man of her dreams in South Africa, but she would surely find the adventure she craved. Either way, she was going to make the best of her newfound liberty.

The chime of a tower clock somewhere in the city brought Olivia's reverie to an end. She was to meet Mr. Quinlan in the lobby of the hotel before the clock chimed the next hour. Mr. Falk had penned a note of reference, informing her that his friend had agreed to escort her to Kimberley. The solicitor had assured her that Mr. Quinlan was a man of faultless integrity, one she could trust without reservation or hesitation.

Eager to begin the final steps of her journey, Olivia returned to her room. Exactly one hour later, punctuality being one of her greatest virtues, she was waiting in the lobby. It was empty, except for the desk clerk, a middle-aged gentleman with a cadaverous face and spectacles perched on the brim of his hawkish, blue-veined nose.

She asked the man if anyone had inquired about her. Receiving a negative reply, she looked around the lobby a second time. Noting the entrance to both the dining room and a small reading parlor, she hesitated.

"If you would care to wait in the garden," the clerk suggested, "I will send your guest there upon his arrival. The weather is very pleasant this evening."

"Thank you," she replied. "I shall wait in the garden."

Olivia walked across the tiled floor, hoping Mr. Quinlan didn't keep her waiting too long. She hadn't eaten since that morning, too excited about the upcoming trip to Kimberley and the possibilities of owning and managing her own business to think about food.

The garden was a pleasant surprise. Surrounded on three sides by the hotel itself, the western boundary was fenced by thick foliage, expertly manicured into a tall green wall that offered the hotel guests privacy. The garden was embellished by wrought iron benches, painted a pristine white, and positioned at spacious intervals along a cobblestone path that led to a large fountain where a sculptured elephant stood high on its hind legs with its trunk curled against its forehead. Dark glossy ferns grew in clusters alongside the walkway, joined by small patches of brightly colored flowers and low-lying shrubs with prickly tips.

The fragrance of grass, recently dampened by the dew, made the air smell sweet as Olivia strolled along the cobblestone path, stopping every few feet to inspect graceful tiger lilies and clumps of blue flax. Ashen clouds, drained of their color by the setting sun, floated slowly across the star-studded sky and large glowing moon. In the distance, the sound of the sea made the night seem almost magical.

Selecting the bench nearest the fountain, Olivia sat down to contemplate the first day of her new life. The voyage from Portsmouth had been pleasant. She'd been guilt ridden at first, knowing her family couldn't comprehend her motives for dashing off and leaving what they considered a well-ordered life, but eventually her adventurous spirit had taken her to the steamer's railing for hours at a time. She'd stared at the sea, enjoying the ever-changing shades of the water as the ship had pushed south.

Now that she was in Africa, there was more to consider than the vague possibilities of dreams come true. The whimsical thoughts that had entertained her during the voyage had suddenly become reality. Looking at the fountain and thinking of the small wooden lion in her pocket, Olivia knew she was just as likely to encounter one of those animals as she was an alley cat. The thought held as much excitement as it did trepidation. Although she wanted what other women wanted, a husband and a family, she was willing to teeter on the brink of spinsterhood a while longer.

Quinn stood at the entrance to the garden. He stared at the woman and frowned. Damn Falk and his cunning manners. The solicitor hadn't given him the slightest clue that the lady was young and pleasing to the eye. Very pleasing if a man considered the wispy honey-brown curls framing her face, the delicate angle of her chin, and the subtle curves of her body. Dressed in a blue skirt, a high-collared white blouse, and a waist-length embroidered jacket, she was a perfect example of British femininity.

Unfortunately, he'd been expecting a spinster with a sagging bosom and gray hair, not an English nymph washed in moonlight.

Quinn didn't like surprises, and Miss St. John was certainly a surprise.

Surprises could get a man killed in the bush country. They could get a diamond shipment stolen in less time that it took to reload the bolt-action Mauser rifle he carried whenever he left the city. Surprises were for children, not for men who earned their living making sure the unexpected was always expected.

Drawn by the noise of boot heels on cobblestone, Olivia looked toward the hotel door. The man materialized out of the shadows like a dark god emerging from the underworld. Tall and lean and powerfully built, he wasn't at all like the gentleman she'd expected to meet. A man of distinction should be much older, and he certainly shouldn't make a woman's heart quicken with nothing more than a cursory glance.

"Miss St. John?"

Inwardly appalled by her reaction to the stranger, Olivia came to her feet. The man towered above her, his raven hair absorbing the moonlight, his blue eyes blazing as they raked over her, moving slowly from the hem of her skirt to the top of her head, then lowering until he was staring at her mouth. His countenance was stern, and she didn't have a clue as to what he was thinking, or why he was thinking it.

Quickly regaining the courage that had brought her to South Africa to begin with, she offered the man a cordial smile. "Mr. Quinlan?" she asked, hoping against hope that the man wasn't the one Sidney Falk had written her about.

"Quinn," he corrected her. "We aren't as formal here as they are in England."

He continued studying her, taking in the narrow expanse of her waist and the finishing school posture that made her seem taller than her five foot two inches. Her expression wasn't hard to decipher. It was a combination of anticipation and apprehension, a natural reaction to being alone and thousands of miles from home. Quinn knew he shouldn't be staring. It wasn't polite, but that didn't particularly bother him at the moment. He was still assimilating the fact that he'd been duped into taking a young, desirable woman where no young, desirable woman should be going.

Strange, unnamed feelings sprang to life as Olivia looked up at Matthew Quinlan. He was wearing formal evening attire. A diamond stickpin winked wickedly in the moonlight, but it was his walking stick that caught her interest. Made of ebony wood, the head was carved into the threatening face of a jackal. Two diamond eyes gleamed in the silvery light as he set the cane aside and withdrew a slim cheroot from the inside pocket of his dinner jacket.

Gentlemen rarely smoked without asking a lady's permission first, but Olivia knew Matthew Quinlan wasn't your typical gentleman. Any man who made a living guarding priceless jewels would have to be as ruthless and cunning as the thieves who would gladly rob him blind. He would also have to be, as Sidney Falk's note had decreed, an honest man.

The conclusion offered Olivia some comfort as she watched him strike a match. The tip of the slender cigar glowed red, then gold, in the increasing darkness.

"Please, sit down," Quinn said. "I've requested a table, but it will be a few minutes before it's ready. In the meantime, we can talk about Kimberley."

As Olivia resumed her seat on the bench, the tingling sensation she'd felt when Quinn had stepped out of the shadows was replaced by a more vivid awareness of the man. He was in his early thirties. His remarkably handsome face was tanned by the African sun, emphasizing the brilliance of his eyes. Dressed like a gentleman, there was still an untamed quality about him, one that made Olivia think of the wild animals that lived beyond the perimeters of Cape Town.

"Mr. Falk told me that you travel between Cape Town and Kimberley on a regular basis," she said, intending to keep the conversation focused on the business at hand. "He assured me that I would be in capable hands."

The thoughts of actually getting his hands on Miss St. John was enough to make Quinn's mouth water, but he'd trained himself too well to ever let his expression reveal his true thoughts.

"It's what I do," he replied simply, knowing that Falk had explained the details of his occupation.

"When do you anticipate returning to Kimberley?" Olivia asked, acutely aware that Mr. Quinlan was studying her far too closely. She waited for the answer as he blew out a ring of pale smoke that drifted slowly over his shoulder then out of sight.

"The day after tomorrow," he replied. "Can you be ready to travel that quickly?"

"I've only unpacked one trunk."

Before Quinn could tell her that the trunks would have to be loaded aboard a railroad car, then unloaded at Clavinia and reloaded onto cumbersome ox carts, a hotel employee appeared to tell them that their table was ready.

"Shall we?" Quinn said, stepping aside and giving her full access to the cobblestone path that led to the hotel's main lobby.

Olivia walked in front of him, consumed by curiosity. She'd never met a man like Matthew Quinlan before. He was confident, bordering on arrogant, if her instincts were right, but at the same time she sensed there was more to him than he wanted people to know. As she entered the hotel with its bright gaslights and polished brass trimmings, she realized she was being foolish. The moonlight had clouded her mind, tricking her into thinking that he might find her attractive. His intense gaze had probably been nothing more than the bad manners he'd displayed in lighting a cigar without first requesting if it might offend her.

Quinn questioned his sanity for the second time in one day. Taking any woman into the bush was folly. Taking a young pretty woman was pure foolishness. Yet, he had little choice. He'd given Sidney his word, which meant he'd keep it. His only recourse was to persuade the lady to change her mind.

Plotting how he'd do it, Quinn followed as the restaurant's maître d' showed them to a small table in the rear of the dining room. Once they were seated, he ordered a bottle of the hotel's best champagne.

"Sidney told me that you recently inherited some property in Kimberley."

"Yes." Olivia's eyes gleamed with enthusiasm. "My uncle came to Africa a good many years ago. He was my father's younger brother, and from what I've been told, a bit of an adventurer at heart. He kept in touch with the family, but after my father's health began to fail, his letters went unanswered, until I wrote him myself. We began to correspond on a regular basis. I would send him copies of the Portsmouth newspapers. He'd write to me about Africa. I couldn't wait to see it with my own eyes."

And what beautiful eyes they were, Quinn thought. The dining room was ablaze with light, so he could see their true color, a deep rich brown. Miss St. John was a gentle-born lady, obviously well educated, and obviously as innocent as the day she'd been born. Everything about her suggested that she was a real lady, a lady who thought only pure thoughts, who always behaved properly and dressed properly. Imagining her in the African wilderness that had become his second home was as difficult as imagining himself standing behind a church pulpit.

"Have you been in South Africa long, Mr. Quinlan?" The effort it took to make casual conversation surprised Olivia. Normally she didn't have trouble talking to people, but Matthew Quinlan wasn't just anyone. He was the most handsome man in the room.

"Quinn," he corrected her, not answering her question until the waiter finished filling their wine glasses. "I've been in Africa for over fifteen years."

"And your family?" Olivia prompted, still curious.

He shook his head instead of replying.

"What of your family, Miss St. John? Were they as fervent in their good wishes as you are in your enthusiasm to reach Kimberley?"

"Not exactly."

"Would you care to explain what 'not exactly' means?"

Olivia sighed under her breath. "It means they think me impulsively foolish and sure to fail in my endeavors," she said candidly.

"And what are your endeavors?"

"To assume responsibility for my inheritance, of course. The prospect of running my own business is quite exhilarating."

Quinn stopped himself before he mentioned that exhilarating might be an understatement. There were ten times as many brothels in Kimberley as there was boardinghouses. He reminded himself that all he had agreed to do was to get the lady from Cape Town to Kimberley, anything beyond that wasn't his business.

There was a stiff silence while Olivia searched her mind for something else to say. What did a lady ask of a man she'd just met, the man who would soon be escorting her to a town she knew nothing about? Thinking she might appease some of her curiosity, she inquired how long the trip would take.

"Three, maybe four weeks," Quinn replied, lengthening the time because there was no way a lady was going to be able to maintain the pace he normally set.

"That long," she sighed, clearly disappointed. "But, I thought the railroad—"

"The railroad runs north to Calvinia," he told her. "Then it takes a turn east, toward Bitterfontein and Alexander Bay. That's the opposite direction of where we'll be going. Kimberley sits north of the Orange River. They finished the bridge a few months ago, so the trains run from the mines to Prieska. Connecting Clavinia to Prieska is going to take at least two more years.

"We'll be traveling by foot most of the way," he added, thinking he'd found the path to her discouragement.

"You mean we'll be *walking* to Kimberley!"

"There'll be an ox cart to haul your belongings," he explained. "You can ride in the cart when you get tired."

"Are there no roads?" she asked. "Horses? I can ride. My father taught me."

"Horses don't do well in the bush," Quinn explained. "They get skittish around wild animals. It's a long ride from here to Kimberley, and horses make a tempting meal for a hungry lion."

Unsure if the man was teasing her, Olivia wasn't certain how to react. Her uncle had written her about the bush country, describing its magnificent sunsets and awe-inspiring isolation, but she'd never imagined having to cross it on foot. She supposed she should have asked Mr. Falk to explain things more clearly, but she'd been so excited by the very idea of the trip she hadn't asked.

Quinn sipped his champagne, waiting for her to come to terms with the cold, hard facts of South African life.

"I'll need some comfortable walking shoes," Olivia announced unexpectedly. "Can you recommend a shop where I can purchase them, along with anything else my wardrobe may be lacking?"

Two

What the woman was lacking was good common sense, Quinn decided, as he put down his wine glass and picked up the menu. Of course the evening was still young, and he hadn't told her about the scorpions, snakes, and countless insects that infested the grassy plateau they'd be crossing mile by weary mile. If that didn't do it, he was sure the prospect of not being able to bathe for days at a time would insult her delicate sensibilities enough to make her think twice.

"I've been told the Kimberley Hole is a sight to see," Olivia said, letting her natural curiosity take control again. "Mr. Averon, a gentleman I met on board the steamer, told me that it's the largest hole ever dug by man."

"Try several thousand men," Quinn replied. "And yes, it's big."

Men had died digging diamonds out of the ground, some had drowned, caught by the torrential rainstorms that could sweep across the peninsula without warning. The Kimberley Hole was both grave and glory, a challenge and a curse. There was no point trying to describe it. It had to be seen to be appreciated.

"What of the city, itself?" she asked after Quinn motioned for the waiter to return, then gave him their order, requesting the hotel's specialty, roasted lamb served with rice and spiced vegetables.

"Kimberley isn't a city, it's a mining town," Quinn said, wondering just how much Benjamin St. John had divulged in his letters. "Diamonds are the only reason it exists," he continued. "The interior of South Africa isn't all that hospitable. Once the diamonds are mined out, if they're mined out, the town will disappear as quickly as it appeared."

"What of the families?"

"Without the mines there isn't any reason to live there. It's in the middle of nowhere."

"I understand."

"I doubt that, " Quinn retorted. "Things in Africa are rarely what they seem to be. It's a beautiful country, but it's also brutal."

"Are you trying to dissuade me from making the trip?" she asked as the waiter approached the table, bringing their meal. "Because if you are, sir, I must tell you that I'm determined to reach Kimberley."

"Sidney mentioned that you were insistent," he said, wondering how quickly that insistence would fade once she realized what getting to Kimberley involved. "As for attempting to dissuade you, on the contrary, I find your dedication admirable. Despite its brutal charm, this country has a lot of opportunities. I assume that's what brought you this far."

"You're correct in that assumption, Mr. Quinlan. I'm

looking forward to taking over the business my uncle left me. Humble though it may be, it does offer me the opportunity to determine my own fate.''

So that was it. The lady had romantic notions about fate and destiny. No doubt she also thought men were motivated by honor and decency. Quinn knew better. The years he'd spent hustling diamonds and avoiding bullets had tarnished his opinion of the human race. He didn't have any grand illusions about what Olivia was going to find once she reached her destination, and he certainly didn't have any false hopes that she'd end up living happily ever after. Kimberley wasn't an easy place to live for men or women. Simple day-to-day life would demand things Miss St. John couldn't even imagine.

Quinn knew that if left to her own devices, the lady would find herself knee-deep in trouble. It was going to take more than talk to bring her to her senses. He could spend hours describing the hardships she was about to face, but with no understanding of the real danger, she'd see only the romance of an adventure into the unknown.

The meal continued with Quinn explaining where and when diamonds had originally been discovered in South Africa. He told Olivia that the first diamond was found accidentally by a young boy. Later, it was seen at the home of a Dutch farmer named Jacobs, south of the Orange River. Thinking it was brighter and heavier than other stones, a man by the name of Van Niekrek offered to buy it. The child's mother wouldn't sell such a insufficient thing as a glimmering stone and gave it to him, instead. From Van Niekerk it was passed to a man by the name of O'Reilly, who was the first to imagine it a diamond. After a thorough examination by Dr. Athestone, of Grahamstown, all doubts faded. The stone was declared an authentic diamond, and the rush to the inland of the Cape Peninsula began.

Olivia listened in amazement, enjoying the story as much as the rich tones of Quinn's voice. Another story followed, that of the "Star of South Africa." The same Van Niekerk, fired by his success in obtaining the first diamond, sought and found one that was in the possession of a tribal witch doctor. The stone weighed eighty-three carats and was claimed to be perfect in its shape and brightness. Eventually it was sold to adorn the neck of a British countess.

While Quinn spoke, he thought of all the ways he might be able to change the path Miss St. John seemed so determined to walk. Although she didn't appear to be overly pampered, she was still young and naïve. She was also very tempting. The longer he sat at the table, watching the way she licked her lips after taking a sip of champagne, the more he realized he'd be a fool to take her into the bush, where she'd be within reach for weeks on end. Sooner or later his good intentions would vanish, and he'd end up doing something foolish, like kissing her.

The meal ended with small chunks of local fruit served with chopped nuts and cream. Quinn laid his napkin aside, then stood. "Would you care for a walk in the garden before retiring?"

Enthralled by the stories he'd told her, Olivia smiled. "Thank you."

He escorted her outside. The moon was still shining brightly, illuminating the small courtyard with soft pale light. They walked for a while, not speaking.

Olivia was thinking of the reasonable clothing she'd have to purchase the next day, hoping she wouldn't diminish her funds too drastically. She'd need the small amount of money she'd saved over the years to repair the damage the months of abandonment had no doubt brought upon the boardinghouse.

Quinn slowed his pace, coming to a stop beyond the fountain, near the tall podocarpus bushes that had been trimmed to create a flat floral wall. The moonlight, suddenly dimmed by a blanket of wispy clouds, still gave enough light for him to see Olivia's face. She was looking up at the sky with wide, optimistic eyes. Quinn frowned. Since gentle persuasion hadn't worked, maybe some cold, hard facts would do the job.

"Are you absolutely certain you want to do this?" he asked, causing her head to turn.

"Yes."

"I wasn't exaggerating when I said we'd be walking most of the way." Quinn focused his steely gaze on her. "I've seen a lion rip out the throat of a stallion easier than a knife slices through warm butter. Even if we don't see any lions, we're going to see other animals. Jackals, hyenas, baboons. None of them are friendly."

Olivia let out a short, frustrated sigh. "I'm not a child, Mr. Quinlan, so don't try to frighten me. Nor, am I impervious to the dangers we'll be facing."

"We'll be sleeping on the ground," he told her. "This isn't a safari. We won't be traveling with two dozen natives, loaded down with tents and all the things you're accustomed to having at your fingertips. The only way to cross the bush country safely is to cross it fast."

Olivia looked at the man who had been such a charming dinner partner. Standing in the darkness, he suddenly looked as dangerous as the land he was describing. Yet, she sensed that she'd be safe with him. Despite his bluntness, Quinn's decency shone through. He was also handsome, dangerously compelling, and totally irresistible. His unusual masculine charms and their ability to make her very much aware that she was a woman might be disconcerting, but they weren't reason enough for her to change her mind.

"I have to go to Kimberley," she replied. "Please don't ask me to expound on my reasons. I'm sure they would sound trivial to a man like you. Nothing you have said, or can say, will change my mind.''

''You're not insistent, you're stubborn.''

''My father said the very same thing when I told him that I'd booked passage to Cape Town,'' Olivia replied, remembering the conversation all too well. ''He spent several hours warning me about the dangers a young woman might encounter along the way. Yet, I arrived safe and unharmed. Actually, the voyage was extremely pleasant.'' She held up her hand when Quinn started to interrupt her. ''I'm aware that the trip to Kimberley will be far more treacherous.''

''Treacherous doesn't begin to describe what could happen,'' Quinn said tightly.

''I'm not afraid,'' Olivia said. She was nervous (what woman wouldn't be) but she wasn't frightened. ''My future is in Kimberley.''

''What if the future isn't all you hope it is?'' he asked roughly. ''You might have inherited a boardinghouse, but what about the hard work it's going to take to open the doors again? To keep them open?''

''I'm not expecting miracles,'' she replied crisply. ''And I'm not totally lacking in common sense, sir. Whatever needs to be done, I'll do.''

''When we make camp you'll be expected to do your share of work,'' he bristled, sensing as he had that morning in Sidney's office that he was fighting a losing battle.

''I have no intention of being a burden,'' Olivia replied with stiff politeness.

Quinn drew in a deep breath, then released it. ''Be sure and write your family tonight. It will be the last letter you'll post for a while.''

Olivia couldn't suppress her triumphant smile. ''When do we leave?''

"The day after tomorrow," Quinn relented, clearly disappointed that he hadn't been able to dishearten her. "Meet me at the depot at ten. The train for Calvinia leaves at eleven."

"I'll be there," Olivia assured him.

Quinn stepped aside, clearing the way for her to return to the hotel.

Olivia hesitated, unsure how to thank him. It was apparent that he wasn't overjoyed by the prospect of escorting her to Kimberley. Deciding a man of blunt words would want the same in return, she looked up at him. "Thank you."

"Don't thank me yet," Quinn told her. His tone clearly said she was going to regret the words along with her decision.

"Then, I shall simply bid you good night." Gathering up the full folds of her skirt, Olivia walked toward the hotel.

Quinn watched her until she disappeared inside, frowning the entire time. The lady had backbone, he'd give her that. She might even have enough backbone to make a go of it in Kimberley, once he got her there. It was the getting her there that had him frowning. Truthful to a fault, because he wanted people to be the same in return, Quinn had to admit that he was going to have one hell of a time remembering that young ladies like Miss Olivia St. John were for marrying.

Marriage was the last thing Quinn wanted or needed. Every time he picked up a shipment of diamonds, his chances of being shot, knifed, speared, or poisoned increased tenfold. The women who weren't affected by the prospect of becoming a widow were the ones who were more interested in his money than his affection. That left women like the one he'd arranged to meet later in the evening. Anna Heerengracht was the merry widow of a Dutch businessman, who liked her lovers to linger all night. Considering the surprises he'd had today, her preferences suited Quinn's current mood just fine

Olivia retired to her room. As she undressed and prepared for bed, her mind swirled with the images Quinn had painted with his blunt words. She told herself he was simply trying to do the same thing her father and Sidney Falk had tried, to dispirit her into deciding that she'd be better off at home.

Some time later, unable to sleep and finding no solace in the volume of poetry she'd taken to bed with her, Olivia stood on the balcony. She stared into the African night, hearing the sweet song of night birds and smelling the exotic fragrance of wild orchids. No amount of adventure could eliminate the pragmatic side of her nature, the side that repeatedly told her to give the sonnets her full attention, letting thoughts of Matthew Quinlan fade into nothingness. No good could come of her being attracted to the man, and her heart would show no profit if she allowed it to be broken.

And Quinn was most definitely a breaker of hearts. It showed in his sapphire eyes and in the arrogant way he smiled. Knowing she'd be better off to concentrate on her inheritance and leave the adventure of romance for another time, Olivia couldn't help but wonder why the enigmatic Mr. Quinlan had agreed to escort her in the first place.

Three

Sidney Falk was waiting at the train station. Olivia was pleased to see the solicitor. He was a stout man in his late forties. Dressed in a stylish suit and starched white shirt, he was far from handsome. Underneath his tanned skin, his features were small and pouched, his nose too wide, his chin too rounded. But he was a pleasing sort, with a calm voice, and a gentlemanly manner, and Oliver was delighted that he'd come to say farewell.

"Miss St. John," he greeted her, taking off his hat.

"Mr. Falk," she replied, wondering where Quinn might be.

"He'll be along, never worry," Sidney assured her as if reading her thoughts. A smile brightened his face. "I see his efforts to convince you to return to England were as fruitless as mine."

It was Olivia's turn to smile. "His effort was a valiant one," she admitted, "but, I'm still going to Kimberley. As you can see.'' She pointed to the trunks that were being loaded onto the train.

''Then, I wish you a safe journey and much success once you reach your destination.''

''Thank you.''

Before she could engage the solicitor in further conversation, Quinn appeared. Dressed like a country squire about to take a leisurely ride across his estates, the man still had the power to hold Olivia's attention. He frowned at her, clearly disappointed that she hadn't changed her mind and was still intent on beginning the most dangerous journey of her life.

''Sidney,'' Quinn said, blatantly rude in not acknowledging Olivia's presence.

''Ignoring me won't make me disappear,'' she said pleasantly.

Sidney Falk laughed out loud. ''This ought to be an interesting trip.''

Still frowning, Quinn turned his blistering blue eyes on Olivia. He let out a long breath as his gaze moved slowly downward to where the toes of two black shoes peered out from beneath the hem of her traveling suit. ''Did you buy a pair of walking boots?''

''I purchased two pairs,'' Olivia replied, her tone not as pleasant as before. ''Don't worry, Mr. Quinlan, my wardrobe won't be a hindrance. I realize that you want to reach Kimberley as quickly as possible.''

Instead of replying, Quinn took Sidney by the arm and led him away, not stopping until they'd reached a distance that prohibited Olivia from overhearing what was being said.

''You're being rude again,'' Sidney censured him.

''You didn't tell me she was young and pretty.''

''It must have slipped my mind.''

''I ought to slit your throat,'' Quinn said acidly. ''What

in the hell were you thinking? That girl doesn't belong in Kimberley any more than I belong in a parlor at Buckingham Palace, sipping tea with the queen.''

The solicitor cleared his throat. ''Now you know why I couldn't trust the Dutchman or anyone like him to escort her.''

''I'm no saint,'' Quinn countered.

''No, you're a sinner with integrity,'' Sidney said, letting a smug grin lighten his expression. ''I trust you, which means, Miss St. John can trust you.''

Quinn wasn't sure he trusted himself. He glared at his friend. ''This is the last favor I'll ever owe you.''

They returned to where Olivia was waiting. The train depot was beginning to throb with people. Tastefully dressed passengers began to board the train, while natives loaded baggage and sacks of supplies into the luggage car. Olivia's nerves sparked with excitement as the locomotive belched thick black smoke into the pale morning sky. Like a small child who had been fed too many sweets, she'd lain away most of the night, her mind racing with endless possibilities. Quinn had never been far from her thoughts, no matter how vigorously she'd tried to think of anything but the diamond jackal. Even now, she was overly conscious of his presence.

''Let's get going,'' he said, once the train whistle had ceased its ear-piercing shriek, announcing its imminent departure.

Olivia nodded, resolved that there'd be no looking back.

''Take care, Miss St. John,'' Sidney Falk said, lifting her hand to place a chaste kiss just above her gloved knuckles. In a lower voice, he added, ''Quinn may be a proverbial pain in the backside most of the time, but I wouldn't entrust you to his care if he wasn't the best man for the job.''

''Thank you for your concern and your friendship,'' Olivia replied.

"I'm at your disposal, if you have any further need of my services."

"I'll keep that in mind," she told him. "And I'll write you once I reach Kimberley."

While the solicitor bid Quinn farewell, Olivia tried not to think of literally being passed from one man's hands into another. She was a very good judge of character, but she wasn't entirely sure of her judgment when it came to Quinn.

"My car is this way," Quinn said, motioning her toward the end of the train.

The car had all the amenities of a moving hotel. The furniture, bolted to the floor for safety, was expensive and extremely tasteful. Green velvet curtains, held open with gold braiding, could be closed at any point along the way, giving the occupants complete privacy. A wood-framed green velvet settee, two matching chairs, a liquor cabinet, an eating table, and a smaller table and chairs for playing cards were among the furnishings. There was a bed, concealed behind a painted silk partition. Olivia was even more surprised to discover that the car had personal facilities. The trek to Kimberley might be primitive, once they left Calvinia, but the initial part of their journey would be taken in lavish comfort.

As she removed her hat and gloves, Olivia realized that the private railroad car was a reflection of Quinn's personal wealth. Silently she wondered how much money the mine owners paid him to risk his life. A substantial amount by the looks of things, she concluded, but what good would it do him if he was killed? Completely baffled by her sudden concern for Quinn's safety, she turned around to find the man staring at her.

"It's very impressive," she said, meaning the private car.

"Make yourself comfortable," Quinn replied with biting politeness.

He shed his jacket, tossing it over the back of one of the chairs circled around the card table, then began rolling up the sleeves of his linen shirt with a jerky motion that said he had work to do and she was keeping him from it.

Feeling suddenly awkward, Olivia made herself comfortable in one of the two plush chairs and stared out the window. The man didn't have to act like she had the plague. How in the world was she going to travel all the way to the Kimberley with him if they couldn't exchange even one pleasant word?

The train gave a jerk as it began to move. Metal wheels rolled slowly over steel tracks as more black smoke billowed and drifted past the windows. Olivia looked toward the door as a tall, dark-skinned man entered the car. He wasn't wearing a shirt under his white jacket, and the trousers stopped several inches short of his ankles. His feet were bare and his head was swathed in a bright red turban. Standing several inches taller than Quinn, his large brown eyes settled on Olivia.

"Echo, this is Miss St. John," Quinn said. "Miss St. John, this is Echo. He's been with me for years. If you need anything, all you have to do is ask."

"Missy John, welcome."

"Miss St. John," Quinn corrected him.

"Missy John," Echo replied, offering his employer a flashing white-toothed smile.

Quinn made a strange grunting sound then turned to Olivia. "Echo always gets the last word, that's why he's called Echo."

Olivia smiled. "I'm pleased to make your acquaintance."

"I pleased," Echo said. "Missy John, delightful," he added unexpectedly, looking at his employer.

Quinn said something in a language Olivia couldn't understand, although she sensed it was a reprimand aimed at the servant. Echo didn't seem affected. Instead he replied in the same language, a musical blend of grunts and clicks, smiling all the while.

"How long will it take to reach Calvinia?" she asked, not caring which man answered her.

"Two days," Quinn replied too curtly for her to think his mood had lightened. "Echo will bring your meals. There are some books in the storage compartment, if you'd like to pass the time reading. You can open the windows if you need fresh air." Heading for the door, he cautioned her, "Women aren't allowed in the club car."

"I'm sure I'll be comfortable here," she replied, knowing the last place she wanted to be was in a club car crowded with men, drinking whiskey and puffing on cigars. Still, it bristled her pride to be reminded that ladies had limitations.

Without a word or a backward glance, Quinn left the railroad car.

Olivia found herself alone with Echo.

"Would Missy John like lemonade?"

"That would be wonderful," she said. "How long have you worked for Mr. Quinlan?"

"Many years," he replied. "Quinn very good boss man."

"I'm sure he is," she responded. "Do you help him transport diamonds?"

Echo shook his head. "No talk about diamonds."

"I'm sorry," Olivia said, realizing that Quinn would be secretive about the details of his profession. She'd have to find another way to appease her curiosity about the man. And she was curious. More curious than she should be, considering the man was a stranger.

"Missy John not sorry," Echo said, heading for the door and the lemonade he'd offered. "Quinn take good care of his delightful lady."

Olivia blushed to the roots of her hair. Echo was certainly

outspoken for a servant. She glanced out the window, knowing Quinn didn't consider her delightful at all. The man's treatment of her this morning had been more than rude.

Soon, the city of Cape Town was behind her, and Olivia became enthralled by the drastic changes of the widening landscape. The buildings of the city gave way to sweeping fields of tall bush grass. Golden-tipped and waist-high, the grass swayed gently, dancing to the silent music of the wind. The farther they moved into the hinterland of the peninsula, the wider the land seemed to become. Olivia gasped in surprise as a herd of wild animals came into view. There were hundreds of them. The impalas were sleek, deerlike creatures with graceful necks and white bellies. They moved lazily over the thick grass, munching along the way, heedless to the iron machine dissecting their pasture.

When Echo returned with a pitcher of lemonade and a plate of sandwiches, Olivia had to force her eyes away from the window. "They're beautiful," she breathed in awe.

Echo bent down to look at the animals with the same cherished expression Olivia was certain shone in her own brown eyes. "You see many more," he said confidently.

Excited by the prospect, Olivia accepted a glass of lemonade. "Tell me about the bush country," she urged.

"It is big," Echo said, smiling. "And wild with many animals," he continued.

"What's your favorite animal?" she asked, realizing she must sound like an excited child but unable to contain her enthusiasm.

The servant searched his mind a moment before answering. "Giraffe."

"I can't wait to see one," she exclaimed, turning back to the soot-stained window.

Quinn didn't return to the private car until late afternoon. His eyes gleamed with emotions Olivia couldn't name as he poured himself a brandy and sat down in the chair closest to the door. "Echo tells me that you've been staring out the window all day."

"It's so beautiful," she said, unabashed by his rough tone. "I never imagined how endless the land would seem."

"It's even more endless once we get in the karoo," he told her.

"The karoo?"

"It's what the natives call the interior," he explained. "It means 'land of thirst.' "

"Aren't there any rivers?" Olivia asked, grateful that he'd returned to the private car. As mesmerized as she was by the African landscape, it was nice to have someone to talk to.

"They're few and far between," Quinn said. "The Orange River is the longest. It flows into the Atlantic Ocean at Alexander Bay. The Vaal River joins the Orange south of Kimberley. A lot of people wash for diamonds along the banks, but most of the big finds come from digging. Then, there's the Limpopo, it runs from the middle of the peninsula into the Indian Ocean."

An awkward silence filled the car as a dozen unspoken questions formed in Olivia's mind. She wanted to ask Quinn about the natives and the how they lived in a parched land with wild animals all around them, but she didn't. His expression said he wasn't in the mood for conversation. He looked tired, and she suddenly found herself thinking about the one bed the car provided. It was large enough for two people, but of course, that was out of the question. Would her escort sleep in another car? Or was he planning on using the long settee with its buttoned back and plump cushions? The thought of him sleeping so nearby brought a certain peace of mind, followed by a rush of unexplainable feelings Olivia didn't want to decipher at the moment. Wordlessly, she turned to stare out the window once again.

A few moments later her mouth formed a soundless O.

"What is it?" Quinn asked, getting up and moving to where she was seated. He leaned down over her, supporting himself with one hand braced on the back of her chair, the other resting on the wall above the window. "It's an ostrich."

"An ostrich!" Olivia exclaimed. "I never imagined they were so big."

"Big and fast," he told her. "The native children chase them, hoping the birds will spread their wings and some feathers will fall out. They exchange the feathers for candy when the tradesmen come through."

Olivia thought of the brightly dyed ostrich plumes that adorned the fashionable hats and dresses of ladies in England and smiled.

Quinn saw the smile and flinched on the inside. Echo was right. Miss St. John was delightful, especially when she smiled. Her eyes were wide with amazement, forcing him to struggle against the natural urge to kiss her. He backed away from the window, knowing that if he continued to tempt fate it was very likely to kick him in the ass.

As much as he wanted to deny it, he was attracted to her. The delectable little lady would make a wonderful bed partner, once he'd got past her prudish disposition. The thought had his body hard and tight within seconds, and he cursed under his breath. He'd promised Sidney to take care of her, at least until they reached Kimberley, which meant seduction was out of the question. He did have a few morals left, but at the moment, he'd gladly ignore them for another one of Olivia's delightful smiles.

"Did you say something?" Olivia asked, focusing those wide, innocent eyes on him.

"Nothing important," Quinn told her. He refilled his brandy glass, knowing he had to get out of the car before he did something foolish. "I'll be in the club car," he announced, reaching for the jacket he'd shed earlier in the day.

Olivia watched him leave, confused by his abrupt mood changes. One minute the man was acting cordial, telling her wonderful things about Africa, the next he was glaring at her as if she had two heads.

It was pitch black when Echo brought her dinner. Olivia was pacing the length of the lavish private railroad car, trying to work the stiffness from her legs brought on by six hours of sitting and staring out the window. She'd seen more impalas and another herd of animals, larger than the impalas and with oddly shaped horns. The beasts had raised their heads and stared as the train went by, then stampeded into a graceful run when the engineer had given the whistle a short blast. If she saw them the following day, she hoped that Echo or Quinn would be available to give her their proper name.

Her escort had yet to return from the club car, and she suspected she wouldn't see him until morning, if then. It was obvious Quinn didn't consider sharing her company part of his job.

Feeling tired but still excited, Olivia sat down to a dinner of spiced chicken and deliciously cooked yams, smothered in butter. Echo turned down the bed before leaving the car, and she looked at the silk screen for a long time before walking to the door and securing the lock. Once she was certain she wouldn't be disturbed while she changed into her nightclothes, she undressed as quickly as possible, putting a blue robe over her batiste nightgown. Her hair came down in a tumble of thick curls to be brushed, then braided.

After a long moment's concentration, she unlocked the door, and retired. A final glance out the window told her that there was nothing to see but a round pale moon. The cotton blanket had barely been pulled up to cover her waist when the door opened and Quinn came strolling into the railroad car. When he peered around the screen, his hair was tousled, as if he'd been running his fingers through the thick black waves. He eyed her for a moment before speaking.

"To bed so soon, Miss St. John?" he queried.

The light of a gas lantern outlined his handsome profile and the broad width of his shoulders, adding to Olivia's anxiety at being found in her nightclothes. Bold eyes scanned her with frustrated impatience while she tucked the blanket more closely around her.

"It's been a long day," she said simply.

"Have you eaten?"

She nodded, profoundly aware that he didn't seem in any hurry to leave her alone. His jacket was missing again, as well as the vest he'd worn that morning. His linen shirt, vastly more wrinkled than it had been earlier in the day, was unbuttoned at the collar.

Quinn was just as busy surveying her. Sitting propped up in bed with the white lace of a virginal nightgown showing above the embroidered necklace of the blue robe, and a thick braid of hair draped over her right shoulder, she looked like a little girl waiting for a bedtime story before being tucked in for the night.

His hand tightened on the wooden frame of the silk partition. If he had any sense, he'd find a berth and get some sleep, but he wasn't in a sensible mood. He'd trekked across the bush too many times to pay for the luxury of having a private car, not to make use of it. Turning his back on the

saintly nymph resting in his bed, he poured himself a stiff
drink.

Olivia listened breathlessly at the sound of the top being
replaced on the crystal whiskey decanter. She could hear
Quinn making himself comfortable, the slight whisper of
cloth against the velvet cushions of the settee as he sat
down, and the exasperated sigh he released once he was
comfortable. She doubted the settee could accommodate his
weight and height, and for a moment she was tempted to
ask if he'd prefer the bed, then changed her mind. He'd no
doubt remind her that he had spent a good portion of his
life sleeping on the ground.

Stretching out felt wonderful after a day of sitting while
the train rolled tirelessly northeast toward Calvinia. Cool
sheets caressed Olivia's feet and limbs as she snuggled down
to what she hoped would be a dreamless night.

An hour later she was still wide awake.

She could hear Quinn snoring. It wasn't a loud snore, but
it was distracting, especially since she was doing her very
best not to think about the man sleeping only a few yards
away. She'd never shared a room with anyone, not even her
sister, and she'd certainly never imagined sharing one with
a man, who was for all intents and purposes a total stranger.

Sitting up, Olivia pulled back the window curtain. She
could see the shadow of the train against the scrub grass as
it moved through the moonlit night.

Quinn snorted rather than snored. The noise was followed
by a loud thump, then an abrupt curse. He'd fallen off the
settee.

Olivia scrambled to her knees, leaning forward to look
around the screen partition, but she couldn't see anything
except the carpeted floor of the rail car. Venturing out of
bed, she peered around the corner to find Quinn sitting up
in the middle of the private car, his arms extended behind

him, his hands palms down as he supported his upper body. The look he gave her was disgruntled, almost childish, and Olivia couldn't keep from smiling.

"What's so damn funny?" he demanded.

"Nothing," she replied, suppressing a giggle.

"Give me the extra blanket," he ordered, "then get back in bed."

Olivia looked around her.

"In the compartment at the end of the bed," he growled.

Moving as quickly as she could, she opened the trunklike bench at the end of the bed and retrieved the blanket. Holding it out to him, she smiled apologetically. "I can sleep on the sofa."

"Don't patronize me." His eyes narrowed into dark blue slits as he looked up at her. "I've slept on harder things than a carpet before."

Olivia didn't argue. She watched as he rolled the blanket into an oblong pillow, then lay down, stuffing it under his head. As his eyes closed, he ordered her back to bed.

"Don't be ridiculous, Mr. Quinlan," she argued. "I'm not nearly as tall or as large as you are. I'm sure the settee will suffice. Please, take the bed. You need your sleep as much as I do."

With his dignity close to failing him, Quinn stared at her. Although he'd turned down the gas fixture, there was still enough light for him to see her standing in front of him, dressed in soft cotton. His mouth began to water. If he moved, it would be to pull the lovely lady into his arms. Once he got his hands on her, he wouldn't stop until . . .

"Go to bed, Miss St. John."

"But—"

"Go to bed, damn it!"

Reluctantly, Olivia obeyed, but it was another hour before she finally slept.

                         * * *

She awoke the next morning to find Quinn gone and the
blanket tossed on the settee. She was about to get dressed
when Echo tapped on the door, announcing himself and a
tray of food. Making sure her robe was properly buttoned,
Olivia told him to enter.

The servant was all smiles as he neatly folded the discarded blanket and put it back in the storage compartment
at the end of the bed. "Quinn not happy," he announced
with a gleaming show of white teeth.

Unsure how to respond, Olivia said nothing.

"Head hurt," Echo told her, still smiling.

Unable to stop herself, Olivia laughed. "He did hit the
floor rather hard."

The servant joined in the laughter as he uncovered a plate
of thin potato pancakes and fresh melon. Pulling out a chair,
he indicated for Olivia to sit down. "You eat. See more
animals today. Maybe lion."

"A lion," she replied, her eyes wide as they glanced
toward the window. "Do you really think so?"

"Maybe. Maybe not," Echo replied, shrugging his shoulders. "Lions hide in grass. Hard to see. You must watch
very closely."

Nodding that she'd do just that, Olivia sat down to her
breakfast while Echo tidied up the railroad car. "I bring hot
water," he said, preparing to leave. "Be back soon."

"Thank you," she said.

"Eat," he commanded politely, getting in the last word
just as Quinn had predicted.

An hour later, wearing a lightweight dress with stiff ecru
lace at the collar, Olivia clutched the tiny wooden lion her
uncle had sent her, while she stared out the train window,
hoping for a glimpse of the real thing. Once or twice, she

thought she saw something moving in the golden grass, but it was impossible to tell what it was.

The day passed hour by hour, while she watched, silently hoping that Quinn might make an appearance just to disrupt the monotony of the train trip. Echo brought her lunch, taking a change of clothes for his employer when he left the private car. Her escort didn't show his handsome face until the sun was a burning golden ball against the western horizon.

The train gave a firm jerk, almost unseating Olivia. "What's wrong?"

"Elephants," Quinn announced. "Care to see them?"

As if the man had to ask, Olivia thought, coming to her feet. She followed him outside the car, onto the narrow platform.

"You'll have to bend over the railing and look," Quinn said. "They're crossing the tracks ahead of the train."

Before Quinn could blink a blue eye, the young lady from Portsmouth was bustle high, leaning over the railing, straining for a look at the herd of elephants marching across the train tracks.

Olivia watched in total amazement as the herd of gigantic animals stepped carefully over the narrow steel rails. Their grayish skin was thick and wrinkled and splattered with dried mud and dust. Their large ears twitched while their massive rumps swayed from side to side.

"They're huge! Do they always cross here?"

"Elephants cross anything they like, anywhere they like," Quinn replied, amused by the animation in her voice and the unladylike way she was leaning over the platform railing. His smiled broadened as he thought of that damnable bustle and her corset being discarded to accommodate the heat of the bush country. "Even railroads don't argue with elephants."

"I should think not," she agreed, then leaned even farther over the railing. "There's a baby one!"

"The herd is being led by an old female," he told her, readying himself to pull her back if she went too far. "The baby you're referring to weighs more than a draft horse."

"It's adorable!"

Quinn shook his head. "If you ever see one in the bush, don't get too close. The mama won't be far away, and there's nothing more dangerous than a mother elephant that thinks her baby is in danger."

"Do you think we'll see more?" she asked, twisting her head around to look at him.

"Probably," he replied with an indulgent grin.

It took a good half an hour for the entire herd to cross the tracks, and Olivia watched until the train steamed up again and began to move. Her eyes were still sparkling with excitement as Quinn held open the door for her to return to the private car.

She hurried to the window to watch the last of the herd lumber off into the distance, their short skinny tails swinging back and forth while their large round feet left a trail of crushed grass behind them.

Quinn helped himself to a brandy, knowing he should return to the club car and the card game he'd abandoned to alert Olivia to the herd of elephants.

"We should get to Calvinia by midmorning," he told her. "I'd spend the remainder of the evening contemplating my decision, if I were you. Once we leave, there's no turning back."

"We've had this conversation before," Olivia replied adamantly. "I'm going to Kimberley."

A deep rush of desire hit Quinn. At the very moment he'd liked nothing better than to kiss the stubborn look right off the lady's face. The thought was followed by a more daring one that had him wondering if he'd lost his mind.

"Since you're set on having your way, perhaps it's time to discuss my fee."

His fee.

Sidney Falk hadn't mentioned anything about Quinn charging her a fee. She had some funds left after paying her hotel bill and buying the practical clothing she'd need in the bush, but she was also going to need things once they reached Kimberley. Hopefully, Quinn's fee wouldn't be too substantial.

"I apologize for the oversight," she said. "Of course, you'd expect to be compensated for your time and effort."

"I'm not talking about money."

Olivia stared at him, slightly disoriented by the tone of his voice. It was as smooth as the wind blowing across the incessant grasslands.

"My profession has it rewards," Quinn said, spreading his hands wide to indicate the luxury of the private rail car. "In fact, I'm a very wealthy man."

"Then what to do require, sir?"

He smiled a devastatingly devilish smile that made Olivia's heart pound against her ribs.

"A kiss."

Her mouth fell open and for a brief moment she couldn't think of a word to say, at least not one that would serve the purpose.

Quinn used the amusing moment to his advantage. "Actually, a kiss a day would be more appropriate. Yes, I think that fee is reasonable, don't you? From this day forth, until we reach Kimberley, you will have to kiss me."

Olivia's inability to speak evaporated into a gasp of rage. Her hands fisted at her side. "Mr. Falk insisted that you were a man of distinction. A man who could be trusted without reproach. Apparently, he was wrong. I have no intention of kissing you, today or any other day. In fact, I find the suggestion disgusting, degrading, and utterly insulting.''

Quinn smiled even more on the inside. Just as he'd expected, the lady couldn't think beyond her genteel upbringing. "What about reaching your destination? I'm not only a wealthy man, Miss St. John, I have influence. Enough influence to keep any respectable guide from escorting you farther than the door of this rail car.''

"Don't threaten me," she hissed. "And don't think that you can bully me into changing my mind just because your talk of hungry lions, stinging scorpions, and slithering reptiles hasn't worked.''

"I never threaten. I'm a man of my word. Ask anyone who knows me." His smile went from devilish to sensual. "Is a kiss too much to pay?''

"You're loathsome, arrogant, and blatantly rude." Her voice quivered with anger. She'd never been more charmingly insulted before. But then, she'd never met a man like Matthew Quinlan before. Gone was the gentleman who had entertained her with tales of diamonds mines. The man standing in front of her was as coldhearted as the hungry lions he'd warned her about, and just as hungry. She could see it in his eyes.

Taking a deep breath, she continued to reprimand him. "Your threats are useless, sir. People travel to Kimberley on a regular basis. I shall find someone to accompany me, or I will find the way myself.''

"Not likely," he said much too confidentially for Olivia to doubt him. "You'll get lost the first day. The bush is like a desert. Everything in every direction looks the same. Some Khoikhoi tribesman will find you wandering around in circles, half-starved and covered with insect bites.''

Olivia didn't have the slightest idea who or what a Khoikhoi was, nor did she care. All she wanted was to see the last of Matthew Quinn. She moved to open the door, but he stopped her by stepping forward and blocking her path.

"What's the matter, Miss St. John? Haven't you ever kissed a man before?"

His gall was beyond belief. "That's none of your business," she bristled. "Now, please step aside. I'm in need of some fresh air."

Quinn didn't budge.

He'd started out to change her mind, but somewhere in the span of a heartbeat, it was his mind that had changed. He wanted that kiss, and he wanted a kiss every day until he opened the door of Olivia's inherited boardinghouse and escorted her inside.

Maybe it was the sparkle in the lady's eyes when she got angry, or the stubborn tilt of her pretty chin, or the way she'd watched the elephants. Maybe it was her determination to reach Kimberley any way she could. Hell, maybe it wasn't anything more then her sweet little mouth looking like it needed to be kissed. The reason wasn't important. What was important was the realization that he wanted her, and he'd do damn near anything to have her. The admission was as much of a shock to Quinn as his proposed fee was to the lady from Portsmouth.

"A kiss a day," he said. "Take it or leave it."

Olivia gritted her teeth. The man had a thing or two to learn. First, she wasn't going to let him scare her into returning to Cape Town. Secondly, the thought of kissing him wasn't all that disgusting.

Why shouldn't she kiss him? She was certainly old enough to kiss a man. But more than that, she had to get to Kimberley. Learning about the boardinghouse had changed her life. Gone were the depressing thoughts of never being anything more than a governess, an invisible servant set apart from the others on staff because she was educated, separated from the family who paid her wages because she was an employee. Always an outsider. Knowing there was property, a deed with her name on it, made everything different. Her uncle had given her more than a building. He'd given her a chance to be her own person, an independent woman.

Olivia thought of all the days and nights she'd spent dreaming about adventure. What could be more adventurous than kissing a man like Quinn? She looked away for a moment, settling her gaze on the carved walking stick resting in the corner of the car. The fashionable accessory with its diamond eyes seemed to be mocking her, warning her that if she backed down now, she'd be forever retreating.

"Very well, Mr. Quinlan," she announced. "A kiss a day."

The lady was full of surprises.

This time Quinn wasn't upset that she'd done the unexpected. In fact, he was looking forward to teaching the pretty Miss St. John how to kiss a man properly. Of course, that would take time. Lots of time. And lots of kisses.

Olivia took a small step forward. When she looked up again, her heart skipped a beat, or felt as if it did. Quinn was staring down at her, his blue eyes gleaming. She was nervous, rightfully so, but she wasn't about to let the irritating man know that. Raising her head, she came up on her tiptoes.

"On the lips," Quinn whispered, knowing she meant to give him a chaste kiss on the cheek, then scramble away.

Olivia stiffened slightly, but she didn't stop. With her eyes wide open, she placed her mouth ever so gently against his lips. It didn't stay there for more than a second, but it seemed like an eternity. An eternity in which she felt the warmth of his breath, tasted the brandy he'd just drank, and experienced the texture of his mouth. As chaste as the kiss was, it left her wanting more. Shocked by the brazen thought, she stepped back, keeping her hands at her side.

"That wasn't so bad, was it?" Quinn asked, thinking it had to be the shortest kiss in history. No doubt about it, Olivia St. John was as innocent as a newborn lamb.

She glared at him. "If we're through negotiating your fee, Mr. Quinlan, may I suggest you return to the club car."

"Until tomorrow," he said, emphasizing his victory with a wink as he left the car.

Once the door was shut, Olivia slumped onto the settee. She closed her eyes, thinking about what she'd just done, what she'd agreed to do for God only knew how many days. Not understanding the gauntlet Quinn had just thrown down, but knowing he expected her to change her mind once the train pulled into the depot at Calvinia, Olivia gathered her resolve. She wasn't going to fail. She was going to reach Kimberley, no matter how many pairs of walking shoes she wore out, and she was going to turn her uncle's boarding-house into the finest, most respected establishment in the province. Matthew Quinlan be damned.

Four

By the time the train pulled into the depot at Calvinia, Olivia was too excited to sit still. She'd put on her new walking shoes, functional short-topped black leather boots with low heels and thick corded strings. After pacing the full length of the railroad car several times, she decided the shoes were both comfortable and ugly. Fortunately, the brown linen skirt the shopkeeper had recommended hid the shoes well enough if she was standing still. In addition to the linen skirt, she wore a lightweight cotton blouse with a high collar and a short-waisted brown jacket with sturdy brass buttons. After braiding her hair and pinning it into a neat bun at the nape of her neck, she put on a wide-brimmed straw hat with a blue scarf that tied under her chin. After a quick glance in the small mirror over the vanity table, Olivia declared herself as ready as she could be.

She didn't see Quinn until she stepped out of the private car. He was already on the short platform, talking to Echo.

Like her, his attire had changed from fashionable to practical. He was wearing dark trousers stuffed into the top of black knee-high boots that were scuffed and well worn. A cream-colored shirt was covered by a loosely fitting jacket. The tailor had apparently used the fabric normally reserved for lapels to add additional pockets to the jacket. Olivia counted six.

Quinn turned to look at her. She was about to offer him a good morning smile, but the expression on his face said he wasn't in a cordial mood. Unsure if she was the reason, she couldn't help but rethink the first thought that had come to mind that morning. Before the day was over with she would be expected to give the insufferable man another kiss.

Quinn couldn't keep his gaze from raking over Olivia from head to toe and back again. He'd gone to sleep thinking about the stubborn young lady. He'd awakened that morning to realize that he was actually looking forward to his next payment. Every ounce of common sense he had told him to keep his distance, but his body wasn't inclined to be that practical. The tiny taste he'd had of her last night had been just enough to tempt his senses. Quinn knew he wouldn't be satisfied until he'd had a second helping of Miss St. John's charms.

Disgruntled with his unruly appetite and his own eagerness, Quinn gave Echo some final instructions before approaching Olivia.

"You won't be walking today," he said, looking down at the shiny black toes of her new boots.

"But I thought—"

"I've got supplies to deliver to the farm before I head into the bush," Quinn maintained.

"The farm?"

"I own a small farm not far from here," he replied.

"We'll spend the night there, then start out again in the morning."

It was hard to imagine Quinn on a farm, but then again he'd said he owned it. Nothing had been said about him actually being a farmer.

"You can ride in the wagon with Echo," Quinn said before entering the depot building.

Olivia waited, watching and listening as other passengers left the train. She strolled up and down the short platform, taking a quick look into the depot. All she could see was one large room with a wooden floor and two long benches. Quinn was standing with his back to the door, talking to the clerk. A chalkboard showed the arrival and departure schedule of the trains that linked Calvinia to Cape Town.

Just north of the depot's main building, a large stack of railroad ties and sections of steel railing filled an open-walled hut with a rusty tin roof, indicating that sooner or later the railroad would be back to finish the job of laying track across the bushland that separated the town from the interior of the country.

Beyond the depot buildings there were several grass-roofed huts shaped like gigantic beehives. Native children played in the grassless area between the shelters while their mothers squatted in front of the huts, cooking over open fires.

The town of Calvinia was across the tracks, hidden from view by the stationary train. Olivia had seen enough of it from the window of the rail car to know it was composed of several shops, two taverns, a blacksmith and livery, and a large livestock pen that was currently empty. A few scattered houses and a single-steepled Anglican church finished off the small community.

The wind was blowing from the east, bringing the heat of the inland peninsula with it. By the time Echo appeared, driving a cumbersome ox cart, Olivia was already regretting her decision to wear a corset.

"Missy John ride with me," Echo announced, jumping down from the seat.

Unsure how to go about getting into the cart, Olivia stared at it for a moment.

Quinn solved the dilemma when he walked out of the depot, marched to where she was standing and grabbed her by the hand. Without a word, he hauled her to the opposite side of the cart, then wrapped his steely hands around her waist and lifted her onto the wooden seat with no more effort than it took Echo to toss her valise into the back of the wagon.

"Don't fall off," he warned, seeing the shock on her face.

"Thank you," Olivia said absently. She was too busy looking at the unappealing rump of the black and white ox to notice Quinn's smile as he walked toward the second wagon.

He climbed into the seat, next to a small native boy, then gave the reins a hard slap. The cart jerked then began to move forward on its awkward wooden wheels. Olivia watched as Quinn reached into one of his large jacket pockets. He called out something in a native dialect, then tossed a handful of candy to the small children playing near the end of the depot platform. Laughing with delight, the children scrambled to catch the treats in midair, grinning all the while.

The gesture touched Olivia's heart, bringing a smile to her face that vanished the moment Echo climbed into the cart, tipping it so far to one side she had to grab the seat to keep from falling over. She gripped it more tightly when the cart started moving, jarring her insides with every turn of its huge wheels.

Glancing over her shoulder, she could see that her trunks

had already been loaded into the cart, along with sacks of coffee beans, flour, and rice. Several wooden barrels sat upright, secured to the cart with rope to keep them from toppling over. She also noticed the rifle lying on top of the sacks, well within Echo's reach if they encountered any unfriendly animals. Looking at Quinn's wagon, she could see the barrel of another rifle resting against the seat, between him and the young boy.

"How long will it take us to reach the farm?"

"We be there before dark," Echo told her. "Not far."

Olivia took one hand off the seat to lift the small brooch watch pinned to her jacket. It was only a few minutes after ten. Dark was hours away. Hours that would be spent on the inflexible wooden seat of an ox cart that was swaying over the treeless grassland like a clipper ship at sea. Grimacing on the inside, she resigned herself to a long uncomfortable day, thinking that walking to Kimberley might have its advantages. At least her backside wouldn't get sore.

The two carts moved through the center of town. Quinn called out a greeting to several men exiting one of the taverns as they moved east. The men waved in return, then stared as Olivia passed by in the second wagon.

The road was a rutted, dirt-packed avenue that soon became a worn path that cut through the grassland. Here and there flat-topped trees with yellowish-brown bark and creamy white flowers broke the monotony of the short, stubby grass that grew in every direction. Olivia could hear birds, but she saw only a few as they left the shelter of one tree to take refuge in the branches of another.

Before an hour had passed, she was perspiring under her clothes and the stays of her corset were poking her with the ferociousness of darning needles. The constant swaying motion of the ox cart was beginning to make her feel seasick, something she'd never experienced during the voyage from

Portsmouth. Quinn kept the first wagon rolling due east. She could hear him talking to the young boy sitting beside him, but there was too much distance between the carts for Olivia to make sense of the words.

"Who is the boy?" she asked of Echo.

"Jerulla's son."

"Does Jerulla manage Quinn's farm?"

"No. She cook and clean," Echo said. "Kruger manage farm."

Olivia was about to ask if Jerulla and Kruger were husband and wife when she saw the giraffes. The animals were munching on the uppermost branches of a wide-canopied tree.

"Oh . . ." she said, pointing to the animals.

Echo didn't bother to slow the cart since it was moving at a snail's pace. Instead, he chuckled as Olivia stared in wonderment at the leaf-eating animals with large brown splotches interrupting their amber coats. Long, gangly legs supported their bodies. The carts rolled by, keeping a respectable distance, while the giraffes enjoyed their lunch.

It was another hour before Quinn stopped the lead cart. Sighing unconsciously, Olivia allowed Echo to help her down. Her knees buckled for a moment, but she managed to keep from falling flat on her face.

"Walk around," Quinn said, coming up behind her. He was carrying the rifle. "Stay close," he added.

Olivia nodded, then licked her lips. "Could I have a drink of water, please?"

He rested the rifle against the cart then reached inside to produce a canteen. After unscrewing the top, he handed it to her. "You might as well get used to drinking without a cup. We don't have time for that kind of luxury in the bush."

Hearing the subtle sarcasm in his voice, Olivia accepted

the canteen with a smile. After two hours in the sun, she'd gladly forsake a cup. Lifting it to her mouth, she drank.

Half-smiling, Quinn watched as she tilted her head back, exposing the pale skin of her throat and neck. He knew she must be roasting underneath all those clothes. He was sweating and he wasn't wearing half the layers she was. Normally, he wouldn't have stopped for another hour, but he knew she'd need water. And she'd keep on needing it as long she insisted on caging herself in corsets and petticoats. The only good thing was that her body needed the fluid too desperately to let any of it go to waste, which meant he wouldn't have to worry about nature calling her into the bushes.

Olivia recapped the canteen and handed it to Quinn. "I never imagined giraffes being so elegant."

Quinn took the cap off the canteen, turned it up, and swallowed. He wondered what Olivia would think the next time she got thirsty and was forced to drink from the same canteen again. After storing it back in the wagon, he looked at her, then smiled. "You should see them run. They're a lot faster than they look."

His comment was the first amiable thing he'd said all morning.

Realizing that he was standing there grinning at her like some besotted schoolboy, Quinn slapped his hat against his thigh to rid it of dust, then told her to get back in the cart. This time he didn't make it easy for her by lifting her off the ground and sitting her on the seat. He stalked toward the first wagon, leaving Echo to do the honors.

The abrupt change in Quinn's mood puzzled Olivia, but she didn't let it consume her thoughts. The short time she'd spent with the temperamental man had taught her there was no rhyme or reason to his disposition. In any case, she was too busy trying to keep herself from toppling off the seat of the ox cart to worry about Quinn's unpredictable personality.

They stopped again during the late afternoon. Silently thanking God for his mercy, Olivia walked around the cart, avoiding the ox and its swishing tail. The landscape was gradually changing. Instead of endless grass and the occasional tree, the foliage was thicker and greener with large clusters of podocarpus bushes and sparsely branched shrubs with untidy crowns and spine-tipped branches. The land rolled into slight valleys with outcroppings of rock and gaunt trees towering over the underbrush. It all seemed wild and untamed to her city-bred eyes.

While Echo unpacked the meal he'd prepared before leaving the luxury of the dining car, Olivia watched a small white-breasted bird peck at the reddish-orange fruit that had fallen off a nearby tree.

"Sour plum," Quinn said as he came walking up to her. "The fruit isn't ripe enough to eat, unless you're a bird."

"A South African lemon," Olivia remarked.

"Not exactly, but close. The taste isn't all that bad, once you get used to it. The natives use the tree bark and roots to make medicine. They squeeze the oil from the seed pods and use it to tan hides."

Quinn gave her a brief glance, torn between admiration that she wasn't complaining about the heat and irritation because she was proving to be one hardheaded young woman. He thought about collecting his kiss but decided against it. Echo might keep a secret almost as well as he did, but Jerulla's boy was all eyes, ears, and mouth.

"You know a lot about this country and its people, don't you?"

"Enough." Quinn shrugged. "I've been here a long time."

"Have you ever thought of going back to England?"

"No one wants to go back to the East End," he said matter-of-factly. He turned to look at her. "Surprised that I don't miss home sweet home?"

"No," Olivia answered candidly. "This is much better than London."

"What about you?" Quinn inquired. "Aren't you going to miss the parties and the gentlemen?"

"I'll miss my family," Olivia admitted. "As for parties and gentleman, there weren't any to speak of."

Quinn wasn't sure he believed her. His ward, for lack of a better word, might not be breathtakingly beautiful, but she was very pretty. Maybe she was running from unrequited love, a handsome young man who'd broken her heart. One thing was for certain, if there had been a man he'd never gotten around to kissing the lady. She didn't have the slightest idea what to do with her mouth. But she would by the time they reached Kimberley. Quinn was going to make sure of it.

When Olivia looked at Quinn, she knew they were both thinking about the kiss he'd demanded the previous evening, and all the ones she'd agreed to give him in the future. The stark blueness of his eyes had softened and there was a half smile on his face, as if he was daring her to take the incentive and kiss him right then and there. If Echo weren't nearby, she might consider getting the kiss over and done with, but she didn't want to give the servant the wrong impression. Her arrangement with Quinn would remain a private one for as long as possible.

Already hot and flushed with heat, she could feel her face reddening as she thought about the anticipated kiss.

Quinn's smile widened. "Any gentleman to speak of, or none to speak of?"

"There was no particular gentleman, if that's what you're asking."

"Just as well," he said in a clipped voice. "Gentlemen don't last long out here. That's one good thing about being born in the slums. It taught me how to survive."

"Yes, I imagine it did," Olivia said softly, realizing some of her curiosity had just been satisfied.

The East End was London's greatest sin. Quinn's ability to rise above the poverty and misery of his childhood attested to his character. It also explained why he was so comfortable risking his life. He'd simply exchanged one treacherous existence for another.

Normally, Quinn didn't offer information about himself to anyone. It was second nature, considering what he did. The less people knew about him, the more difficult it was to predict what he'd do or when he'd do it. He wasn't sure why he'd revealed his meager beginnings to Olivia. Maybe it was the legendary honest streak he'd acquired since coming to Africa. He didn't want her getting any romantic notions about the kisses he'd demanded.

"Let's eat," he said, knowing he'd said enough. "I want to be at the farm before nightfall, and I've already lost an hour stopping so you can rest."

"I'll do better tomorrow," Olivia predicted. "Even I can walk faster than an ox."

"We'll see about that," Quinn said before turning away.

Blessedly the farm came into sight before Olivia's strength gave out. Stiff, hungry, and hot, her skin and clothing were covered with a fine layer of dust. The farmhouse with its gabled roof and rustic porch looked like a palace to her weary eyes.

The sun was setting, sending long streams of golden light over the lush grassland that surrounded the farm. Although the house was modest, it was well kept. Olivia glanced at

the outbuildings. Most of them had tin roofs and looked as
well maintained as the house. There were paddocks and
holding pens and she could see what looked like an orchard.
A shout from Echo brought several men out of the barns
and work sheds. They hurried toward the arriving carts and
the supplies that would have to be unloaded and stored
before night robbed the last of the light from the sky.

Quinn stopped his cart. The man hadn't so much as
glanced over his shoulder during the last half of their trip.
But now that they'd arrived at the farm, Olivia couldn't
help but think about the kiss she'd be expected to deliver
sometime between now and midnight.

The young boy, who hadn't been introduced to her and
who had kept to himself whenever they'd stopped, scrambled
out of the cart and ran toward the house. The front door
opened at the sound of his voice, and a young woman stepped
outside.

Her skin was several shades lighter than the boy's, more
bronzed than brown. She was tall and slender with thick
black hair, large dark eyes, and the most exotically beautiful
features Olivia had ever seen. Her slender body was exhib-
ited to perfection in the traditional native wrapping. The
pale yellow cloth accented her unusual skin coloring. She
smiled as the young boy came running toward her, and
Olivia assumed the woman was his mother, Jerulla.

Echo confirmed her assumption by calling out the woman's name, then waving. Jerulla waved back, then turned
her attention to Quinn, who was heading for the porch with
long, determined strides. Olivia sucked in her breath as he
walked straight into the woman's open arms.

They exchanged words after a very affectionate embrace.
Not that Olivia cared, she told herself. All she was wanted
was a hot bath and a good night's sleep. As hungry as she
was, food could wait until morning.

With Echo's help she was able to get out of the cart with her dignity intact. Her bottom felt bruised and her legs felt stiff. She stood by the cart, waiting for Quinn to introduce her to his housekeeper. When he finally turned, motioning for her to come forward, Olivia wasn't sure how he'd explain her presence.

"Jerulla, this is Miss St. John. I'm taking her to Kimberley with me."

Up close the native woman was even more beautiful. Her smile was just as lovely as her large ebony eyes. "Welcome," she said in a soft, pleasant voice.

If Olivia's presence came as a surprise, it didn't show on Jerulla's face.

"Jerulla takes care of the house for me," Quinn said simply. "Montagu is her son."

"I'm very pleased to meet you," Olivia said, noting that there was no mention of a husband.

Once they were inside, Olivia was amazed by the decor. Instead of a velvet settee, there was a long comfortable sofa with a zebra skin draped over the back. The chairs, upholstered in dark leather, sat next to tables fashioned in the simple, artistic style of German furniture. The walls were decorated with native African masks, spears, wooden shields, and colorful woven mats. Gas lanterns provided a soft light that made the large room appear cozy despite its unusual furnishings.

"This way," Jerulla said, motioning for Olivia to follow her.

The house wasn't large, so it didn't take long for Olivia to be shown the room where she'd be sleeping. Like the front parlor, the furniture was simple but sturdy. The bed was draped in mosquito netting. It looked so inviting Olivia thought twice about the bath she craved.

"Echo will bring your things," Jerulla said, speaking

flawless English. "I will have the tub in the bathing room filled with hot water. You will want to refresh yourself before you eat. Then a good night's sleep. The journey to Kimberley will be a long one."

"Have you been there?" Olivia asked.

"I was born in Kimberley," she said. With that, the lovely housekeeper was gone, her bare feet silent on the polished wooden floor.

The last thing Olivia wanted to do was sit down. Her bottom felt numb. She walked to the open window and watched the last rays of the setting sun linger on the edge of the horizon. The amber light washed the land, lending its golden color to the grass and trees. Birds were beginning to roost in the branches of a nearby paperbark thorn, chattering and flapping their speckled wings as they fought for the best branches.

Echo delivered the valise Olivia had packed that morning. Still smiling in spite of the bone-weary day, he put the small case on the floor next to the bed. "I carry water," he said. "Missy John have bath."

"Thank you," Olivia said, thinking it couldn't be too soon.

"Missy John, welcome."

The servant had no sooner vacated the doorway before Quinn appeared. He was munching on an orange. "Don't take too long in that tub," he warned. "I want a bath, too."

Unaccustomed to discussing her toiletries with a man, Olivia nodded instead of replying.

When Quinn continued standing in the doorway, she thought he might be thinking about collecting his daily kiss. But he didn't make any move to come into the room, simply looking at her instead, as if he knew what she was thinking. The man seemed to enjoy monopolizing her thoughts.

"Jerulla is very lovely," she said, too tired to restrain her curiosity.

"Yes, she is."

"She told me she was born in Kimberley."

"Her father was French. Like most men in Kimberley, he was a miner. Jerulla's mother was the daughter of a Khoisan chieftain and a Dutch plantation owner."

It took a few moments for Olivia's tired mind to assimilate what he was saying.

"Shocked, Miss St. John? You shouldn't be. White men have been sowing their seed in South Africa for over two hundred years."

Unsure what he expected her to say, Olivia remained silent.

"When a tribal chieftain finds himself in debt to a white man, he usually repays the favor with a gift. The present can be anything from a zebra pelt, like the one you saw in the front room, to a daughter."

"They give away their children!"

"Only the females ones."

Olivia gave him the scowl she normally reserved for children who misbehaved in the classroom. Quinn didn't even blink.

"I won Jerulla in a card game," he explained casually. "Her father was running out of luck and money. He only had two things of value. A mine claim and a daughter. He chose the daughter. She was only twelve."

"That's—"

"The way things are done in Africa," Quinn said, talking over her outrage. "Get used to them."

"Parliament outlawed slavery over fifty years ago."

"Jerulla isn't a slave," Quinn countered. "She's here of her own free will."

"I wasn't implying . . ."

"I don't care what you think," Quinn interrupted her. "Just be damn sure you don't say anything to hurt Jerulla or her son. I don't take kindly to people insulting my friends."

"I meant no offense," Olivia said, angry that he'd think she could be so callous. "Do you always expect the worst of people, Mr. Quinlan?"

"The name is Quinn. And it's better than expecting more than you're going to get," he said before popping the last of the orange into his mouth.

They stared at each other for a long moment. Quinn chewing the orange, enjoying its sweet refreshing taste, as he wondered why he'd taken the time to talk about Jerulla. He didn't owe Olivia any explanations, but then he didn't need to be standing in the doorway to her bedroom, either. The truth was, he'd simply wanted to see her for a moment, to ensure himself that she was as tired as she looked. With any luck, she'd refuse to get out of bed in the morning, realizing that today was only a small sampling of what was in store for her if she didn't change her mind and go back to England where she belonged.

Miss Olivia St. John was a stubborn bit of news, but Kimberley was going to demand more than tenacity. With any luck, she might actually find a boardinghouse waiting for her, but then what? She'd have to work, harder than she'd ever worked in her life, to make a go of it. And even if she did, what kind of future would she have? Sooner or later, some miner would forsake a dry claim and decide that the income from a boardinghouse was better than nothing. She'd end up married with children hanging on her skirts, an old woman before her time.

Why the hell should I care? I'm her escort, not her father.

Wordlessly, Quinn turned to leave. It was time for a good stiff whiskey.

Olivia watched him go, thinking it must be terrible to go

through life always looking over your shoulder, expecting to find a knife in your back.

Finally clean, Olivia walked into the small dining room. Dressed in a black skirt and white blouse, she felt much better than she had upon her arrival. Quinn was nowhere in sight, but the table was set for two, so she assumed he'd be joining her.

He appeared a few moments later, looking as handsome as ever. His hair was damp from a rushed bath; she'd only abandoned the brass tub a short time ago. With a taunting smile, he pulled out a chair and seated her, then tapped on the door between the dining room and the kitchen to announce that the meal could be served.

Jerulla appeared, carrying a tray of food.

"Jerulla's an excellent cook," Quinn said, giving the servant a smile that made Olivia's heart feel vaguely injured.

In spite of the uncomfortable feeling, her appetite was hearty, and the meal progressed with little conversation until Quinn reached across the small table to refill her wine glass.

"We'll leave at sunrise," he said.

She nodded, knowing he was once again trying to intimidate her. The only thing his remark accomplished was to make Olivia increasingly aware that *the kiss* would be due soon.

Quinn relaxed with his own wine, knowing that his dinner guest was thinking the same thing he was thinking. When and where would he collect his daily reward? Let her worry, he decided. Anticipation could be fun, if you were awaiting something pleasurable, and he intended to make their next kiss as pleasant as possible for both of them.

"We'll finish our wine in the front room," he announced when Jerulla appeared to clear away the dishes.

She replied to his instructions in her native language. Whatever she said made Quinn smile, and once again Olivia felt a stab of jealousy. She couldn't help wishing that she could coax the same gentle expression out of Quinn that Jerulla did. It would make the upcoming trip more pleasant if she knew he wouldn't be snapping at her heels every time she wanted a drink of water or needed to rest for a few minutes.

They adjourned to the front parlor where Quinn made himself comfortable on the long sofa, stretching his legs out and resting his booted feet on a low teakwood table. Olivia sat down in one of the leather chairs, avoiding Quinn's bold blue eyes by studying the strange masks and weapons that adorned the walls.

"The shield was made by a Zulu tribesman," Quinn said. "They're fierce warriors. Tall, brave men who hunt lions with nothing but spears and courage."

The admiration in his voice brought Olivia's gaze away from the long wooden shield with its unusual red markings. "My uncle wrote me about them."

"You have to see a Zulu warrior in action to appreciate his talents."

"Then I hope to see one," she replied. "And a lion."

"Be careful what you wish for," he said in a husky whisper.

His tone sent a shiver of expectation up Olivia's spine.

"Lions are one of the most beautiful animals I've ever seen. From a distance," he added. "But they're not overgrown house cats. They don't purr. They roar."

Like you, Olivia thought.

The dim lighting in the room, plus the hearty meal she'd eaten, was making her sleepy. She yawned in spite of her impeccable manners.

"Get some sleep," Quinn said. "Tomorrow is going to be a long day."

Olivia hesitated, then stood up. "Good night."

"Good night."

She walked down the corridor, pausing midway. Did Quinn mean to come to her room to gather his daily kiss? Surely not. And even if he did, she had no intention of opening the door to let him in. A frown clouded her face as she resumed walking. Maybe he'd forgotten about it? Maybe the one kiss they'd shared hadn't left him wanting more?

Torn between relief and disappointment, Olivia closed the door to her room and began undressing. She looked at the long nightgown, draped over the back of a chair. The night was almost as warm as the day had been. Deciding her camisole and drawers would do just as nicely, she unpinned her hair and brushed it until it crackled.

She was reaching for the gas lantern, sitting on the table beside the bed, when she realized that although her body was tired, her mind was wide awake. Taking the book of Shakespeare sonnets out of her bag, she climbed into bed, being careful to close the mosquito netting before snuggling back against the feather pillows. Reading always helped to clear her mind.

Half an hour later, she closed the book. That's when she saw it.

Whatever *it* was, it was sitting in the middle of the bedroom floor. It was round and furry, a cross between a rodent and a squirrel, with rusty-brown fur and a bushy tail. When its pointed ears twitched and its beady black eyes blinked, Olivia screamed.

She was standing upright in the middle of the bed, still screaming loud enough to be heard in Cape Town, when Quinn came rushing into the room. He followed her pointing

72   *Patricia Waddell*

finger toward the dim corner of the room where the *bush rat* had fled. Quinn got a quick glimpse of the oversized rodent, huddled in the corner with its round bushy rump backed against the wall.

Grabbing Olivia's nightgown from the chair, he told her there was nothing to be afraid of, then walked toward the small animal that was more frightened than the lady stomping around in the middle of the mattress as if the rat meant to climb into bed with her.

Quinn tossed the nightgown over the rat, then gathered it up like a hen in a sack and carried it out of the room. Echo met him in the hallway.

Between the racket their houseguest was still making and the wiggling form of something trapped in the makeshift pouch, the servant reached the right conclusion. Laughing, he waved Jerulla and Montagu back into their room, then carried the uninvited visitor outside to be set free.

Quinn went back into Olivia's room. "Shut up," he ordered. "You'll wake the whole damn province."

"I . . . I didn't know . . . It didn't look harmless," Olivia managed to say between gasps for air.

It only took a moment for Olivia to realize she was standing in the middle of the bed wearing nothing but her undergarments. A double dose of humiliation hit her as she blushed and reached for the blanket. Anxious to cover herself up, she snatched without looking and ended up with the edge of the coverlet and a sizable amount of mosquito netting.

Quinn just kept staring at her.

Olivia wished the man had taken the time to put on some clothes before he'd come rushing to her rescue. He was barefooted and bare chested. His black trousers weren't completely buttoned. They were riding low on his hips, and she could see his navel, circled by the same dark crisp hair that covered his chest.

"You can leave now," she stammered.

Quinn watched as she tangled more of the blanket and netting around her. When he didn't move, she gave the inadequate shield a hard jerk. The netting came away from the frame, covering her like a transparent shroud.

Olivia didn't scream this time, she grunted with disgust. Quinn laughed.

He kept on laughing as she flopped down on her knees with her arms going in every possible direction, trying to free herself from the sheer mesh that had her trapped like a fish in a net.

"Stop wiggling," Quinn chuckled as he walked toward the bed. "You're only making things worse."

Thinking nothing could be worse than making a fool of herself in her underwear, Olivia continued to struggle against the netting and the blanket that was tangled around her ankles.

"Hold still, damn it!"

She went as still as stone when she felt Quinn's hands. They felt as if he'd dipped them in fire before coming into the room. Still chuckling, he began sorting through the mosquito netting and the bedcovers, gradually separating her from the bedclothes and netting.

When her head was freed, she glared up at him.

"This isn't funny," she snapped.

"Yes, it is."

She tried to push him away, but her arms and hands fluttered like a pair of useless gauze wings.

"Be still," he said impatiently.

Olivia made an unladylike sound. There wasn't much else she could do. Her legs were wrapped up like a mummy's and her arms were . . . She wasn't sure where her arms were. But she definitely knew where Quinn's were. They circled around her, pressing her against his bare chest.

After Quinn freed her head and shoulder, he used the netting to pin her arms against her sides, then gently pushed her back against the mattress. "If you don't be still, I'll never get you out of this."

His voice wasn't impatient or amused. It was whisper soft.

Olivia knew he was going to kiss her. Her mind raced with the memory of what it had felt like before, and her body betrayed her, relaxing as he leaned closer.

"That's better, butterfly."

Her expression went from frustrated to inquisitive.

"That's what you look like," he whispered. "A pretty brown-eyed butterfly who can't get free of her cocoon."

"Don't be silly," she said, although she rather liked being called a butterfly. It was the most romantic thing anyone had ever said to her. As for getting out of her cocoon, Olivia wasn't sure she was all that eager to escape. It was nice being held in Quinn's arms.

"I'll let you go once I've collected my wages." His smile was very smug and very male. "You thought I'd forgotten."

Olivia's breathing increased, but she didn't say a word. Quinn's smothering gaze had her trapped more securely than the bed linens and netting.

Slowly his head lowered and his mouth pressed gently against hers. When his tongue darted out to tease the seam of her lips, she gasped.

"Shhh," he said against her moist lips.

She felt the velvet texture of his tongue again, coaxing her to react. Unable to stop herself, she parted her lips, and Quinn pressed forward, tasting her. The penetration of his tongue was shocking, drawing a moan from deep in her throat.

The sound was music to Quinn's experienced ears. He continued the kiss, slowly easing his tongue into her mouth again, then withdrawing it just as slowly, teasing himself as much as he was teasing her.

Pleasure rippled through Olivia's body, like an endless tide rolling onto an imaginary beach. She arched up, instinctively wanting more of the sweet pleasure, needing to be closer to the tempting heat of his body. She was a woman, but she'd never felt like one until now. Her femininity had been denied for too long, smothered by social rules and a Victorian conscience. Now at last, she was free to let herself experience all the things she'd only been able to entertain in her dreams.

Quinn could feel her hard nipples straining against the cotton camisole and the thin layer of netting he hadn't removed. His lips moved slowly over hers, the same way he wanted to move slowly in and out of her, prolonging the pleasure until she was clawing at his back, begging him to end the sensual torment. She'd be tight and hot and . . . a virgin!

The realization that he was quickly losing control of the situation was enough to make Quinn end the kiss. With his heart hammering against his ribs, he stood up.

Olivia didn't move as he began to untangle her again. She was too embarrassed to open her eyes. She never knew men kissed with their tongues as well as their lips. It was . . . she wasn't sure what. She only knew that she couldn't look Quinn in the face. Not now.

After the netting was returned to its wooden frame and the blanket covered her from the neck down, Quinn let himself breathe again. "Good night."

"Good night," Olivia whispered.

He turned down the lantern, then closed the door behind him.

After reaching his own room, Quinn pulled the cork out of a bottle of whiskey and flopped down in a chair, cursing the bulge in his pants and the long night ahead of him.

Five

Olivia woke to gentle predawn light seeping through the drawn curtains. Half-remembered dreams clouded her head as she sat up, stretching slowly, then grimacing at the painful memory of yesterday's long cart ride. The moment she was fully awake, Quinn sprang to mind. She'd fallen asleep with the taste of him on her lips. The kiss hadn't been at all what she'd expected and now, facing another day and another kiss, Olivia knew she had a lot to learn about men and their personal appetites. Never in all her wild imaginings had she suspected a kiss could be so intimate.

Pushing aside the mosquito netting, she climbed out of bed and began to get dressed, making sure to give her boots a hard shake before slipping her feet into them. Once she was wearing the practical brown linen skirt and a cream-colored blouse with modest eyelet trim at the collar, she closed her valise and announced to herself she was ready for another day in the bush country.

She left the valise sitting on the floor. Carrying her straw
hat and a lightweight tan jacket with large pockets, she left
her room. She could hear voices and recognized Quinn's
immediately. Her short walk to the front of the house took
her past his room. Olivia paused when she heard Jerulla
replying to something Quinn had just said. The lovely young
housekeeper was in his room, the door was slightly ajar,
and the sun was barely over the horizon. What was she
trying to do, make the bed with Quinn still in it?

The jealous thought forced Olivia to take a deep breath.
Her relationship with Quinn, if you could call it that, was
strictly business. The thought was a contradiction, considering the fee he'd required, but it was true, nevertheless. She
had no right to be thinking what she was thinking. Unfortunately, that didn't stop her from thinking it.

"This trip is going to take longer than usual," Quinn
announced. "Don't expect me back for at least two months."

"You will be missed," Jerulla replied.

Her words made Olivia grit her teeth. She squeezed her
eyes shut, trying to block out the image of Quinn leaving
her only to invite Jerulla into his room for the night. Surely
not, but then who was she to say? It was Quinn himself
who had blatantly told her that things in Africa were done
differently, and Jerulla was extremely beautiful.

Forcing herself to focus on the physical demands that
would be placed on her for the next few weeks, Olivia
continued down the hall toward the front of the house, leaving Quinn and Jerulla and their conversation behind her.
Echo was in the kitchen, slicing a large melon that would
be part of the morning meal.

"Good morning," Olivia said cheerfully.

"Good morning," the servant replied, giving her a wide
friendly smile. "Missy John eat plenty. Long walk today."

Olivia nodded, then returned to the dining room. She was

helping herself to a cup of the strong coffee Quinn preferred to tea when her escort walked into the room. The smile she'd forced to her face quickly vanished as he pulled out a chair and sat down as if he'd rather be anywhere in the world than in a room with her.

With a brusque manner, Quinn reached for the coffeepot sitting in the center of the table. He filled a cup almost to overflowing, then glared at her. "It's now or never, Miss St. John. Once we start, there's no turning back."

Everything about his brisk tone and the set of his jaw said he'd completely forgotten that he'd held her in his arms and kissed her the night before. Wounded that the kiss had stirred her to dream about the insufferable man all night, Olivia glanced toward the door and took another sip of the coffee she'd weakened with a hefty dose of sugar and cream. "I never intended to turn back, Mr. Quinlan."

Quinn drew in a long breath, then let it out with a frustrated rush. He'd said everything he could say, done everything he could do. Even though he didn't owe Olivia so much as the time of day, he disliked the idea of having to sit back and watch while she learned things the hard way.

"Very well," he relented with a noticeable lack of enthusiasm. "I'll have Echo load the cart."

Olivia met his gaze for a brief moment. There had been no mention of the way she'd reacted to the bush rat or the brazen kiss that had followed the event. Quinn was being his usual abrupt self, but there was something about the way he was looking at her now that made her think he hadn't completely forgotten the kiss after all.

"Did you sleep well?" he asked unexpectedly.

"Yes." She paused to take another sip of coffee. "I apologize if I . . ."

"Don't apologize," Quinn said, cutting off what she would have said. He'd spent most of the night thinking about how she'd looked lying in the bed, tangled up in white linens and mosquito netting, with her wild mane of hair falling around her shoulders. He ought to be sorry that he'd taken advantage of the situation, but he wasn't. It had been a very long time since he'd enjoyed kissing a woman as much as he'd enjoyed kissing Miss Olivia St. John.

That, and a pulsing headache that he couldn't blame on anything but a bottle of whiskey and his own stupidity, was the reason for his current dilemma. He was torn between the logic of wanting to send Olivia back where she belonged and his own desire to have her remain in his life a while longer. There was a definite disparity in what he knew should be done and what he was actually doing, and Quinn didn't like the discrepancy. It meant he couldn't keep things in clear tones of black or white, right or wrong. It meant he was letting his personal feelings get in the way of the job he'd agreed to do, and he never let his personal feelings get in the way. At least he never had before. But then he'd never been paid with kisses. A really stupid idea now that he thought about it.

"No more arguments?" Olivia prompted, thinking he'd given in too easily.

"We leave in an hour," Quinn said neutrally. He refilled his coffee cup, then left the table, taking the cup with him.

If Olivia thought her second day in the South African bush was going to be any easier than her first, she was badly mistaken. Quinn started the march from the farmhouse, heading northwest. Olivia followed with Echo walking behind her. The ox cart, loaded with water barrels and sacks of supplies, came last, driven by another native while yet another man walked by its side. All of the men were armed. The two natives carried long spears. Echo had a rifle slung over his left shoulder, a long menacing knife sheathed at his waist, and a small pistol tucked into the waistband of his faded trousers. Two bandoliers of bullets crisscrossed Quinn's chest to supply the Mauser rifle he had slung over his shoulder. An intimidating machete was tied to his belt, alongside a small knife with a narrow blade. Like Echo, he was carrying a hand revolver, but Quinn's was tucked into a leather holster within easy reach of his right hand.

Olivia's first glimpse of him had been an eye-opening experience. Her father had hunting rifles and a pair of dueling pistols he'd inherited from a great uncle, but she'd never seen a one-man arsenal. Quinn was definitely ready to take on anything that came his way.

The five of them moved at a casual pace to begin with, giving Olivia hope that things might not be as bad as Quinn had painted them, but her hope faltered after two hours without so much as a minute's rest. When they did stop, it was just long enough to quench their thirst.

Quinn didn't speak as he handed her the canteen, but Olivia knew he expected her to complain as soon as she'd washed the dust out of her mouth. When she didn't, he capped the canteen, handed it to Echo, and began walking again.

The trek continued throughout the morning, with Quinn glancing over his shoulder on several occasions to make sure everyone was keeping up. He held the pace at a brisk walk over the rolling land. The knee-high grass clung to Olivia's skirt like tiny fingers, hampering her steps as she struggled to keep pace with Echo. She watched the almost fluid movement of Quinn's body as he walked several yards in front of them. He moved through the tall bush grass with the ease of a jungle cat, completely comfortable with every stride.

Olivia tried not to think about the way he'd looked the

previous night when he'd come rushing into her room, half-naked, but she couldn't watch him without remembering the long lean muscles and the dark sprinkling of hair that had covered his chest. Nor could she forget the way it had felt to have Quinn's body looming over her, his smothering gaze holding her in place as he told her that he intended to collect his wages for the day.

The kiss that had followed was still uppermost in her mind, making her wonder when the next one would be claimed, and if it would be as intimate and as powerful as the one they'd shared the previous night. For the hundredth time, she cautioned herself about becoming overly occupied with thoughts of Quinn. There was no future in allowing herself to become infatuated with a man who could kiss her passionately one minute and stare holes through her the next.

By noon, the sun was blazing like a furnace, and Olivia couldn't feel her feet because they were numb. She squinted against the bright sunlight. Overhead the sky was a faultless blue, unbroken by clouds. The land stretched out before them, a vast expanse of dry, undulating grass and an occasional tree. In the distance, she could see a herd of grazing animals silhouetted against the horizon.

When Quinn held up his hand, indicating that they'd stop for the noonday meal, Olivia used what breath she had left to mumble a grateful "amen."

They stopped beneath a baobab tree. The massive tree was as least twenty meters tall and another twelve meters in diameter. Its sheer size was staggering, its branches snarled and twisted. Olivia had to tilt her head back to see the top.

While Echo joined the two native men, she slumped against the ox cart. Her jacket had been unbuttoned a good hour ago. She took it off now, knowing she'd never be able to survive the heat if she kept it on. The starched collar of her blouse was limp, hanging down over the row of tiny buttons like a wilted lettuce leaf. She ran her fingers inside the collar, pulling it away from her neck, letting the air get to her hot, damp skin.

She was taking deep breaths when Quinn marched up to her.

"Are you wearing a corset?"

Too shocked by the question to answer it, Olivia simply stared at him. She stood there, so ill at ease she could barely meet his gaze, while the breeze caught her skirt, billowing it out around her legs. The longer she avoided answering him, the madder she got. How dare the man walk up to her and ask so personal a question?

Quinn's piercing eyes didn't even blink. It was apparent that he wasn't used to people ignoring him, and although Olivia yearned to tell him that she wasn't under his umbrella of authority, she didn't quite dare.

"Take the damn thing off," he said with a contemptuous snort.

"I most certainly will not!"

"You're going to faint if you don't," he told her. "When you do, I'll take the damn thing off you myself."

His words weren't a threat, they were a promise. She also knew he was right, but it boiled her pride to have to admit it. The thought of him touching her, of him removing her clothing, fired another emotion. A blush crept over her face, softening her defiance.

"You can go behind the tree," Quinn said matter-of-factly. "No one's going to peek."

He didn't have to peek, he'd seen a lot more than her corset last night. He grinned, and she knew he was remembering how she'd been dressed, or rather undressed, when he'd come rushing into her room.

"I'll be fine," she argued. "All I need is a drink of water and a few minutes to rest."

"Neither one is going to help you once we start walking again," Quinn insisted. "You can't get any air in your lungs when you can't get a decent breath."

Olivia couldn't argue with his logic, but that didn't mean she was going to start taking off her underwear whenever he suggested it.

He watched her as she tried to think of a way to keep her pride and her corset. Her chin had the same stubborn tilt he'd seen at breakfast that morning, and her eyes were sparkling with indignation. Quinn almost smiled, but he stopped himself in time. Something indefinable had changed between them since that first kiss. It wasn't just Olivia St. John doing her best to reach Kimberley, it was Olivia St. John doing her best to prove him wrong.

He had to admire her backbone, along with every other part of her pretty little body. But, either way the corset had to go. "What's it going to be?"

"Very well," Olivia snapped. "Kindly step aside."

She reached for her valise, but Quinn had it in his hand before she could grab it. He started walking, forcing her to follow. When they were on the far side of the huge baobab tree, he stopped, setting the valise on the ground next to a large protruding root.

She couldn't see the others, so she had to assume they couldn't see her or Quinn, either. For a moment Olivia wondered if her escort was going to claim his kiss, then decided there was no way she was going to give him one after his current rudeness. He'd have to wait until her temper cooled.

"Thank you," she said, dismissing him with her tone.

Quinn gave her a starchy glare. "Be quick about it."

He walked away, then turned his back.

It was on the tip of Olivia's tongue to ask him to join the other men, but she doubted he'd do it. The man was as stubborn as the ox pulling the supply cart.

Unfortunately, there was no quick way out of a corset. She unbuttoned her blouse, then removed it and draped it over the valise, acutely aware of the fact that she was standing out in the open in broad daylight. Her skirt had to be unfastened, as well. She let it slide to her hips as she unlaced the corset, watching Quinn the entire time and remembering that he'd seen her in a lot less than she was wearing at the moment.

The laces hadn't been tied all that tightly, but it took both her hands and a good deal of effort to untie them. The moment the corset fell away from her body, Olivia sighed with relief. She wasn't sure, but she thought she heard Quinn chuckling as she hastily slipped her arms back into the blouse, refastened her skirt, then stuffed the corset into the leather valise.

"You can turn around now," she said, once she was sure every button on her blouse was securely fastened.

"Why don't you leave the damn thing here," he said, glaring at the valise as if it contained some vile creation.

"Can I have a drink of water, please?" she asked, ignoring his comment the same way she intended to ignore the man for the balance of the day. Instead of looking at his face, she focused on the canteen suspended from a woven strap hanging over his left shoulder.

Quinn uncapped the canteen, then passed it to her. While she drank, taking small sips the way he'd told her to that morning, he felt slightly disappointed that she hadn't offered a more fervent argument before forfeiting the corset. He rather liked the idea of stripping her out of her clothes. In fact, he liked it too much.

"Thank you," Olivia said again, handing him the canteen.

She was back to being stodgy and overly polite, which
meant she was still embarrassed. Quinn thought about giving
her another reason to blush, but decided against it. She
needed food more than she needed another kissing lesson.
And he needed to remember that once he got Miss Olivia
St. John to Kimberley, she wasn't his concern anymore. If
he let the game of their daily kisses get out of hand, he'd
have a deflowered virgin on his hands, which meant he'd
also have a big problem. Women like Olivia were for marrying, and marriage wasn't something he wanted.

He picked up the valise. "Sit down before you fall down."

Olivia bristled at his tone, but she took his advise. When
she walked around the tree to discover that Echo had put a
small woven mat on the ground, she gratefully sat down on
it, spreading out her skirt to cover her legs. It had been hours
since she'd eaten, and she was hungry.

They ate a cold lunch, prepared and packed by Jerulla.
Olivia sat silently, enjoying the food almost as much as she
enjoyed being still for a while. Quinn sat cross-legged on
the ground, not far away, eating heartily and talking to Echo.
The other two bearers, whom Echo had introduced as Amura
and Tiburo, sat nearer the tree, as silent as they had been
all morning.

Olivia watched Quinn shyly from beneath her lashes as
he began to move around the camp, checking the cart to
make sure the ropes holding the water barrels upright were
securely fastened, checking the cart's axles to be certain the
rolling, bumpy land hadn't dislodged anything. When he
walked away, then disappeared behind a clump of short
bushes, she realized what he was doing and averted her gaze,
hoping none of men had noticed how closely she'd been
watching him.

Quinn returned a few minutes later. He pulled two oranges
out of the food basket and tossed one in her direction. Olivia

caught it, being sure to thank him before she began peeling away the fruit's tough skin.

"Eat it slowly," Quinn told her.

She nodded, then made a small sound of enjoyment as she tasted the juicy orange. She looked up to find Quinn standing over her, smiling.

"You made that same sound last night when I kissed you," he said, keeping his voice low and soft so he wasn't overheard.

The glint of surprise in her eyes and the blush of color on her cheeks said he'd embarrassed her again. Not sure why he did it, and not particularly caring, Quinn squatted down on the balls of his feet. "Lick your lips."

Belatedly, Olivia realized she was doing as he asked because she couldn't stop herself. His mouth brushed gently over hers, his body hiding their actions from the men gathered around the cart.

"Again," he whispered. "You taste like oranges and sunshine and . . ."

His words stopped as his mouth lightly covered hers a second time. The kiss wasn't as intimate as the one he'd given her last night, but the results was just as powerful. Olivia closed her eyes, but not before she caught a good glimpse of the wedge of dark hair revealed by the open collar of his shirt. She remembered how he'd looked last night, all tight bronzed skin and supple muscles and a flat, hard stomach that had flared into lean hips.

She'd never thought of a man's body being something special, but having seen Quinn bare chested with his hair tousled and his eyes shining like blue diamonds, she had to admit that he was a remarkable example of the male gender.

All her thoughts scattered when Quinn moved his tongue over the seam of her closed lips, enticing them to open. She trembled under the pressure of his mouth, unable to move any other way. It felt so wonderful.

Unconsciously, she leaned into the kiss, letting Quinn know that she wasn't upset that he'd claimed it.

For an instant, Quinn cursed his impatience in not waiting to claim the kiss when they were alone, but it was too late now. With a forced combination of resolve and self-control, he brushed his mouth across hers ever so lightly, then withdrew before he stretched out on the ground and took her with him.

Despite the hunger that leaped inside Olivia, she was able to keep herself from begging for another dose of Quinn's intoxicating medicine. Her lips trembled as he slowly lifted his away, leaving her feeling incomplete.

"Ride in the cart for a while," he said, his voice a whisper of breath against her moist lips. "You don't have to prove anything your first day in the bush."

Momentarily distracted and disappointed because he wasn't still kissing her, Olivia blinked, unsure if the man in front of her was the same one who'd rudely ordered her out of her corset less than an hour ago. Quinn was a chameleon, changing in the blink of an eye. *Part jackal, part gentleman,* she thought, almost smiling.

"The sacks aren't as comfortable as a mattress," Quinn said, standing up, "but, you might be able to take a nap."

"I'm not a child," she said, thinking he was back to belittling her again.

"No, you're not."

His gaze felt hotter than the sun as he looked down at her. Nothing more was said as he turned and walked toward the cart, but Olivia knew, as surely as she knew her own name, that Quinn enjoyed kissing her. The realization sent a sweet stab of sensation through her body. Her legs trembled as she stood up, but it wasn't from walking too much. The certainty that she was battling her first encounter with real passion made her feel weak inside and out.

She wanted more of Quinn's debilitating kisses, not less of them.

Diamond in the Rough

Six

By the time they stopped for the day, Olivia ached from her head to her toes. Her body felt bruised from the three-hour cart ride, and her mind felt battered from all the thoughts that had been rolling around inside it. She groaned and closed her eyes for a moment, but the memory of Quinn's kisses burned like a radiant sun. Finding the strength to take a step, she staggered for a moment, then quickly regained her footing. She glanced around, praying that Quinn hadn't witnessed her moment of weakness.

He hadn't.

"Rest," Echo said, helping her to sit down on the same woven mat he'd supplied when they'd stopped earlier.

"Thank you."

"Eat, then sleep," Echo instructed, before leaving her to unload what they'd need from the cart.

Olivia looked at the dry ground around her. She was tempted to lie down, close her eyes, and never wake up, but she found the strength to stay awake. Camp had to be made and a meal prepared before she could sleep. The men took care of the camp quickly enough. While Amura and Tiburo set up two tents, Echo unloaded the supplies from the cart. Quinn gave her a quick glance before he stomped off to gather firewood.

In no time at all, he was back, his arms loaded with dead tree branches. He dumped them on the ground not far from where Olivia was sitting, then returned to the cart for a shovel. Again, she watched while he dug a shallow hole. He filled the bottom with dry grass, then crisscrossed the branches inside the hole before lighting the fire. The ensuing orange flames competed with the blazing colors of an African sunset.

"I can cook," she offered, intending to be whatever help she could.

"That's Echo's job," Quinn said curtly. "Just sit still and stay out of the way."

"I'd like to freshen up," she said flatly, deciding there was no use wasting a smile on the irritating man.

Quinn made a grunting sound, then stomped back to the cart. When he returned he had a canteen slung over his shoulder and a small metal basin in his left hand. His right hand was gripping the Mauser rifle. "Here."

Olivia looked at the basin. It would be like taking a bath in a teacup, but she wasn't about to argue. Quinn's cold eyes said he was waiting for her to complain.

When she tried to stand up, Quinn dropped the basin on the ground and reached out to help her. An aching groan escaped her mouth before she could stop it. His steely arm tightened around her waist, a brief reminder of the way he'd held her last night, just before he released her and stepped back.

"You don't have the strength to wash your face," he grumbled.

"Please stop belittling my stamina," Olivia grumbled right back. "I'll manage."

Silently Quinn admitted that she'd managed just fine all day. Any other lady he knew would have insisted she be taken back to civilization by now, but not this one. Looking worn out and frayed around her pretty edges, Olivia St. John was still as determined as ever.

"As soon as you eat, go to bed," Quinn said stiffly. "We've got a lot more days like this one ahead of us."

Smiling in spite of the ominous prediction, Olivia made her way to the far side of the makeshift campsite. She emptied the canteen into the basin, then splashed her face, washing away the thin layer of dust that had collected during the long, hot day. Keeping her back to the men, she unfastened the top buttons of her blouse and used a hankie to wash her neck, sighing out loud at how wonderful it felt.

Wishing she could strip down to her bare skin, then plunge into a tub of hot scented water, and knowing the wish was as empty as the canteen hanging over a nearby tree branch, Olivia did the best she could with the small amount of water Quinn had allotted her. She rolled up the sleeves of her blouse, washing as much of her arms as possible. Once she was as clean as she could get, she hung the hankie next to the canteen, tossed the water onto the ground, and carried the basin back to the cart.

Quinn watched, realizing that he wanted Olivia more than he'd wanted any woman in a very long time. Silently, he gauged his stupidity against the desire that hadn't left him since she'd given him a quick, chaste kiss in the railroad car. As he watched her walk back to the mat and sit down, he told himself he had every reason in the world to get her to Kimberley as quickly as possible, and absolutely no reason to think beyond that point. But he couldn't seem to shake the idea that depositing her on the doorstep of her boarding-house, or whatever she'd inherited, wasn't going to be as easy as he hoped it would be.

By the time the sky was a blanket of blinking stars, decorated with a shiny pale moon, Olivia could barely keep her eyes open. She handed her tin plate to Echo with a mumbled word of thanks, then looked at the tents. They weren't very big, but the thought of stretching out on a blanket was heavenly.

"Go to bed," Quinn said, reading her mind.

Olivia did just that, pushing aside the mosquito netting that covered the entrance to the military style tent with a weary hand. Quinn had already lit a small lantern. The soft light illuminated the smooth dry ground and Olivia's valise that he'd fetched from the cart earlier. The only other thing in the tent was a stack of blankets.

Spreading one out on the ground, Olivia sat on it before untying her shoes and putting them aside. She'd never slept on the ground before, but she was too tired to worry about the lack of a mattress. Once she'd stripped down to her petticoat and camisole, she reached for a second blanket. She was sitting upright in the primitive bed, brushing the tangles from her hair when Quinn pushed back the tent flaps and joined her.

The brush went flying as Olivia reached for the blanket, bringing it up to her neck as quickly as possible, but not fast enough to keep Quinn from seeing more of her than he should have seen.

"What do you think you're doing?" Her voice cracked with anger.

"Going to bed," he said flatly.

"In here?"

"That's right, Miss St. John," he replied, reaching for

the last of the blankets. ''Two people to a tent. One standing guard. It's the way we do things here in the bush.''

''But—''

''But nothing,'' Quinn snapped, more aggravated over finding Olivia in her underclothes than he had a right to be. ''This is my tent. I've been walking all day, just like you. I'm tried.''

And grumpy, and rude, and too close for comfort, Olivia finished silently.

As Quinn made his bed, she listened to the sounds beyond the tents. It was quiet except for the hum of insects and the muffled voices of the natives as they decided who would stand the first watch. Inside the tent, the air vibrated with the tension that existed between the man and woman who would be sleeping next to one another.

Unwillingly, Olivia admitted she shouldn't be surprised by anything Quinn did or said, but she was having a difficult time adjusting to his proximity and the casual way he was going about taking off his boots and jacket.

The boots came first. Once Quinn was standing in his socks, he lifted the bandoliers off his shoulders, laying them aside, followed by the holster and revolver. The Mauser rifle was placed next to the blanket, within easy reach.

Olivia watched the entire time, compelled by the muscular grace of Quinn's movements and the knowledge of what he'd looked like once his shirt was removed. But she was disappointed. Quinn didn't take off his shirt. He simply stretched out on one blanket and bunched another into a pillow, tucking it under his head.

''I'm turning down the lantern in five minutes,'' he said. ''Finish brushing your hair, then get some sleep.''

Olivia reached for the brush that had landed a short distance away, halfway between her sleeping blanket and Quinn's. The two beds were less than a foot apart. She gave him a quick glance to make sure he wasn't looking at her before she lowered the blanket to her waist and began pulling the ivory handled brush through her thick hair, wanting to get the job done as quickly as possible.

"You don't have to pull yourself baldheaded. I'm not seeing anything I haven't seen before."

With a quickness that belied her exhaustion, Olivia jerked the blanket back up, deciding she could sleep with tangled hair as easily as she could without it. She put the brush in the valise, fastened the leather straps one-handedly, and reached for the lantern.

Quinn's hand was already on the small metal knob. He said something profane under his breath as he stared across the small gap that separated them. Olivia's hand touched his, then jerked back as if the lantern had burned her, but both she and Quinn knew that wasn't the reason. His eyes held hers for a long sensual moment, their depths as deep and blue as the ocean she'd sailed to reach Cape Town.

All thoughts of sleeping vanished as Olivia looked at Quinn, his face ruggedly handsome and tanned by the African sun, his eyes clear and bright. She didn't want to think about the kisses they'd shared or the fact that she wanted one now, but she couldn't stop the thought from taking shape inside her head any more than she could stop herself from licking her lips as Quinn's gaze moved to her mouth.

He grumbled another profanity, this one in some strange African dialect, before softening his voice and adding. "You look pretty with your hair down."

Olivia bristled, then moved back, sitting on one blanket and holding the other clutched to her breast like a woolen shield. "I'm not pretty."

Quinn smiled the knowing smile of a man who knew when a woman was fishing for a compliment. "You're pretty enough, and you know it."

Olivia knew nothing of the kind, but she wasn't going to argue. In truth, she liked knowing that Quinn found her attractive. She liked it almost as much as she liked his kisses. The honest admission of her attraction to the strange man wasn't as shocking as it had been earlier in the day, but it still brought a blush of color to her cheeks.

"Lie down," Quinn said, turning out the lantern and pitching the tent into total darkness.

He listened to the rustle of cotton petticoats and woolen blankets as Olivia made herself comfortable. Cursing silently this time, he reached down and unbuttoned the top two buttons of his trousers, making himself as comfortable as he was going to be for a long time. He had to get his unruly body under control or he'd be in a helluva shape by the time they reached Kimberley.

Lying flat on his back, eyes closed, Quinn thought about forsaking the few manners he'd learned over the years and reaching for the woman lying so close he could hear her breathing. He didn't. Instead, he tried to think about the shipment of diamonds he'd be carrying on the return trip. Normally, he enjoyed using his mind to outwit the greedy thieves that always thought they could get something for nothing more than a fight. But tonight the challenge of outsmarting them wasn't satisfying enough. He was as hard as a baobab tree, and all he could think about was satisfying himself with the brown-eyed virgin sleeping a few feet away.

It was going to be a very long night.

"I didn't expect it to be so quiet," Olivia whispered into the darkness.

Quinn flinched at the sound of her soft voice. "If we were in the tropical jungles, nearer the equator, it wouldn't be," he told her. "They're noisier at night than they are in the daylight. But this isn't jungle. The bush is flat and wide and as quiet as a church."

"There is something reverent about it," Olivia agreed.

"I thought you were tired," Quinn said dryly.

"I am. In fact, I'm exhausted," she admitted. "But my mind doesn't seem to be the slightest bit sleepy."

Quinn chuckled in spite of himself. "Go ahead and talk then."

"I don't know what to say."

"Say whatever's on your mind and get it over with," Quinn told her. "Then, maybe both of us can get some sleep."

His voice belied the sexual tension that was making his body harder and harder with each soft word that left Olivia's mouth. He shifted on the blanketed ground, telling himself he deserved the discomfort for letting a pretty little butterfly get under his skin.

"I think I'm beginning to understand why Uncle Benjamin loved this place," Olivia said. "It has a raw beauty, like the ocean. Untouched and wild and far more lovely than anything man can create."

Quinn smiled in the dark. One of the things he liked most about Africa was that it didn't remind him of the slums where he'd been born and raised.

"Uncle Benjamin said he couldn't bring himself to leave," Olivia continued, interrupting his private thoughts. "He wrote my father and tried to explain why he didn't want to come home and work in the family business, but I don't think my father ever really understood. I don't think he could, unless he came here."

"Some men belong in cities," Quinn said. "Some don't."

"I suppose so," Olivia said, then yawned.

Folding her hands under her head, she smiled. Quinn certainly didn't belong in a city. He was as wild and unpredictable as the land around them. And strong and intriguing and sleeping so close she could almost imagine him holding her during the night, keeping her warm and protecting her with his body, the way primitive men had protected their women.

She drifted off to sleep with that thought in mind, and awoke to find it had become a reality. She was lying with her back to Quinn. He was curled around her, spoon-fashion, with one hand resting on her hip. She could feel the heat of his breath against the nape of her neck. His chest rose and fell in a gentle, methodical rhythm, pressing against her back.

For the longest time, Olivia lay perfectly still, afraid to move because she didn't want to awaken Quinn, fearful that when she did, he would accuse her of seeking him out during the night. She couldn't imagine how she'd ended up so close to him. Had she moved? Or had he?

Either way, they were snuggling like a married couple.

It was still dark outside and the night was silent, intensifying the feelings that were flowing through her body like sun through glass. It was unnerving to be this close to the man, so close she could feel every inch of his body touching hers, so close she could almost hear his heart beating. Whenever she thought of Quinn, it was with pragmatic caution, but whenever he touched her, intentionally or accidentally, that caution went the way of the wind.

Quinn moved. His hand slipped over her hip to rest against her belly. The intimacy of the touch stole Olivia's breath for a moment. She lay as still as stone, trapped between the impropriety of the moment and the coursing ripples of sensation that overtook her body. This was nothing like being held for a kiss. Quinn was asleep, his movements involuntary, his intentions unselfish.

Holding her breath, Olivia eased onto her back, thinking she could scoot to the side and claim her own blanket again. The air wedged in her throat when Quinn's arm lifted, then returned, pinning her to the ground. Her movement had only served to disturb his sleep. Grumbling an incoherent word under his breath, he gathered her closer, his right arm draped around her middle.

Olivia shivered, then went still again, fearful of what her next movement might bring.

Quinn smiled to himself. If he were the gentleman he should be, he'd turn over, freeing Olivia, but he wasn't in a very gentlemanly mood. He liked the feel of her in his arms. She was soft and warm and very feminine, a fact he'd seen with his own eyes and one he was relearning now in the quiet darkness just before dawn.

The wind brushed through the tall grass around the tent, rustling the mosquito netting that covered the entrance. The sheer fabric shivered and swayed its way back into place. The campfire wasn't giving off enough light for Olivia to see Quinn, but she could feel him. Letting out a weak sigh, she realized she was going to have to move before dawn awakened him naturally and he found her tucked up against him. Holding her lower lip between her teeth, she slowly began easing away from him.

The movement turned into a caress as Quinn's hand moved over her belly.

He muttered something in his sleep, and Olivia stopped, leaving several inches of space between them. Unfortunately, his hand was resting just below her ribs.

Quinn felt the sensual shiver that raced through Olivia's body and smiled again. Although he wasn't touching anything but petticoat and the lace stitched into the bottom of her camisole, he could feel the heat of her body, seeping through the cloth, warming the palm of his hand. Desire coiled inside him. Hot and hard and more tempting than anything he'd felt in years.

A sound pierced the night. Long and loud, the barking

laugh vibrated like an echo. Olivia sat upright, momentarily frightened, forgetting the closeness of Quinn's hand.

A instant later, the campfire flared anew as one of the men outside the tent tossed more wood onto the flames.

"A hyena," Quinn said sleepily.

Olivia used the interruption to put as much distance between herself and the bushman as the small tent would allow. "Are they dangerous?"

"No," he assured her in a groggy voice. "The fire will keep them away."

Settling back down, on her side of the tent, Olivia closed her eyes, hoping that Quinn hadn't noticed how close they'd been.

In the darkness, Quinn was cursing the animal that had interrupted what could have been an interesting dawn. He slept again, but only for a few minutes. When the blackness of the night was broken by faint streaks of light on the horizon, he left the tent.

Olivia woke a short time later. She could hear the men moving around outside, preparing to leave once they'd eaten. Still stiff, but determined to move, she slowly came to her feet, frowning at the tangled mane of hair that fell over her shoulders. She opened the valise and took out her brush. Once her hair was tamed and braided, she got dressed.

She carried the blankets outside, giving each a firm shake before she folded it. She stacked the blankets neatly by the tent door, then went back inside to retrieve her valise. Her nose wiggled with disgust as she found several large black ants crawling up the side of the small leather suitcase. She brushed them away, then stomped her feet to make sure none of the busy little insects got into her shoes.

Echo greeted her with a wave of his hand and a bright smile. The other two men followed suit. She was putting the blankets in the cart when Quinn appeared, carrying his rifle.

Seeing him in the soft morning light reminded Olivia just how close she'd been to him during the night. She turned away, avoiding his direct gaze. Walking to where she'd hung the canteen the previous evening, she unhooked it from the tree branch, stuffed her dry hankie into her pocket and walked back to the ox cart.

"I'll fill it for you," Quinn said, holding out his hand.

Olivia gave him the canteen.

Quinn sat the wooden stock of his rifle on the ground, resting the long barrel against the cart. He filled the canteen with water, then handed it back to her.

"Do you take that everywhere?" Olivia asked, as he picked up the rifle.

"Even into the bushes to take a piss," he replied curtly.

Olivia rolled her eyes toward the sky. "Really, Mr. Quinlan, I've never met a man who thrives on being rude. It's beyond me to comprehend why you insist on being ill-mannered. And, please, don't use Africa as an excuse. It's an unacceptable one."

"I don't need an excuse, when I have a damn good reason, Miss St. John. I like staying alive. In this country that means keeping a gun close at hand."

Echo used a tin plate and a wooden spoon to announce that breakfast was ready. Grateful that she had something to concentrate on besides Quinn's dreadful manners and the long march ahead of them, Olivia walked toward the tent, turning her back on the man and his irritating ways.

The day was long and tedious. Olivia got through it by putting one foot in front of the other, moving forward with each step the same way she was determined to move forward with her life. As they walked through the bush grass, she tried to sort out her feelings about Quinn, the opportunity her inheritance was giving her, and her dreams for the future, but they kept getting tangled up in each other.

Quinn was the hardest man she'd ever encountered. There was no give in him. He was what he was and the world be damned if they didn't like it. While Olivia admired his ability to make his own way in the world, she had to admit they had nothing in common, nothing upon which to build a relationship, and that's what she wanted for the future. She wanted a man who could tolerate and accept her need to make her own way, to set her own goals, and to speak her own mind.

She had no illusions about marriage. Men expected their wives to become an extension of themselves, to accept their male viewpoint as the only way of looking at things. She'd seen her sister change since her marriage, bowing to her husband's authority in almost every facet of her life, slowly losing her identity. Olivia didn't want that. What she did want was a man who could respect her as a partner, not overwhelm her like an invading army.

Quinn was definitely overwhelming her.

She couldn't shake the memory of what it had been like to kiss him, to wake up in his arms, or the tingling anticipation of what it would be like to kiss him again.

Since she'd accepted his outrageous proposal in the railroad car, their daily kiss had become the focal point of her existence. It had to stop, or she'd find herself paying the piper in more ways than one.

As they moved farther north, the golden-tipped bush grass began to wane, growing shorter and thinner. Soon the landscape was a great desertlike plain, rolling from horizon to horizon. The trees were fewer and farther between, and the sun beat down with the ferocity of a fiery furnace. Nothing could be more different from the rich, green countryside she'd left behind in England, but Olivia still found herself awed by the land. She was fascinated by its solitude, by its stony flat-topped hillocks that Echo called *koppies*. The dry earth was dotted with karoo bushes, a few inches tall with fingerlike leaves, while the sky overhead was as wide and blue as an ocean.

Herds of animals grazed on the vast plain, munching the grass to its roots, moving lazily in no particular direction, simply existing as they'd existed since God's creation. She saw impalas and giraffes and elephants and flocks of birds, flying to the small ponds the rainy season had left behind.

Quinn stayed in the lead for the entire day, keeping a good distance ahead of the cart. By the time they stopped for the night, Olivia was beginning to have second thoughts about her stamina. Her feet were burning and her legs felt itchy. She slumped down on the ground, forsaking the mat Echo usually supplied, and removed the cap of her canteen. The water was warm, but delicious, and she drank her fill, vowing to never take the wet commodity for granted again.

Quinn had been right about one thing. The bush country had a way of separating illusion from reality, of forcing a person to accept their insignificant place in the grander scheme of things. After only two days, Olivia realized that it was going to take every ounce of energy she possessed to reach the railhead at Prieska.

After eating, she carried the tin basin, her water canteen, and her valise into the tent. Echo had, as he'd done the previous night, pitched the tent and put the sleeping blankets inside. Olivia draped one of the blankets over the flaps, signaling to Quinn that she wanted a few minutes privacy, then quickly stripped down to her drawers and camisole. The sponge bath that followed wasn't the luxurious tub bath she craved, but it was better than nothing.

As she slipped on a clean pair of muslin drawers, she felt the bite. It was on the inside of her right thigh, several inches above the knee. Slightly red and swollen, she gave the spot an extra good scrubbing, hoping the itching that ensued would gradually go away.

When Quinn entered the tent, a good hour later, Olivia was in her nightgown with the blanket pulled up to her chin. His smile said all the nightgowns in the world wouldn't erase the memory of what he'd seen before.

Olivia bid him a curt good night, then turned onto her side, offering him her back. A few moments later, she felt his hand tugging at the blanket. She rolled over, fully intending to give him a firm piece of her mind only to find him grinning down at her.

"Aren't you forgetting something?"

His expression was soft yet mischievous, like a little boy's.

Olivia knew exactly what he thought she'd forgotten. Unfortunately, the kiss he expected for his daily wage had been centered in her thoughts the entire day.

"It was a long day," Quinn said, his voice deep and low. "I've earned my pay, and then some."

"You've earned one kiss and nothing more," she said primly.

Quinn's eyes were literally sparkling as he tugged the blanket off Olivia's shoulder, revealing the soft cotton of her white nightgown. "All laced up tight," he mumbled.

Olivia glared up at him as she jerked the blanket back in place.

Quinn moved from a squat to a kneeling position. His knees rested on the blanket, keeping her from drawing it any closer. "Give me my kiss," he said as casually as if he were asking for a drink of water.

Olivia raised her head, willing to meet him halfway.

Quinn drew back.

"I can't kiss you if you keep moving away," she told him. "I'm too tired to play games."

"I don't play games," Quinn replied, hinting that although he was being his usual cantankerous self, he took his payment arrangements very seriously.

Letting out a frustrated sigh, Olivia came up on her elbows, making sure the blanket covered as much of her as possible. "Very well, Mr. Quinlan, shall we get it over with?"

Quinn chuckled deep in his throat, then smiled. "Close your eyes."

"Is that really necessary?"

"It is if you want to get some sleep."

Reluctantly, Olivia closed her eyes. She waited for what seemed like an eternity before she felt the warmth of Quinn's breath against her mouth. The tip of his tongue teased her lips into parting. "That's it, butterfly," he whispered. "The day deserves a real kiss."

She shivered on the inside, feeling the excitement build as he pressed his mouth more firmly against her. She melted against him as he slid one arm around her waist and held her against his body. Wanting to believe that she could share a kiss without having it affect her to the point of caring about the rude man didn't keep Olivia from feeling the soft texture of his mouth as acutely as she felt the hard ground under the woolen blanket.

Quinn couldn't understand his reaction to the prim little governess from Portsmouth. He'd never favored virgins, and he'd certainly never seduced one, but there was no denying that's exactly what he was doing tonight. He wanted the kiss he was about to give Olivia to haunt her until it was time for the next one. He wanted her to want him as much as he wanted her, and his conscience didn't seem overly concerned how he went about achieving his goal.

Olivia made a startled sound as his tongue penetrated her mouth, but she didn't push him away. Quinn caressed the sensitive underside of her tongue with his own, tasting her and sending a shimmering current of sensation flowing all the way to her toes. The sensation was followed by a strange warmth, centered in the pit of her stomach, as his mouth lingered, tasting her.

Daringly, Olivia touched Quinn's tongue with her own, discovering that she could make him shiver, as well.

He kissed her harder, more deeply, until she whimpered and her hands pressed against his chest. But she was kissing him back with an innocence that was as enticing as the feel of her soft, trembling body. Quinn knew he should let her go, but he couldn't, any more than he could contain the overwhelming need she aroused so easily.

He wanted to toss the blanket aside and inch up the hem of her nightgown so he could see her legs, then he wanted to touch them. He wanted to bury his body deep inside hers, to feel her warmth, to lose himself in her femininity. A hot flush of desire raced through his body. The sensation brought a groan from deep within him, a raw primitive sound that warned him just how close he was to losing control.

Olivia felt herself being gently pushed back, until she was resting on the blanket and Quinn was hovering above her, his mouth touching her as lightly as a butterfly touched a flower.

Olivia liked the taste and feel of his mouth too much to protest the gentle kiss. The slow, gentle brushing of his tongue, the light suction of his mouth, the alluring heat of his male body combined to create a magical spell, and she was its willing victim.

Quinn eased his hand into the long skein of silky hair spilling over Olivia's shoulders. He twisted it around his fingers, holding her in place, although it wasn't necessary.

She was kissing him back, now, her tongue hesitantly touching his, her body lifting to press against him.

His mouth lifted, not enough to end the kiss, but enough for Olivia to take a breath. Then his mouth returned full force, covering hers almost savagely, stealing the breath she'd just drawn. The heat of the kiss was enough to make her forget that she was a lady and that he was more stranger than friend. When Quinn was kissing her, there didn't seem to be any right or wrong about it. It was simply the most wonderful thing in the world. When he finally pulled away, disappointment splintered the glowing warmth that had engulfed her moments before.

"I drew the first watch," Quinn said, his voice thick and husky. "Get some sleep."

With that, he was gone, leaving her to stare into the darkness and wonder what other magic her diamond jackal could weave.

Seven

Olivia awoke shortly after dawn the next morning. Grayish light filled the tent as the day became more than a vague promise. She looked at the wrinkled blanket spread on the ground besides her. It attested to Quinn's presence sometime during the night.

Frowning she pushed aside her own blanket and stretched, forcing the aching muscles she'd gone to sleep with to come awake. Her right leg felt stiff and tight. She frowned, remembering the insect bite. When she raised the hem of her drawers to inspect the area she saw that it was even more red and swollen than before. The bite had inflamed from the size of a pin prick to the size of a small coin. It itched, but Olivia didn't scratch it, knowing she'd only make matters worse.

Thinking Echo must have a native remedy, she shook her clothes vigorously before putting them on, trying to dislodge any insects that might be hiding in the folds, then left the tent.

Echo was cooking over the open fire. The staple food of the bush was a thick corn porridge made with curdled milk. Having eaten it the previous morning, Olivia knew it tasted much better than it looked. She was approaching the benevolent servant to inquire about a possible salve for the irritating insect bite when Quinn came walking up to the campfire.

"Eat fast," he said without any preliminaries. "I found some lion tracks just east of camp. The more distance we put between the cat and ourselves the better."

Olivia looked toward the rising sun, glowing like a large vanilla ball against the horizon. Had the lion been close to camp? For the first time since leaving the farm, she was grateful for the exhaustion that had claimed her last night. If she'd known about the lion, she was sure she wouldn't have slept a wink.

Nervously, Olivia claimed the wooden bowl Echo passed her way, then sat down on the mat to eat her meal. She avoid looking directly at Quinn, scanning the landscape instead, thinking about a golden lion lying patiently in some random patch of amber grass. Actually, it was a relief to think about something besides her escort. The kiss Quinn had given her last night was still a very strong memory, one Olivia didn't want to spend the day reliving. It would only make things worse, and she was already suffering from an overblown case of infatuation.

It had to be infatuation.

Falling in love with a man like Quinn would be the biggest mistake of her life. No matter how hard she tried, and she'd given it her best effort, she couldn't imagine him domesticated with a wife and family. Like he'd said, some men were born to live in cities, some weren't. Likewise, some men were meant for marriage and some weren't. Quinn was of the later category, which meant Olivia was wasting her time by allowing him to creep into her dreams.

After breakfast, they broke camp, loading the wagon in a tense silence. Echo reassured her that a lion preferred four-legged game to men with rifles, but Olivia wasn't entirely sure she believed him. The servant had assumed the role of her guardian angel since leaving the farm, making sure he stayed by her side, matching her step by step, encouraging her when she got tired, smiling that bright flashy smile of his when she was near tears.

"Miss John, no worry," he said as he covered the sacks of supplies in the wagon with the tents he'd just collapsed and folded. "Quinn best shot in bush country. No lion going to bother you."

By the middle of the day, Olivia was worried more about a pesky insect bite than a hungry lion. Her clothing was damp from all the perspiration it had absorbed since the sun had come into its full glory. Muslin underwear was rubbing against her legs with each step she took. The constant scraping of damp fabric against the soft skin of her inner thighs was gradually turning the irritating bite into a full-fledged sore.

Echo noticed that she was favoring one leg over the other. His normal expression, a perpetual smile, turned into a frown. "Something wrong?"

"No," Olivia lied. "I'm fine."

"I don't think so," he said worriedly, stopping for a moment to let her catch her breath.

"I'm fine," Olivia insisted, looking past the tall native to where Quinn had stopped to glance over his shoulder. "You'd think my feet would be accustomed to walking by now. That's all they've done for the last two and a half days."

She managed to get through the day, but the painful price

she paid for her stubbornness showed on her face when they stopped to make camp for the night.

When Quinn approached her, his brow was furrowed and he was scowling.

"You're limping." he said accusingly.

"My feet hurt," Olivia told him. It wasn't a lie, even if it wasn't the entire truth.

"Why don't I believe you?"

"I'm too tired to care what you believe or disbelieve, Mr. Quinlan."

He went from looking skeptical to looking outright angry. "You only call me Mr. Quinlan when you don't want to tell me something."

"I've never called you anything but Mr. Quinlan," Olivia reminded him. "As for my current state of exhaustion, the reason is apparent. Now, if you'll excuse me."

She started to turn away from him, when a stab of pain moved through her right leg. It crumpled under her and she would have fallen if not for Quinn's callused hand. Once she was standing upright again, Olivia tried to move ahead of him.

"That's it," Quinn said. "What's wrong? And don't bother lying this time."

Olivia squared her shoulders, thankful that no one but Echo could understand what was being said. "You're making a scene," she hissed.

"No, I'm asking a question," he retorted. "And I want an answer."

"Well, you're not going to get one," she replied angrily. "I'm tired and hungry and I want to sit down."

"Not so fast," Quinn demanded, catching hold of her arm.

She tried to swat his hand away, but there was no stopping him as he hauled her off in the direction of the tent Echo had just finished setting up. She looked around his towering body to where the native workers were going about their business, seemingly unconcerned that Quinn was manhandling her.

"I'm not your woman to be pulled hither and yon!" Olivia snapped.

Quinn knew he shouldn't be doing what he was doing, but he didn't care. The dainty little lady had a way of making him lose his temper, especially when she did her very best to ignore him, which was most of the time. She'd slept in his arms, and the way she'd kissed him was enough to give him certain rights, even if they weren't legitimate ones.

Once they were inside the tent, she turned on him like a cat, but her claws didn't get a chance to do any damage. Quinn grabbed her arms, pinning them to her sides. "You've got exactly one minute to tell me what's wrong with your leg."

"And if I don't?" she said passionately.

"Then I find out for myself."

"You wouldn't dare!"

Quinn didn't say a word. He simply stared at her, poised for the fight she was determined to give him.

"Sit down," he demanded, releasing her arms.

"Get out of this tent and leave me in peace," she said, so flustered she couldn't think straight. The man simply refused to be a gentleman about anything.

"This is *my* tent," he informed her. "And you're *my* woman. Or at least everyone thinks you are. That means no one is going to come rushing to your rescue."

"Echo knows better," she insisted.

Quinn chuckled. "You've slept next to me for the last two nights."

"But that doesn't . . ." Comprehension dawned in her brown eyes. "You scoundrel! You . . . You . . ." She didn't know the kind of words her rage demanded. "You're deliberating giving those men the wrong impression."

"It's for your own protection," Quinn said, defending his motives.

"I don't want your protection," she said, facing him, her hands clenched angrily at her sides. "I want you out of this tent. Immediately!"

"Sit down and shut up."

"I will not."

"Have it your way," he mumbled under his breath as he snatched her off her feet. She wiggled and squirmed, but he didn't drop her, and he didn't let go until she was sitting flat on her bottom with her legs spread out in front of her.

He reached down to untie her shoes.

Olivia kicked out, almost catching him under the chin with her right foot.

"Do that again and it won't be your leg hurting," Quinn warned. He added a lethal look to his words, and Olivia knew she'd be better off to sit still.

With her arms stretched out, she supported herself with her hands while Quinn unlaced her shoes.

He found the thick socks she'd purchased when she'd bought the walking boots. After they were jerked off her feet and tossed aside, he still had to deal with the cotton stockings. But before that, he cradled her right foot in the palm of his hands, flexing it gently to make sure she hadn't sprained it. "Does that hurt?"

"No," Olivia answered stiffly. "Are you satisfied?"

It's going to take a lot more than this to satisfy me, Quinn thought.

As he continued the tender examination, Olivia felt the heat of his hand turn into a hot rush of warmth that raced throughout her body. Her heartbeat increased as it always did when Quinn touched her in the slightest way, and she shut her mouth to keep from groaning with pleasure.

He rested her feet on his thighs, then began the task of rolling down her stockings. It only took Olivia a quick blink of her brown eyes to realize what he was about to do. She jerked her feet away, holding her skirt firmly in place. Her voice was jagged and shaky, but she managed to get the word said clearly enough for anyone to understand. "No."

"I want to check your feet for blisters," Quinn said.

"I don't have any blisters," she told him.

"Take them off."

Or I will, his gaze said.

Olivia looked over his shoulder at the canvas tent flaps, but freedom wasn't an option. Quinn was blocking her path and he was twice her size.

"Very well," she relented. "But turn your head."

He chuckled wickedly. "I've seen—"

"I don't care what you've seen," she said rigidly. "You're not seeing anything else. Now, turn your head."

Grinning, Quinn turned around so his back was to her.

Olivia hastily unrolled her stockings, then rearranged her petticoat and skirt so Quinn could examine her feet and nothing else.

"You can look now," she told him.

He shook his head, silently rebuking her for acting like a child. But when he cradled her bare foot in his hot hand, Olivia felt anything but childish. She struggled against the urge to let him go on touching her until there wasn't an inch of her body that hadn't felt the sensual abrasion of his strong hands.

"No blisters," he announced. His frown intensified as his gaze moved slowly up her body. His voice was tight and hard when he spoke, "Are you going to tell me what it is, or do I have to strip you bare and find out for myself? And don't lie to me," he added harshly.

Olivia swallowed hard, frantically searching for a way to keep her dignity intact.

"I'm losing my patience," Quinn pointed out. His hands were wrapped around her bare ankles, keeping her in place. Inch by slow inch, they began to move, easily forcing the hem of her skirt up despite her efforts to the contrary.

"Something bit me," she blurted out. "Some kind of insect, I think."

"Where?" His hands stilled.

"On my leg."

"Where on your leg?"

"Above my knee," she admitted hastily. "Are you satisfied now that I'm completely humiliated?"

"If you've got a bite that's making you limp, you're going to be even more embarrassed," Quinn informed her. "Pull up your skirt and let me see it."

"I'll do nothing of the kind."

He made a frustrated sound under his breath. "This isn't the time to remember all the things your mother taught you," he said impatiently. "This is Africa. A bite can be as bad as a broken bone. Now pull up your skirt. I've seen legs before."

Olivia pushed his hands away.

Quinn cursed.

The words were African, but Olivia didn't need an interpreter to know he'd reached the end of his rope.

He stood up, glaring down at her. "I'm going outside. Take off whatever needs to be taken off and cover up the rest. I'm going to have a look at that bite. With or without your cooperation," he finished sternly.

"You're—"

"I'm bigger and stronger and more stubborn than some

prissy little governess who'd rather have her leg rot off than show it to a man,'' he inserted. "Ten minutes," he told her.

Olivia stared at the canvas flaps that fluttered behind him. There was no use thinking she could keep Quinn out of the tent. Her leg throbbed as she came to her feet. After a few minutes of frantically searching her brain for a way out of the indelicate situation, she realized there wasn't one.

She wasn't afraid of Quinn; he'd been too gentle when he'd examined her feet for blisters, but she wasn't looking forward to having him examine her leg the same way. And she had no doubts that he'd have a good look at the bite, even if he had to sit on her to do it.

Exactly ten minutes later, Olivia froze in the act of slipping her nightgown over her head.

"I'm coming in," Quinn said from outside the tent.

"Not yet!"

He started counting, and Olivia knew he wasn't going to pass ten before the tent flaps opened, so she hurried, pushing the nightgown past her hips. Since the bite was midway up her thigh, there was no way Quinn could examine it while she was wearing her drawers, not unless he cut the leg open, and she wasn't about to have a perfectly good pair of muslin drawers ruined. She was naked under the nightgown, but she'd figured out a way to reveal the least amount of herself as possible, if Quinn would only give her time.

On the count of ten, he marched into the tent.

Olivia's fingers were tying the laces at the throat of the nightgown. She turned around, glaring at him.

"Sit down," he said, dropping the leather satchel that held his personal clothing onto the ground.

Using the robe she'd packed as a lap shawl, Olivia sat down on the blanket she'd unfolded after Quinn had left. Keeping her back to him and her mind focused on what had to be done, she raised the hem of the nightgown until she could see the bite. It was as red as a strawberry and almost as large. The center was slightly bruised from being rubbed all day, and it felt hot to the touch.

Once her entire right leg was bared, she draped the robe over her lap, tugging it under her left leg and over the junction of her thighs before she raised her hip. Once she sat down flat again, there was nothing for Quinn to see but her right leg. Too embarrassed for words, she told him she was ready.

He knelt beside her and looked at the inflamed area. "This didn't happen today," he said, seemingly unaffected by the sight of a woman's naked thigh.

"I'm not sure when I was bitten," she told him.

"Why didn't you say something?"

"I didn't think it was more than an ant bite," she told him, forcing herself to speak as if they were discussing the weather. "I brushed some off my valise yesterday morning."

Quinn frowned. "One thing the bush has plenty of is ants. And scorpions, and . . . It doesn't matter. Whatever it was, you've managed to turn it into a full-fledged boil."

Olivia struggled to keep her composure. Quinn was acting as if she'd invited the ant to nibble on her flesh, then deliberately done everything within her power to make herself miserable afterward.

Instead of touching her leg, Quinn pressed his hand against her forehead. "It's hard to tell if you're running a fever, you're blushing so hotly."

Olivia pushed his hand away.

"Sit still for a few minutes, butterfly," he said, smiling gently. "I'll be right back."

Olivia's shoulders slumped the moment Quinn left the tent. She was so dazed by the tenderness she'd heard in his voice, and the use of the nickname he'd given her, that all she could do was sit and stare as the sunset turned the western side of the tent into a red and gold canvas.

She heard Quinn talking to Echo, but she couldn't understand what was being said. An eternity passed before the tent flaps moved again and Quinn returned. This time he was carrying several canteens and the small basin she used to take her sponge baths.

He didn't say a word as he emptied one canteen into the basin. The water steamed and Olivia realized that it had been heated over the fire. She watched wordlessly as he lit the kerosene lantern, then opened his satchel. He took out a small leather case. When it was open, she could see what looked like medical instruments.

"One thing the bush teaches you is self-reliance," Quinn said. "I've taken out bullets, sewn up skin, and set broken bones. Hell, I even delivered a baby once."

No wonder a bare leg doesn't make him blink an eye, Olivia thought, then frowned at just how much life Quinn had experienced. Compared to her, he had lived a dozen lifetimes.

Quinn put the small medical case within reach, took a bar of soap out of the satchel and washed his hands in the steamy water. When he turned to look at her, his expression was as gentle as the sunset that was filling the tent with rich golden light.

"I'll try not to hurt you," he said.

Olivia braced herself for the touch of his hands. When it came, she flinched. Not because Quinn was being rough, but because the swollen area felt as if it were ready to burst.

"Easy, butterfly," Quinn whispered softly.

His tanned fingertips were a sharp contrast to the white skin of Olivia's inner thigh. With her legs sprawled out in front of her, it was too easy to imagine what she would look like lying naked on a feather mattress. Her skin was as pale and soft as the petals of a lily, and he wanted to do a hell of a lot more than touch a few benign inches of it. Just thinking about the parts hidden by the nightgown and robe were enough to make Quinn's body tighten with a hard, quick rush of desire.

"Does that hurt?" he asked as he lightly touched the reddened skin surrounding the bite.

"Yes," she admitted with a gasp of air.

Quinn forced his attention away from Olivia's young innocent body. He took a small scalpel out of the medical pack.

"What are you going to do?" she asked nervously.

"That boil has to be lanced. If I don't, you won't be able to walk at all tomorrow."

Before Olivia could consent to the procedure, Quinn pulled a square dressing out of the kit and placed it under her right thigh. Then he sterilized the scalpel with the small flame of the lantern. "It won't be more than a pin prick," he assured her.

Olivia wasn't afraid of having the boil lanced. It was the idea of Quinn playing doctor that had her emotionally disoriented. It seemed he was always having that affect on her, making her think one way and feel another.

"Do you want a drink of whiskey? I have a bottle in my satchel."

"Whiskey for a pin prick? I think not," she told him, then added, "but thank you for asking."

"Just take a deep breath and relax," Quinn said, kneeling by her side. The tip of the scalpel was hot, but no longer glowing. He rested his left hand against her naked thigh to keep her from flinching. "Ready?"

Olivia nodded, thinking his palm felt as hot as the inflamed area he was setting out to cure. Despite the unladylike way she was sitting and the seriousness of having a tiny insect bite turn into a boil, she couldn't help but enjoy the feel of his bare hand on her leg. The thought of curling up against his body and sleeping away the night was far more appealing than it should be.

Quinn watched Olivia for a moment, repeating to himself all the reasons why he shouldn't think of her as anymore more than a prissy pain in the ass, but the reasons fell away with each beat of his heart. He disliked the idea of causing her pain, even if it was for her own good.

He gave her a reassuring smile before he bent his head and concentrated on what had to be done. With a steady hand he cut a miniscule slice in the center of the swollen bite. It started to drain immediately. He watched the tiny stream of dark red blood flow over the curve of her white thigh and onto the dressing.

"I barely felt it," Olivia said. "And it feels better already."

"The pressure is gone," he told her. "It should drain naturally. Once the bleeding has stopped, I'll put some salve on it. You should be as right as rain, come morning."

"Thank you."

"You're welcome," he said. His expression turned pensive, then hard. "You should have told me about the bite this morning. If you had, I wouldn't be cleaning a scalpel right now."

Olivia wasn't in the mood to admit that she deserved his gentle scolding. Now that her leg was feeling better, all she wanted to do was sleep.

"What was it?" she asked.

"What was what?"

"The baby you delivered. Was it a boy or a girl?"

"A boy," Quinn said smiling. "Jerulla's son, Montagu."

"Oh," Olivia said, truly surprised.

"It's not something I'd want to do again," he admitted.

"But there wasn't time to find a woman to help her, and Montagu wasn't going to wait to be born."

"I'm sure you'll be a comfort to your wife, if you should ever marry. Most men don't know anything about babies, except how to make them." She blushed as soon as the words came out. A week ago, she'd wouldn't have dreamed of saying such a thing, but the time with Quinn had changed her so much she didn't know herself anymore.

"I've never made a baby and I don't plan on getting married."

If Quinn chose to spend his life alone, it was none of her concern, but the surety of his words unraveled the daydreams she'd been carrying around inside her. Averting her gaze, Olivia subdued her disappointment, reminding herself that when they reached Kimberley she had an inheritance to claim and a future of her own to build. If she was preoccupied with Quinn now, it was simply that circumstances had him ruling the stage. All that would pass as soon as the bush country was behind them.

Quinn turned his back, busying himself with the instruments he'd bought from a retiring physician and the salve he'd use as a poultice once the wound finished draining. He didn't want to look at the dark lashes framing Olivia's big brown eyes or the pale skin of her bared leg or the way her breasts pushed suggestively against her nightgown. As soon as he had her settled for the night, he was going to take himself away from camp and find a nice lonely spot where he could drink the whiskey she'd refused.

He walked to the opening of the tent, tossed the water he'd used to wash his hands onto the ground, then refilled the basin with hot water from the second canteen. After dampening a cloth, he handed it to Olivia.

She bathed the small wound, washing away the infection and the blood. The area was still red, but the swelling had diminished to almost nothing. When Quinn opened the tin of salve, Olivia covered her nose with her hand. "It stinks."

"That it does, Miss St. John," he agreed laughingly. "It's baobab bark, ground into a fine powder and mixed with God only knows what. It's Echo's recipe, not mine." He put some of the smelly salve on a clean square of cloth. "It won't sting, even if it does stink."

After the dressing was in place, he smiled. "You can cover up your leg now."

With a sigh of relief, Olivia tucked her nightgown into place, but not before Quinn caught a quick glimpse of the soft brown curls between her legs. He gritted his teeth. The temptation to lay her back onto the blanket was almost more than he could resist. He wanted to touch the soft curves of her body, to let his hands roam as they pleased, to taste the sweet mouth that he'd been thinking about all day, to take her right then and there.

He had the temptation under control by the time Olivia looked up at him, her dark eyes glowing with an emotion he couldn't identify. He wasn't expecting the small smile she gave him. It drew her name from him in a rough caress of breath as he held her by the shoulders and covered her mouth.

Her body, forbidden to him moments before, was suddenly accessible. He ran his hands from her shoulders to her wrists, feeling the tension melt as she leaned into the kiss rather than away from it. Her hands fluttered hesitantly. He placed them against his chest, palms down, letting her feel the hammering reaction of his heart. Slowly, he turned the kiss into an event, a long lingering melting of mouths and tongues, of breath and heat, and an undeniable wanting that began to run out of control as his hands continued their sensual exploration. He lifted her upward, arching her body into his, and nibbled at the corner of her mouth.

"Do you know what you do to me, butterfly?"

The question went unanswered because Olivia didn't have the breath or the wits to reply. She could feel his hands resting just below her breasts and they ached for him to touch them. When he did, her nipples went taut, begging for something she didn't understand. All she could do was kiss him back, leaning into his embrace, wanting time to stand still so this wonderful feeling could go on forever.

"One kiss isn't enough," Quinn whispered, if a moan could be called a whisper. His mouth opened over hers again, his teeth gently teasing, his tongue dipping and tasting while his body wanted to do so much more. His hands moved in the same slow sensual rhythm, fondling her breasts, making her ache in the very center of her body, forcing all logic from her mind.

Olivia's hands responded. Her fingers curled like talons, digging into the front of his shirt, holding onto him because there was nothing else in the world she wanted more.

Slowly, Quinn lowered her to the blanket, covering her upper body with his. The kiss went on and on while her heart pounded and her blood ran wild. She didn't make a sound, but he could feel her response, feel the female warmth of her pressing closer and closer, silently begging for him not to stop. He had just enough sanity left to refuse the sensual plead.

"Butterfly," he said tentatively, his mouth resting against the sensitive skin of her throat. He drew in a deep breath, trying to calm the riotous sensations that had his body so hard he couldn't stand up and walk away from her.

A sob caught in Olivia's throat, but it wasn't caused by pain or fear or embarrassment. She was simply reacting to the turbulence inside her heart and body, a storm fed by confusion and desire and sensual awareness. Her hands were still knotted in the front of his shirt. She forced them to relax, to release him because she sensed he wanted to be free.

Quinn looked down at her, feeling more in that moment than he'd ever felt before. Her eyes were closed and her mouth was swollen from his kisses. His right hand was still cradling her breast. Desire was burning his body, but what he was feeling wasn't entirely physical. It was . . . What the hell was it about this woman that made him forget every ounce of common sense he'd ever possessed?

"Get some rest," he said huskily, struggling to his feet. He didn't dare look at her as he stuffed the medical kit into the leather satchel. "Echo will bring you some dinner."

Then he was gone.

How many times have I seen that man turn his back and walk away? Olivia asked herself once she was alone. *More times than I want,* she had to admit. Intelligently, she was grateful that Quinn hadn't taken advantage of the opportunity she'd given him, but that was her mind talking. Her body was screaming for more kisses, more touching, more of everything Quinn had taught her to want so desperately. Wiping away a traitorous tear, Olivia turned onto her side and stared at the canvas wall of the tent, feeling empty and more alone than she'd ever felt in her life.

Eight

It was a quiet night, bright and cool, the sky as black as pitch, the moon pale and shimmering. Quinn drew a deep breath. The air had the scent of bush grass and dust and animals mixed with it. The stillness was broken only by the whisper of wind over the ground and the hum of insects. But he found it hard to enjoy the tranquility surrounding him. Even while staring at the countless stars dotting the heavens, he was thinking about the woman sleeping in the tent. The warm whiskey he was sipping wasn't helping him to forget the way Olivia had felt in his arms. Its raw burning taste couldn't wash the essence of her from his mouth. The cool night air wasn't easing the heat in his body. He was still aroused, still unsatisfied.

Taking another sip of whiskey, Quinn cursed his inability to sleep. No, not sleep. He might as well be honest with himself. He could fall asleep standing up, he was so tired. He didn't trust himself to go back to the tent, to lie down beside her, knowing she was within easy reach. He wanted her too much to refuse himself a second time in one night.

And she wanted him.

He'd felt it this evening. Her reaction hadn't been shock or curiosity or uncertainty. Miss Olivia St. John had been just as aroused, just as wanting, and just as willing as he'd been.

That was something he hadn't expected, and he hated the unexpected. It threw him off balance and put him on the defensive. What was even more irritating was knowing that he hadn't been on the defensive for years, not with a woman. As much as he enjoyed female beauties, he had never cared enough to feel threatened by them.

Quinn contemplated all this while he watched thin ghostly clouds drift across the moon, darkening the already black shadows of the landscape. Gazing across the distance to where the campfire burned bright orange in front of the two tents, he sorted through the events that had him sitting in the dark, sipping whiskey, when he should be sleeping.

First, Sidney Falk had tricked him into taking a pretty brown-eyed governess under his wing. He'd get even with the solicitor in time. Secondly, he, himself, had been foolish enough to think he could intimidate her into backing down from the trip to Kimberley by insisting that she routinely kiss him along the way. He was paying the price of his folly this very minute. And last, but not least, if he could go back to Cape Town, to that day in Sidney's office, and undo everything, he wouldn't.

Quinn took another swig of whiskey. The simple truth wasn't easy to face for a man who prided himself on being honest. His reluctance to change things had to be blamed on something, so he blamed it on his zest for challenges and danger. Keeping his desire for Olivia under control was definitely a challenge. The danger was in wanting the woman in the first place.

The sensual impasse was going to get worse before it got better, which meant he was a damn fool for thinking he could stop what instinct and Mother Nature had started. Olivia wasn't going to be content until she'd experienced what she'd just discovered was hovering on the horizon.

Maybe it was for the best, he told himself, as he pushed the cork into the top of the whiskey bottle, then reached for the rifle resting by his side. If Miss Olivia St. John of Portsmouth really wanted to be an independent, self-reliant woman, she was going to have to do a lot of growing up in a very short time.

South Africa was long on hardships and short on compassion.

A woman alone was prey for more than wild animals, especially in a mining town. Once they got to Kimberley, the lady would find herself at the mercy of unscrupulous men who wouldn't give a damn about her vulnerability or her heart. Olivia had lived her whole life surrounded by family, protected by her parents, sheltered from the crude hard facts that were as much a part of African life as the lions that fed on the weakest members of an impala herd.

She was a proper lady with a fine English upbringing. But most of all she was innocent. Too innocent to understand what he wanted from her, and too vulnerable to handle the consequences if he took her. She'd give herself with a bunch of romantic notions attached and cry her eyes out when she realized passion and love didn't always go hand in hand. Young ladies of the day were taught that sexual pleasure was something dark and unseemly, something they submitted to only after a wedding ring had been slipped on their finger. They filled in the void with daydreams of love, expecting a man to honor those dreams and be a gentleman.

What those young ladies didn't know, what Olivia didn't know, was that men weren't naturally pallid and courteous. The male gender was ruled by the same primal instincts as any other male of any other species. They were sexually aggressive. Society established the rules, and the men who lived in civilized places accepted them, but civilization and society barely had a toehold in Africa.

Olivia was ripe and ready for picking by the first gentleman who came along, but who said that man would be any better than he was? The odds were that the gentleman would be a hell of a lot worse. At least Quinn wouldn't lie to her, whispering sweet promises in her ear, then forgetting them as soon as he got his pants back on.

So, if Olivia wanted to become a woman in his arms, Quinn was more than willing to oblige her. He wouldn't blindside her with kisses, and he wouldn't seduce her. He'd go back to their original arrangement, one he'd altered without her even knowing it. She'd be doing the kissing from now on, not him. And if she wanted more, then he'd make damn sure she understood that marriage wasn't part of the bargain. His body might not like the decision, but at least his conscience wouldn't beat him black and blue.

Olivia couldn't believe it. Quinn was acting like a stranger again.

He'd stomped into the tent that morning, seconds after her eyes had opened, to shove a canteen and the tin of smelly salve into her hands. "Clean the bite and put more salve on it. You'll be riding in the cart today."

She hadn't had time to reply yea or nay. He'd left as quickly as he'd entered, making her wonder if their last encounter might have been an illusion, a fever dream brought on by the insect bite.

It was late afternoon now and her escort hadn't spoken another word. When she'd asked Echo if something was wrong, the servant had opened the flap of Quinn's leather satchel, pulled out a half empty whiskey bottle and smiled in wordless explanation.

So Quinn had been drinking, had he?

A week ago, Olivia would have applauded the man's obvious headache, but a lot had changed in the course of a few days. Mostly her.

She was beginning to understand Quinn, or at least she was beginning to understand why he'd been reluctant to bring her into the bush. Everything he'd warned her about, the fatigue, the heat, the insects, had all been true. So far, she wasn't displaying herself well, but she didn't think Quinn had consumed half a bottle of whiskey because she'd been bitten by an ant. She suspected that he might not like what was happening between them, even though he'd initiated it with his unorthodox payment arrangements.

As the cart rolled and swayed over the uneven ground, rocking her insides until she thought her kidneys might come loose, she wondered what Quinn was thinking. As he had all through the day, he periodically stopped walking to scan the horizon. Whenever he did, Olivia followed suit, but all she saw was more rolling grasslands, speckled with scrawny trees. She'd grown accustomed to the sight of animal herds grazing in the distance. Seeing what she'd seen for the last three days, she wondered if Quinn was actually looking for something or simply following his natural wary instincts.

Probably the latter of the two, she decided. He was a diamond jackal, after all. A man who lived looking over his shoulder, expecting the worse. For him, being cautious was simply something he did without thinking, a reflex of the life he'd chosen to live.

When they pitched camp for the night, Quinn made himself scarce, reaffirming Olivia's suspicions that he planned on avoiding her if at all possible.

Since her leg was feeling much better, she helped Echo wash the wild yams he'd dug for dinner. In the distance, lilac-colored clouds lay on the horizon while thin streaks of gold, the last of the sunset, pierced the evening sky. There was an unusual calmness to the air. Not a leaf was moving as the sounds of the night began to be heard.

"Quinn told me that he delivered Jerulla's son," Olivia said, taking advantage of the privacy she and Echo had been allotted to ask a few questions. God knew she had a thousand she didn't dare ask Quinn himself.

"Quinn scared that night." The big native laughed. "Echo scared, too. No women to help and Jerulla crying, calling out to the spirits to help her bring her son into the world. No place for men."

"Was Montagu born at the farm?"

The servant shook his head, then pointed north. "Two, maybe three days from here. We come back from mines . . ." He handed her another yam to scrub. His customary smile faded as his ebony face expressed the feelings that came with the memory. "Quinn not want to bring Jerulla. Warned Zaruara against it. But he no listen."

"Zaruara?"

"Jerulla's husband," Echo told her. "Good man, but stubborn."

"I know what you mean," Olivia mumbled her breath. "Did Zaruara work for Quinn?" If she didn't ask, she'd never know. It was obvious that Quinn wasn't going to tell her anything.

"Many years," he replied. "When Jerulla come to farm, Zaruara like her, but she too young. Quinn said no. So Zaruara wait."

"So he waited, and eventually he married Jerulla with Quinn's blessing," Olivia surmised.

"Big wedding feast." Echo was back to smiling.

"What happened to Zaruara?"

"Killed. Carrying diamonds." Echo looked toward the small koppie where Quinn was sitting, taking the first evening watch. "Many diamonds that time. Much trouble."

Olivia put aside the yellowish yam she'd just washed. "Someone tried to steal the diamonds and Zaruara was killed."

Echo pulled up the sleeve of the coarsely woven tunic he was wearing to show Olivia a white scar that slashed across his upper arm. "I shot. Quinn shot. Zaruara killed."

A sudden weakness stole Olivia's breath. Quinn had told her that his work was dangerous, and she'd told herself that he was a man at risk, but seeing the scar on Echo's arm, hearing the words spoken, made the reality even more acute. Quinn had been shot. He could have been killed. He could be shot again, or murdered for the diamonds he carried back from the mines. What kind of man purposely made himself a target? A man who didn't care if he lived or died? No, not Quinn. He was too full of life to be suicidal. Money? Olivia didn't think so. His home in Calvinia had been built to function as a farm, not a country home for holiday retreats. And he seemed content in the bush, despite the danger.

"Jerulla was with you?" she prompted, taking the last of the wild yams from Echo's large hands and putting them in the basin to soak.

"Quinn push her out of the way. Madness," Echo said, trying to describe the confusion that had come with the ambush. "Six men. All dead before Quinn put down his rifle."

Olivia closed her eyes, fighting the image that was forming in her mind. Quinn wounded, but still fighting. Echo shot,

as well. Zaruara murdered. And Jerulla . . . Had the shock
of seeing her husband killed brought on a premature labor?
Was that why her son had been born in the bush, in the
middle of nowhere with no one to help her but Quinn and
Echo?

Did Quinn feel responsible for her? Of course, he did,
Olivia told herself. That's why she lived at the farm with
her son.

As she opened her eyes, Olivia looked toward the small
rise of land where Quinn was sitting, his back resting against
the stump of a dead tree. As always, the Mauser rifle was
by his side. Her heart swelled with respect as the jealousy
she'd harbored over Jerulla faded. The exotically beautiful
housekeeper had been a child when she'd come into Quinn's
custody. He had watched over her, blessing her marriage to
Zaruara only when he knew she was ready to be a wife.
Then, when she'd been turned into a widow, he'd brought
her back to the farm, giving her and Montagu a home.

The acknowledgment of Quinn's compassion for others
only increased Olivia's concern. That's why Sidney Falk
trusted him. Not because he was honest, but because he truly
cared about people. He'd protected Jerulla that day in the
bush the same way he'd protect his current ward, with his
own life.

The short conversation with Echo had revealed much
more than Olivia had expected. Her reaction, the clutching
fear that had gripped her heart at the thought of Quinn being
killed, was an exhibit of just how much she'd come to care
about him. The way he had kissed her last night, whispering
that one kiss wasn't enough, could be taken as a sign that
he was beginning to care for her in return.

*Of course, you couldn't prove that by the way he's been
treating me today*, Olivia thought. *Will he avoid me all*

evening? What about later, when we're in the tent? Will he kiss me like he did last night?

Three hours passed before Olivia had her answer. The only light was the pale halo around the moon and the dancing flames of the campfire when Quinn finally entered the tent.

Olivia pretended to be sleeping. The lantern was out and she doubted Quinn could see her face. Lying on her side, she watched his shadowy shape as he sat down on the blanket to pull off his boots. She heard the soft rustle of the spare blanket as he rolled it into a pillow, and the weary sigh that followed when he finally stretched out to sleep.

"How's the leg?" he asked.

Olivia smiled in the darkness. She hadn't fooled him at all. "It's much better. No itching and the swelling is gone. I'll return the salve in the morning."

"Keep it," Quinn said. "If you get bitten again, use the salve right away. Don't be stubborn about it."

"I wasn't stubborn the first time," she argued lightly. "I was—"

"Being a lady," Quinn finished for her, reminding himself at the same time.

"And you dislike ladies?" She tried to see his face in the dark, but she couldn't. All she could make out was the darker shape of his long, lean body resting a few feet away. Much too far if he planned on collecting his daily kiss.

"Go to sleep," he said, avoiding an answer. He turned over then, offering her his back.

Disappointment replaced anticipation as she realized Quinn wasn't going to kiss her good night.

Disappointment reigned for another three days and nights. They continued through the bush country. The wheels of the ox cart rolled across the arid ground as Olivia walked

by its side, always aware that Quinn was just a few yards
ahead. He moved with the natural ease of a man at home
in the wild landscape that stretched out in all directions.

Beneath the shield of her wide-brimmed hat, Olivia looked
around her. The more she saw of this country, the more she
felt at home in the heat and dust and isolation that was such
a contrast to the rain-drenched city she'd once called home.
Had her uncle felt that way? Loving the vastness as much
as he had once loved England?

Reaching into the pocket of her skirt, Olivia wrapped her
fingers around the small wooden lion. It had been the symbol
of her dreams until she'd arrived in Cape Town. Now it was
the symbol of her determination. She would make a life in
this raw beautiful country, a satisfying life, a life where she
could simply be who and what she wanted to be.

Up ahead, Quinn stopped walking. He watched the horizon for a long moment, but his eyes were gradually drawn
to the ground he'd already crossed. He looked over his
shoulder, seeing Olivia beside the cart. She was keeping up
far better than he'd expected. In fact, the three-week trip
across the bush wasn't going to take as long as he'd predicted. They were halfway to Prieska. Another week at the
most, and they'd be boarding the train that would take them
to Kimberley and the inheritance she'd come all the way
from England to claim.

Slowly, Quinn's gaze returned to the rugged land in front
of him. He concentrated on the sights and sounds around
him: the dust from hundreds of hooves, a fine powder kicked
up by the animals grazing lazily only a few miles away, the
chatter of birds hidden in the tangled branches of paperbark
and sour plum trees, the soft almost soundless whisper of
the wind, but none of the things pushed the memory of
Olivia from his mind. Time wasn't helping him to forget
the way she'd felt in his arms or the taste of her mouth

when he'd taken it so passionately. The long days and star-studded nights only intensified the wanting.

When Olivia and Echo stopped only a few feet away from where Quinn was standing, he could see the deep hue of her eyes, shining with the same excitement he always felt when he was in the bush. He felt that excitement radiate through his own body, making the desire he'd sworn to control leap to life again. As she smiled at him, the shy fleeting smile of an innocent young woman, Quinn knew that she was coming to love this wild land the same way he loved it, with his every soul.

It took all his willpower not to reach for her then, to pull her close, so he could smell the scent of the lilac soap she used every night, mixed with the fragrance of woman. He wanted to wrap his arm around her waist, to keep her by his side, as they both studied a landscape as old and primal as life itself.

As Olivia took off her hat to let the faint breeze that had been blowing all day cool her skin, Quinn looked away. He didn't want her to see the hunger in his eyes.

They stopped long enough to quench their thirst for water, then started walking again. This time Olivia didn't keep pace with Echo and the sluggish ox cart. She walked beside Quinn, determined to end the brooding silence that had existed between them since the night he'd stolen her breath with kisses so sweet and wonderful she couldn't think of anything else.

They walked in silence for a few minutes, putting some distance between themselves and the others. Olivia used the time to think about what she wanted to say. How did you remind a man that he'd forgotten to kiss you?

Quinn tried not to think at all. He could deal with wanting a woman. He'd gone weeks without one before. But this woman had him fighting more than physical desire. Her steadfastness, getting up every morning for the last week, putting on her boots, and walking mile after lonely mile, had earned his admiration. Her appreciation of the land most women would call too wild and too lonely created a bond between them that he'd never shared with another female. Sleeping in the same tent, listening to her breathe, had spurred an intimacy unlike any he'd ever known before.

It was distracting and more disturbing than Quinn wanted to admit.

"You can't avoid me," Olivia said, giving him a quick glance.

Quinn didn't say anything for a long time. He'd known this conversation was coming. He'd postponed it as long as he could, thinking she might get her temper up and figure out she was better off without him. Obviously, that hadn't happened.

"We'll reach a Khoikhoi village tomorrow," he said after a few long steps that didn't keep Olivia from matching him stride for stride. The lady wasn't going to be assigned to the rear ranks any longer.

"Echo told me about them," she said, greedy for any conversation Quinn was willing to share with her. "He said they're herdsmen."

"Goats," he explained. "Centuries before Vasco da Gama, the Portuguese navigator, ever reached the Cape of Good Hope, the Khoikhoi were hunters like their cousins the Khoisan. Now they tend their herds and move across the karoo like the seasons, following the grass and the water."

"What water? I haven't seen more than a footprint full since we left Calvinia."

Quinn sighed and tugged his hat lower over his eyes. "The first real water you'll see is the Orange River. We'll cross it by train."

Grass crunched under their feet as Olivia tried not to

think about reaching civilization again. Once they did, Quinn would go his separate way.

"Why haven't you kissed me for the last three days?" There, she'd said it.

Quinn kept walking as he answered her. "Our arrangement was that you'd do the kissing. Why haven't you kissed me for the last three days?"

"But . . . you kissed me the last time," Olivia pointed out, slightly embarrassed by the conversation but determined to finish it. Hastily she added, "And the time before."

"I thought you needed a few lessons to get the hang of things," he said, sounding like his old arrogant self again. "Now that you know what to do. Do it, or forget about it."

She looked at the toes of her walking boots, scuffed from miles of walking, then at Quinn, then back at the ground. "Okay."

"Okay?"

"Okay," Olivia said. She moistened her dry lips with the tip of her tongue.

Quinn thought she was going to kiss him right then and there.

"I'll kiss you this evening. A good-night kiss."

Quinn began to wonder just where Miss Olivia St. John had gotten her gumption. She hadn't learned it at finishing school. Maybe she'd inherited it from the uncle who had come to South Africa years ago. Wherever she'd gotten it, she was giving him fits.

"What if I want more than a good-night kiss?" Quinn asked, glaring down at her as if he'd like nothing better than for her to disappear in a puff of smoke. "What if I told you that I'm no city gentleman who's willing to settle for a chaste kiss on the cheek and a little hand-holding when your chaperone isn't watching? What if I told you that I want you naked the next time I kiss you, as naked as the day you were born? Does that make you blush all the way to your pretty English toes, Miss St. John? It should. I like women. I like them too much to be satisfied by prissy little kisses that don't come close to satisfying a real man.''

"Hell, you'd swoon dead away if I told you what it really takes to satisfy a man," he added gruffly. "Hold onto your fancy daydreams, pretty lady. I've been around too long, and lived too hard, to think they'll bring you anything but trouble.''

Olivia stood still under the insulting remarks, not because she liked them, but because she could heard the sadness in Quinn's voice. He was trying to drive a wedge between them, trying to force her to dislike him. If he cut her sharply enough with his words, she wouldn't come back for more. If she took his insults to heart, she wouldn't want his attention. Well, the man was too late. She didn't dislike him. And she wanted to be kissed again.

Their bone-weary trek through the bush country had taught Olivia a very valuable lesson. She wasn't weak. In her own way, she was just as strong as Quinn. Strong enough to withstand his glaring looks and standoffish ways.

"Then I'll be sure not to give you a prissy good-night kiss," she retorted sweetly.

This time it was Quinn who watched her turn and walk away.

The Khoikhoi village appeared on the horizon just before sunset. The tribe had moved south, letting their herds graze on the last of the spring grass before heading north toward the fertile basin that followed the Orange River. The cluster of huts and the half-naked children playing nearby brought a smile to Olivia's face. They were greeted by the tribal chief, a short man with bowed legs and black wrinkled skin.

His small ebony eyes gleamed like black diamonds as he surveyed Olivia's wrinkled appearance.

When he spoke, the words, formed by pressing his tongue against the roof of his mouth, sounded almost poetic.

"We've been invited to a feast," Quinn explained.

"It sounds wonderful," Olivia replied, no longer so much of a lady she couldn't admit when she was hungry.

"That depends on whether they roast a monkey or a goat," Quinn said. He laughed at the expression that came over her face, then leaned down, closer than he'd been in days, and whispered into her ear. "Be careful. Offending a tribal chief's hospitality can get you into a lot of trouble."

Olivia gave him a scalding look before she glanced back at the chief. The little man smiled back, revealing a large gap in the top row of his white teeth. He motioned for her to follow him. After an encouraging nod from Quinn, she did, and was led to a large hut. When he pulled back the coarse blanket covering the doorway, Olivia stepped inside.

A short time later Echo brought her valise and a earthen jar of water. The hut wasn't large, but it was far more spacious than the tent she'd been sleeping in for the last week or so. Animal skins covered the floor. Using the privacy to its best advantage, Olivia took a quick sponge bath and changed into the last of her clean blouses. The first thing she was going to do when they reached Prieska was take a two-hour bath.

The feast was a modest dinner of baked yams and, as Quinn had predicted, roasted goat. The men drank a crude type of beer, brewed from local grains and honey. Olivia refused the dark goat meat with a cordial smile, noticing that no one took offense when she passed the wooden platter to Quinn. "Afraid to taste a delicacy?" he teased her.

"Your opinion of a delicacy and mine are two different things," she said, before turning her attention back to the

group of natives that had gathered into a large circle. There
were as many women as men. Their curiosity made her feel
uncomfortable until one of the women pointed at Quinn
and smiled. Olivia looked at the handsome bushmen sitting
crossed-legged by her side and shook her head in the univer-
sal gesture that meant no. The women laughed out loud.

"Will you please tell these people that I'm *not* your
woman?" Olivia hissed, wishing all the while that she were.

"Why? They aren't going to believe it," Quinn replied.
"I've been traveling across this country for years. I've never
brought a woman with me before."

"What about Jerulla?"

"What about her?"

"She traveled with you," Olivia reminded him.

"Echo's been telling tales."

"Don't be upset with him," she said. "He didn't give
away any secrets."

Quinn's expression turned skeptical, then bland. "Jerulla
was born in this country. She may have white blood, but
her heart is African."

Olivia was about to say something, but her mouth ended
up shaping a wordless sound as a woman sitting across from
Quinn casually dropped the shoulder of her native dress and
began nursing her baby. Olivia had seen her own breasts,
but never those of another woman, and she'd certainly never
seen a woman nursing a child in full view of anyone who
cared to watch.

"I told you things were done differently here," Quinn
said following her gaze to where the infant suckled greedily
at his mother's dark nipple. He'd seen hundreds of bare-
chested native women and almost as many nursing infants.
"That doesn't make these people immoral. It just makes
them different."

Olivia watched the infant nursing and felt her own maternal instincts respond. Under the heavy cotton of her stiff-collared blouse her nipples turned taut, the same way they did when Quinn kissed her. Her gaze moved from the nursing mother to the man sitting at her side. "You're jumping to conclusions again. I don't think these people are immoral."

"Most Europeans do," he replied curtly. "They come here thinking it's their Christian duty to convert them, to civilize them, when the truth is these people are more religious, more committed to their beliefs, than any missionary I've ever met."

"What do they believe?" Olivia asked, curious and sincere at the same time.

"Their religion is as pragmatic as the lives they lead," he told her. "The high god is too remote, so they depend on the myriad spirits inhabiting the world to listen to their prayers. They also believe that animals have souls, just like men. The spirit of a lion can be as powerful as the warrior who slays it."

"Spirits?"

"The essence of the people and animals that once walked the same earth we do. Their chiefs and witch doctors use the past to explain the present and the future," he instructed her.

"And the spirits lived in the past."

He smiled at her keen insight. "Without their faith, the harmony and unity of the tribe would cease to exist. They see their faith as clearly as they see the land around them. To most of them, it's one and the same."

Olivia's heart skipped a beat at the reverence in Quinn's voice. He understood these people because he accepted them for what they were, demanding nothing from them in return. He shared his supplies; they shared the warmth of their fire.

She looked at the nursing mother. The infant was asleep

now, its tiny fist curled against the woman's full breast. When the woman smiled, Olivia smiled in reply.

Quinn watched her from the corner of his eye. The young lady was becoming more and more of a mystery.

He turned to the chief, rattling off some words. The man nodded, then waved his hand toward the horizon.

"Come on," Quinn said, unfolding his long legs and standing. "I want to show you something."

"What?"

"Just come on," he urged her, holding out his hand.

She took his hand long enough to stand, then released it. It wasn't what she wanted to do, but her manners were too well-engrained for her to forget them completely.

They walked beyond the circle of huts, moving toward the gold and red light of the setting sun. Just being with Quinn, close enough to reach out and touch him if she chose, was enough for now. It was shocking to realize just how deeply this man had touched her heart and her senses, much deeper than she'd ever thought another person could reach.

They left the village behind, moving toward a high koppie where several sour plum trees grew so closely together their branches had become entwined. As they walked, Olivia tried to calmly solve the puzzle she and Quinn created. On the surface, they had nothing in common, nothing to give her hope that the attraction and affection she felt for him could or would be returned. Deeper down, in the very center of her heart, she wondered if she'd ever understand him. Could love flourish without understanding? Could it grow when there was nothing but dreams to give it roots?

When they were standing under the twisted branches of the largest tree, Quinn put down his rifle and reached into the pocket of his jacket. He pulled out a small spyglass. The burnished brass gleamed in the fading sunlight. He held the magnifying instrument up to his eye, his head moving slowly as he scanned the basin of land lying at the bottom of the hill.

"There," he said, keeping his voice low and soft. He handed Olivia the glass. "Look toward that patch of bushes, then just a little to the left."

She followed his instructions, then sucked in her breath. The lion was resting on its belly with its large paws spread in front of him, like an Egyptian sphinx. It was a male with a bushy black mane. The animal's reddish-gold coat gleamed in competition with the sunset. Its amber eyes blinked lazily just before it opened its mouth to yawn. Olivia saw the large pointed teeth that could bite through muscle and bone as easily as a human bit into a piece of soft bread. But she wasn't afraid. Looking at the lion was like looking at Quinn. All she could think about was its muscular grace and strength. And like Quinn, the animal represented a land she longed to understand and embrace.

"He's magnificent," she said in awe. "I never imagined how magnificent."

She lowered the spyglass, turning to look at Quinn. "How did you know he was here?"

"The chief told me. Most of the men will be up all night, making sure your magnificent beast doesn't make a dinner out of one of their goats."

Olivia looked toward the bushes again. The lion blended into the landscape, a respected foe that ruled by strength and reputation. *Like Quinn*, she thought. He's admired and feared because the men who have tried to rob him have failed.

"Thank you for showing me the lion," she said.

"You're welcome."

Silence stretched between them as Quinn collapsed the spyglass and returned it to the pocket of his bush coat.

"I'd like to kiss you now," Olivia heard herself say.

Quinn replied with a hoarse sound deep in his chest. He didn't move as she stepped closer, raising her hands to rest them just below his shoulders. She could feel the heat of his body and the fierce beating of his heart. Standing on her tiptoes, she pressed her mouth gently against his, surprised by her own daring and the wave of sensation that engulfed her the moment their mouths touched.

Quinn couldn't stop his arms from wrapping around her or the groan of pleasure that came when the tip of her tongue gently caressed his lips.

"That's one," Olivia whispered softly, leaning back just enough to look into his brilliant blue eyes. "It's been three days. You've earned two more kisses."

Nine

The golden sunlight was fading to the colorless shades of twilight when Olivia leaned toward Quinn's mouth a second time. She'd never seen his eyes burn so brightly, but the heat was mixed with a longing she recognized easily now. She felt the same sweet urging racing in her own blood. The knowledge that she was risking her heart was blotted out by the overwhelming need that was bubbling up inside her.

The fear and doubts and vulnerability she'd carried for the last three days were brushed aside by the soft breeze that came with the darkening of the sky. The only thing that mattered was the hard line of Quinn's mouth, softening even as she reached for it. This man was what he was, hard and honest, fearless, and beyond the reach of her dreams. But she wasn't dreaming now. The evening was real, he was real, and she was in his arms again.

Quinn experienced a momentary rush of regret that faded

as quickly as it came. A shiver ran through him; his chest tightened with agony and pleasure combined. He could feel the warmth of Olivia's breath against his mouth. Her velvety eyes had taken on the darker sheen of passion, and he could feel the slight trembling of her body as he tightened his arms, drawing her nearer.

When the kiss came it was warm and open-mouthed and more than Quinn could resist. His mouth pressed firmly against hers for a long moment. Then needing more than the chaste touching of mouths, his tongue eased between her parted lips. Her eyes closed, their dark lashes resting against skin that had been warmed by the sun, glowing with health. She relaxed, accepting his embrace, enjoying the kiss like the young, curious woman she was.

When the kiss ended, he rested his mouth against her temple, close to her ear. She was leaning against him, allowing his body to support her weight, trusting him in the instinctive way God had intended for female to trust male.

"Butterfly," Quinn whispered while he rubbed her back with his left hand, stroking slowly from neck to waist, before inching his hand down to the very base of her spine and pressing gently, urging her even closer.

His right hand moved to her neck, pushing aside the starched eyelet lace so he could caress her throat with the callused tip of his index finger. He planted a kiss there, where her pulse was beating rapidly, blowing against the same spot when he lifted his mouth.

A breeze, carrying the scent of the bush country, wrapped her skirt around her legs, but all Olivia could feel was Quinn's warm breath. He shifted her until all she could feel was him. He was a steamy warmth that engulfed her. She shivered as if she was cold, but there was nothing but heat inside her. A deep, hot, coiling heat that demanded something she knew she shouldn't want. If kissing Quinn was sinful, if enjoying the feelings he brought to life was wicked, then she was damned for eternity, because she couldn't deny herself the third kiss.

Quinn was feeling just as damned. Every thought in his head was screaming for him to release the soft woman in his arms, to free her and himself from something that had no future, only momentary pleasure and the certainty that no matter how much he wanted her, he didn't want marriage and all the things that went with it. But even while his head was telling him to let Olivia go, his hands were drawing her closer, enticing her with the smooth pressure of his left palm pressed against her lower back while his right hand continued to caress the sensitive skin of her neck. His fingers began undoing buttons, slowly revealing more of Olivia's soft skin. He gently rocked her against him, letting her feel the power of his desire, teasing himself and her until there was nothing but an unanswered desire burning so brightly it shone like the sun that was slowly vanishing beyond the horizon.

His mouth sought hers this time, kissing her with a searing tenderness, cherishing her in a way he'd never cherished another woman. She trembled in his arms as he taught her about dreaming and sexual hunger and how much pleasure a man could give a woman. He wanted to lose himself in her arms. The simple truth of just how much he wanted her was frightening. He'd had women before, but he'd never had the innocent passion Olivia was giving him.

More buttons came undone as his hands did what they wanted, touching starched cotton and tiny shell buttons, then soft muslin and lace, then an even softer woman. With hot caresses, he traced the swell of her breasts while his mouth seduced hers, overwhelming her senses with his touch and taste.

Keeping her eyes closed, Olivia followed the wordless commands of his hands, lifting herself against him, swaying within the circle of his arms as her knees went weak. The moonlight became silver fire, the air a musky blanket that covered them. Her sighs and gasps mixed with the sounds of the night. He whispered words she didn't recognize but instinctively understood.

"My God, you're beautiful." His voice was tight, his breath hot and rushed as his mouth moved from her swollen lips to the swell of her breasts. His tongue licked and tasted, his teeth nibbled and teased, and all the while Olivia clung to him, her fingers digging into the folds of his shirt.

When his mouth closed over a taut pink nipple, her head arched backward, unconsciously offering him her body. Her lips parted in a soft moan as Quinn accepted the invitation, sucking more of her into his hot mouth, teaching her that passion was both painful and sweet, wonderful and unbearable.

Feelings exploded inside Olivia, sensations that made colors dance beneath her closed eyelids. She wanted him with a savage urgency that belied her Victorian upbringing. Her breasts felt achy beneath his greedy mouth, her belly tight, and her legs so weak she could barely stand.

Quinn sank to his knees, taking Olivia with him. The ground felt cold compared to the hot, willing woman in his arms. He could feel her heat, radiating like the sun, warming his hands and mouth as he continued sucking one breast, then the other.

Even kneeling was too much effort. He shifted his weight to the side, stretching out on the ground, then fitting her against his hard length. His knee slid between her legs until he was pressing against the very center of her. He could feel how hot she was, how ready.

Olivia clung to him, unwilling to give up the passionate

reality that would too soon turn back into a dream. Her eyes fluttered open and she saw his face, hardened with passion, but more handsome than she'd ever seen it before. Her body burned to know the touch of his, all of him against all of her.

Quinn's mouth moved to the lilac-scented valley between her breasts, then over and under them as his hands cupped her like a priceless treasure. Desire danced in Olivia's body, from her head to her toes and fingertips, then to the very center of her body, where the heat had coiled so tightly she felt as if she would burst.

Lying side to side, kissing, their arms and legs entwined as tightly as the branches overhead, Quinn could feel her body surrendering inch by sweet inch. The number of kisses no longer mattered, all that mattered was getting closer to the shimmering passion that was making Olivia gasp for breath as Quinn pushed his leg tightly between hers, creating an unbearable pressure against the warm moist cradle of her body.

Her fingers, no longer knotted in the front of his shirt, sought metal buttons and the hard plane of his chest. When she found it, her nails raked over his heated flesh, making him grit his teeth. Nothing had prepared her for this . . . this incredible wanting that seemed to go on and on with no reward, yet the wanting was a deep frustrating pleasure in itself.

"You're killing me," Quinn said with a trembling voice.

Olivia couldn't say anything. She felt as wild as the land around them. Wild and free and primitive. The passionate hum of her body had become a song that had to be sung or lost forever. She combed through the hair on Quinn's chest, loving the sounds she drew from him, loving the heat of his skin, and the knowledge that she could make him tremble as fiercely as she was trembling.

Her hands explored, hesitantly as first, then more boldly. She pushed his shirt off one shoulder and kissed the skin she discovered. It was hot and salty and her tongue lingered, teasing him the same way he had teased her.

''My God,'' he groaned, jerking his shirt free so she could reach more of him.

She did, running her hands from the waistband of his trousers to the muscular ridge of his shoulders, feeling the power of his body and loving it, marveling at the strength and play of muscle as he moved up and over her, covering her completely with his body.

Then his hands were tracing a line from her ankle to her waist, pushing up the hem of her linen skirt as he found his way beneath the cotton of the one petticoat she was wearing. He touched the same skin he'd touched three nights ago, but this time there was no pain. All Olivia could feel was the burning caress of his hands and the longing of her own body.

She twisted and squirmed, vainly trying to get closer to the sweet dream.

When Quinn felt the heat of Olivia's desire, he cupped his hand over it, feeling her shake with wanting. His fingers curled gently, stroking and teasing the hot slick flesh, teaching her that wanting a man could grow and grow until she cried his name out loud then trembled even more violently in his arms, unable to stop the passionate explosion that seemed to tear her soul from her body and set it free.

A flash of raw, blind passion raced up Quinn's spine as his free hand moved to his trousers and the remaining buttons that were keeping him from becoming a part of the passion that had Olivia willing to yield her sweetest secrets.

His breath was a painful groan as he looked down at her, knowing that if he took her, there'd be no walking away once they reached Kimberley. There'd be no walking away ever. He'd be as bound to her by his conscience as he would be by a wedding ceremony.

Olivia felt the change that swept over Quinn as quickly as desire had swept through her own body. She opened eyes that were gleaming with passion. For the first time since he'd introduced himself in the hotel, she called him by the name she'd been afraid to voice until now. "Quinn."

He'd never heard it said so sweetly. But the sweetness turned bitter with the knowledge that he couldn't take what she was offering. Virginity was a prize meant only for a husband.

Cursing under his breath, Quinn pushed himself away from her. He closed his eyes against the reality of what he almost hadn't had the strength to stop.

"Quinn?"

He heard the confusion in her voice and took a deep breath, drawing air into his lungs as he sat up. He looked at the land instead of the woman. How many times had he walked through the bush? Too many to count in the fifteen years he'd been jackaling diamonds. He knew the wild country like he knew his own wild heart. He wanted Olivia, but he didn't want the complications that came with her.

"No more kisses," he said gruffly. "If I unbutton my pants, you won't find a wedding ring inside them. And that's what a *lady* expects, isn't it?"

Olivia sucked in her breath as humiliation and shame replaced passion. She struggled to her feet, saying nothing because Quinn's words cut too deeply for her to speak.

"Isn't it?" he repeated viciously.

"I . . . I'm sorry," she stammered, hating herself for her decency and her common sense. Her head hung low as she righted her clothing and thought of them rolling around on the ground like two animals, of how she'd clawed at his chest, silently begging him to touch her.

Quinn was right. If he hadn't stopped, if they had made love, he would be duty bound to offer her marriage. Slowly her eyes lifted and she looked at the wild land, wondering if it had bewitched her into forgetting that a lady didn't do the things she'd done. She hadn't just kissed Quinn, she'd blatantly invited him to make love to her. That invitation had taken her beyond the bounds of propriety into a place she didn't belong.

"No more kisses," she relented so softly she wasn't sure Quinn heard her. *And no more daydreams about a man who wants nothing more than to be rid of me as soon as possible*, she added silently as she forced her chin up and her eyes toward the fire that burned brightly in the circle created by the thatched huts.

They walked back to the village side by side, but with more distance between them this time, a distance Olivia feared she'd never be able to cross.

Prieska rested in the foothills of the Doringberge, or Thorn Mountains, on the southern bank of the Orange River. It had its beginnings as a fording place, but unlike other towns that had been given colonial names, Prieska retained its native name. The local bushmen knew it as Prieskab, "place of the lost goat."

The Orange River, flowing aggressively through the northern province, created a lifeline that reached to the Atlantic Ocean, and the railroad had spent a year building the bridge that crossed at Prieska, a bridge that would eventually connect Kimberley with the cities of the southern peninsula.

Olivia's first sight of the trading post and mission school brought a bittersweet smile to her face. She'd gladly give all her worldly goods for a hot bath and a feather mattress, but reaching civilization also meant her time with Quinn was limited.

As the ox cart rolled into the main street, a dusty avenue bordered by businesses and bawdy taverns with their doors wide open, she wished Quinn would at least talk to her. Since that night in the bush, when he'd shown her the lion and kissed her for the last time, their relationship had gone from passionately volatile to nerve-rackingly mute.

He refused to speak to her at all, walking ahead of the one cart caravan. At night, he took the first watch, then slept outside the tent under the stars. If he had any instructions, they were passed on to her by Echo, who knew something was amiss, but had the good sense not to ask. The native servant had become even more solicitous of Olivia, doing his best to offer her what comfort he could. But nothing could console the humiliation and regret she carried now.

She'd flung her morals to the wind that night, forgetting herself and her upbringing completely. Yet beneath the regret, she couldn't help but remember how it had felt to be held in Quinn's arms. Knowing that she might never feel that way again was her biggest regret.

They entered the town as dusty pilgrims and joined the people milling around in the streets. There were natives and railroad workers and farmers, going about their daily business. Everyone in sight seemed to know Quinn, calling out his name as they raised their hand in greeting. They gave Olivia more than a cursory glance, but she was too exhausted to care.

The Prieska Lodging House wasn't nearly as elaborate as the hotel in Cape Town, but two and a half weeks in the bush had drastically altered Olivia's opinion of luxurious housing. She'd settle for anything that had a wooden floor and a real bed.

"I'll see that your meals are served in your room," Quinn

said, speaking to her directly for the first time in days. "Stay there until the train leaves tomorrow."

His abrupt tone set fire to Olivia's vulnerable temper. "I have no intention of being confined to my room like an ill-mannered child," she retorted sharply.

Quinn glared at her, his eyes warning her that his temper was just as unstable as hers. "This isn't some fancy hotel that caters to people on holiday," he said in a low lethal voice. "Most of the rooms are rented to railroad men. They're a rough bunch. I don't have time to keep you out of trouble."

The very suggestion was enough to bring Olivia's chin up another inch. "Any trouble I've encountered so far, Mr. Quinlan, has been of your doing. As for mingling with the local residents, I will do so if it pleases me."

"Stay in your room," he demanded, taking her by the arm. It was the first time he'd touched her since he'd come to his senses that night in the bush. This time his hand wasn't up her skirt, caressing her soft thighs. It was gripping her arm none too gently and hauling her toward the staircase.

"Let me go," she hissed, thankful the desk clerk with his wire spectacles and curious eyes had left the lobby to tend to business elsewhere.

Quinn paid her no mind as he dragged her down the hallway, not stopping until they reached the last door. He tugged her inside, kicking the door closed behind them.

Every emotion Olivia had been feeling since she'd arrived in South Africa swelled up inside her: hope, embarrassment, regret, pain, loneliness. They exploded the moment Quinn released her. She turned on the toes of her scuffed boots, swung back her hand, and slapped him for all she was worth.

Caught completely off guard, Quinn's head snapped back. While he was stunned speechless, she marched to the door and opened it. "Kindly leave this room, Mr. Quinlan. And don't bother returning until you've found your manners."

Quinn clenched his hands into fists, so angry it was all he could do keep from dragging her to the bed and bending her over his knee. The only thing that stopped him was knowing that if he got her that close to a bed he'd do a hell of a lot more than give her tit for tat.

"The train leaves at noon tomorrow," he said as he stomped through the door.

She slammed it so hard it bounced back open.

After he was gone, Olivia felt the tears coming. There was no stopping them. They streamed down her face as she looked around the sparsely furnished room. She'd traveled with Quinn for weeks, slept on the ground beside him, eaten with him, kissed him, and let him touch her in ways she was still too embarrassed to think about, and the man had the audacity to treat her more rudely now than he'd done before. He was as cold-blooded as the snake Echo had discovered in the cart that morning. Cold-blooded and cold hearted.

Olivia told herself that, but she didn't believe it anymore than she believed that she'd gotten over her infatuation. The infatuation had already advanced into a heartthrobbing, heartbreaking case of unrequited love.

Stricken anew by her true feelings for Quinn, she slumped down on the edge of the bed. She'd come to Africa to claim her inheritance and the promise of a new life. It was what she wanted, not this frustrating emotional storm that had been raging since she'd met the insufferable diamond jackal. There was no peace, no future, in caring for a man who had so rudely assured her that he'd never marry.

She studied the unpolished wooden floor at her feet, berating her heart for not listening to her head, while all the while she prayed that Quinn would come back, bathed and dressed, to take her to dinner in the small downstairs dining room.

But Quinn didn't come back.

It was well into the evening when Olivia pulled back the curtains and stared out the window. She'd had a nap and her bath, a long lavish hour in a tub of hot steamy water. She'd eaten a well-prepared meal, alone. Now, dressed in a clean pink blouse and a doe brown skirt with two petticoats underneath it, she knew she couldn't sleep until she'd spoken with Quinn.

Whatever existed between them, she couldn't let it end with a stiff goodbye in front of her Kimberley boarding-house.

The memory of that night in the bush had been nagging at her ever since, making her dream fanciful dreams, making her want Quinn's arms around her again. The train ride from Prieska to Kimberley would take less than two days, and she knew he'd continue to avoid her unless she sought him out. He wanted her body, but he didn't want the love and commitment that came with marriage.

She wanted . . . what?

The only thing she could be certain of at this very moment was that she wouldn't be able to sleep a wink until she and Quinn talked out their differences.

She slipped down the stairs, hoping she wouldn't meet Echo in the lobby. The servant wouldn't approve of her leaving the hotel at such a late hour, and he'd be sure to follow her if she insisted on doing so. Thankfully, the lobby was empty; the clerk had retired for the evening.

Olivia paused at the doorway, took a deep breath, then opened it and stepped outside into the night air. Muffled voices and the sound of a badly played piano carried in the dark distance. The shops were all closed for the night, but the taverns were doing a thriving business.

She hesitated at the end of the plank sidewalk that fronted the hotel. Where would Quinn be? Drinking and gambling, no doubt.

With that thought in mind, and no idea of what she'd say once she found him, Olivia moved down the street, stopping every few feet to listen, half expecting to have Quinn jump at her from out of the dark. A large establishment, nearly as big as the lodging house, stood at the end of the street, near the river. A slanted thatched roof covered the front porch. The doors were opened, letting the gaslight escape.

She paused outside the tavern, straining her ears to hear Quinn's voice among those inside. The fingers of her right hand ventured into her skirt pocket to clutch the wooden lion, stroking it like a talisman as she stepped onto the porch and up to the open door. Unnoticed for a moment, she peered inside.

The tavern was filled with men. Dressed in working clothes with unshaven faces, they sat drinking whiskey and playing cards. Smoke from their cigars filled the air, drifting lazily toward the beamed ceiling.

It wasn't difficult to spot Quinn. He was sitting at a card table with a whiskey glass in one hand and a voluptuous, half-naked woman perched on his knee. The woman had hair the color of straw. Her breasts were spilling out of a blue satin dress and her painted lips were whispering something into Quinn's ear. Whatever she said made him smile. He leaned down and kissed the top of her breast, then laughed.

Olivia swallowed the anger rising up like bile. Swaying on her feet she turned to leave, wishing she'd never come, knowing she'd never be able to forget the sight of Quinn touching that . . . that woman. A sorrowful sound was ripped from her throat as she vowed never again to dream about the despicable man. Her skirt caught on the bottom edge of the open door. She jerked it loose, causing the door to close halfway then swing open again. It slammed against the outer wall of the tavern.

Every eye in the tavern turned toward Olivia, but Quinn was the only man that cursed out loud. Standing up so quickly he almost dumped the bosom-heavy woman onto the floor, he marched toward the door.

Olivia whirled around and started to run. Tears blurred her vision, but she kept on running, praying she could reach her room in time.

Her prayers were in vain.

Quinn's hand reached out of the dark to stop her. Holding her despite her efforts to get away, he turned her around, cursing under his breath. "What in the bloody hell do you think you're doing?"

"Nothing. Leave me alone!" She turned her face aside, not wanting to look at him, not wanting to remember that he'd kissed her breasts the same way he'd kissed those of the woman in the tavern.

Her face was wet with tears as he stomped toward the hotel, dragging her alongside him. But he didn't take her inside. Instead, he pulled her into the narrow alleyway between the hotel and one of the closed shops. Her chest was heaving with anger, her heart pounding with pain as Quinn turned on her. She couldn't see his face in the dark, but she could feel the pressure of his hand around her wrist and hear his labored breathing.

"What are you doing out here?" he demanded roughly.

"Please . . . Let me go."

"Answer me," he said, releasing her wrist only to put his hands on her shoulders. He shook her hard. "What in the hell did you expect me to be doing?"

Olivia shook her head. Her heart was hurting, but she couldn't let him know how badly he'd crushed it. She wouldn't humiliate herself again. She may have lost her heart to Quinn, but she wouldn't sacrifice her pride along with it. Lifting her chin, she forced some strength into her voice.

"I don't expect anything of you," she said, thankful the darkness hid her tears.

"Don't you? You expect me to be a gentleman. Well, I'm not, Miss St. John." he said, his tone accusing. "I'm a man who drinks and plays cards. A man who's used to having a woman after three weeks in the bush. Is that the kind of man you want? Do you want to warm my bed tonight? Because that's all I've got to offer you."

He took a step closer, pressing Olivia back against the building, trapping her between the hard wooden wall and the heat of his body. "I warned you that night in the bush. I warned myself," he added so softly she wasn't sure she'd heard him correctly.

Her breath came in short gasps as he leaned toward her. She could smell the whiskey he'd been drinking and the cheap perfume of the woman who had been sitting on his lap. She tried not to think of what he planned on doing with that woman.

"You should have stayed in your room." He shook his head as if he were trying to regain his senses. "Damn it."

He was close enough now for her to see the glint of his eyes. Then he pulled her hard against him and his mouth came crushing down, cutting off any protest she might have made. The kiss was hard and punishing, almost brutal. She tried to twist away, but he held her firm, forcing his tongue into her mouth and sending shivers of delight down her spine.

She should hate him, but she didn't. She should push him away, but she couldn't.

She fought against herself, knowing her feelings were the

real enemy. The heat of Quinn's body sank into her, warming her the same way his kiss was warming her. Her hands swept up his arms and around his neck. She arched against him, feeling the thunderous beating of his heart. Her own matched its rhythm, pounding inside her chest, expanding with love and all the dreams she'd vowed to forsake only moments before.

Suddenly his mouth softened. The kiss became passionate instead of punishing. He pressed against her from knee to shoulder, letting her feel the hard evidence of his desire. His hands knotted in her hair, holding her in place even though she'd stopped trying to get away.

Heat and something even hotter spread through Olivia as his hands moved slowly down her body until he was cupping her bottom. He lifted her, pressing her against the hard bugle in his trousers. She wanted to wrap herself around him, but he was holding her too tightly.

It was shameful, this wanting, but she couldn't end it. She didn't want to end it. She wanted this, her and Quinn, the night and the passion, to go on forever.

A soft moan escaped her throat, and Quinn shuddered. His tongue dipped into her mouth one last time. He felt her melt against him, willing to give him anything he wanted. His heart beat hard then went numb as he reached up and grabbed her hands, freeing himself from her embrace. This was insanity.

A rough breath filled his lungs as he stepped back. "Go inside, butterfly. And stay there this time."

Olivia wanted to argue, but the cold tone of his voice said it would be useless. She staggered toward the hotel entryway, her lips tingling from his kiss; her body shivering as if she'd been dunked into a vat of cold water. But on the inside she was burning with fever, a passionate fever she knew only Quinn could cure.

Ten

You expect me to be a gentleman. Well, I'm not . . . I'm a man who drinks and plays cards. A man who's used to having a woman after three weeks in the bush. Is that the kind of man you want? Do you want to warm my bed tonight? Because that's all I've got to offer you.

Quinn's words echoed inside Olivia's head as the train moved toward Kimberley. She'd had a lot of time to think in the last forty-eight hours.

What did a woman offer a man when all he wanted was physical pleasure?

Friendship?

Friendship implied a mutual respect, a sharing of ideas and principles, some sort of common ground. She wasn't even sure Quinn liked her. Their relationship wasn't what one would call a casual acquaintance. In the last few weeks, they had argued, kissed, and come very close to being as intimate as a husband and wife, but the truth of the matter was, she didn't have the slightest idea how to describe their association.

Right now her diamond jackal was acting more like a mule.

They hadn't exchanged a single word since that night outside the hotel. So here she sat in the De Beers's private railroad car, surrounded by luxury, while he sat in the club car sipping whiskey and playing cards with several railroad engineers.

Outside the window, the morning was bright and fresh. The intense blue of the sky mixed with the bright reds and greens and purples of the landscape as the railroad ran through the Thorn Mountains. The light and color were a sensual pleasure that Quinn had taught her to appreciate, like the golden red sunsets they'd sat and watched all those evenings in the bush.

Olivia looked around her, taking in the splendor of the rail car. No expense had been spared in making the car a small private haven for the kings of the diamond industry. There were candlesticks molded into the shapes of animals, resting in silver holders, and a ceramic teapot fashioned like an elephant. Tea would pour out of the curled trunk and into white china cups edged with gold trim. An elaborate teakwood chess box held playing pieces carved from jade and ivory. A small bookcase, built into the wall, displayed leather-bound volumes of classic literature, just in case a pampered passenger wanted to idle away the time reading.

But no amount of civility or comfort could ease the biting recollection of Quinn's words or the fiery memory of his kiss. The longer he avoided her, the more Olivia longed to see him. She was tempted to make her way to the club car and insist that the man stop acting like a child. They would reach Kimberley soon. She didn't want him exiting her life as if he'd never entered it. And she knew that was exactly what Quinn was planning to do. He'd escort her to her uncle's boardinghouse, then walk away, thinking he was doing the gentlemanly thing.

He was going to break her heart to keep from hurting her.

Thus, her dilemma.

What could she say or do that would keep Quinn from turning on his heels and marching away once the train reached Kimberley? How did a woman go about keeping a man who didn't want to be kept?

Olivia had another hour to ponder the question before she saw Quinn. He opened the door to the private car and walked in, surprising her.

"It's time to put on your bonnet and open your parasol," he said sarcastically. "We should be seeing the Kimberley depot in a few minutes."

Olivia looked wistfully out the window, but as much as the thought of finally claiming her inheritance thrilled her, thoughts of Quinn not being with her each day stabbed at her heart.

Even now, with him glaring at her and being deliberately rude to keep her at a distance, she couldn't help but notice how his mere presence brought her to life. The moment her eyes caught sight of him her body betrayed her, a blood-humming, heart-pounding betrayal that told her she'd never be rid of this man, even when he left her.

"I suppose you can't wait to be rid of me," she said, reaching for her bonnet and the filigreed pin she used to keep it in place. "Once I'm deposited in Kimberley, you can get back to carrying diamonds across the bush."

"That's what I do," Quinn said pointedly.

"And I shall reopen my uncle's boardinghouse," Olivia replied proudly. "Perhaps we will see each other from time to time."

Quinn gritted his teeth. Damn the woman, didn't she know

the sooner she didn't lay eyes on him the better off she'd be? That night in Prieska should have told her that his control was hanging by a loose thread. He'd come close to having her right there in the alley. The only thing that had stopped him was his conscience, and it was wearing thin.

No goodbye kiss, he reminded himself as the train belched out thick puffs of black smoke that drifted by the windows like menacing clouds. Olivia never took her eyes off him as he stood near the door. Her chin was held high, but he could see the anguished gleam of betrayal in her gaze and it made him feel guilty about the one thing he should be proud of. He hadn't seduced a virgin.

"Aren't you excited about beginning that independent life you've been dreaming of?" he asked, needing to fill the void with words that would remind her how many differences existed between them.

"Of course I'm excited."

"You don't look very excited."

Olivia looked at her reflection in the window, shoving the hat pin into the brim of her bonnet with more force than necessary. The man made her so angry. This could very well be the last private moments they'd have together, and he was scowling at her as if she were personally responsible for every fault to be found in the world. When she turned to look at him again, he was helping himself to a drink.

If he was going to stay long enough to enjoy a brandy, then maybe she'd have a chance to say what was on her mind. Choosing her words carefully, she licked her lips before she began. "There are a few things I'd like to say to you, Mr. Quinlan."

He chuckled. "So it's Mr. Quinlan again, is it?"

She licked her lips again, unaware that the nervous gesture was making Quinn grit his teeth. He sipped the brandy, letting the heat of the French liquor distract him for a moment. She was perched like a nervous butterfly on the edge of the velvet settee, looking very pretty. Her back was as straight as a poker, and he knew she was struggling to maintain her composure. He should take pity on her, knowing that anything they discussed would have a sheen of embarrassment to it. But he wasn't feeling compassionate at the moment. The last two days had been pure hell. From the moment she'd run away from him in the alley to now, he'd felt as if something inside him was about to rip open at the seams.

He'd drank his misery away that night, falling into bed, thinking that once his eyes were closed, his body would relax and he would sleep. But he hadn't slept. He'd stared at the ceiling instead, aroused and aching and damning himself for wanting a lady with velvet brown eyes and a smile that was pure hot sunshine. Since then, he'd kept to himself, gambling in the club car, finding any and every excuse to leave her alone.

But he couldn't make himself leave her now. Even looking at her was a sensual thing. Watching her tongue dart out to moisten her lips made his body leap with desire, and seeing the nervousness in her eyes made him want to gather up all her hopes and dreams and lay them at her feet like some fairy-tale prince. She was naïve and stubborn and inspiring all at the same time, and he . . . What the hell, he was fooling himself if he thought she'd give up her morals for a few hours of pleasure. And it would take hours. If he ever got his hands on her the way he wanted, he'd make sure any man who came after him would have the impossible task of besting him as a lover.

The thought of someone else discovering all Olivia's sensual secrets turned the expensive brandy bitter inside Quinn's mouth.

He sat down in a nearby chair, stretching out his legs. "Say whatever's on your mind, Miss St. John."

His tone of voice wasn't making Olivia's task easier, but then she hadn't expected it to be. Still, she had to say something. She began hesitantly, hoping Quinn wouldn't mock her for revealing a few of her feelings. "I'm sure the task of seeing me safely to Kimberley hasn't been the most enjoyable thing you've ever done, but nevertheless, I am grateful."

Grateful enough to take some of the starch out of your principles and let me make love to you? Quinn asked himself the question, already knowing the answer was no. He could seduce Olivia out of her virginity, but she'd never give it willingly, sacrificing her gentility and morals for the sake of pleasure rather than marriage.

She was about to thank him for all the things she'd learned during their trek across the bush when she realized just what he'd taught her. It was Quinn who had shown her how intimate a kiss could be. It wasn't proper to thank a man for teaching you that passion was one of life's most intense feelings. Yet she couldn't find fault with the lessons Quinn had taught her so well. All those things seemed right and natural with him.

The train's high-pitched whistle shattered the fragile silence between them. Olivia looked anxiously toward the window, suddenly wishing she hadn't arrived at the destination she'd set out to reach months ago. She needed more time.

Quinn downed the last of the brandy, then set the glass aside and came to his feet "Kimberley," he announced. "You're here at last."

His words sounded like an epitaph. Olivia masked her disappointment by averting her gaze and reaching for her parasol. When she stood, her forced smile wasn't as brilliant as it should have been, but it was the best she could do.

Quinn fought the urge to pull her into his arms and kiss her fears away. He'd agreed to bring her to Kimberley and the deed was done. He couldn't go on being responsible for her. Or feeling guilty because he'd made a mistake and collected a few kisses along the way. The lady had come all the way from England to stand on her own two feet. It was time to let her.

The depot was as busy as London's Paddington Station. Kimberley had sprung up in the barren landscape because untold wealth was hiding beneath the ground. The town existed because humans were obsessed by things that glittered, and nothing glittered as brightly as a diamond.

There were people everywhere: native porters loaded down with luggage and railroad workers shuffling cargo from the supply cars onto flatbed wagons pulled by lean mules and clumpy fat oxen. The dialect of half a dozen African tribes mixed with the European accents of the depot workers, responsible for seeing that the right supplies got to the right people.

Olivia sat quietly in front of the railway office, her gaze taking in everything, her mind jumping from one thought to another as she waited for Quinn to come and claim her.

As the minutes ticked away, she grew more eager. Now that she was here, she wanted to find her uncle's boardinghouse and get on with things. The short conversation she'd had with Quinn was more than enough to let her know the man wasn't going to be receptive to anything she had to say.

The door of the depot office opened and closed, catching Olivia's attention. She looked up to find a tall, rather handsome man staring at her. His blond hair was so fair it bordered on being silver. He was dressed similarly to Quinn: dark trousers, a bushman's jacket, and knee-high boots. Eyes of the lightest blue-gray looked at her as a smile came to his face. Hat in hand, he bowed at the waist. "Welcome to Kimberley," he said. "I hope it isn't a husband that's brought you here."

Olivia blinked, surprised by his remark and needing a moment to comprehend its meaning. Just what she needed, another arrogant man. But unlike Quinn, this man wore his conceit much too comfortably.

"Hans Van Mier, originally of Amsterdam, at your service," he introduced himself. "And you are . . ."

"Olivia St. John."

His smile widened. "Miss St. John."

Olivia nodded.

"Excellent," Van Mier said. "Where is your chaperone? I shall waste no time in pleading for the opportunity to take you to dinner." He looked around, frowning slightly. "Unfortunately, the town has little to offer in the way of culinary delights. Perhaps a walk in the moonlight?"

"Perhaps a kick in the pants would do instead," Quinn said.

Olivia watched as the Dutchman turned to face her escort. His expression went from solicitous to cold in the blink of an eye. "Quinn."

"Van Mier," he said, his tone implying that the man wasn't held in high regard.

The two men appraised each other in a lethal silence that had Olivia fearing they'd engage in fisticuffs with no further provocation, but suddenly the Dutchman's smile returned, slightly roguish this time. "So, she's the one."

"This is Miss St. John," Quinn said bitingly. "The *lady* I escorted from Kimberley."

"The bush had been buzzing about it," Van Mier replied, then cast a quick glance in Olivia's direction. "The natives carry gossip faster than a telegraph."

"I've never been inclined to believe gossip, Mr. Van Mier," she said, coming to her feet. The Dutchman might be handsome and consider himself well-mannered, but she didn't care for him.

Apparently, Quinn didn't either, because he wasted no time in telling Olivia that the wagon was ready.

Giving Hans Van Mier a polite but stiff nod of her head, she followed Quinn down the depot steps. The wagon, already loaded with her trunks, was waiting. She lowered her parasol as Echo jumped down to help her.

"The Dutchman is more trouble than you can handle," Quinn told her, keeping his voice low but his tone sharp. "Stay away from him."

Pricked by Quinn's misconception that she'd sought out the man's company in the first place, Olivia turned to face him. "Stop telling me what to do," she replied haughtily. "I'm a grown woman who can chose her own friends."

"The Dutchman isn't interested in friendship."

"And I suppose you are?" she challenged him in an accusing whisper.

The woman might not know one end of a rifle from the other, but her aim was perfect. Quinn flinched inwardly, knowing he deserved the sharp words.

"Get in the wagon," he said, glaring at her as if he might change his mind about escorting her to the address Sidney Falk had furnished and strangle her instead.

Echo stood nearby, smiling all the while.

Olivia turned around and raised her foot, determined to gain the wagon's seat all by herself, but the skirt of her traveling suit wasn't wide enough unless she hiked it up.

Swearing under his breath, Quinn wrapped his hands

around her waist and lifted her. For a moment they were eye to eye. He felt the pull of her gaze as surely as he felt the corset she'd rummaged out of the trunk. He'd find Van Mier as soon as Olivia was delivered and make sure the Dutchman understood that if he so much as looked in her direction again, he'd find the fight he'd been looking for ever since Quinn bested him at cards three nights in a row.

Jealousy!

Quinn had never felt it before and the first time was a burning green flame that stole his breath. Realizing how dangerously close he was to actually making Olivia ''his woman,'' he dropped her onto the wagon seat as though she'd burnt his hands. ''Hull Street isn't that far away. Let's see what your beloved uncle left you.''

With her pride slightly bruised and her emotions so tangled it would take hours to unravel them, Olivia kept her gaze riveted on the town and not the man sitting beside her. Quinn was driving the wagon while Echo sat in the back. They hit a bump in the dirt road that sent her pitching toward him. She righted herself, but not quickly enough to keep from feeling his hard muscular thigh. She sat stiffly beside him after that, telling herself to ignore him the same way he was ignoring her.

They drove through the main part of town. There were shops and taverns, more taverns than she'd seen in Prieska. Two church steeples rose above the business rooftops, but the holy structures were assigned to secondary streets, blatantly proclaiming the preferences of the town's residents.

Again, Quinn was recognized by almost everyone they passed. By the time they turned onto Hull Street, Olivia realized he was legendary in the diamond fields.

The mules plodded forward, pulling the wagon down the packed dirt avenue. The change in the town ripped Olivia's concentration away from Quinn and focused it on the boardinghouse she was about to claim. Once they left the main business district, Kimberley became row after row of shabby ill-kempt houses and even shabbier taverns. The people she saw were mostly men with gaunt faces, dressed in grimy clothes. Olivia couldn't be sure if their haggard expressions were caused by the fatigue of mining diamonds or the despair of not finding any.

Her optimism waned as they came to the end of the street. A large, two-story house stood to her right. The shutters were closed, adding to its abandoned appearance. The front door, weathered to a dull gray, hung on rusty hinges. The roof was tin, rusty around the stone chimney, and sure to leak. A front lawn, if the few yards of gravelly dirt could be called a lawn, was inhabited by clumps of weeds. All in all, her inheritance appeared to be ready to collapse in the first good wind that came its way.

Quinn flicked the reins, preparing to turn the wagon around. "I'll take you to the Duggan Hotel. The rooms are clean and the food is good."

"No," Olivia said, reaching out to still his hand. When he looked at her, she shook her head, reaffirming her decision. "My uncle lived here. So will I."

"I can't leave you here," he announced. "Look at this place."

"I am looking," she told him. "This is *my* boardinghouse. It may not flatter you with its appearance now, but it will. All it needs is a coat of paint and a little work."

Echo said something that Quinn seconded in a disgruntled tone.

"I'm staying here," she insisted, knowing that Quinn expected her to fail in resurrecting the house the same way he'd expected her to turn back after her first day in the bush. Well, she hadn't turned back, and she wasn't going to fail. Not now, not after coming all this way.

Her hopes and dreams were inside the clapboard building that needed far more than a coat of paint, and she wasn't going to desert them the way Quinn was about to desert her.

"Of all the stubborn, harebrained ideas," he grunted, getting down from the seat. "If I thought you'd stay, I'd haul your pretty butt to the hotel," he grumbled on, "but you'd be out the door the minute my back was turned."

"I'm glad you realize it would be a waste of time," Olivia crooned sweetly.

He lifted her off the wagon seat with a steel grip around her waist, his face so close to hers she could see the anger sparking in his eyes. "You're more trouble than you're worth," he complained, belying his words by setting her feet on the ground as gently as he would a child.

Olivia disregarded his words and looked at the house. "I'll need to open my trunk and retrieve the key to the front door."

"Don't bother," Quinn said over his shoulder as he stomped toward the house. He gave the door a hard tug. Creaking hinges announced his success. "Come on," he called out before disappearing inside.

Filled with a dreadful kind of anticipation at what she'd find, Olivia followed him, frowning at the weeds sprouting around the front steps. The interior was so dim she couldn't be sure what she was seeing until Quinn walked into what would be the front parlor and began banging open shutters with the ferocity of a military sergeant wanting to awaken his troops.

Sunlight streamed into the room, revealing furniture draped in dingy sheets and discolored blankets. Cobwebs hung from the corners and ceilings like silky drapes. The bare floor was carpeted in a layer of dust that revealed Quinn's footprints as he moved from window to window, grumbling under his breath about stubborn English ladies and their silly notions.

He turned to watch Olivia's reaction, but all he saw was her back as she turned to explore the other rooms. "Don't go up those stairs until I've made sure they're safe," he yelled as she disappeared into the hallway.

Olivia could hear him following her as she made her way into the large room on the opposite side of the house. There were more closed windows, but she could make out a long table framed by a dozen chairs. More cursing accompanied the sound of windows being opened and shutters being thrown back so hard they bounced off the outside wall.

Wordlessly she surveyed the room: the empty cupboards standing against the far wall; a ceramic pitcher, sitting in the center of the deserted table, dressed in fragile cobwebs that danced in the first fresh air to hit the room in months. The dining room was as filthy as the parlor, but Olivia didn't see the dust and dirt. She saw possibilities: tall windows covered with Irish lace curtains; a vase of wildflowers decorating the center of a table covered with a crisp linen cloth; and the faces of her boarders, eagerly awaiting their evening meal.

"The kitchen must be through there," she said, pointing toward a door.

Quinn followed her, admiring the way she was hiding her disappointment. The place was even worse than he'd imagined.

The kitchen wasn't much better. A large cast-iron cooking stove, blackened from use, had taken on a grayish tint now that it was covered in a layer of fine dust. More cupboards, their glass doors cracked and scarred, displayed stacks of dishes. A small scorpion that had been crawling across the bare wooden floor crunched under the heel of Quinn's boot as he headed for the back door. It opened to the music of rusty hinges and rotting wood.

Olivia closed her eyes for a moment, locking in the whirl-wind of emotions that had her legs trembling. So many emotions, she couldn't count them all. But the biggest one, the one she couldn't let take control, was her love for the tall, dark-haired man who was cursing under his breath again.

Slowly, she opened her eyes and saw him framed in the sunlight seeping into the dirty kitchen. She could sweep floors and clean windows, dust furniture and dispose of cobwebs, but she couldn't stop loving this man. "It's going to take a lot of work," she said, forcing her eyes away from Quinn's handsome face.

"I'll take you to the hotel," he said. "You can think about it."

She shook her head. "There's no thinking to be done," she told him. "I have enough money to buy paint and other necessities. The rest is simply a matter of soap and water and enough hands to scrub everything." She looked at him. "Could I borrow Echo's services for the balance of the day? Tomorrow, I'll have him post a notice in town. I'll need a cook and a housemaid and—"

"Blast it, woman, look at this place!"

Calmly, Olivia reached up and pulled the filigreed pin from her bonnet. She held the hat in her hand, not wanting to soil it by putting it on the small cutting table beside her. "I have looked," she told him. "And I'm not leaving the only thing in the world that truly belongs to me."

Quinn clenched his jaw to keep from . . . what? He didn't have the right to make her do anything. He didn't have any rights at all where this particular woman was concerned, so what could he do but let her have her way? He stomped out the back door, calling for Echo at the top of his lungs.

Olivia remained in the kitchen, hoping he'd be back. She needed to say goodbye to him, to try to make him understand.

Moments later, Quinn reappeared, looking as unhappy as he had when he'd stormed out of the room. "Echo will unload your trunks, then take the wagon back to town. You'll need a few things before you can stay the night here. He'll be back before dark. Until then, don't go upstairs."

"Thank you," she said, knowing he wasn't going to keep her company until Echo returned.

"For what?" Quinn demanded. "Leaving you in this hellhole?"

She bit her bottom lip, trying to hold back the tears that wanted to flow like a spring rain. True, she was disappointed with the condition of the boardinghouse, but that wasn't the reason she wanted to cry. Quinn was leaving her.

"I appreciate all you've done for me," she whispered, hating herself because she knew she wouldn't be able to stop the tears. They were brimming against her closed lashes.

Quinn saw one escape, rolling down her cheek to become trapped in the corner of her mouth. Women and tears had never bothered him in the past. The two went together like aged brandy and expensive cigars, but seeing Olivia cry made his stomach muscles clench like he'd just taken a gut punch.

"Hell," he grumbled as he marched across the room and pulled her into his arms. He held her tight, letting her wet the front of his jacket with silent tears.

Olivia's arms slipped around his neck.

"Stop crying," he said, feeling like an ass for bringing her all this way. He should have turned around that night in the bush when he'd almost made love to her. But he hadn't turned back, and now he'd do almost anything to keep her in his arms.

"It's not what you think," Olivia whispered shakily. He

smelled so good and she felt so secure in his arms. Her heart was breaking as she looked up at him.

"What?" he asked roughly, wanting to understand this complicated woman, needing to know that she was going to be all right.

She reached up and touched a shaky fingertip to the center of his bottom lip. "One last kiss," she whispered. "Your final payment."

Quinn looked into her beautiful innocent, tear-dampened eyes and felt his insides turn to mush. He was too aware of how good she felt resting against him, the swell of her breasts, and the scent of the lilac soap she used, to push her away. Each breath he took was infused with her presence and the knowledge that kissing her would be a mistake. A mistake he was going to regret but couldn't stop himself from making. His eyes didn't leave her face as he slowly lowered his head and covered her mouth.

Olivia moaned softly as her fingers dug into the shoulders of his jacket. His mouth was hot and hard and more wonderful than she'd remembered. She clung to him, wanting this last kiss more than she wanted all the dreams she'd brought with her from England.

Quinn's tongue dipped deep, tasting her over and over again, until both of them were trembling with need. His hands cradled her head, holding her in place, while he walked her backward. The edge of the cutting table pressed against her thighs. Then she was sitting on it, the dust forgotten, everything forgotten but the need of two people to be as close as they could be. He crushed his mouth to hers, revealing the deep frustration that had been with him for the last few days, letting her know that he'd wanted to kiss her before now, but had somehow managed to control himself. There was no control now. He kept kissing her, his hands exploring, his body hard and tight against hers.

His knee pressed between her legs, forcing them open, pushing up her skirt as it accommodated his thigh. His hands moved from her hair to her hips, holding them as he pushed against her, letting her feel the desire she kindled.

He raised his head and looked down at her parted lips. *God,* he thought, returning for a second kiss. *Why can't I get enough of this woman?*

His hips rotated against her, pressing as deep as her clothing would permit. Her hands left his shoulders to press against his chest. He pulled back again, catching his breath as his hands began undoing buttons, pushing her jacket off her shoulders, reaching for the small buttons on the front of her blouse. She moaned his name. The sound was heaven to his ears as he found the lace of her camisole, then the soft womanly skin he'd been searching for.

His mouth bathed her skin with wet kisses as his teeth nibbled at her collarbone. Desire rushed through him, destroying the last of his common sense. He pushed her blouse down, pinning her arms against her sides, as he nibbled and tasted every inch of her that he could reach. Damn corsets and lace and all the things that kept him from tasting her breasts!

Olivia let her head fall back, reveling in the glory of his touch, wanting it more and more with each caress of his tongue. Her fingers knotted in thick waves of black hair as she held him close.

He rotated his hips against her, so hard with desire he was actually hurting. "I want you," he whispered. "But . . ."

"I know," she whispered in return, hating the reality neither one of them could change.

Their words hung in the heated silence that followed. Quinn took a ragged breath, then slowly pushed himself away from the table. He gazed at her face, glowing with passion, and the exposed skin of her upper chest that had been rubbed pink by his unshaven face.

He raked his fingers through his hair as he turned to leave. The door creaked in protest as he held it open. He turned to look at her one last time. She was still sitting on the dusty table, her clothes undone, her mouth swollen from his kisses, her eyes wide and luminous, shining with passion and tears.

"Echo will stay with you until . . ." He took a deep breath.

"I'll be fine," she managed the words, knowing that no matter how successfully she turned the boardinghouse around, she'd never be victorious in freeing her heart from Quinn's grasp. She began buttoning up her blouse. "Don't worry about me."

Quinn turned, closing the door behind him, but a closed door wasn't enough to keep him from calling himself the biggest fool in the world as he walked around the house and headed for town.

He needed a drink. Hell, he needed more than a drink. There wasn't enough whiskey in all of Kimberley to wash the taste of the little English lady out of his mouth. He'd visit O'Reilly's place—the Irishman kept the cleanest whores in town. Once he'd had a woman, he'd be able to think straight again.

Eleven

Quinn walked into the Irish-style pub with the determined steps of a man intent on getting as drunk as possible. O'Reilly, the stout proprietor with graying hair and keen eyes, gave him a knowing smile, reached for a bottle of his best, and planted it on the bar within Quinn's reach.

"Heard you were back," the Irishman said, watching Quinn wrench out the cork with his teeth and then pour himself a drink. "Heard you brought a lady with you this time."

The gossip that had spread faster than a bushfire earned the proprietor a stern look as Quinn lifted the bottle to his mouth and swilled down a long hot drink. Wiping his mouth with the sleeve of his bush jacket, he carried the bottle to a corner table and plopped down in a chair.

He sat there until the bottle was empty, downing one drink after another, but not finding the relief he sought even when he could see the bottom of the amber bottle. By that time it was dark. The confusion of the day had eased. The crackling whips and bawling oxen had ceased their endless trips up and down the dirt streets. The dust that hung in the air like a red haze over the landscape had settled with the sun. The night was a quiet blanket over the town, filled with the muted sounds of voices whispering over card tables and into the ears of the taverns' talented ladies instead of shouting over the rattle of mining buckets.

Quinn raised his hand, signaling for another bottle of O'Reilly's best.

A tall whore carried it to the table. She was younger than she looked, with long legs and dark hair. The dress she was wearing revealed more than it covered, showing a goodly portion of her lush full breasts. Her eyes were brown, but they lacked the innocence of the ones Quinn was trying so hard to forget.

"Want some company?" the whore asked, sitting down before he answered one way or the other.

Quinn recognized her, but not because he'd had her before. O'Reilly's was one of his favorite haunts. The whiskey was pure Irish, not watered-down like the other taverns. The miners came here to drink and gamble and have a woman for the night. The Irishman ran a tight ship. No fighting was allowed inside where it could damage the furniture, and no guns allowed upstairs where one of his girls could get hurt in the cross fire. A man put his money on the bar and paid for what he got in advance, and O'Reilly made sure he got his money's worth.

"What's your name?" Quinn asked.

"Margaret."

"Let's go upstairs, Margaret."

He stood up, more sober than he should be after a whole bottle of whiskey, and strolled to the bar. Digging into his pocket after being told the price by O'Reilly, he dropped more than the necessary coins onto the scarred mahogany bar. "That enough for the whole night?"

"That'll do it," the Irishman said, giving Margaret a wink as she headed for the staircase and the room where she always put a smile on her customer's face.

But Margaret was the one smiling as she led the way to her room. Quinn had a reputation for being quite a man once his trousers came off. She pushed the door open, then stepped back so he could walk in ahead of her.

Quinn strolled into the room, whiskey bottle in hand, wondering what in the hell he was doing buying a woman for the night when there was a willing one on Hull Street. The answer was simple. Margaret wasn't a virgin. Her reputation wouldn't be ruined when he stripped her naked and mounted her. There'd be no attack of conscience when the sun came up tomorrow morning, and most of all, he wouldn't be expected to produce a wedding ring in the name of gentlemanly honor.

A wedding ring! It was a golden cage, that's what it was. A circular trap that kept a man from breathing freely, from doing what he wanted, from wandering where he chose. Marriage wasn't for him. And neither were ladies, damn their pretty smiles.

He plopped down on the edge of the bed, looking at the whore as she began to peel away her dress. When she was standing in front of him in nothing but her bare skin and a wide smile, he gulped down another drink. Margaret had nice tits. Round and full and crowned with coral tips that were begging to be pinched and suckled. But the part of Quinn that had been harder than a baobab tree for the last three weeks lay passively inside his trousers, limp and disinterested.

The little English governess had turned him into a goddamn eunuch. *Damn her and her innocent eyes. Damn her and her stubbornness, but most of all, damn her and her sweet mouth.*

He stared at the whore, feeling nothing, wanting nothing more than the woman he couldn't have. He took another swill of whiskey and fell back onto the bed, looking at the ceiling this time.

"What's the matter, honey?" Margaret crooned as she straddled him and began undoing buttons. "Tired? Don't worry. I'll take care of everything."

Quinn pushed her hands away as he sat up, cursing at the whiskey he spilt in the process. "Put your clothes on," he grumbled.

"But—"

"But nothing," he growled. "I paid for you. Do what you're told."

Thinking there must be two Quinns, the whore reached for the flimsy robe draped over the brass foot railing and slipped it on. Not sure what to do next, she simply stood next to the bed and waited.

"Sit down," Quinn told her.

She sat down on a stool in front of the vanity table with its cracked mirror. The night was still young, and Quinn was a fine-looking man. If she left him now, O'Reilly would think she wasn't worth keeping, and she needed her share of the money he'd dribble out come morning.

Quinn shook his head, letting his eyes drift closed. The whiskey wasn't helping him to forget, but it was making him sleepy. "I'm a damn fool for even thinking about her," he mumbled.

Margaret didn't hear what he'd said, but a few seconds later she heard the soft snoring sounds he made. Disappointed that she hadn't had the man, and the pleasure she was sure he could bring her, she frowned into the mirror. An hour later, with the sounds of a busy tavern drifting through the crack under the door, she stretched out at the foot of the bed and slept.

On Hull Street, Olivia stared at the mattress Echo had carried downstairs and laid on the dining room table. He'd swept off the dust, then covered the mattress with one of the blankets from the cart. The kerosene lantern had been turned down, concealing the dirt that hadn't been cleaned away yet.

It was almost midnight and she was bone tired. She'd stood in the kitchen, staring at the door Quinn had closed behind him, for almost an hour. Then, telling herself that crying wouldn't bring him back, she'd inspected as much as the house as she dared. Once Echo returned from town, she had rolled up her sleeves and gone to work. The kitchen was clean enough to prepare breakfast and the dining room had been swept clear of cobwebs. The real scrubbing would start first thing in the morning.

"Missy John no sleep on floor," Echo said, carrying in another blanket. "Use chair for step."

He pushed one of the chairs close to the table, then held out his hand. Smiling with gratitude that the servant would be nearby during the night, Olivia held onto his hand and stepped onto the chair. A short second later, she was lying on the mattress, fully clothed.

"Busy day tomorrow," Echo said, making himself a pallet in the corner. "Lots of work to make this place whole again."

"Yes," Olivia admitted wearily. "But I'll do it. With your help."

"Echo help," he said. "Not leave Missy John."

She lay on the makeshift bed, staring at the dark ceiling, too tired to sleep. Every so often, she looked toward the corner where Echo was sleeping. The servant was proving to be the most steadfast person she'd ever met. Part of her wanted to ask him about Quinn, to probe the servant's mind for information that might explain why the man was so set on keeping her at arm's length, but she didn't dare. Echo worked for Quinn, and she didn't want to put him in the middle of a situation that seemed to have no reasonable solution.

What was happening between herself and Quinn was like nothing she'd ever encountered before. She lay there, alone on a mattress on a tabletop, staring at the ceiling and thinking about the events that had brought her to South Africa and into Quinn's arms. There was no rhyme or reason to what she felt for the diamond jackal, no logic in the yearnings of her body and heart, only the deep-rooted knowledge that she loved him.

Gradually her eyes drifted closed and memories drifted into dreams. She felt Quinn's arms again, holding her close, his body hot and hard against hers, his mouth wet and demanding. She clutched the pillow, dreaming that she was holding the man she loved.

When she woke, it was to the sound of Echo singing in the kitchen. The song was clicks and grunts that flowed methodically to a rhythm as old as Africa itself.

Quinn woke with a pounding headache. He blinked, then cursed at the pain that shot through his temples. The whore, Margaret, was sleeping near his feet. The robe had risen up during the night, exposing her legs and part of her right hip, but Quinn looked away, disgusted with himself and his inability to take the woman.

He rolled out of bed, coming to his feet with a groggy awareness that it was late morning and the sunlight, once he stepped into it, was only going to make his head hurt worse. Still, he moved toward the door, telling himself a hot bath and a shave could work wonders.

God knew he needed a miracle.

Feeling guilty that he hadn't lived up to his reputation and shown the woman a good time, he reached into the pocket of his trousers, leaving a stack of coins on the dresser.

He was at the cottage the De Beers supplied for him before he questioned the insanity of the previous day and night. He'd vowed that he wouldn't kiss Olivia again, sworn an oath to himself that was just as binding, or should have been, as the promise he made whenever he accepted an assignment from De Beers. But he'd broken his word, kissing her, almost seducing her again. His willpower couldn't hold a candle to the tempting young lady.

After two cups of strong coffee, he stripped and climbed into a hot hip bath. The water eased the fatigue from his aching muscles, but it didn't soothe his conscience. Echo didn't help when the native knocked on the door, then strolled unceremoniously into the room. The servant's customary smile vanished the moment he saw Quinn lounging in the tub.

"Missy John need help," Echo announced. "Plenty help."

"I know," Quinn admitted. "Go into town and hire men you can trust. And women to do the cooking and cleaning. Put anything you need on my account."

The servant grunted. "Missy John no want your charity."

"I know that, too," Quinn relented, realizing Echo had changed camps on him. The native's loyalty now belonged to a young woman with soft brown eyes and the innocence of a newborn butterfly. "You don't have to tell her that I'm paying for anything. Just make sure she gets that damn boardinghouse looking decent."

"She know the money come from you."

"Then let her throw a conniption fit. I don't care. Just make sure she doesn't hurt herself trying to turn that dilapidated old house into a palace."

"I get help."

"Good. De Beers will have me running back to Cape Town in a few weeks. You're staying here. I'll put out the word that Miss St. John is under my protection. That should keep the troublemakers away."

"Quinn troublemaker," Echo said, looming over his naked employer. "You want woman. Woman want you. Don't understand."

Quinn came out of the tub with a string of curses and a splash of water. "There's no understanding women. Especially ladies." He caught the towel Echo tossed his way and began drying a body that was springing to life at the mention of Olivia's name. "She's a lady. A real lady. And I'm no gentleman."

"I watch over Missy John. Good woman. Better than Quinn deserve."

Quinn didn't argue. Olivia did deserve better than the likes of him. He might be wealthy now, but all the money in the world couldn't erase what he really was—a hellion from the East End, a man who survived by his gut instincts. And he liked it that way. Hell, he had it made. He had a house in Cape Town, a farm in Calvinia, a cottage in Kimberley, and servants to take care of him no matter which roof he slept under. He had the ear of Cecil John Rhodes and Barney Barnato, the two biggest diamond magnates in South Africa. Life was good, but most of all it was free. He wasn't about to give up that freedom just because some brown-eyed angel made his crotch stand up and take notice.

Quinn told himself that for the next six days. That was as long as he could keep his curiosity on a leash and stay away from the boardinghouse.

When he saw it again, he was amazed at how much work Echo and the three men he'd hired had accomplished. The house had received a coat of white paint. The shutters were a dark green, framing windows that had been washed and polished until they reflected the afternoon sun like a mirror.

He looked up at the roof, where two workers were replacing the old tin with new. Realizing that he'd paid for the repairs, and would probably keep on paying until the house met Olivia's sterling standards, Quinn didn't bother knocking. He walked in unannounced.

The foyer smelled like lye soap.

"Gentlemen knock on a door," Olivia said, hiding her surprise behind the stern words.

The unpredictable man would pick this day to come calling. She'd been cleaning the parlor. Her hair was covered with a scarf, her muslin dress streaked with dirt and grime. She had a mop bucket in one hand and a soiled rag in the other.

Quinn thought she looked rather pretty with dirt on the end of her upturned nose. He smiled, then frowned. "I told Echo to hire someone to do the cleaning."

"He did," Olivia told him. "Ignoring my orders completely in lieu of yours, I might add. The women he hired are upstairs, cleaning the bedrooms." She sat the mop bucket on the floor. Just seeing Quinn made her wish for things she'd promised herself she wouldn't wish for again. He stood straight and tall in front of her, as handsome and as stubborn at ever. Well, she was stubborn, too. "I'll repay you as soon as I have some boarders. I can manage once the bulk of the repairs are made."

"Hire another woman," Quinn said. "I don't like you hauling mop buckets."

"Why not? It's honest work and these are my floors. I'll mop them if I want to."

Making a frustrated sound, Quinn stared at her.

Olivia stared right back. Quinn hadn't deliberately stolen
her heart, so she couldn't blame him. He didn't know that
he had it tucked in his pocket along with the hard candy he
tossed to the native children. And she couldn't tell him. It
was bad enough when he walked away from her after kissing
her senseless. If she saw pity in his eyes, it would be the
end of her pride.

The impasse lasted for several moments. Quinn glaring
at her, she glaring back, both wanting the same thing but
too stubborn to admit it.

Quinn disliked the idea of Olivia ruining her soft hands
doing the work of a scullery maid almost as much as he
disliked the bland expression on her face. He didn't realize
until that moment that he'd come to the boardinghouse with
one thing in mind—to see her smile. But his appearance
was having the opposite effect. The longer she stared at him
the more insipid her expression became. He gave the mop
bucket a scathing look. "You're working too hard."

"There's a lot to be done."

"Not today," he announced. "If you plan on living in
Kimberley, it's time you saw what the town's all about."

"Meaning?"

"Meaning, I'm going to show you a diamond mine."

"Right now?"

"As soon you wash the dirt off your nose," Quinn
chuckled.

The remark brought a blush to her cheeks and a twinkle
to her eyes as she drew back her hand and let go of the rag.
It missed Quinn completely. "A gentleman doesn't point
out a lady's shortcomings."

"Why not?" he asked, stepping over the wet rag.
"You've been pointing out mine ever since I met you."

The closer he came the higher the confusion rose inside

Olivia. It seemed as though Quinn was forever stalking her only to turn his back once he'd had his fun. And he turned away so easily, seemingly unaware that his departure caused her pain. Yet, he was here again. Standing in front of her, seeking her company. Why?

The possibility that he could *feel* something was enough to keep Olivia from declining his invitation.

Her eyes, meeting his gaze, showed her confusion at his unexpected appearance, but Quinn had no more of an answer for her than he had for himself. He knew she was remembering the last time they'd been alone. Her blouse had been undone then, her breasts flushed by the heat of passion, her body melting naturally against his own. The image of how she'd looked sitting on the dusty table hadn't left his mind once in the last six days. It insisted on hovering there, just beyond the edge of reason, taunting him and a conscience that had once been crystal clear.

"I need to change my dress," she said. "You can wait in the parlor. The windows are bare of draperies and the sofa is in the back of the house to air, but there's a comfortable chair. I won't be long."

Quinn tipped his head, then walked into the room, surprised by the transformation a little soap and water had accomplished. He waited, wondering why he'd come when he knew damn well he should stay away. The only excuse he was willing to accept was the flimsy one that he still felt responsible for Olivia, and until she was firmly settled and the boardinghouse was operating profitably, he'd keep an eye on things—from a distance, of course.

Upstairs, Olivia hastily stripped out of the old muslin dress, washed her face and hands, then brushed her hair, pinning it loosely at the nape of her neck. She donned a dove-gray skirt, accenting its color with a silky peach blouse.

With an Italian cameo pinned to her collar, she returned to the parlor.

Quinn gave her an admiring smile as he reached for the hat he'd tossed onto a freshly polished table. "Shall we?" he said, offering his arm.

His sterling manners brought a smile to Olivia's face. She suffered fanciful thoughts as he escorted her outside. The buggy, drawn by a sleek horse, was the first she'd seen in Kimberley.

"A tour of the legendary Hole is the best place to begin," Quinn said, helping her into the seat with the a firm grip on her hand. "It won't be what you expect."

They rode through the town, drawing the attention of the people on the street. Most of Kimberley was made of corrugated iron and lumber and not very appealing to the eye. There had been no rain for several weeks, making the streets dry and dusty. Under the rim of her parasol, Olivia could feel the curious stares. *Quinn has a woman.* She could almost hear the words milling around in the peoples' mind, but she held her head high, slightly proud at the idea that if any woman could claim the diamond jackal, it was she.

Olivia soon discovered that the town was actually built around the Hole to supply the wants and needs of the mining population. As they approached the focal point of the diamond industry, Quinn told her that the small hill had originally been called Colesberg's Koppie. Upon reaching the point, Olivia had to admit that he had been right. The Hole wasn't at all what she'd expected.

The koppie was hardly a hill at all, its summit having been shaved away by mining shovels. There was a rise of land, however, a circular mound created by the mining debris. It was a few feet high. Quinn stopped the buggy. "We have to walk from here."

Eager now to see what had drawn so many fortune hunters

to South Africa, Olivia departed the buggy with an enthusiastic smile.

"Stay close to me," Quinn cautioned her.

Olivia's bright expression changed to one of complete awe as they reached the brim of the mine. Everything was gathered in one place. The mine wasn't a narrow entrance into an underground cavern but a large earthen bowl, containing thousands of workers.

"The Hole covers nine acres," Quinn told her. "It's hard to imagine a hole being that big, but it is. And those men," he pointed down into the earthen pit that owed its creation to human greed, "bees in a hive. Those are the men who will be renting your rooms. Dirty, bone-weary men, who'll come to your table with dirt under their nails because they'd have to soak their hands for a week to them get clean. Is that what you expected?"

So the invitation was another means to discourage her. Olivia was disappointed, but she wasn't surprised. Quinn seemed determined to bring about her eviction.

"Dirty hands or not, they will need a place to sleep and a hot meal," she responded, knowing he wanted to hear her say that the miners and their grimy appearance disgusted her. Although she didn't like the idea of having her newly scrubbed floors tracked over, she was practical enough to know that the success of her boardinghouse depended on the men who worked in the mines.

Quinn waited for her to say more, but she didn't.

She stood on the narrow road that circled the brim of the Hole, gazing down into the entirety of the Kimberley mine. The men digging did resemble bees, working diligently to find the small hard stones that nature had buried deep in the earth. They worked on tiers that spiraled downward from the top of the pit like the colors and patterns found on a child's toy. The earthen shelves allowed the men at the bottom of the mine to gradually reach its top. The dirt itself was hauled up and out of the hole by means of a wire tramway.

"See those boxes?" Quinn said, pointing again.

Olivia's gaze followed his hand. The boxes were the size of a small house.

"They're the first sorting sheds," he explained. "The tram is worked by mules. Once the bucket tram reaches the box, the sorting begins. The higher the box, the more thorough the sort."

The tram and boxes worked on a simple principle. Two buckets coming up. Two going down. The process was repeated, time and time again, as the dirt was sifted like flour. The wires converged at the bottom of the mining basin. They dropped down and crept back up with a gentle trembling resonance, like the strings of a harp being plucked. The musical vibration mixed with the voices of the miners, creating an unique sound.

"This is blue ground," Quinn said.

Olivia gave him a puzzled look. "Dirt isn't blue."

"The darker the dirt, the better chance of finding diamonds," he explained. "The geologists have an explanation for it. Volcanoes. This whole region was created by them. But miners don't care about science. To them it's just blue."

With the sun shining down into the pit, Olivia could see the various layers. Near the surface and for some distance down, the sides were a light brown, but there were other colors on the earthen walls, as well. Varying shades that darkened toward the center of the pit. The variation gave the large bowl a peculiar appearance as the sun reflected off the piles of gravel and debris.

"It's astounding," Olivia said, staring at the men busy with their picks and shovels, working along the earthen dikes and channels that formed the walls of the mine. "I've never seen the inside of a beehive, but I imagine it's very much like this.''

The peculiar beehive was guarded like a golden treasure. Armed men with bandoliers across their chests and rifles in their hands patrolled each layer of the pit. There was a cluster of guards at each sifting point, watching each bucket of dirt as it was dumped and sorted.

Olivia continued to stare at the workers. They were a mixture of black and white, old and young. All dirty, all sweaty, and all greedily gouging at the earth.

''I can't imagine finding a diamond in all that dirt,'' Olivia mused. ''It must be like looking for the proverbial needle in a haystack.''

''Miners are as sharp-sighted as vultures. The largest stones are found during the mining process, when the dirt is knocked around and dumped into the buckets.''

Olivia glanced over her shoulder, reluctant to give up the fascinating sights and sounds of the mine. Quinn urged her on with an arm wrapped around her waist. He continued explaining the process of finding a shiny needle in a haystack of dirt. ''When the 'blue' comes up it's deposited in wooden troughs. The watering takes place near the river. De Beers uses a puddling-trough where the dirt is broken up and converted into a muddy paste. Diamonds are the heaviest stones, so they sink to the bottom of the trough. When the washing is finished, whatever's at the bottom of the trough is sifted, washed again, and examined until all you have left is diamonds.''

He helped her into the buggy, then walked around and got in beside her.

''What happens next?'' Olivia asked as she opened her parasol.

''The sorting house.'' He gave her a quick glance as he carefully turned the buggy around. ''Diamonds come in all shapes and sizes and colors. Once they're sorted for clarity and color, they're sent to the brokers.''

"That's where you come in," Olivia said.

Quinn's expression changed immediately. Instead of expounding on his part in the scheme of things, he said nothing at all.

She could feel the walls going up as they made their way back to the boardinghouse. *The secrets of his trade,* Olivia told herself. *No wonder he never talks about himself. He's so used to hiding things, it's become second nature.*

Is he hiding his real feelings for me, too?

Does he have any feelings for me?

By the time they reached Hull Street, she was back to wondering if she'd ever know the real Matthew Quinlan. Although he hadn't kissed her today, he had shared time and conversation, things he didn't normally share. That made the day special.

When the buggy stopped in front of the boardinghouse, Quinn looked at her for a long moment before he climbed down, then walked around to help her down from the seat. His hands felt strong around her waist and Olivia longed to have them touch her more intimately. She wanted to feel those shivering sensations again, the ones that always erupted inside her whenever Quinn pressed his mouth to hers.

"Thank you for showing me the mine," she said.

He looked at her as if he wanted to say something, but his dark lashes lowered and when they came up the fortress was back in place, firmly erected to keep anyone from getting inside.

Instead of saying you're welcome, Quinn smiled, almost sadly. His hands dropped away from her waist and he stepped back.

The possibility of being kissed goodbye dissolved as

Olivia watched him climb back into the buggy. He gathered the reins in one hand, then reached up and tapped a finger to the brim of his hat. "Don't work too hard, butterfly."

Twelve

Another week of scrubbing, dusting, polishing, and painting turned the boardinghouse into a clean establishment, if not a renowned one. The yard had been weeded and flowers planted along the front of the porch, the rugs beat clean, and the linens freshly starched. Although the house still had a long way to go to meet her expectations, Olivia felt confident she could attract some boarders once a notice was posted in town.

She sat in the parlor, hemming a pair of curtains for one of the upstairs rooms, when a firm knock on the door forced her to put the task aside. Hoping the visitor was Quinn, she pressed the wrinkles from her black skirt and stopped by the mirror on her way to smooth her hair. Keeping her expression cordial, she opened the door.

Her visitor was a middle-aged man. Thin with a haggard look about him, he stared at her from dull brown eyes. "Quinn said you might have a room to rent."

"Yes," Olivia replied, opening the door wider and motioning him inside.

"Name's Mailer. Edward Mailer," the man said, taking off his hat. "I'm a sorter at the De Beers's shed."

Mr. Mailer was a cordial man who accepted the tea she offered with a gracious smile. Once they were seated in the front parlor, Olivia felt a twinge of discomfort at the thought of discussing the rent, but she knew she had to get over the awkwardness. She decided the best way was to find out a little something about the potential boarder.

"Where are you from, Mr. Mailer?"

"My father was English. My mother was born in Alexander Bay, second-generation German. I was born there, too. Didn't care much for farming or fishing, so I came to the mines. I've been working the sorting tables for the last five years."

After a few minutes of amiable conservation, Olivia got down to business.

"I have several rooms available," she began. "How long do you think you'll be needing one?"

"Until the mines play out," Mailer said with a slight smile on his face. He shrugged the bony shoulders under his brown jacket. "That could be forever. The Hole's just getting bigger. They could be digging diamonds here for a long time to come."

"Very well," she replied, then told him the weekly fee. "The rent includes two meals, breakfast and dinner. Visitors can be entertained here in the parlor, or on the front porch, but not upstairs. My gentlemen boarders are welcome to smoke their cigars or pipes outside." She hesitated, hoping the last rule wouldn't undo the deal. "Liquor of any kind is prohibited. Is that acceptable?"

"Sounds fine to me," he responded. "Can I move my things in today?"

"Of course, but wouldn't you like to see the room first?"

"No need," he told her. "Anything's better than the place I've been living in." He looked around the parlor, admiring the clean floor and polished mantle. It was easy to see that Miss St. John was a respectable young lady who intended to run a respectable boardinghouse. "You'll have more boarders than you can handle once the word gets out. Most of the boardinghouses around here are . . . Well, they're not near as comfortable as this one."

Olivia breathed a silent sigh of relief. Perhaps renting the other rooms wouldn't be as difficult as she'd expected. Goodness knew she needed the money. Her funds were almost depleted, and she didn't have any idea how much she owned Quinn. Every time she asked Echo, the manservant just smiled at her and said nothing.

Her first official boarder came to his feet, thanking her for the tea. "I'll be back before dark. I'll give you the rent money then."

"That will be fine, Mr. Mailer."

She walked with him to the front door, hoping she'd see Quinn soon, so she could thank him for recommending her boardinghouse. Mr. Mailer was a likable sort.

So were the next five men who knocked on her door. Each of them worked for De Beers. They were all over forty, all friendly, with the exception of Robert Reynolds, who was the youngest at forty-two and downright shy. By the end of the following day, Olivia had only two rooms left. Both of them had boards over the windows awaiting glass that had been ordered from Cape Town. The next man accepted one of the rooms anyway, saying he didn't mind the inconvenience. That left one room.

Olivia was determined to rent it without Quinn's help.

She poured herself a cup of tea while she pondered having seven boarders without the benefit of a single notice or advertisement. Each of the men had arrived following a recommendation from Quinn, which meant he was personally selecting her boarders. Why? Didn't he trust her to do it herself, or was he intentionally surrounding her with older unattractive men who didn't present any temptation? Maybe he was simply making sure that she rented to reliable workers who would pay on time, thus insuring the monies she owed him would be repaid? Whatever his reason, Olivia didn't like it.

After finishing her tea, she went into the kitchen to help Taila, the oldest of the two women Echo had hired. Dinner was over, and the men who hadn't already retired for the night were outside on the front porch, smoking their cigars and discussing the day's events. The plump native woman, with short-cropped hair and enormous ebony eyes, was an excellent cook, which was of considerable help now that there were seven hungry men to feed. With farms stretching east and west along the Vaal River, produce was readily available, along with a fresh supply of poultry, beef, mutton, and pork.

Putting an apron over her dress, Olivia began drying the last of the dishes. Taila had a limited English vocabulary, but they were able to discuss the following day's menu. After the dishes were put away, Taila wished Olivia a good night, then left for the night. She lived nearby in a small corrugated tin hut with her husband and two sons, all of whom worked in the mines.

The back door was open, the screen closed, allowing the exotic song of a night bird into the room. Feeling restless and knowing she wouldn't be able to sleep, Olivia sat down at the kitchen table, watching the flames of the kerosene lantern and thinking of Quinn.

She was angry at him for so many things, but underneath the anger was the growing hope that she wasn't wasting her heart on the man. Now that the boardinghouse seemed to have a future, she couldn't stop from thinking about her own.

The muffled sounds of men coming in from the porch and climbing the stairs to their rooms on the second floor were barely heard by Olivia as she sat in the kitchen, hands folded on the table in front of her, her mind elsewhere. There was only the soft sounds of a South African night and the flicker of lantern light to keep her company.

The parlor clock struck ten and still she sat there, staring into space while her thoughts turned inward. The soft rattle of the screen door brought her out of her contemplations.

"Hello, butterfly."

Quinn was standing on the other side of the door, half in shadow, half in light. She studied his broad shoulders, the crispness of his white shirt, stretched taut over his muscular frame, and the raven black hair that curled over his collar. *God help me, I love this man.* She came to her feet, thinking she'd spend the rest of her life loving him because there was no substitute for the feelings he evoked with no more than a whisper of the affectionate nickname he'd given her.

"It's late," she said, unlatching the door anyway.

"I didn't want to interrupt your dinner," he replied, stepping inside the room.

Olivia accepted his explanation although she sensed it was more. If Quinn had come calling earlier in the evening, knocking on the front door instead of gently rattling the kitchen screen, his visit could be construed as a formal visit, a gentleman calling upon a lady.

As always, his physical presence overwhelmed her. She returned to the table, but she didn't sit down. Instead she watched him as his sapphire eyes surveyed the now neatly arranged kitchen. He reached out and touched the pale petals of a wild orchid, transplanted from the river bank to a clay pot on the sideboard.

"What is it about women and wild things? If something grows free in the woods, they always want to stick it in a pot and grow it in the parlor."

Olivia knew Quinn wasn't talking about flowers. He was talking about himself.

In many ways he was as wild as the orchids, thriving in a land that too frequently brought other men to their knees, free to come and go as he pleased, to live as he pleased.

Disliking the reminder that he wasn't a man who wanted a permanent woman in his future, Olivia untied her apron and draped it over the back of a kitchen chair.

"Women and their fixation with flowers isn't all that different than man's obsession for gold or diamonds. Whenever men find something shiny, you seem compelled to dig it out of the ground. Explain one and you've explained the other."

A slow lazy smile came to Quinn's face. "You look like you want to slap me again."

"I'm tempted," she told him.

He smiled the mischievous, mysterious smile that always made her blood hum as she moved around the kitchen, straightening things that didn't need to be straightened, lifting the lid of the empty teapot, then setting it back into place. She turned her back on him as she walked to the pantry to get what she'd need to put a fresh pot on to boil.

He could see that she was sizzling under the collar. She was acting all indignant and self-righteous. He took a long breath. "Get it said."

"Get what said?" she snapped as she turned to face him, the tea forgotten. "Would you take the time to listen if I told you that you're interfering in my life? I doubt it. No, not the legendary Matthew Quinlan. You'd just go on doing whatever you like, whenever you like it, and think of me as a prissy lady for saying otherwise.''

"You really are mad, aren't you?''

"No. I'm not mad. Neither am I angry nor upset. I'm merely ready to take charge of *my* life and *my* boardinghouse. Something I can't do as long as you insist upon playing guardian angel.''

He could see angry flames dancing in her brown eyes. "Your last room will be filled by tomorrow,'' he said, thinking she was almost as pretty when she was angry as she was when she was melting in his arms. "The man's name is Hudson. He works in one of the box sheds near the southern end of the Hole. He's a little gruff at times, but he's a good man.''

When she spoke her voice was calm but firm. "I'm afraid Mr. Hudson will be disappointed. I have no intention of renting out the last room until the windows are replaced. That will be several weeks, according to the merchant who ordered the glass for me. At that time, if he's still interested, I'll take Mr. Hudson's application into consideration.''

She paused, knowing what he was up to, but unable to understand his motives. Like the man, they were mysterious and secretive. "There may be other applicants,'' she said. "Regardless of the number, I shall like to make the selection without your intervention.''

Quinn didn't say anything. He just stood there, looking at her as if he had every right to be in her kitchen late at night, directing her life as he saw fit. Olivia suspected his thoughts were similar to her own, the recollection that he'd kissed her in this very room, of how she'd kissed him in return, and that if he ever kissed her again, there'd be even more memories between them. But memories didn't give him the right to dictate her future. Only a wedding ring could do that, and Quinn wasn't interested in taking a wife.

It took some effort, but she was able to keep her voice from shaking. "Please don't think me ungrateful. I do appreciate what you've done so far," she told him. "But, it's time—"

"For me to mind my own business," Quinn finished for her.

"Aptly put."

Their eyes met again. Her gaze resolved, his possessive. In that moment, Olivia knew why he had sent her boarders, and why he was insisting that she rent the last room to Mr. Hudson.

Quinn was leaving Kimberley.

Leaving her.

He was standing there so tall and imposing, so handsome it made her heart hurt. She tucked her hands into the pockets of her skirt to keep from reaching out to him. A dull pain inched from her heart, weaving its way throughout her body. Touching him wouldn't keep him from leaving. There was no holding a man like Quinn, unless he wanted to be held.

Quinn stayed where he was. Olivia looked young and vulnerable, and for the first time he wasn't looking forward to the challenge of another hike through the bush. The game of cat and mouse he always played with potential thieves wasn't one-tenth as appealing as the lady from Portsmouth.

"When are you leaving?" she asked resignedly.

"Who said I'm leaving?"

"That's why you're here, isn't it? To tell me goodbye."

Quinn felt a twinge of regret that all too quickly became a full-fledged attack of conscience. Why couldn't he walk away from this woman, the way he'd walked away from so many others? What was it about her soft voice and angel eyes that had a stranglehold on him?

The lack of admission didn't keep Olivia from knowing she was right. Quinn was leaving. Maybe not today, or tomorrow. But soon. He wouldn't tell her, of course. He distrusted everyone. She doubted if Echo even knew, although he was probably the only man with whom Quinn shared confidences, and even that faith had its limitations.

"I don't know why I'm interfering," he admitted in a soft voice. "Maybe it's because I know this town better than anyone. I've watched it grow, and I've watched the men in it get greedier and greedier as the Hole expands. You're a woman alone, with no family to take care of you."

It wasn't an apology, but it was something, an explanation of his actions that only made her hurt all the more. Quinn didn't feel any real affection for her, he was simply continuing the job he'd taken on in Cape Town, watching out for her like an older brother. If he felt anything, it was obligation and perhaps some guilt that he'd taken liberties with her.

"It was my decision to leave my family," she told him, taking herself to the cupboard for a clean cup. She still couldn't look at him. "I know it's difficult for men to accept, but women can take care of themselves. Even ladies from Portsmouth."

Quinn couldn't see the tears brimming in her eyes, but he could hear the hurt in her voice. It made him feel as low as the dirt on Hull Street. She was making it sound like he was deserting her, but he wasn't. He was leaving Echo behind for the first time in years. He should have been gone already, but he'd stayed, making sure she had boarders. He'd even come to say goodbye, although it would have been easier to stay away.

Stricken anew by the depths of her feelings for this man, Olivia gathered her composure and turned to face him, knowing he wasn't going to leave until she did. Her heart was hammering inside her chest, but she didn't let it show. She couldn't let it show. She had to get Quinn out of here, before she . . . Using the prim, schoolteacher voice that she'd often had to call upon when tutoring children, she looked across the kitchen. "Thank you for coming. But as you can see, I'm fine. Now, if you'll excuse me, it's late and—"

"Don't," Quinn said, striding across the room. He grabbed her by the shoulders, stopping the exit she was determined to make. "Don't do this to yourself."

"Do what?" she snapped at him, keeping her voice low because she didn't want anyone to know that Quinn had come calling after hours. It would only increase the gossip that had arrived in Kimberley the same day they'd departed the train.

"Torment yourself," he said, holding her despite the hands that were trying to push him away. "Don't torment me."

"I'm not doing anything," she hissed. "You're the one who insisted that we kiss. You're the one who keeps showing up on my doorstep. Just go away! Go away and let me be."

She was sobbing by this time, the words spoken raggedly, the sound of her distress ripping at Quinn like the claws of a lion. He held her, anchoring her struggling body against his stronger one. God, she felt so good. So right. He'd missed that rightness, the knowledge that this particular woman fit against his body so perfectly, that he'd fit within her so perfectly. He wanted that perfection like he wanted his next breath, as naturally as if of all the men in the world he was the one who had been created solely to hold Olivia in his arms.

Quinn's arms imprisoned her. There was nothing she could do but stand there, captured by his strength, unable to resist the dangerous temptation he presented.

"I should . . ." Quinn relented in a throaty whisper. "I should walk out that door and never come back. But I can't, butterfly. I can't."

His confession brought her eyes up. She looked at him through the tears, unsure what she was hearing.

One of his hands found its way to the nape of her neck, holding her for the kiss they both knew was inevitable. She watched as his face came closer and closer, his dark lashes lowering to shield those soul-piercing blue eyes. His breath was warm, scented by the whiskey he'd drank before showing up at her back door. Warm lips came down on hers. She felt the forbidden lick of his tongue, the gentle nibbling of his teeth, and surrendered to the soft probing. Her body betrayed her better judgment as she molded it to his, wanting to feel the power he always brought with him, that undeniable need that robbed her of reality, leaving only hopes and dreams and possibilities. Wonderful possibilities that didn't seem so far-fetched when Quinn was kissing her.

The kiss was gentle and tender, demanding and possessive. Still holding her tightly against him, Quinn taught her what torment really was, a longing so deep and keen that it was beyond any tangible explanation.

Enough of Quinn's common sense intruded for him to realize that he couldn't make love to her in the kitchen. And he was going to make love to her. That's why he'd come here tonight, not to say goodbye, but to lay claim to her in a way that would keep her from turning to another man while he was gone.

Olivia felt his hands moving slowly down her body, pressing her more snugly against him until she could feel the hard proof of his need through layers of broadcloth skirt and cotton petticoats. He held her there, breathing into her ear, mumbling things she didn't understand, allowing her to learn as much of him as she could while they still had their clothes on.

Her breasts were hard and tight and aching against the muslin of her camisole and she suddenly, desperately needed to be free from the clothing that kept her from feeling the hot callused caress of his hands. She twisted against him, silently begging because she was too embarrassed to say the words.

"I know, butterfly." He lifted her in his arms then, cradling her against his chest as he walked out of the kitchen, through the dining room, and down the short darkened hallway that led to her bedroom.

The door was slightly ajar. He pushed it open with his knee, never loosening his hold on her. Once they were inside, he latched the door, shutting out the real world. The world they'd have to face come morning.

When Quinn reached the bed, he let her slide down his body, enjoying the tormenting caress as she rubbed over him. He meant to enjoy every minute of this insane night, because it was insane. Every thing about their relationship was insane. Impossible. He shouldn't be here, but he was. He shouldn't touch her, but he was. He'd sort out the consequences later. For now, there was only insanity and desire, the night and the woman.

He tunneled his fingers through her hair, loosening pins, sending them to the floor. She was helpless to do anything but return his kiss. A myriad of emotions started to swirl around inside her—love, desire, need—each had its part in the sensual dance, this prelude to becoming real lovers. There was no making sense of things; they'd gone beyond that point. There was only the desire burning deep within her and the surety that she'd never love another man the way she loved Quinn.

Olivia felt the cool fabric of the coverlet, the soft breeze fluttering the lace curtains she'd finished hemming that morning, and the heat of Quinn's hands as he measured her from shoulder to thigh. It was too dark to see more than his body silhouetted against the pale moonlight, but she could feel the heat of him, seeping into her bones and muscles and blood, the warmth of him slowly taking over her heart and mind.

She'd forfeited her corset because of the climate, but there were still layers of clothing to remove. Quinn removed them with taunting caresses, stripping away her skirt and tossing it aside. The buttons on the front of her blouse came undone, slowly, sensually, letting the night air touch her skin the same gentle way his hands were touching her. Petticoats were untied and tossed aside. The action was accompanied by the deep resonant sound of his voice, whispering how much he'd been wanting to rid her of them and the muslin camisole. Thin ribbons unraveled and cloth parted in the same sensual dance, until she was lying naked on the bed.

"I knew you'd look like this," Quinn said, staring at her. He was still fully clothed.

She looked up at him, her heart fluttering, beating so erratically she could barely get her breath. His eyes seemed to be branding her, turning the gossip into truth, making her "Quinn's woman."

He continued to hold her with his gaze as his hands moved to his own clothing. His jacket and shirt were tossed to the floor, not hastily but fast enough to show her the impatience of a desire held in check too long. He unfastened his trousers, one button at a time, teasing her as the male always teased the female before mating. He put his thumbs in the waistband pushing them down as he turned around to sit on the edge of the bed. In the moonlight she could see the lean muscles of his back and hips. A soft thump came with each boot, pulled off and discarded. Then socks and trousers were kicked aside, and he was stretching out on the mattress next to her.

Everything was new and shocking. The heat of his naked skin, the crisp texture of the hair on his chest and arms and legs, the sounds of his breathing as his hands leisurely roamed over her, starting at her collarbone then slowly moving downward, touching and feeling, savoring her like an admirer of art might savor a sculpture.

But Olivia wasn't made of bronze or polished marble, she was alive. More alive in this moment than she'd ever dreamed of being.

The moonlight gleamed on his naked skin as he raised himself, leaning over her. "Don't hate me," she thought she heard him whisper as his mouth joined his hands and gentle kisses made her tremble. His mouth moved slowly over her breasts, learning the soft mounds with sensual breaths and licks of his tongue, making her ache for what she'd felt that night in the bush when he'd suckled her like a hungry babe. And then his mouth was there, drawing her inside, making her back arch to get closer.

Her hair lay across the pillow in soft waves. Quinn knotted one of his hands into the thick mane of honey-colored silk in a desperate attempt to keep his control. Tension tugged at his body, demanding release, but he held it in check, knowing pleasure would be a long time coming, wanting to make the sensual trap he'd willingly walked into last forever. She smelled like lilac soap and orchid blossoms and warm African nights. His hands ran over her, feeding his starving senses, arousing the denied desire that had been his constant companion.

Olivia moaned his name and the sound of it suited the sultry night and the naked bodies and the passion that was about to be unleashed. Her lips fell open as his mouth became more demanding, drawing on her breast until it was almost painful, making something hot and wonderful pool in the very depths of her.

His hands drifted to her waist, then lowered, rubbing softly against her belly, then lower still. Finally he touched her. His fingers circled and stroked, making her gasp with shock, but he didn't stop. It was too late to stop, insanity ruled now. Insanity and all the things they both had kept bottled up inside them for weeks.

She responded hesitantly at first, keeping still while his fingers gently probed, learning her secrets. But the passion was too high, the need too much, for her to stay still for long. Her hands, clutching his shoulders, began to move. She began to explore, shyly at first, then more aggressively as those stroking fingers made her blood run hotter and hotter.

When her fingers combed through the thick hair below his navel, it was Quinn's turn to groan. He was hard and tight and tingling with anticipation. Olivia could feel him throbbing against her bare thigh.

Then he was pushing her back, holding her more firmly against his body. "Spread your legs, butterfly."

She blushed in the dark, but did as he asked, making a place for him. He filled it, rubbing his hard smooth length against the moist sensitive place he'd touched with his fingers. His hands were braced near her shoulders, his upper body teasing the hard erect nipples of her breasts while his hips moved slowly from side to side, then back and forth, a slow sensual dance that made her want more. So much more.

They watched each other now, her face flushed with excitement and just a tint of embarrassment, his features intense, his mind and body focused on just one thing, drawing the pleasure out for as long as possible.

He rolled gently against her, teaching her the differences between them, the way they would eventually fit together. She was ready for him, but it wasn't going to be easy. She was small and tight. So damn tight, it was all he could do not to lose control. He wanted to be inside her, to feel her hot satiny channel surrounding him, milking him until he couldn't hold back any longer.

Her body shuddered, arching, pushing upward as his hips rolled within the cradle of her thighs, demanding that he stop tormenting them both, letting him know that she too was beyond the point of no return. His body probed gently, finding the entrance to hers. "Hold on to me," he breathed heavily. "Don't let go."

His upper body lifted as his hips pushed forward. He entered her then, hard and quick.

She gasped, but he trapped the sound with a kiss. She pushed against his chest with her open palms, but his weight held her in place. "Shhh, butterfly, it won't hurt for long. Just relax. Relax and trust me."

She gasped again as his hips lifted then returned, pushing again, stretching her until there was no escaping his possession. She arched up, thinking to dislodge him, but her movement accomplished just the opposite. He moved deeper into her.

Their bodies pressed together. He lifted and returned, filling her. She tensed, then relaxed. "That's better," he whispered into her ear. "Move with me, not against me. Lift when I lift, follow me, don't let me get away."

Quinn wasn't so far gone that he'd forgotten they weren't in the house alone. So he made love to her as slowly as possible, as quietly as possible. His mouth absorbed the soft sounds she made as she did what he asked, lifting up as he retreated, following him, keeping him inside her.

Her hands rested on his hips as he moved. His were fisted in the silken hair lying on the pillow as he continued move slowly, surely within her. He watched her face, the changing expression that came with increased pleasure. "God, you're beautiful."

The words brought her eyes open. He was close enough

to see them shining with passion. "It's only going to get better," he promised as he pushed deeper, straining to find that one point, that one moment, when he'd push her over the edge.

Olivia couldn't keep her eyes open for long. They drifted closed as Quinn kept pushing against her, into her, and with each stroke she felt herself dissolving, like sugar spooned into a cup of hot tea, disappearing until they were one and the same. The shocking pleasure, the intimacy of their joining, brought tears to her eyes.

He held her hips now, lifting her hard against him as he pushed down. Harder and deeper with each thrust. Then it happened. The pleasure exploded. She couldn't stop it. Her entire body trembled and her mind went blank, spinning away from her as a riot of sensations moved from the center of her body to the tips of her toes.

Suddenly the mysterious, indefinable need she'd felt since the first timid kiss she'd shared with Quinn wasn't a mystery anymore. This was the answer, this wonderful thing she was experiencing. This giving and taking, this sharing, this ecstasy.

A deep satisfied sound escaped Quinn as he pushed hard one last time and pulsed within her. His forehead rested against hers moments later, his breathing deep and ragged, his body drained of strength. But it had been a sweet draining, better than he'd ever felt before, so damn good he wasn't sure he had the strength to roll off her and onto his side.

A smile lifted the corners of his mouth as Olivia's arms circled his neck. She pressed up one last time, needing the contact as much as he did. He rolled to the side, taking her with him, holding her tightly. His hands gently caressed her hips, his fingers spreading wide to knead her soft bottom, his smile growing wider as she nestled closer.

They slept for a while, then made love again, neither

speaking this time. They didn't need words to express what they were feeling, wanting, needing from each other. The night was an all-consuming desire, and they were caught up in the storm, willing victims until dawn.

The soft colors of a South African sunrise were filling the room when Olivia opened her eyes. The window was still open, the mosquito netting down, covering the bed where she slept alone. She smoothed her hands over the sheets, feeling their coolness, realizing that Quinn had left her hours ago.

An emptiness, unlike anything she'd ever felt before, inched its way into her mind and heart. He was gone. How was she going to get through the day?

The same way you got through the bush, she told herself, sitting up slowly because her body ached from all the things Quinn had taught her to enjoy. *One step at a time, one hour at a time, one day at a time. Quinn will be back. Until then, you'll live with the questions and the doubts the same way you lived with the dreams until last night.*

Thirteen

The days stretched into weeks, a month, then two months, as Olivia focused all her energy on the boardinghouse and the six men she fed on a regular basis. Although she couldn't be sure, she sensed that Echo knew something extremely intimate had transpired between herself and Quinn, because the servant was even more solicitous than before. Every so often she'd turn to find him looking at her, his dark eyes glowing sympathetically, as if he knew how badly her heart ached for Quinn.

The only way she could survive the long, lonely days was to keep her mind focused on the small details: brewing a perfect pot of tea, making sure the transplanted orchids that decorated each of the downstairs rooms received just the right combination of water and sunshine. Each task became a quest, a deed that had to be completed to perfection. There was no room for thought, because if she stopped to think, she'd cry, and she refused to let the tears start.

There was no guarantee that Quinn was giving her more than a cursory thought as he went about his business, wherever he was. There was no guarantee that what had happened between them meant more than a tinker's damn to the man, but her heart kept on hoping. Every time she closed her eyes, so exhausted she should sleep without hesitation, that flicker of hope kept her awake until her thoughts turned to Quinn. Sometimes the nights seemed endless, an infinite period between activity and nothingness, filled with an aching loneliness that made her realize how empty her life had been before meeting the legendary diamond jackal.

But the morning light outshone the flickering candle of hope, and with each sunrise Olivia was forced to face the fact that when Quinn did return, things weren't likely to change. He would still be a man who thrived on freedom and danger, and she'd still be a woman who wanted marriage and children.

She found herself fearing that she'd be forever wanting what she couldn't have, living in a boardinghouse in Kimberley while Quinn continued migrating between the mining community and Cape Town, loving him from a distance that would only grow greater with time. When those thoughts took hold, the future became a blur, a disheartening image that sapped her hope. What if Quinn didn't love her? What if he returned with the idea that she'd be his woman any time he was in the mood? Could she live with that? Olivia knew she couldn't. No matter how much she loved Quinn, her pride wouldn't allow her to be his mistress.

It was Tuesday, the day Olivia normally went into Kimberley to do her shopping. She dressed as she always did, in a dark broadcloth skirt, an organdy blouse, and a linen jacket. The merchant had delivered the glass for the last room, and

Echo was upstairs, setting the expensive panes that had been crated and shipped from Cape Town. She thought about going upstairs and inviting him to accompany her, but it really wasn't necessary. She knew the local merchants now. Whatever she purchased could be picked up later in the day.

Opening the door, Olivia let out a short gasp of surprise, then stepped back.

"Sorry, I was about to knock," Hans Van Mier said, lowering his hand to his side.

"Mr. Van Mier," she said, surprised to find the Dutchman on her doorstep. He was naturally handsome, with his pale hair combed back from his tanned face and his eyes gleaming blue beneath blond brows.

"I just returned to Kimberley," he said, as if she should have known or cared that he'd left in the first place. "I'm looking for a room. Please tell me you haven't rented all of yours."

"I do have one room left, but there have been several applicants. I couldn't rent it to you without taking them into consideration," she replied, knowing Quinn wouldn't approve of her inviting the Dutchman into her boarding-house.

I have to stop connecting Quinn to every thought I think, she rebuked herself as she looked up at the Dutchman. *So what if I rent Mr. Van Mier a room? He has to have a place to sleep and eat just like everyone else.*

"I'm very interested in retaining a permanent residence," he said. "I move around a lot, hiring out my services as a guide, but I'd like to know I have someplace I can call home. Even if it's only a room on the second floor of your boardinghouse."

If he was trying to flatter his way inside, it wasn't impressing Olivia, but she was too well-mannered to tell him so. "We can talk about the room," she said, allowing him to follow her into the parlor. "But I feel an obligation to the men who have already applied. They aren't as well paid as you, Mr. Mier, which makes your ability to find accommodations less of a problem."

She was about to offer the Dutchman a cup of tea, something she did for each of her prospective tenants, when she turned to find Echo standing in the foyer just beyond the parlor door. She'd never before seen such an expression on his face. There was no hint of a smile, just cold dark eyes staring at the Dutchman.

Van Mier stared right back, daring the native to say anything offensive. Right or wrong, white men ruled Kimberley, and the servant knew it as well as anyone.

"Mr. Van Mier is inquiring about the room," Olivia said, keeping her back to the Dutchman while her eyes beseeched Echo not to start any trouble. "I told him that I've already had several inquires."

Echo dropped his lethal gaze, his eyes softening as they settled on her face. He didn't say anything, but, then, he didn't have to. They both knew Quinn would raise hell if he returned and found Van Mier sleeping under Olivia's newly inherited roof.

"You're being dismissed," Van Mier said arrogantly.

Olivia pivoted on the toes of her well-polished shoes. "Echo is my employee, not yours," she said with a snap to her voice. "Kindly remember that, if you please."

"He's—"

"A loyal friend," Olivia inserted before the Dutchman could apply one of the crude terms so many white men used when referring to the natives. "I expect my guests to show him the same respect they show me."

The Dutchman weighed her words for a moment, then smiled. "I meant no offense."

Both Olivia and Echo knew he was lying, but it didn't

matter. The damage was done. All she wanted to do now was get the Dutchman out of her parlor as quickly as possible.

"I was on my way into town," she said. "Since I have several applications to consider before the room is assigned, if you'd leave me the address where you're currently staying, I'll send you a note informing you of my decision."

"I'd like the matter settled now," Van Mier said, sitting down on the settee as if he meant to stay until she rented him the room. "If you're worried about the rent, don't be. I'll pay you three times what you normally charge. As I said, I want to retain it as a permanent residence."

Like bloody hell you will, Olivia thought as she gestured Echo away from the door. The servant stepped out of sight, but he didn't leave the foyer. Turning to face the haughty Dutchman, she kept her expression bland and her voice businesslike. "I won't be bribed into renting you a room, Mr. Van Mier. I treat all my boarders equally."

"Even Quinn?"

"Mr. Quinlan doesn't retain a room in this house," she replied stiffly. "I understand De Beers provides him with a very comfortable residence when he is in town."

"De Beers gives its best jackal anything he wants," Van Mier said, letting his jealousy show much too easily for Olivia to overlook it. "But one day, he's going to meet his match. All jackals do."

"Perhaps," she replied, masking her alarm behind a cold façade that was growing increasingly difficult to continue. "However, Mr. Quinlan's association with the De Beers isn't the subject we were discussing. May I again ask for your current address? I will let you know if and when a room becomes available."

"Try a cold day in hell!" Quinn's voice sliced through the parlor. "You're not welcome here, Van Mier. Get out and stay out."

Olivia felt her heart stop. She swirled around to find Quinn standing in the doorway with Echo slightly behind him. Both men were staring at the Dutchman with vengeance in their eyes. Once her heart started beating again, Olivia was flooded with a deluge of feelings. Elated that Quinn had returned, she couldn't help but wonder how long he'd been in town. And what did he think he was doing, picking and choosing her boarders, as if he had a right to dictate her life?

Hans stood up, facing Quinn's insulting remarks with a confident smile. He opened the jacket of his double-breasted suit with a gentlemanly flair. "I'm not armed," he said casually.

"I'm not challenging you to a duel," Quinn said coldly. "But if you're in the mood, we might as well settle this once and for all."

"Don't be ridiculous," Olivia said, glaring at Quinn.

He refused to meet her gaze, looking past her to where the Dutchman stood by the settee. Without a word Quinn shed the dark jacket he was wearing, handing it to Echo. His hands moved to the buttons of his waistcoat. The striped silk-lined vest followed the jacket. As he rolled up the sleeves of his shirt, he turned toward the front door, calling back over his shoulder, "Come on, Van Mier, we've both been looking for an excuse to beat the hell out of each other. It might as well be today."

Olivia couldn't believe her ears. She looked at Echo. The servant was one big smile as he folded Quinn's jacket and vest over his right arm. Seeing that she'd get no help from that quarter, Olivia turned to the Dutchman. He was unbuttoning the stiff collar of his shirt.

"I suggest you stay inside, Miss St. John."

"Are you out of your mind?" she retorted hotly. "Grown men don't fight over rented rooms."

"This isn't about renting a room," Van Mier said, stepping around her.

Olivia followed him outside, determined to stop the altercation before it began, baffled as to why Quinn had deliberately initiated it, and growing angrier by the minute that he was using her as an excuse to settle some unnamed feud between himself and the Dutchman. By the time she reached the front door, the two men were squared off for battle.

"Stop them," she said to Echo.

"Missy John go inside," the servant replied. "Wait for Quinn there."

"I'll do nothing of the sort," she fumed. "And you won't be getting the last word this time, so don't even try. I will not have two grown men rolling around in the dirt in front of my boardinghouse." She yelled out the last words, but she might as well have been talking to the lilies she'd planted beside the front porch, because neither man so much as looked her way.

Before she could take a step off the porch or blink her astonished brown eyes, Quinn drew back and threw a punch that nearly knocked the Dutchman off his feet. After that it was grunts and groans and dirt flying as the two began to fight in earnest. They rolled around in the yard, punching and slugging. Mr. Mailer, who was working the second shift at the sorting house that week, opened the window of his room and leaned outside. Wearing a dull gray union suit and a smile, he cheered Quinn on, declaring it was time someone taught the Dutchman a thing or two.

Quinn and Van Mier were almost matched in height and weight, but the diamond jackal had the advantage of having been born in the East End, where fighting meant winning any way you could. There was nothing gentlemanly about the way he scrambled to his feet, blocking the Dutchman's next punch only to land one of his own, a sharp right hook that sent the blond man back to the ground.

Olivia stood speechless, her eyes wide with disbelief as the two men literally tried to kill each other with their bare hands. By the time Van Mier was lying unconscious, the street beyond the boardinghouse was filled with onlookers. One man, dressed in grimy overalls and wearing a battered hat, was collecting money from the other men who had arrived early enough to place bets.

Quinn staggered to his feet. His lip was bleeding, and Olivia could see that his left eye would be swollen shut within seconds. His shirt was ripped under one arm. He pushed his hair away from his face and spit on the ground, barely missing the end of the Dutchman's bleeding nose. "Haul his carcass out of here," he said to no one in particular. "When he comes to, tell him the next time I see him will be the last time."

Several men stepped forward. One grabbed Van Mier's feet, the other hooked his hands under the Dutchman's armpits. They carried their unconscious cargo down the street toward one of the taverns.

Quinn took a step toward Olivia.

Embarrassed, angry, and thoroughly frustrated, her eyes bore a hole through him. "Of all the childish . . ."

"Later," Quinn mumbled, grimacing as he touched his split lip. "I need a drink."

"I don't keep spirits in the house," she said coldly, turning toward the door. At that moment she didn't care what Quinn wanted. Let the man follow the Dutchman down the street. There were more than enough taverns in Kimberley to satisfy his need for whiskey and female sympathy. She was sure that was what he had in mind. He expected her to nurse his cuts and bruises, to pamper him. Well, he was in for a surprise. She was done pampering the irritating man.

Despite her resolve not to give Quinn one moment of undeserved compassion, Olivia went directly to the kitchen and put water on to boil. She didn't look at him as he came into the room, pulled out a chair and sat down. While the water was heating, she gathered what she'd need, including the tin of Echo's medicinal salve.

Echo appeared with a bottle of whiskey.

"Where did you get that?" Olivia asked sharply.

Instead of answering her, Echo sat the bottle on the table within reach of Quinn's bruised hands and exited the room. It was plain to see another fight was brewing.

Quinn sat patiently while she washed the blood off his mouth, unaware that she wanted to press her lips against his swollen ones so badly her insides were fluttering. Still, Olivia maintained her dignity, knowing if she didn't she'd be crying all over the man. Seeing his handsome face bruised, his left eye swollen and turning purple, she did her best to let her temper cool. It would serve Quinn right if she gave him a tongue-lashing, but what she had to say was too important to be spoken angrily. She had to make him understand that by protecting her, he was only making things worse. If there was gossip about them, and she was sure there was, he'd only added fuel to the fire by challenging Van Mier to a fight.

"Talk to me, butterfly," he said as she placed a wet compress against his swollen eye.

With more effort than her expression showed, Olivia kept her voice calm. "What should I say, Mr. Quinlan? Are you the least bit interested in my opinion? I think not. If you were, you wouldn't have enticed Mr. Van Mier into a fight." She reached for the tin of salve. "And you did entice him. Why, I'm not sure. Whatever vendetta you have for the man can't possibly have anything to do with me. Today was the first time I've laid eyes on him since we arrived in Kimberley."

"He's trouble."

"I'll accept your evaluation," she said blandly. "But I won't condone your actions."

He looked at her, his one good eye unblinking. "He doesn't want a room. He wants you."

"You're being ridiculous again." She turned away from him, but his hand wrapped around her wrist, capturing her.

"Am I?" he asked, studying her face as she did her best to hide what his touch was doing to her. "You're young and pretty and unattached."

Unattached. That was one way to describe her current circumstances. She could feel the tension in Quinn's grip. It wasn't anger or frustration that had him holding her wrist so tightly. It was passion. The same passion that always erupted between them when they got this close.

"The Dutchman may look like a gentleman, but he isn't," Quinn said stiffly. "You're not the first women he's tried to charm, and you won't be the last."

She watched his chest rise and fall, saw the shuddering of his breath as he tried to make light of his own feelings while he blamed another man for wanting the same thing. The hypocrisy of the moment almost made her laugh. "Are your motives any better?" she asked him in a surprisingly calm voice. "You don't want a wife, so you come calling in the middle of the night, then sneak away before dawn. Two months later, you have the audacity to stroll into my house without so much as a knock, exiling another man. You perpetuate the gossip that I'm your woman by starting a brawl in front of my home." The tone of her voice grew with a firm intensity that almost had her shouting. "I'm sure the whole of Kimberley is as convinced as Mr. Van Mier that I'm your woman."

"You are my woman."

She jerked away from him. "Does that make you proud? Does it give you a sense of accomplishment to know that—"

"God," Quinn groaned. He wrapped his arms around her waist and pressed his bruised face against her middle. "No," he mumbled, moving his head from side to side, luxuriating in the feel and scent of her. "I ought to be shot for what I did. But I wouldn't undo it. Every minute I held you in my arms was pure heaven."

Olivia was too close to tears to say anything. Instead she forced herself to stand still while he buried his face against her, his breath so hot she could feel it through the thin layers of her organdy blouse and muslin camisole. Her breathing was tremulous, her heart pounding so hard she knew he could feel it, but still she said nothing.

What was there to say? She'd been Quinn's woman for one night, but if he didn't love her, then she had no choice but to cease being anything to him.

"Please let me go," she said, hating the words almost as much as she hated the realization that Quinn would gladly take her as his mistress.

His arms slipped away as he raised his head to find those dark brown eyes looking down at him. He leaned back in the chair while she opened the tin of salve and begin applying it ever so gently to the small cut on his jaw. He'd never seen her like this before, halfway between tears and anger, her face taut with tension, her teeth almost grinding together to keep from lashing out of him. He deserved whatever insults she wanted to sling his way. He'd taken her virginity, then left in the middle of the night. If she wanted to rant and rave at him, then he'd damn well sit there and take it.

"You may dislike Mr. Van Mier," she finally said. Her mother would be proud of her. She was being as gracious as a queen, when she actually wanted to finish what the

Dutchman had started. "But at least admit that your reasons have nothing whatsoever to do with me. I was in the process of showing Van Mier to the door when you came rushing to my rescue like some medieval knight. An unnecessary rescue, I might add."

She turned her back on him and walked to the sideboard. She knew Quinn wasn't going to explain why he and Hans Van Mier hated each other. He was too used to keeping secrets to share anything with anyone, especially his heart. Her hands were shaking as she used a pair of sewing scissors to cut a small towel into strips. Determined to make Quinn understand that he couldn't keep popping in and out of her life like a jack-in-the-box, she took a deep breath before returning to the table. Before she could speak, he did.

"Why didn't you rent the last room? I know at least three men who were willing to take it, with or without glass in the windows."

He pulled the cork out of the bottle and turned it up, flinching as the whiskey found its way into the cut on his bottom lip. When he put the bottle down, Olivia was scowling at him. What in the hell did the woman expect him to do? The last time he'd seen her she was lying naked in the bed with just enough of the sheet over her pretty little rump to make him think twice about leaving. He hadn't been able to get that image out of his mind. He hadn't been able to get *her* out of his mind. This last trip had been the fastest one he'd ever made. He hadn't walked across the bush, he'd run. And for what? To find her with the Dutchman.

"When I rent the room it will be to someone of my choosing," she said, keeping her distance while she soaked a cloth in the warm water. She was about to hand it to him so he could wash the blood off his neck when she got a good look at his hands. His knuckles were bruised and bleeding. His right hand, the one that had connected so firmly with the

Dutchman's mouth and jaw, actually had teeth marks on it. Instead of giving him the cloth, she pushed the basin closer. "Soak your hands," she said.

He put his right hand into the basin and reached for the whiskey bottle with his left. She was about to take the liquor away, but stopped when he poured it into the basin instead of taking a drink. A smile lifted the corners of her mouth when he started cursing.

"It serves you right," she told him.

Quinn didn't argue. Instead, he turned the bottle up again and took a good long drink. When he set it down, he glared at her. "If you were in the process of the showing the man to the door, why get upset because I did it for you?"

"Beating a man unconscious isn't the same as cordially asking him to leave," Olivia pointed out.

"It got the job done," Quinn replied smugly.

"That's not the point," she said, crossing her arms over her breasts.

"Then what the hell is the point?"

"Don't get surly with me," she countered, raising her chin a good inch. The man couldn't be that dim-witted. "You're the one who insists on being my guardian angel. Well, I don't need one. I can manage to rent out the last of my rooms using my own judgment."

"People aren't always what they seem," he cautioned her.

"Really! How gallant of you to remind me," she snapped. "And how to do I go about judging a man's true character. Do I base my opinion on his actions rather than his words? If so, how should I judge you?"

Quinn flinched as if he'd taken another punch. He'd almost forgotten how well his butterfly could turn words into a weapon. He shook the water off his hand and stood up. He wanted to say something to defend himself, but he couldn't. There was no defense for seducing a virgin. And he had seduced Olivia. He'd lured her into his arms, knowing all the while that he shouldn't. But knowing hadn't stopped him. He'd wanted her too damn bad. He still wanted her.

With her insides trembling and her heart pounding, Olivia backed away from him. It was killing her to say what had to be said. She wasn't blaming Quinn. There was no one to blame but herself. She'd gone willingly into his arms. If her heart was as bruised and battered as his handsome face, it was her own fault.

Confused by all the emotions the man could inflict upon her without saying a word, she turned away to stare out the window. She had hoped to talk to Quinn, but if she spoke from her heart, it would be a confession of love. Quinn didn't want her to love him. He wanted . . . She didn't even know that much about him. The man wouldn't open up and tell her anything. Even the night he'd come to say goodbye to her, he'd never spoken the words.

Quinn saw the slight tremor of her bottom lip as she turned away from him. He reached for the whiskey bottle, but his hand stopped midway. Liquor wasn't the answer. God help him, he didn't know what say. He'd mentally kicked himself a hundred times during the last few weeks. Every step he'd taken away from Kimberley had ripped his guts out. He'd left her in the middle of the night, without a word, sneaking out the back door the same way he'd come into the house. He'd rushed back, knowing with each return step that he wasn't going to be welcomed. But he'd come anyway, because he couldn't stay away.

Suddenly, he found himself standing behind her. His hands went to her shoulders.

"Don't." She jerked away from him. After a forlorn breath, she sighed, "I think you should go."

"We need to talk."

"Talk!" She turned on him like a she-cat. "It's a little late for that, isn't it? I tried to talk to you in the bush, but you ignored me. I tried to talk to you that day on the train, before we arrived in Kimberley, but you made sure we didn't have time for more than a few words. And that . . . that night," she stammered she was so close to tears. "I wanted to talk to you, but you kept kissing me, making me want things . . . It doesn't matter now. When I woke up, you were gone." She straightened her shoulders, forcing herself to be blunt. "For a man who wants to talk, you don't say much, Mr. Quinlan."

"Damn!" Quinn blurted out. "What in the hell do you want me to say? That I'm sorry I had you. Well, I'm not. And neither are you. Look me in the eye now and tell me that you aren't glad to see me."

"I am glad to see you," she confessed softly. Her eyelids closed and a tear rolled down her face. Then they opened again. "But I can't keep . . . *We* can't keep interfering with each other's lives. You feeling responsible for me, me letting you. It isn't right. The boardinghouse is doing well. The men you sent are all respectable and hard-working. I'm already beginning to show a profit. I should be able to repay you, if only you'd tell me how much."

"I don't give a damn about the money."

"I do," she said stubbornly. "You didn't have to help me."

"It wasn't charity," he said more harshly than he intended.

"Which is exactly why it should be repaid."

His eyes drifted down her body to where the now blood-stained organdy blouse was tucked into the waistband of her skirt. It was easy to envision her without her clothes, to remember the softness of her skin, the way she'd come alive in his arms. "Is there going to be a baby?"

"No," she said, almost sadly.

He looked at her trembling lips and the tears gleaming in her eyes and hated himself. His hand reached out, damp with water and a small trickle of blood, and curled around the nape of her neck. "Tell me to leave, butterfly."

Olivia knew he was going to kiss her. *One last time*, she told herself.

His mouth settled gently over hers. The flavor of whiskey mixed with the coppery taste of blood as his lips moved tenderly. It was the goodbye kiss he should have given her weeks ago.

Olivia's arms wrapped around his waist, hugging him tightly. She squeezed her eyes shut and more tears flowed down her face. Quinn kissed them away, his breath a warm caress on her cheeks. Filled with love and longing, Olivia's heart ached. She allowed him to hold her as she tried to absorb his presence, to fill her senses with the feel and scent of him, to delight in this moment if she could find no joy in anything else.

"I never meant to hurt you," he whispered as he cradled her against his chest, his chin resting in the soft curls atop her head.

Wordlessly, they both remembered what it had felt like to hold each other in the dark, to lie skin to skin, heartbeat to heartbeat. But she needed more than memories. She needed all the things Quinn wasn't willing to give.

Slowly her hands inched their way up to the middle of his chest. Gently, she pushed him away. Her eyes lingered on his face, the bruised jaw and the swollen lip and the puffy eye. With a soft sigh, she stepped back. Mustering what little dignity she had left, she smiled. "I don't think you should come calling again."

Quinn wanted to pull her back into his arms, to kiss her until she was begging him to stay, but he didn't. She was half his size, but right now, she was twice as strong. If he gave a damn about her, he'd leave. And he'd stay away. Sooner or later the gossip would settle down. He'd go about his business, and she'd go about hers.

So why wasn't he rushing out the door, away from a woman who rightfully deserved a marriage proposal and all the things that went with it? He ought to be thankful there wasn't a baby. He liked children, but he'd make a lousy father. He liked women, but not enough to let one have that kind of hold on him. Especially this woman. She was already too close for comfort.

"Take care of yourself, butterfly."

He reached for the whiskey bottle sitting on the table. After a long lingering look, he lifted it in salute, then turned and walked out of the kitchen, taking the liquor with him.

In the silence that followed, Olivia whispered, "Goodbye, my love."

Fourteen

Olivia set the table in the dining room. The men would begin filing in as soon as the sky darkened. They would wash up first, in the backyard shed that Echo had finished painting that morning. Once the grime of the Hole and the fine dust of the sorting houses had been disposed of, the men would sit down and begin to eat, tucking away an enormous amount of food in a short time. Then she'd serve coffee and dessert and the conversation would begin.

She would sit quietly at the head of the table and listen while her seven boarders—she'd rented the last of the rooms to a Frenchman who had shortened his lengthy name to Jon Laforge—discussed the mine and politics and whatever else came to mind. She enjoyed listening because she learned more each evening. South Africa was as complex in its politics as England. There were the Boers, most of whom were of Dutch descent, who disliked the heavy British presence and who, everyone agreed, would one day take their rebellious actions into a full-fledged war. The provinces north of the Orange and Vaal Rivers had been originally settled by the Boers, and they maintained a strong base of sympathy despite the British imperial policy demanding support of each colony's administration through local taxes.

Then there was the rumor of gold being found in the Transvaal valley, adding speculation to the after-dinner conversation as her boarders projected what other surprises were in store. Fortune hunters were already starting to arrive from Australia, New Zealand, Europe, and as far away as America. Each new batch of men brought a frown from the Boer leadership in Pretoria, but once the rumors of gold had escaped, there was no stopping the stampede of invaders. Like it or not, South Africa's future would be determined by the glittering minerals hidden beneath its wild plains and majestic mountains.

Like her boarders, Olivia thought about the future. It loomed in front of her, as lonely as her past had been, now that Quinn had disappeared from her life. More than a month had gone by since she'd watched him walk out of the kitchen. He was still in Kimberly. She'd gone into town yesterday to shop and she'd seen him, walking along the main street, looking ruggedly handsome in his dark trousers and bush jacket. He hadn't seen her because she'd been inside one of the shops, purchasing oil for the lanterns. Echo had disappeared for almost an hour, and she was sure he had sought Quinn out to ensure his friend that she was still alive and well.

And she was, if one could call her daily existence being alive.

She ate. She slept. She walked. She talked. But her heart wasn't involved in any of her actions; it lay numb inside her chest. Lying in the darkness of her room, after everyone else in the house was asleep, she would relive each and every moment she had spent with Quinn. The arguments, the long silences, the kisses, and the few short hours she'd spent as his lover. She cursed the adage that time cured all things, because it wasn't true.

Time didn't cure love. It only intensified the emotion, making it almost unbearable.

The question of whether or not she would go on loving Quinn for the rest of her life wasn't one she asked herself any longer. There were no questions at all, because nothing seemed to matter, not the trumpet lilies she'd planted on the eastern side of the house, or the new dress she'd finished sewing that afternoon. There was no past or present or future, only the empty aching moments she survived one at a time.

Her only solace was the wild landscape and the peaceful sounds of the Vaal River that could be heard just before dawn, when the whole world seemed quiet. Each passing day brought a new appreciation for the country and its people and the animals that roamed free only a few miles beyond the bustling mining community. The only thing her heart seemed capable of loving, besides the stubborn, blue-eyed diamond jackal, was the land.

Olivia was sitting in the parlor, reading a collection of essays written by the first Dutch colonists to settle in Cape Town, when a sharp knock on the front door brought her head up. For a moment she let her heart soar, hoping it might be Quinn, but she quickly forced her foolishness aside and, putting down the book, walked into the foyer. The visitor turned out to be a stout woman in her mid-forties with dark auburn hair and hazel eyes. She was carrying a large shopping basket in one hand and a wide-brimmed straw hat in the other.

"You'd be Miss St. John."

"Yes."

"I'm sorry it took me so long to get here," she said.

"I'm Maude Billingsley. I worked for your uncle before he took sick."

Elated by the unexpected guest, Olivia invited her inside. "I can't tell you how much your visit means to me. Several people have told me that they knew my uncle, but he seemed to have been a man who kept to himself. Can you tell me something about him? I know it's an unusual request, but he left England when I was only a child. All I can remember is that his hair was dark brown, like my father's."

Maude's smile was sympathetic. "Benjamin wasn't an easy man to get to know. He liked his privacy. I worked for him for almost ten years. He was fair and decent. I always got my wages on Tuesday, and he never asked me to work on Sunday. I did most of the cooking and cleaning."

Olivia felt tears forming in her tears. "He wrote me such beautiful letters."

"I know. I'm the one who posted them. Do you still have the little lion?"

"Oh, yes," she said cheerfully. She reached into the pocket of her skirt and pulled it out. "I saw a real one on my way here."

"I heard about Quinn bringing you across the bush country," Maude said, giving her a knowing look. "It set tongues to wagging, I'll tell you that."

"I'm sure it did," Olivia conceded. She couldn't allow thoughts of Quinn to keep her from enjoying the moment. Maude had actually known her uncle, worked for him. It was like discovering a long-lost cousin. "I was determined to get to Kimberley. I can't tell you how much it meant to me when I found out that Uncle Benjamin had left me the boardinghouse."

Her visitor gave the parlor a long appreciative look. "You've got the place looking better than ever," she said. "Benjamin wasn't wrong about you. He said you had spirit."

Olivia found herself blushing with pride. "It feels like home to me."

"That's what Benjamin wanted. When he went to Cape Town to find a solicitor, he didn't have any doubts that you'd come to Kimberley. I meant to be here," Maude said. Her expression turned pensive. "I kept the house open as long as I could. Then I got word from my sister. She and her husband have a station near Kuruman—that's north of here." She took a deep breath. "Maggie broke her leg, and with three young ones to look after, she needed all the help she could get. So I closed the house. I sent Mr. Falk a letter before I left."

"The letter and I must have crossed paths while I was on my way here," Olivia told her. "But that's not important now."

"No, I don't suppose so," Maude agreed. "I came back as soon as I could. Mr. Travis, the clerk at the train depot, told me that you had arrived and reopened the boardinghouse."

The two women visited for several hours. Maude told Olivia amusing anecdotes about the ten years she had worked for Benjamin St. John, and Olivia filled her in on the latest news from England. "Bustles are becoming more fashionable," Olivia said, wiggling her nose.

"Not much use for that kind of finery here in Kimberley," Maude said laughingly. "Unless you're planning on having dinner at the big house."

Olivia didn't need to be told who owned the big house. Cecil Rhodes, the man behind De Beers Consolidated Mines, occupied the grandest house in Kimberley. Everyone knew it was only a matter of time before he became the prime minister of the Cape Colony.

Once again Quinn came to mind. Olivia knew he mixed and mingled with the Rhodes family, although he rarely mentioned the mine owner's name. Still, she had to wonder if the ladies on the higher side of town were as stricken with the diamond jackal as she was. Knowing they must be, she pushed her jealousy aside, refusing to let it overwhelm the happiness she felt at finally meeting someone who knew her uncle.

As the dinner hour approached, Olivia invited Maude to join them in the dining room. The older woman agreed, but only if she could help Taila in the kitchen first. By the time the meal was over, Maude had installed herself back into the household, greeting the boarders with a bright smile as she filled their plates. It seemed as natural as breathing for Olivia to offer her a job. Maude didn't hesitate in accepting it, admitting that she had hoped for just that thing.

It was late when the older woman tapped on Olivia's door.

"I don't mean to keep you from your rest, but with all the excitement I almost forgot to give you this." She reached into the large shopping basket she'd brought with her and produced a small wooden box. "Benjamin gave this to me the morning before he died. He made me promise to put it into your hands and no one else's. I've had it with me ever since."

"Then he was certain that I'd come," Olivia said, taking possession of the small wooden box. The intricate carving on the top and sides were undeniably African.

"Almost certain," Maude remarked. "He told me to wait a full year. After that, I was to send the box to Mr. Falk in Cape Town with a letter asking him to send it on to you in England."

"That won't be necessary now," Olivia said, cradling the unexpected gift to her chest. "I wonder what it is."

"Only one way to find out," Maude mused with a twinkle in her eye. She stepped away from the door. "I'll spend the night at the inn, since I've already paid for the room, but I'll be back bright and early in the morning.''

"Perfect," Olivia said, feeling lighthearted for the first time in weeks. "Are you sure the attic room will be big enough?"

"It was big enough for ten years," Maude said. "Good night, miss."

"Good night," Olivia said, knowing Echo would make sure Maude reached the inn safely.

Once the bedroom door was closed, Olivia carried the small box to the bed with her. Sitting on the blue coverlet, she placed the gift in her lap and looked at it for the longest time, admiring the dark wood and the elaborate carving. It was smaller than the jewelry box that held the pearl earrings and necklace her mother and father had gifted her with on her eighteenth birthday, but the size wasn't as important as the giver. She ran her fingertips gently over the wood, knowing that her uncle had probably done the same thing. Finally the wonderment of receiving a third present from him (the first had been the tiny wooden lion, the second the boarding-house, and now this) won out and she looked at the lock. It was large in comparison to the box and she wondered if Maude had forgotten to give her the key. The question slipped away as she remembered the key Sidney Falk had given her that day in Cape Town, the one she had assumed fit the front door of the boardinghouse, the one she hadn't used because Quinn had simply pulled the door open. When Echo had repaired the front door, he had also replaced the rusty lock with a new one.

Setting the box aside for the moment, she went to the closet and found the round hat box that held the collection of letters she'd received from her uncle, the letter Sidney had sent her informing her of her inheritance, the deed to the boardinghouse, and the unused key. She'd kept the key for sentimental reasons, but now realizing its true purpose, she quickly returned to the bed and the anticipation of unveiling another surprise.

The key fit perfectly. Once the lid was open, she stared at the contents of the box. There was a folded note. With shaky hands she opened it to find her uncle's bold writing.

My Beloved Olivia:

This will be my last letter to you, dear child, but of all the words I have written over the years, know that these are the most heartfelt. It pleases me to imagine that you are reading this letter where it is being written, in my beloved Africa, but if that is not the case, do not be concerned that I am disappointed. As I followed my conscience, I understand that each person has their own path in life. Whatever course you have chosen, I wish you happiness.

Please accept this small gift in appreciation of the devotion you have shown me over the years. Of all my family, you are the closest to my heart.

In fond admiration
Your uncle, Benjamin St. John

With tears in her eyes, Olivia studied the contents. There were two more miniature animals: a giraffe, Echo's favorite; and an elephant. She handled the wooden animals as though they were made of pure gold, reverently rubbing her fingertips over them, feeling the tiny details that made them look so alike. After several minutes, she laid them on the bed, next to the lion she had withdrawn from her skirt pocket. The last item inside the box was a small leather pouch. She assumed another animal was waiting inside, but when she loosened the leather string and turned the pouch upside down to empty its contents into her open palm, she couldn't believe her eyes. She'd never seen a raw diamond before, but she was sure she was looking at one now.

It was smaller than a hen's egg, but large enough to make her mouth gape open in wonder. The color of expensive French champagne, it was more oblong than circular, rough instead of smooth. She held it up to the lantern. The stone seemed to momentarily capture the light in its crystallized depth before reflecting it like tiny rays from a miniature sun.

She stared at the diamond for the longest time, unable to believe what she was seeing.

Suddenly a soft chuckle began to shake her chest. The longer she looked at the diamond the more amusing she saw things. Finally, she laughed out loud. How like her Uncle Benjamin to leave her a small fortune and not even mention it. Holding the raw gem in the palm of her hand, she lay back on the bed, laughing so hard the tears rolled.

She was rich! Unexpectedly, marvelously rich!

It was almost midnight before Olivia decided what she was going to do with the diamond. Since she hadn't readied herself for bed it was easy enough to brush her hair, tie it away from her face with a ribbon, and slip into her shoes. The first floor of the house was dark, but she knew it so well she didn't bother lighting a lantern. Once she reached the kitchen, she stopped just long enough to get the shawl she kept on the pegged coat rack near the door. Draping it over her shoulders, she stepped out into the darkness. The sky was a vast black bowl, touched here and there by sparkling dots of white light. The moon hung heavily, its glow pale and ghostly.

She was halfway to the shed that had been divided into two rooms: one, a bath for the boarders, the other, Echo's private retreat. The door creaked open as the tall native stepped outside, blending into the darkness.

Olivia didn't need to see his face to know that he would be concerned about her sudden appearance. Keeping her voice low, she announced, "I need to see Quinn."

"Missy John have trouble?"

She shook her head. "No. I just need to see him. Will you take me to his house?"

Echo hesitated a moment, then reached out, touching her arm ever so lightly. "Stay close," he instructed her.

She followed him, not down the dirt-packed street, but through the grassy meadow behind the boardinghouse. The moon, three-quarters full, lit their way as they kept their distance from the row of houses that skirted the edge of town.

Olivia walked silently by Echo's side, mentally preparing herself for another meeting with Quinn, reminding herself that she had to stay in control of her emotions. She couldn't confront him with her heart on her sleeve.

Although it was late by her standards, Kimberley was alive and well. The taverns were doing a booming business, their doors open wide while the beer flowed and male laughter mixed with the natural sounds of an African night.

When they reached the cottage, Olivia looked at it, trying to picture Quinn living inside the neat little Queen Anne house with its pillared veranda and lattice-trimmed windows. There was a small garden, perfectly proportioned to the size of the residence. The scent of blooming flowers filled the humid night air.

Instead of approaching the first door, Echo led her down the gravel path that wound through the garden like a lazy ribbon. The soft glow of lantern light warmed the windows of one room, and Olivia's heart skipped several beats when she saw the shadow of a tall, lean man pass by the window.

"Missy John wait here," Echo said, leaving her to stand by the moon-washed branches of a wisteria tree.

He walked toward the house. The whistle of a night bird broke the silence and she realized that it was Echo making the sound. A signal that Quinn would recognize.

Olivia closed her eyes against the onslaught of emotions that began to run rampant the moment the garden door opened and Quinn's silhouette filled the gap. She could hear the sound of the two men's voices, low and urgent. Then Quinn was standing in front of her, wearing a white shirt, unbuttoned and hanging loosely over his dark trousers.

"What's wrong?"

"Nothing," she said. "I need to talk to you."

"Now? It's the middle of the night."

Her eyes devoured him, standing there in the moonlight, looking wild and handsome and worried that she'd gotten into trouble. His concern eased some of the apprehension she was feeling. It was so good to hear his voice again. The deep resonant tone made her skin tingle. "It's important," she assured him.

"Is it Van Mier? Is he bothering you again?" Quinn wasn't sure what was going on. He'd been hoping against hope that Olivia wouldn't completely shut him out of her life, but he found it hard to believe that she'd come to his home in the middle of the night to resurrect an illicit romance.

"No one is bothering me," she said, stepping around him. She walked toward the open door, knowing he was at her heels.

Once she was inside, she looked around the room. It was a combination library and study. A large secretary with pigeonholes crammed full of papers rested against the western-most wall. A gold-and-blue patterned carpet covered the floor. The furniture was more stylish than the farmhouse in Calvinia.

A whiskey glass was sitting on an oval table next to a large, comfortable reading chair.

"What's going on?" Quinn insisted as he shut the door. As usual, Echo had made himself scarce.

Olivia turned to look at him, loving the sight and sound and smell of having him close again. All thoughts of keeping this meeting strictly business vanished as she studied his beard-stubbled jaw. Being his lover had made looking at him objectively impossible. She was too aware of the blueness of his eyes, the lean muscles of his body, the crisp texture of the dark hair that covered his chest.

He studied her in return, thinking she looked different, but unable to decide just what it was about her that seemed out of place. Her hair was down, pulled back from her pretty face. He liked it that way. It made her eyes seem larger. God, how he adored those big brown eyes. She was wearing a dark shirt and a pastel blouse, familiar clothing, but . . . "What is it?" he insisted impatiently.

Now that she was here, Olivia wasn't sure how to put the events of the evening into words. Deciding it would be easier to show him, she reached into her skirt pocket and produced the pouch. "It's from Uncle Benjamin."

When the diamond tumbled into Quinn's palm, he let out a soft curse.

"It's part of my inheritance," she told him. "Maude Billingsley delivered it."

"Who's Maude Billingsley?" Quinn asked suspiciously. His gaze moved from the uncut diamond to study Olivia's face again.

"She worked for Uncle Benjamin," she explained, then went on to describe the day's events. "She brought the gift box. There are two small animal carvings and a letter my uncle wrote just before he died." She smiled. "He left me quite a legacy."

"Does Maude know about the diamond?"

"I don't think so," she said, shaking her head. "Then, it is a diamond? I wasn't absolutely sure."

"Oh, it's a diamond all right," he said, cocking a brow. He held the stone up to the light, turning it slowly. "It isn't the *Star of Africa*, but it's damn close."

She watched as he moved to the secretary, holding the diamond in one hand as he opened a small drawer with the other. He pulled out a tiny magnifying glass and studied the stone more closely. When he looked up at her, his expression seemed guarded. "This stone is going to make you very rich. Surprised?"

"I'm flabbergasted."

Quinn wasn't sure if there was a word to describe what he was feeling. Just seeing Olivia had him standing on his ear. Seeing the diamond put a whole different light on things. The stone was superb, a real find. The color was rare, neither yellow nor white but somewhere in between. An expert diamond cutter could turn it into a work of art. She'd have enough money to return to England and live a life of luxury.

That's what he wanted, wasn't it? To put the temptation she represented out of reach. He wasn't as sure as he'd been a month ago. Hell, he wasn't sure of anything anymore.

One thing he did know was that he'd never think of women as the weaker gender again. It was amazing how much damage a female could do without even knowing it. Three months ago, he'd been certain that he'd never feel more than sexual desire for a woman. But this woman, this persistent governess from Portsmouth, had brought him to his knees. She was never far from his thoughts, always lurking in the back of his mind. He was beginning to question just what in hell he wanted out of life.

"The color reminds me of the champagne we drank in Cape Town," Olivia said.

"It's unusual," Quinn agreed, not wanting to think about that night and the innocent young woman who wasn't so innocent now. But how could he not think about her, especially when she was standing a few feet away, looking soft and oh, so kissable?

"Is that bad?" Olivia asked, sensing he wasn't all that happy about her unexpected wealth.

"No." He returned the diamond to its pouch. "Have you told anyone else about the stone?"

"No, not even Echo."

"Good. Make sure you don't. Not a word to anyone."

"What now?" she asked. "Can I sell it to De Beers?"

"They mine diamonds; they don't buy them," Quinn told her. "If you want to cash in the stone, it has to go to Cape Town. Selling a diamond is a lot like selling a thoroughbred stallion. You put it on display first. Once the brokers have seen it, the bidding starts."

Relieved that she hadn't been wrong in her assumption, Olivia held out her hand. "May I have my diamond back, please?"

Quinn shook his head as he reached for the whiskey glass sitting on the table. "It stays with me." He looked at her over the rim of the crystal. "Assuming, of course, that the diamond is the reason you came to me tonight."

A strange fragility filled the room. It was as though the air had turned to crystal and the smallest sound might shatter it. Quinn continued watching her, his eyes as bold as ever while the remainder of his features remained devoid of emotion. Olivia was tempted to tell him that the diamond had been an excuse, a logical reason for seeking him out in the middle of the night, but no words left her mouth. Instead, she stared back at him, her mind filled with memories while her body yearned for the comfort only his could offer.

Suddenly she had the awful urge to tell him that she loved

him, that her life was nothing without him, but still the words didn't come. She'd done more than her share, surrendering to his kisses, taking him into her bed. It was Quinn's turn to say or do something. Until she knew what he felt, if anything, she'd keep her feelings to herself.

"Of course, I want you to take the diamond to Cape Town," she said, making it sound as though he were a fool to assume otherwise.

The fragility was still there, an indefinable tension that reminded Olivia of the night she and Quinn had made love. He'd looked into her eyes then, the same way he was looking into them now, as though he were surveying her soul.

Couldn't he see how much she missed him? How much she loved him?

His bland expression turned pensive as he set the glass on the table. "I want you to go home and act as if nothing unusual has happened. You can tell Maude about the carvings and the letter, but don't breathe a word about anything else. I'll have Sidney deposit the funds in an account for you."

She blinked then, his words freeing her from the visions that always muddled her mind whenever he was nearby. "I'm going to Cape Town with you."

"No."

"Yes."

"No, you're not," he repeated, sharply enunciating each word.

Olivia's retort was just as adamant. "If I don't go, then neither does *my* diamond."

Fifteen

She stood there with an outstretched hand, her eyes bright and more determined than he'd ever seen them. Did the woman think he was made of stone? Did she honestly think he could take her into the bush again and not make love to her? She'd be damn lucky to get out of the room; he wanted her so badly he was shaking with it.

"It's my diamond," Olivia reminded him.

"I know who it belongs to," Quinn grumbled. He stomped across the room and poured himself another whiskey.

If he took Olivia with him, it would be easier than worrying about Van Mier sniffing around her again, which was one of the reasons he hadn't taken another commission from De Beers and been on his way already. But that didn't solve the real problem, which was controlling himself when she was completely at his mercy. After leaving the boarding-house the last time, he'd convinced himself that he was doing the right thing. Keeping his distance might be hell on his body, but at least it kept his conscience from roaring at him. Not that he didn't have enough to feel guilty about. He'd taken a virgin without taking a wife.

His thoughts quickly changed direction as he realized what Olivia would face if she returned to England. What if she married? She'd be an attractive bride if she came with a fortune attached, and the diamond was worth a fortune.

"I'm going to Cape Town," she said matter-of-factly. "It's not that I don't trust you," she added quickly. "But the diamond is my inheritance and—"

"You want to take the money and hurry back to England," Quinn finished for her.

Olivia almost told him differently, but something changed her mind. His smugness bothered her in more ways than she cared to admit. Did he really think she could pack up and leave without giving him or what they had shared a second's thought? Maybe he did. Maybe he expected her to act that way because that was how he felt. Whatever had existed between them was over and done, a night to remember, nothing more, nothing less. If that was the case, then he could go on thinking she was eager to return to the civilized world. It would serve him right if she could forget him. But Olivia knew that wasn't going to happen. There was no forgetting a man like Quinn.

Confused once again by the spectrum of emotions he always aroused, she looked toward the door. "When do we leave?"

"Whenever I get damn good and ready," Quinn snapped. Without any forewarning, he marched across the room. "You're more trouble than you're worth."

He captured her arms, forcing her to endure his embrace when she would have escaped it. God, how she wanted this. But with the same breath, Olivia knew she shouldn't let it happen again. "Please, let me go," she said, albeit weakly.

"Why?" he breathed the word against her ear. "You want it as much as I do. I can feel you trembling. Tell me you've forgotten how good it was between us. Tell me you don't want to feel that way again."

His mouth moved hungrily over hers, sealing off any protest she might have made. His hands moved to hold her close, so close she could feel the evidence of his desire pressing against her. The kiss was impatient and urgent, reflecting all the things that had happened between them and would happen again unless Olivia regained her senses. It was a battle she was sure to lose if Quinn had his way. He'd done the noble thing; he'd stayed away from her. But this time, she'd come to him.

Slowly, his hand lowered to cup her breast and squeeze it ever so gently. His mouth lifted enough to whisper her name, then pressed down again, firm and hot and hungry. An all-consuming desire flashed through him, heating his blood, his entire body. The restlessness that had been his constant companion was gone, replaced by a need that was setting fire to his body.

Unable to resist, Olivia leaned into the kiss, abandoning herself to the desperate, sensual storm, to Quinn and his insatiable mouth, to his touch, to anything he wanted from her. Deep inside, where the passion was swirling in a pagan dance of raw need, she knew she could have waited until morning to seek him out, but she hadn't. She'd come hoping that he'd do exactly what he was doing.

His mouth moved from her lips to her throat, then lower, as buttons came undone and clothing parted. She was able to regain a moment of sanity as he kissed the top of her breasts. "Quinn." It was all she was able to say.

He breathed into the valley between her breasts. "Stay with me," he said, kissing each breast through the muslin of her camisole. He looked up at her, his eyes soft and darker than normal, his voice husky. "That's why you came, isn't it?"

His hands moved inside her blouse, upward and over her shoulders as he peeled it away. It hung from the waistband of her skirt as he returned to taste her again and again, licking at her nipples until they were hard kernels against his tongue. "Tell me why you came," he insisted as his mouth continued tormenting her, making it almost impossible for her to speak.

She combed her fingers through his dark hair, loving the warm thick texture, loving the man so much it hurt. There was no point denying it. "Yes, that's why I came," she whispered the confession as she cradled his face in her open palms. Her eyes glistened with unshed tears. "I've missed you. I've missed you so very much."

Quinn knew from the anguished look on her face that she'd fought her desire for him, that she was still fighting it. He wanted to reassure her that everything would be all right, but he wouldn't lie to her. They were lovers, lovers destined to go their separate ways.

But not tonight.

He scooped her up in his arms and began walking toward the dark interior of the house. Her arms wrapped around his neck as she kissed his throat. The silent surrender was as inevitable as the love she was hiding inside her heart. Was living like a spinster, alone and heartbroken, more honorable than taking what few moments of happiness life had to offer her?

Quinn continued down the darkened hall and into his bedroom. But instead of carrying her to the bed, he put her down, then pressed her gently against the closed door. His body was strong and warm as he started kissing her all over again, rekindling the fire he'd started in the other room. His hands bracketed her waist as he held her prisoner, sending waves of delight through her body as his thumbs slowly caressed the undersides of her breasts. His mouth teased first her collarbone, then her bared throat, and finally her waiting lips. His tongue mastered her, dipping and probing, tempting her senses until she was breathing fast and hard.

At last he stepped back. His gaze was tempestuous as she watched him shed his shirt. He continued holding her with his gaze as his hands reached out. Her blouse was jerked loose from her skirt and tossed aside to join his shirt on the floor. Then his touch turned tender. Fingertips traced the lace straps of her camisole. "Take your clothes off, butterfly. I want to watch."

This was what she wanted: Quinn looking at her, his eyes hot with desire. Quinn wanting her. It wasn't love, but Olivia knew it was as close as this man dared to get. As her hands moved slowly to the straps of her camisole, she realized that in many ways she was far more adventurous than Quinn. At least she was willing to risk her heart in the name of love. Quinn had shielded his for so long, he'd forgotten he had one.

With her heart racing wildly, Olivia shed her clothing, one garment at a time. Her breathing eased as she realized she wasn't the least bit embarrassed for Quinn to see her naked. In fact, she liked his eyes on her, following each movement of her hands, lingering on her breasts, then lowering as she stepped out of her pantalets and moved toward him. Had the wildness of Africa seeped into her veins without her knowing it? Because she felt wild. Wild and totally unashamed.

"You're beautiful," he said.

They stood there, staring at each other. Slowly a faint smile came to Quinn's face, followed by a soft chuckle. "I tried to leave you alone," he said as he took a step forward, meeting her halfway. "I really tried."

"I know," she told him as he pulled her back into his arms.

He moved slowly, sensually rubbing his body against her, letting the hair on his chest teasingly graze the tips of her breasts. She trembled with anticipation as he continued moving, teaching her about the mating ritual. Her palms pressed against his bare chest, then gradually moved lower. When she reached the buttons on his trousers, he moved his hips away, giving her just enough room to undo them, kissing her all the while. When her hands ventured inside his pants, Quinn shuddered from head to toe. Her hands were hot as they stroked him; her words a bare whisper as she told him what he felt like. His hands were just as busy, kneading the softness of her bottom as he lifted and pressed her against him.

It wasn't close enough.

He carried her to the bed, his dark head lowering to kiss her breasts, then her belly, then the top of her thighs. With an agonizing tenderness that brought tears to Olivia's eyes, he continued worshipping her body, kissing the hollows of her hips and the flatness of her stomach before moving slowly, tenderly upward until his mouth closed over the aroused peak of one breast.

She arched and stretched under his knowing hands, luxuriating in the way they teased and tormented until she was pulling at him, bringing him down on top of her. When his hard length was pressed against her, she moaned with satisfaction.

"Don't leave me this time," she whispered feverishly.

"I won't," Quinn promised.

At least for a while. Olivia heard the words although he never said them. She'd wake up to find Quinn sleeping beside her, but this was only one night in a lifetime of nights.

Don't think about tomorrow, or next week, or next year, she told herself. *Love him now, while you can.*

And love him she did. She hugged his body close, wrapping her legs around his waist as his hands slid beneath her. They fit together perfectly this time, no hesitation, no pain. Her body held his possessively, lifting when he tried to retreat, sinking into the mattress when he pressed down. They moved instinctively, lovingly, giving and taking unselfishly.

Quinn saw tears shimmer then slip from the corners of her eyes. He kissed them away. His long, slow strokes gradually increased in tempo. He drove harder and faster into her, until ecstasy erupted, then slowly faded into an elemental satisfaction that left them clinging to each other.

Quinn rolled to his side, tucking her tightly against his body.

Smiling, Olivia rested her head in the curve of his shoulder. She whispered his name.

"What?" he asked, before yawning like a contented house cat.

"Nothing," she replied, unable to explain why she simply liked saying his name.

He drifted off to sleep while she stared into the darkness. She may have forgotten her morals, but it was a temporary setback. Sooner or later, she'd have to reconcile her feelings for Quinn with the cold, hard possibility that he didn't care as deeply as she did. They had so little in common. He risked his life to deliver diamonds, while she'd gladly forfeit the one she'd just inherited if only he'd say three little words. If she gambled as readily as Quinn did, she wouldn't wager her money in favor of their relationship continuing beyond the bedroom. Yet she couldn't forsake the tenderness she heard in his voice when he called her "butterfly" or the gentleness of his touch.

After experiencing Africa, Olivia knew she wouldn't be

content if she returned to England. After loving Quinn, she knew she'd never be able to love another man. His natural distrust of people was one obstacle, but she sensed that it went deeper, much deeper. Finding the key wasn't going to be easy. Before she fell asleep, Olivia decided there might be a way to gain the happiness she so desperately wanted to share with Quinn. She'd have to be careful, but the risk was minimal since she'd already lost her heart.

"Wake up, butterfly. It's time to go back to your cocoon."

Somewhere between a sweet dream and consciousness, Olivia felt the light caress of Quinn's hand as it traveled from the curve of her hip around her stomach and upward to the tip of one breast. Not wanting the dream to end, she kept her eyes closed.

"It's almost dawn, sweetheart. I have to get you back to the boardinghouse."

Slowly she opened her eyes to the pale gray light heralding in another day. "Quinn," she whispered.

He was leaning over her, his gaze soft but sensual as he silently appraised the body he'd loved so thoroughly a few hours before. She was small and delicately built, but she'd matched his passion. Unaware that he was smiling, Quinn lowered his head to place a chaste kiss on the tip of her nose. "I'd keep you here forever, if I could. But . . ."

"I know," she said, stopping his words with the tips of her fingers. She rolled onto her back, raising her arms to him. He came into them, resting his head against her bare breasts, allowing her to hold him close. "Will we leave today?"

"No questions," he told her. "But I will give you one last kiss."

The kiss was lush and warm, awakening Olivia at the

same time it soothed her. Then it was over and Quinn was pushing aside the netting and reaching for his pants.

She watched him dress, wondering how many nights she'd have to wait until she could fall asleep in his arms again. There was an intimacy in watching him dress that touched Olivia as deeply as their lovemaking. These were the simple things she longed to share with Quinn, these special moments when a smile said more than words.

He sat on the side of the bed to put on his socks and shoes. She saw the scars then, a round puncture wound that had healed just below his ribs on the left side and another, long and jagged, on his upper arm. Echo had told her that he'd been shot. A few inches higher and it could have killed him. Silently thanking God that it hadn't, Olivia reached out and touched him, letting her fingers trail down the length of his spine, then across his lower back, following the waistband of his trousers. He looked over his shoulder and smiled.

She smiled back, hoping the trip to Cape Town would provide her with the time she needed to win his trust. In medieval times, castles were captured by laying siege to them. The process took longer than an outright battle, but the results were the same. The drawbridge was eventually lowered, and the victorious knight claimed the fortress. Olivia was determined to claim Quinn's heart the same way. If she was successful, her diamond would be the last one he'd deliver.

Quinn gathered up her clothes and placed them on the end of the bed. Once again his gaze roamed over her. "Get dressed before I change my mind and say to hell with reputations."

A short time later they were walking through the dewy scrub grass, side by side, close but not touching. From the ecstasy of the night, they were once again strangers, silent and brooding, consumed by individual thought. There was just enough light for Olivia to make her way without having to hold Quinn's hand. They walked south, their path paralleled by the shanty houses and the taverns that had long since closed their doors. Somewhere in the dimly lit distance, the river bubbled over rocks smoothed by the endless current. Here and there something moved in the taller grass, but Quinn seemed unconcerned so Olivia kept walking.

When they reached the boardinghouse, she prepared herself for another one of his stiff goodbyes. She moved ahead of him toward the door, but his hand reached out and gently brought her to a halt.

Quinn felt her body go as straight as a hunter's spear. She was such a puzzlement at times. One minute she was looking at him with those velvet eyes, the next she was acting as if he had no right to touch her. "Pack a small bag," he said casually. His hand drifted from just below her elbow to wrap around her wrist. His thumb dropped down to lightly caress the center of her palm. "When I decide it's time, I'll come for you. Be ready to leave."

"What will I say to Maude and Taila?" she asked, knowing Echo would be going with them. She tried to keep her voice as calm as his, but it wasn't easy. His thumb was still rubbing sensually over her palm. The movement was creating queer little sensations in the pit of her stomach.

"Nothing," he replied.

"But—"

"Nothing," he repeated, his voice low but firm. "You can send them a wire once we reach Prieska. Until then, not a word. Understand?"

Olivia nodded. Their eyes met and locked. She struggled to contain the emotions that rose inside her, emotions she fought each time Quinn left her. She wanted to cry, to fist her hands and beat them against his chest. Maybe then his heart would feel something. But instead of letting her feelings reign, she stood stiffly in front of him, holding back the tears.

His hand dropped away, but the release was only momentary. His arms encircled her shoulders, pulling her against his chest. "You have to trust me," he said. "I'll get you and the diamond to Cape Town safely."

I'm not worried about me, Olivia thought. *I'm worried about us. Oh, Quinn, can't those beautiful blue eyes see a thing? Can't you see how much you mean to me? How much Africa means to me? Can't you see the irony in asking me to trust you, while you continue to distrust everyone and everything?*

"Go inside," he whispered. "I'll be back before you know it."

She stepped away from him, but the yearning was still in her eyes. The wind blew over the land with a hushed whisper, and Olivia longed to tell Quinn that she loved him. He smiled before leaving her. The tenderness of the expression increased the hope that she wasn't wrong about him, that somewhere in his well-defended heart, Matthew Quinlan just might love her.

True to form, Quinn showed up when Olivia least expected him. He stood in the doorway of the kitchen, straight and tall. The screen door uttered a creaky complaint as he opened it and stepped inside. "It's time to go."

"Now?"

It had been four days since he'd left her standing in the predawn light.

"Now."

Olivia untied the white apron she'd placed over her skirt, despairing that she'd ever find any coherency in the man's actions. She nibbled on her lower lip as she went into her bedroom and withdrew the valise she'd packed from underneath the bed. It didn't seem right to just up and vanish, offering no explanation to the women who worked for her, but she'd promised Quinn that she wouldn't say a word, so she hadn't. When she returned to the kitchen, carrying the valise and the linen jacket she'd bought in Cape Town, Quinn was there, talking to Echo.

As their eyes met, a taunt awareness caught and held them. Echo must have sensed it because he took the valise from her hand, then left the room, giving them a few moments alone.

"Did you bring the diamond?" she asked, realizing she hadn't even thought about it since she'd turned it over to him.

"Wouldn't be much use in going to Cape Town without it," he replied dryly.

He stared at her, standing there in the middle of the room, her eyes big and luminous, her face prettier each time he saw it. Unsmiling, he wondered what she'd do once the diamond was sold. An unconscious scowl drew his eyebrows down. What difference did it make? Once he got her to Cape Town, what she did wasn't any of his business. *That's what you said the first time around. You thought you could drag her across the bush, dump her on the steps of the boarding-house, and forget her. It didn't work then. What in hell makes you think it's going to work now?*

"Is something wrong?" Olivia asked, seeing the change in Quinn's expression.

"Let's go," he said more harshly than he'd intended.

They boarded the train for Prieska a short time later. Once again, Olivia entered the De Beers's private car, but this time she didn't give the lavish accommodations a minute's thought. Quinn was back to being all business. He hadn't given her so much as a cursory glance since they'd left the boardinghouse.

Grumbling under her breath, she gasped in surprise as he came up behind her, cinched one arm around her waist and pulled her close. "Kiss me, woman," he whispered into her ear.

"I will not," she told him, doing her best to pry his arm away. She slapped at his hand as it slipped around her body, then upward, not stopping until it rested just below her breasts. "Let me go! You're impossible."

"I'm hungry for a kiss," Quinn said, pushing against her backside, letting her feel what she could do to him. "It's been a long time, butterfly."

"And it's going to be even longer," she huffed. "Just because I let you make love to me doesn't mean I answer commands like a leash dog. Now, let me go."

He did, albeit reluctantly.

When she swirled around to face him, her eyes were sparkling. "We need to come to an understanding, Mr. Quinlan."

"So, it's Mr. Quinlan again, is it?"

"I think it's always been," she said, almost sadly. Taking off her hat, she placed it on a small marble-topped table. "No more kisses," she announced, meeting his gaze to see how he'd react.

The train whistle screeched as the assembly of passenger and freight cars jerked forward. Olivia swayed precariously for a split second, then caught her balance. Quinn didn't move at all. His feet were planted firmly on the green carpet while he stared at her. It wasn't happening exactly as she'd planned, but then she hadn't expected him to pounce on her the moment the door was closed.

"The first time we traveled together, you demanded a

kiss a day as compensation for your services," she said. "Well, this time I have a demand."

Quinn continued staring at her. From the tips of her well polished shoes to the honey-brown curls atop her head, she was all woman. *His woman.* At least until he got her to Cape Town. Wondering what she had up her sassy sleeve this time, he pulled a cheroot from his jacket pocket and rolled it between his fingers. "What?"

"Where's the diamond?"

"It's safe," Quinn replied impatiently. "What demand?"

Doing her best to conceal her real feelings, Olivia assumed her teaching tone of voice. "Instead of a kiss a day, I want a question a day."

"A question?"

She removed her jacket, folding it neatly before she draped it over the back of the settee. She heard Quinn strike a match to light his cigar. Using time to her advantage, she lowered the window, then took a long, deep breath of fresh air. When she looked at him again, she almost smiled. Her diamond jackal looked perplexed. It was the first time she'd ever seen him appear anything but arrogantly confident.

"I shall ask a question, and you will answer it," she explained.

"What kind of question?"

"Whatever comes to mind," she replied, making herself comfortable on the settee. She had to lean her head back to meet his gaze. "And you will answer each and every one of them."

"What if I don't answer them at all?"

"Then I shall ask for my diamond back," she retorted. "I'll postpone the trip to Cape Town until I've retained another guide."

He blew a ring of pale smoke, then watched it drift lazily out the window. "We've had this conversation before."

"As I recall, you told me that you had enough influence to keep anyone from taking me anywhere. Unfortunately, that won't work this time. I'm not as easily intimidated as I was three months ago."

A quiet intensity filled the rail car. Quinn almost told her that she'd never been easy to intimidate, then changed his mind. She certainly wasn't the innocent young woman he'd met in Cape Town. Centuries had passed in the short amount of time she'd been in South Africa. Now, she was a woman in every sense of the word. He'd made her one, insisting on a kiss a day, then slowly, cunningly seducing her until she'd given him her virginity. He'd unpinned her hair and watched it tumble down her naked back. He'd watched her shed her clothing, moving toward him like a moonwashed nymph, soft and womanly and willing. He'd kissed her and joined their bodies in the most intimate of acts. He'd slept with her in his arms. And she'd asked nothing in return. Nothing but her original request, that he see her safely to Kimberley. Whatever she demanded now, she deserved.

He laughed lightly, admitting defeat. "Very well, butter-fly. A question a day." His eyes grew suddenly piercing, their color darkening to the intense shade that reminded her of sapphires. "But be forewarned, you may not like the answer."

"As long as it's an honest one," she replied, feeling triumphant.

"I don't know any other kind," Quinn returned candidly.

It was almost midnight before Olivia had an opportunity to present her first question. Quinn had left her shortly after relenting to her demand. She'd spent the day staring out the window, wondering if she dared to push this man to the limits of his patience. She looked up as Quinn entered the rail car. *I'll know soon enough*, she said to herself, as he strolled to the chess table and idly fingered one of the ivory pieces.

"I thought you'd be in bed by now," he said, giving her a quick glance.

She noted the shadow of beard on his face and the scent of tobacco that clung to his clothing. He'd taste of Irish whiskey, if she kissed him.

Quinn lowered one of the windows, then sat down and lit a cheroot. His eyes moved appreciatively over her. An unexpected stirring, deep down inside, made him shift his weight restlessly in the chair. He wanted to toss the cigar out the window, turn down the lantern, and make his way to her in the darkness. "What will you do with the money?" he asked unexpectedly. "Buy a house in London?"

"The questions are supposed to be mine," Olivia reminded him.

He stretched out his legs. "Then ask one."

She pondered the unasked question for so long, Quinn thought she might decline asking it. He remained silent.

"Why were you so eager to fight with Hans Van Mier?"

Quinn leaned back in the chair. Another puff of cigar smoke was exhaled before he replied in an unemotional voice. "There are several answers to that question."

"It's still one question." She turned so she was facing him. Folding her hands in her lap, she waited.

Quinn tossed the cheroot out the window. After several long moments, he exhaled a low sigh, then met her gaze. "The night I won Jerulla, Hans was taking cards at the same table." He paused, mulling over what he was about to say. "Apparently, he'd seen Jerulla before. I'm not sure of the circumstances. All I know is that he wanted her bad enough to cheat.''

"But you won."

A wicked smile lifted one corner of his mouth. "I cheat better than he does."

"You said the question had several answers."

He gave her a disgruntled look. Beyond the window, there was nothing to be seen but darkness. No silver moon, no blinking stars, nothing but the empty void of the night.

Olivia sat patiently.

"Some things can't be explained," Quinn said gruffly. "I've never liked the man. Call it a gut feeling."

"So you used his interest in renting a room as an excuse to . . . to exercise your instincts." She sensed that there had been more than one encounter between Quinn and the Dutchman, but she didn't want to push the issue. Whatever Quinn added to his daily answer had to be added of his own free will.

"Something like that," he admitted. What he didn't admit was that he would have gladly beat the Dutchman into the dirt for no other reason than finding him sitting in Olivia's parlor.

Olivia was struck by the realization that Quinn had probably never vocalized his reasons for disliking Van Mier to anyone before. He'd simply kept them inside himself all these years, letting people assume whatever they wanted.

She longed to ask him a dozen more questions, but she couldn't without giving him a reason to refuse them all. Standing up, she looked toward the decorative partition that separated the sleeping section from the parlorlike interior of the private car. "Did you have Echo rent you a berth, or will you be sleeping on the settee?"

"Is that tomorrow's question asked in advance?" he teased.

"No, it is not. I'm merely inquiring, so I'll know if I should offer you a pillow and a blanket."

"You're being stubborn," he remarked, setting his boots aside before he pulled off his socks. He stood up then, stretching his arms high and wide.

"I'm being practical," Olivia countered. But while she prepared herself to list all the reasons their liaison should come to an end, she was thinking about how much she loved this man in spite of his fixation for secrecy, for he was honest to a fault, caring and generous with other people, and, she suspected, very lonely. "What happened between us before can't happen again. You know it as well as I do."

Quinn did know, but he didn't like it. He moved to where she was standing. His heartbeat became more pronounced as he looked down at her. "Being practical isn't one of my strong suits."

"I know," she said, smiling up at him.

"Do you?" he questioned softly.

"I won't be your mistress," she said. "And you don't want a wife."

No. He didn't want a wife.

She turned her head to look at the settee, because if she kept staring at Quinn's handsome face she knew she'd yield and find herself in his arms again. "You can have the bed," she told him. "I'll sleep on the sofa."

"Damn!" The curse caressed the top of her head as he stepped angrily around her. A few moments later he reappeared with a pillow and a lightweight blanket. He tossed them onto the velvet sofa, then turned his back on her. "Good night," he said gruffly.

"Good night."

From the corner of her eye she could see him shed his shirt and stretch out on the settee that was too short by almost half a foot. She waited until he was as comfortable as he was going to get, then lowered the wick on the lantern and retired behind the silk partition. As she slipped out of her clothes and into a soft cotton nightgown, Olivia hoped she was doing the right thing. If her scheme didn't work, she'd find herself sleeping alone for the rest of her life.

Sixteen

The train pulled into the depot at Prieska. The African sun was making a spectacle of itself, throwing deep golden-red light over the wild landscape as it slowly sank beyond the horizon. Olivia couldn't wait to get off the train. The last day and a half had been miserable. Quinn was being coldly polite, keeping his distance while she sat listlessly and stared out the window. Even the splendor of the animals, grazing on the sparse bush grass, couldn't hold her interest for more than a fleeting moment.

As she left the private car with Echo at her side, she saw Quinn standing on the platform. She took a deep breath, swallowing the smile she wanted to give him. It wouldn't do to let him think that her resolve had weakened. The next few weeks would be the longest of her life, yet she hoped she would have the time she needed.

Quinn walked to where she was standing. He nodded at Echo, a silent signal that the servant was to take her small valise to the hotel and wait for them there. Olivia's eyes followed the servant, remembering the night she'd gone hunting for Quinn and found him in the tavern, and the way he'd followed her down the street, pulling her into the alleyway to kiss her, then warn her away.

The sign on the depot door, alerting people to the services of the telegraph, caught Olivia's eye. "You said I could send a wire."

Reluctantly, Quinn stepped back, clearing the way for her to enter the depot office. There was a desk behind a counter that looked as if it hadn't been polished in decades. The windows were bare. The clerk poked his pen into its ink-stained holder when he looked up to find Olivia waiting.

"Can I help you?" he asked, coming to his feet so quickly the swiveled chair he'd been sitting in crashed into the wall behind him. Paying it no mind, he smiled at her as he approached the counter. The smile faded the moment Quinn's shadow darkened the doorway.

"I'd like to send a telegram," Olivia informed him. "To Kimberley."

"Sure thing," the middle-aged clerk said, reaching into the pigeonholes underneath the counter for the form. "Just write out what you want to say. I'll send it off as soon as you're done."

He stepped back, offering her privacy in which to pen her message, although it wasn't necessary. Being the one to transcribe it into the metallic clinks that would turn back into words once received, he'd know soon enough what she had to say to the people in Kimberley.

Quinn's voice was a husky whisper as he joined her at the counter. "Send it to Maude," he told her. "Tell her . . ."

"What?" Olivia glared at her. "How do I explain vanishing like a puff of smoke?"

"Tell her that your father is ill. That you're returning to

England. Tell her that she's in charge of things for the time being.''

"An ill father doesn't excuse me rushing out of my own house with little more than a change of clothes to my name,'' Olivia pointed out. "She'll know something isn't right.''

"It doesn't matter,'' Quinn said impatiently. "You can write her a long letter once we get to Cape Town. It won't make any difference by then.''

By then. He made it sound so simple.

"Very well,'' she relented. She wrote out the brief explanation, then handed the paper to the clerk, asking, "How much do I owe you?''

Quinn cursed under his breath, then tossed a coin onto the counter. He clutched her elbow and hauled her out of the depot office. When they reached the shaded platform, his hand slipped down to her wrist, then completely away.

They walked to the hotel and into the lobby. The desk clerk remembered her and smiled. Olivia signed the register, counting the seconds before Quinn would find an excuse to leave her again.

"Are you hungry?'' he asked as they made their way up the staircase to the second floor.

"Somewhat,'' she replied. "I'd like a bath first, and perhaps a nap.''

When they reached the room, she stared at the tarnished brass doorknob to keep from looking at Quinn's face. A shudder of remorse filled her, a moment's hesitation as she questioned if she was doing the right thing by shutting him out so that she might open his eyes and heart to what the future could hold.

"I'll meet you downstairs for dinner,'' he said stiffly, wondering what was going on in that pretty head of hers. She was acting all prim and proper again, refusing to meet his gaze, her words short but polite. "Eight o'clock," he said, taking the key from her hand, then opening the door.

He set the valise he'd retrieved from the lobby on the floor near the foot of the bed, then turned to her. Her hands were on their way up, to unpin her hat when he caught them, pulling her forward. "This is ridiculous," he grumbled, holding her against him as she did her best to push him away. "Can't I at least kiss you?"

"No," she pleaded in a jagged whisper. "It will only make things worse."

He saw the tears then, shimmering in her warm brown eyes. He hated knowing that he was causing her pain. All he wanted to do was hold her, but even that wasn't right. She was still a lady, a woman who expected a man to do the right thing.

He pulled her tightly against his chest. He felt his body responding to her nearness, the sweet pain of arousal growing as she moved vainly against him, seeking her freedom. The sensation was quickly joined by another more startling awareness. He had come to care about this woman, but he wasn't the kind of man she needed, or deserved.

"I'm sorry," he whispered gruffly.

"Don't be," she said, lifting her head. "I'm not a child. I knew what I was doing."

"Did you? You're a lady, raised to expect things I can't give you."

"I never asked you for anything. I'm not asking now," she managed to say although her heart felt shattered. Wind whipped against the windows causing the glass panes to rattle. It was the only sound in the room. Finally, Olivia drew on the strength that had brought her to South Africa. "What happened between us happened because we both wanted it."

Quinn considered kissing her then, just to appease the

frustration he'd been feeling for the last two days, but in the end he just held her close. He released a pent-up breath. "Then why?"

"Because you can't see the forest for the trees." Her palms flattened against his chest and gave a hard push. His arms fell away. Olivia stepped back. "If you still want me to join you for dinner, I'll meet you downstairs at eight o'clock."

"Dinner," he said simply, looking into her large eyes. For a moment the animosity between them ceased to exist. They stood in the fading sunlight as lovers, all pretense stripped away as both remembered the intimacy they'd shared.

Saying nothing more, Quinn left the room, thinking all the while that he'd been a damn fool to let her come along, knowing all the while that he wanted her more each day. It was a corner he'd never found himself painted into before, and it perplexed him more than it should have. He should be glad that she didn't have to spend the rest of her life renting out rooms to strangers. She'd have a good life once she returned to England, a future with a husband and children.

He knew that she thought she was in love with him. He'd seen the adoration in her eyes, felt it in the way she'd touched him that night in the cottage. But he was the first man she'd ever had. It was infatuation, nothing more. A woman's first taste of passion was always unpredictable. It was natural for them to think their hearts were as involved as their bodies.

By eight o'clock, Quinn had bathed and shaved and changed into fresh clothes. A few minutes later Olivia joined him. She looked rested, with her hair neatly brushed and swept into a stylish coiffure. Her skirt had been pressed. It fell from her waist in neat folds supported by a single petticoat. Her blouse was white with a stiff clerical collar trimmed in dainty blue lace.

Her glance moved away from Quinn to the hotel's open lobby doors and the gaslight that seeped outside, fading a few feet beyond the thick-leaved *strelitzia* that framed the front steps. The bright orange flowers were in full bloom, their petals almost birdlike, perched atop dark green stems like brightly colored nightingales. The plant was commonly called a bird-of-paradise, and Olivia's mind wandered back to the boardinghouse and the *strelitzia* she'd planted with Echo's help.

Paradise. The plant was properly named, she thought. It was lush and colorful and beautiful, just like the land where it grew so bountifully. Africa, or at least the small part of it she'd seen, was a paradise of sights and sounds and scents, a wonderful place that offered countless opportunities, if only a person was wise enough to make the right choices.

Her gaze shifted back to Quinn. He was standing in the lobby, watching her with eyes that hid his true feelings. Her heart accelerated as he stepped toward her, offering his arm. Wordlessly, she accepted it and allowed him to escort her into the dining room.

The room was empty. The train had left on its return trip to Kimberley, taking the hotel's few guests with it. A table in the far corner had been draped with a linen cloth and set for dinner. Candles flickered playfully in the breeze that found its way through the open windows. Tucked carefully into the corner, behind the dining table, a sprawling fern dipped its green head toward the floor.

"The menu is limited, so I've already ordered," Quinn informed her as his intense eyes focused on her face.

She could read the message written in their sapphire depths. This was the last night before they took to the bush, the last night they'd be eating at a table, the last night they'd be sleeping in real beds. He was trying to make it special for her, using the hotel's restricted resources to their best advantage.

"Thank you," she said as he pulled out the chair to seat her.

"You're welcome," he returned, acting as formally as he had that first night in Cape Town. They'd been strangers then, but no longer.

Since that night, Olivia had learned the most intimate things about him, yet she knew nothing at all. He was still distant, still a puzzle waiting to be solved, still a secret. As she looked across the table at him, she felt her heart expand with love. Like the man, it was a bewilderment. How could she feel so strongly about someone when she knew so little about him? But what she felt when she looked into Quinn's eyes was stronger than anything she'd ever experienced before, deep and real and heartfelt.

A tense hush fell over the dining room after their meal was served. They ate spiced chicken served with wild rice and steamy baked yams smothered in butter. Quinn watched as Olivia cut her food, then tasted it. He thought about what it was like to kiss that mouth with its full bottom lip. He let his gaze drift down to where her breasts pushed against the starched bodice of her blouse. She wasn't the kind of woman a man turned into a mistress.

A short time later, Olivia pressed the napkin to her mouth before laying it aside. Quinn reached for the silver coffeepot. After refilling their cups, he leaned back in his chair. "Do you want dessert?"

Olivia shook her head. The tension between them was thicker than the fog on the Portsmouth coast as she reminded herself that Quinn assumed she was returning to England. If he really wanted to know her plans, he'd ask. Since he hadn't, she was content to let them go unsettled for the time being. So much depended on what he said once they reached Cape Town.

"Why a farm?"

"What?" Quinn blinked as he reached inside his jacket pocket for a cheroot. He always smoked one after a good meal.

"The farm in Calvinia," she said, clarifying the question. "Why did you buy a farm?"

He paused for a moment, then he leaned forward, taking a sip of coffee before he answered her. "The orange trees, I suppose."

She didn't ask him to explain himself. Her expression did it for her.

"I'd never tasted an orange until I came to South Africa. I love them," he confessed with a crooked smile. "The farm had a grove of orange trees."

Olivia looked at him, then laughed. "You bought a whole farm because you like oranges."

Quinn shrugged, then lit the slender cigar. "It seemed like a good reason at the time."

"Was this before or after you won Jerulla in a card game?"

"That's two questions."

"There were times when you got more than one kiss," she reminded him brazenly.

Quinn's memory didn't need refreshing. He remembered each and every kiss they had shared. "After," he grunted out the short reply.

Olivia smiled even brighter on the inside. The man tried so hard to hide who he was from the world. He might use the excuse of liking oranges, but she knew he had bought the farm so Jerulla could have a real home.

"When I was little, my father took me to visit his great-grandmother," Olivia told him, wanting to share something of herself. "She was a wisp of a woman, barely five feet tall with silver-gray hair and wrinkled skin that made her look like she'd been soaked in vinegar water. She lived in the country, away from the coast." She smiled with the memory. "I played in the woods around her cottage for hours on end. She had an herb garden and a huge apple tree. I picked enough apples for her to make a pie, then ate so much of it I went to bed with a bellyache."

Quinn puffed on his cheroot, imagining a little brown-eyed girl plucking apples off a tree. She'd never talked about her family, except to tell him that they didn't share in her enthusiasm when it came to South Africa. He supposed she missed them and said as much.

"Yes, I miss them," she replied, reaching for her coffee cup. "My father can be gruff and unbending at times, but he's a good man. My mother doesn't have an unkind bone in her body. Meredith, my sister, is reserved, like our father, but I love her dearly. She married last year. Her husband adores her. I'll probably find myself an aunt before too long."

She glanced over the rim of her cup, silently asking him about his own family. Quinn didn't say a word. What was there to say? His mother had died from neglect, too young to carry the burden of earning a living in the East End and feeding a son at the same time. Quinlan was the name his mother had used, but he didn't know if she'd been born with it or had earned it by marrying a man who had abandoned her later. There weren't any brothers or sisters, just cold lonely memories of growing up on stench-filled streets with nothing to look forward to but a drafty one-room apartment on the third floor of a crumbling tenement house.

Thinking about brothers and sisters and the possibility of Olivia being an aunt, Quinn couldn't forget that another possibility existed. Olivia could be carrying his child.

"What about you? Our relationship may be platonic now, but there's still the chance that you could be pregnant."

Olivia put down the cup and met his unwavering blue eyes. "What if I am?" Before he could reply, she offered her own remedy. "I could become a widow. I wouldn't be the first woman to cloak herself in such a fashion, if necessity demands it. My family wouldn't question me if I returned to England to tell them that I had met a man, married, then lost him to the wilds of Africa. They think the country uncivilized and barbaric." She paused just long enough to take a breath. "Thanks to my inheritance, I can well afford whatever the future holds. You needn't worry," she went on. "You didn't force me into your bed. I went willingly, which means I'll bear the consequences, if there should be any, just as willingly."

Her words cut Quinn to the core, but he didn't so much as blink. If a man didn't want a wife, common sense said he wouldn't want the children that went along with one either. Of course, neither one of them knew if she was pregnant. It was too soon to tell. *What if she is? What kind of father would you make?*

The question went unanswered as Quinn announced, "So you've got it all figured out. You'll go back to England, wealthy and widowed, with an answer for everything."

"I'll do whatever needs to be done."

Olivia hated giving him such a callous answer, but what did the man expect? If she was pregnant, she'd cherish the child, but she wouldn't marry Quinn out of pity or obligation. She wanted him to love her enough to look her straight in the eye and say it loud enough for all the world to hear. Until he did, she'd keep chipping away at his heart, a little at a time, the same way the miners in the Kimberley Hole looked for diamonds.

Quinn tapped his cheroot against the rim of the saucer,

shaking off the ashes, before he stood up. "I want to get an early start in the morning."

Obligingly, Olivia left the table. Having made the long trek from Cape Town, she knew she was going to need all her strength to retrace her steps. Quinn left her at the bottom of the staircase. "I'll see you in the morning, then."

"Good night."

Seventeen

The summer season was nearing an end, and the karoo reflected the effect of months of a hot African sun. The grass was brown to its roots, short and cropped and completely eaten away in places where the animal herds had lingered for more than a day. Once again, Olivia walked beside the ox cart. This time there were six additional men, all heavily armed and spaced out, two walking directly behind Quinn, two more bordering the cart, with the last two bringing up the rear, far enough back to avoid the dust churned up by the ox's hooves and the large cart wheels.

They'd left Prieska just before dawn, a caravan of travelers headed south by southwest with a supply cart and a diamond, hidden Olivia knew not where. She supposed Quinn had the diamond tucked into one of the many pockets in his jacket, but she couldn't be sure, and she knew asking would get her a fierce frown rather than an answer.

As the sun came up, the land absorbed the sunlight's

color, becoming a majestic painting of golds and browns and greens. Olivia watched as a nimble-necked giraffe made a breakfast of the pea-shaped, pale blue flowers of a nearby wisteria. The animal wasn't the least bit disturbed by the parade of humans walking a few hundred yards away.

Olivia smiled, filled with an unspeakable appreciation for the land she now felt comfortable calling home. Uncivilized as some might think it, Africa called to her soul the same way Quinn called to her heart. She couldn't imagine returning to England, to the fog-filled streets of Portsmouth, crowded with houses and chimneys that belched thick black smoke into the air. As much as she had loved living near the ocean, the bush was better. Since the land was wide and endless, she felt more free here than she'd felt in her entire life.

Only her heart was held prisoner. Quinn had captured it somewhere along the way. She couldn't remember the exact moment when she'd tumbled head over heels in love with him. It didn't matter. What mattered was knowing she did indeed love him, and that with a little cooperation on his part, they could be very happy together.

She walked to the front of the caravan, being careful not to step into one of the small anthills that speckled the ground. Quinn gave her a scowl when she appeared beside him, but Olivia didn't let it discourage her. She gazed down at the stubby grass, then up at his face, wishing he'd say something, anything, so she didn't have to force a conversation. When he kept on walking, not saying a word, she used the time to analyze her current circumstances. Oddly enough, she didn't feel shamed by the fact that she'd shared a bed with a man who wasn't her husband. What others might consider a disgraceful act held nothing but beauty for her. What she'd experienced as Quinn's lover, what she'd felt while being held in his arms, was too wonderful to associate with guilt or dishonor. It brightened her heart, bringing an unconscious smile to her face.

"What are you smiling about?" Quinn asked, moving his gaze from her face the moment she acknowledged his question. He scanned the horizon, keeping one hand on the Mauser rifle slung over his shoulder.

"I was thinking that it's a beautiful day," she said. "Did you see the giraffe? It didn't so much as blink when we walked by."

Quinn shrugged, not replying.

"Now who's being stubborn?" she quizzed him.

He stopped walking. The sun was a blaze of color and heat around them. The hot wind whipped at her skirt, buffeting it against her legs as she stared up at him. Quinn stood with his feet spread wide, one hand on the rifle, the other tucked into the pocket of his bush jacket.

"What do you want me to say?" he asked in return. "I've never been much for words."

"You could try a few now and again," she prompted him. "They're only words."

They were a hell of a lot more, and Quinn knew it. He kept his eyes forward, studying the lay of the land, looking for anything that didn't belong to the wildness of the karoo. Everything seemed as it should be, but he wasn't one to trust in appearances. All he had to do was to think back to the day when Zaruara had been killed to know that appearances could be deceiving. Nothing had seemed out of place that day, either. But he'd lost a good man, and Jerulla had lost a husband and a father for her son.

"Echo said we might get some rain," Olivia remarked, refusing to let Quinn's silence end what she'd set out to accomplish. "It's been so long since I've seen it, I'm not sure I'll recognize it."

Quinn grunted under his breath. Why did the woman have

to keep on talking? Didn't she know the sound of her voice was enough to heat up his blood? How in the hell was he going to get her to Cape Town if she kept chatting away like some magpie? He wouldn't, that's how, and then his conscience would raise its guilty head, and he'd be right back where he'd started, wanting a woman who didn't have any place in his life.

His instinct for perseverance kept Quinn silent as they trekked slowly south. What could he say to Olivia to make her understand that he wasn't the kind of man who thought too far into the future? He'd grown up living day by day, and he still existed that way, taking each day as it came and liking it that way. *Only a few more days,* he told himself. *Once she's on her way to England, I can put things back the way they were.* But he wasn't going to be able to forget her, and Quinn knew it. For the first time in his life, he'd given the future more than a casual thought. It was scary to think just how much this woman had affected his life. He pushed the thought aside, knowing that if he allowed it to linger, he wouldn't be able to prevent the ones that were sure to follow. Thoughts of emptiness and disappointment would swell like a tide inside him, and he'd start second-guessing himself.

Olivia kept the conversation going, jumping from one topic to another. She admired a flock of birds, flying back and forth between a placid sour plum tree and a giant baobab tree, with such eloquent words that Quinn's dark brows lifted inquisitively. Still she kept on talking, sharing her thoughts with him, wanting him to know how much she enjoyed the majesty that surrounded them, refusing to let him shut her out again.

When they stopped for lunch, she gladly accepted the canteen he offered, downing a third of it before handing it back to him with a smile. "Walking in this heat makes me thirsty."

Her lips were moist from the water, a pretty kissable pink that drew his eyes and held them. How many times had he kissed that mouth? Quinn didn't like the temptation it represented or the need this particular woman created in him. It was a warning well worth heeding. If he was smart, he'd keep his distance. "Sit down and rest for a while," he said. "I'll see what Echo's got on the menu."

The menu consisted of dried meat, tough but chewable, and fresh fruit. Olivia sat quietly, smiling inwardly as Quinn peeled an orange and popped one of the juicy wedges into his mouth. If the man liked her half as much as he liked oranges, she wouldn't have a head full of questions and a heart full of doubts. Sighing, Olivia closed her eyes. They popped open a few seconds later.

Quinn was squatting in front of her, holding out his hand. "Want one?"

"Yes, please."

But instead of giving her one of the orange slices, he held it a few inches from her mouth. "Open up, butterfly."

Obediently, Olivia opened her mouth. Quinn gently put the dripping orange inside it, then chuckled as the juice ran down her chin. Her hand moved to wipe it away, but his tongue was faster. He licked her closed lips, sipping at the escaping juice.

Olivia's heart stopped dead in her chest. Quinn always seemed to catch her unprepared. The lightest touch from him and all the sensations she was trying so desperately to control surfaced again. She tried to imagine any other man arousing such feelings inside her, but she couldn't. There was only one Quinn.

"It wasn't a real kiss." He licked his own lips this time.

Olivia chewed then swallowed. "You're cheating."

Instead of denying the accusation, he smiled and helped her to her feet. "It's time to get moving."

His attitude changed after that. They walked side by side for the remainder of the day. She asked questions about the plants and animals that populated the South African peninsula. Quinn told her what he could about the bountiful land. By the time they made camp for the night, Olivia's heart was alive with joy. Unfortunately, her jubilation didn't last long.

The distant rumble of thunder grew nearer and nearer, its proximity forcing their evening meal to be hurried along. Quinn had chosen the top of a large koppie for camp, hoping the hill would allow the rain to drain so they wouldn't be sleeping on wet blankets. He helped Echo set up the tents, then ushered Olivia inside one.

"Stay here," he ordered. "A storm like this can get nasty."

Within minutes raindrops were splattering against the sides of the tent. They rolled off to be soaked up by the thirsty ground. Inside the lantern glowed invitingly as Olivia spread out the blankets. After shedding her jacket and boots, she peeped outside. The rain was coming down in thick gray sheets that had the campfire sizzling, reducing it to a clump of soggy black ashes. Thunder rumbled over the landscape, echoing like primitive native drums.

She stepped away from the tent flap just in time for Quinn to come barreling inside. He was dripping wet and cursing under his breath.

"Damn storm." He tossed his hat into the far corner before letting the rifle strap slide down his arm. He propped the Mauser against the tent framing. He was still cursing as he took off the twin bandoliers and began unbuttoning his jacket.

"Will it rain all night?" Olivia gave him the spare blanket.

"All night and all day tomorrow from the look of things." He dried his hair, muttering something she couldn't understand, then tossed the blanket back to her.

She returned it. "You need it more than I do."

He draped the blanket over his shoulders, then glared at her. "You might as well get some sleep. There's nothing else to do."

"We could talk," she suggested.

"We talked all day," he grumbled.

"It's something to pass the time," she told him. "I'm not sleepy."

"You should be."

She drew a deep breath and made herself as comfortable as possible, sitting down and spreading her skirt out so it covered her feet. The lantern light danced while the raindrops splattered with increasing force. The tension inside the tent grew long and strained.

When Quinn finally looked her way, Olivia's eyes challenged him, then traveled over his body from the dark wet hair sticking to his forehead to the toes of his bare feet. She folded her hands in her lap and said, "Talk to me."

"About what?"

"About anything that comes to mind."

A suggestive smile came to his face. "Let's see," he mused. "You and I, alone, in a tent on a rainy night. That brings several things to mind."

"Anything but that."

"Why not that? It's on your mind, too."

"Not at the moment, it isn't," she lied. "Besides, I haven't asked my question yet."

He laughed boldly, then shrugged the blanket off his bare shoulders and spread it out. When he was lying on his back, arms folded behind his head, staring at the spiked ceiling of the tent, he smiled. "Okay, butterfly, ask away."

Olivia glanced around the tent. It was easier than looking at Quinn. The hair on his chest was wet and matted. She could see his nipples, dark and puckered from the chilling rain that had soaked through his jacket. His upper torso gleamed in the lantern light. His skin was bronzed and taut. She knew a heart was hidden beneath those lean, solid muscles. All she had to do was find it.

Her mouth felt dry, so she licked her lips. "Why did you agree to take me to Kimberley in the first place?"

She could see the uneasiness sweep over him. He took a long, deep breath, then held it as if he were counting to ten. Finally he answered her. "I owed Sidney a favor. He called in the debt, so I agreed to take you to Kimberley."

"In other words, he blackmailed you into taking me."

"Something like that."

He turned his gaze on her. She was sitting on the blanket like a young lady at a picnic, looking all fresh and pretty despite the long day. The muted light of the lantern made her honey-colored hair appear more gold than brown. Her gaze moved around the tent, taking in everything, then returning to him.

"I don't suppose you'd care to tell me what the favor was?" she asked, sounding so polite he was tempted to laugh.

Quinn considered the question and the answer. As far as conversations went, he'd talked more to this woman than he had any other in his entire life. Hell, she probably knew him better than any woman had ever known him and that was saying a lot, since he'd kept a few mistresses over the years. Still, he'd never told anyone what she was asking him to divulge now.

He rolled onto his side, facing her, his arm bent as one open palm supported his head. He assessed her dispassionately, trying to decide if his pride could take the beating the answer would require. It might be worth it, if it would put an end to her ridiculous idea that they could be friends after they'd been lovers.

"I was barely fifteen when I hit the docks in Cape Town." He paused for a moment, then went on. "I could take care of myself, but that's about all I could do. After my first skirmish in the bush, the broker thought I was some kind of hero. He called me into his office in Cape Town, gave me a long speech about loyalty and how hard it was to find in South Africa, then handed me an envelope. Before I left, I was working for him."

"That seems sensible, considering what you did," Olivia inserted, comforted by the fact that Quinn was actually talking to her.

"I was staying in a cheap hotel down by the docks. I asked someone to point me in the direction of a solicitor's office. That's when I met Sidney. I walked in, put the envelope on his desk, and waited."

"I don't understand."

All was silent for a moment with the exception of the rain pelting the canvas tent. The wind whistled through the tent flap, the air cooler now that the rain had come. Quinn seemed to be waiting, debating whether or not he should finish what he'd begun.

"I couldn't read the letter or the bank draft," he said. "I couldn't sign my name at the bank because I didn't know how to write, so I hired Sidney to do it for me. He wrote my name out on a piece of paper and watched while I copied it over and over, until I got it right. Then he went to the bank with me, as my solicitor, and helped me open an account."

Olivia didn't know what to say. She sat there, staring at Quinn, seeing a completely different man. Gone was the arrogance, the smug self-confidence that so often had her wanting to slap his handsome face. This was the real Quinn, a proud man plagued by the childhood insecurities he'd brought with him from England.

His gaze was locked on her, and she knew he was waiting for her reaction. But how did one react to such a confession? Quinn had just bared his soul to her. He'd put his pride on the line, and now he was waiting for her to say something condescending or pitiful, because he always expected the worst.

A memory flashed through Olivia's mind—Jerulla and her flawless English—and she knew that Quinn had had the young girl tutored so she'd never feel the sting of ignorance.

Suddenly, so much was clear. Quinn's standoffishness and his determination were both results of his upbringing. He'd come to South Africa to make a life for himself, but he'd never fully escaped the slums of London. Inside, he was still uncertain of himself and the future.

She knew that he'd wanted to shock her with the confession that he'd come to South Africa an ignorant man. It was another way to reiterate the differences between them, differences that might cause any other woman to have second thoughts. She felt tears pooling in her eyes, not because she pitied Quinn, but because she loved him so much it hurt.

"Don't shed any tears for me," he said, seeing the glimmer of moisture in her eyes and misunderstanding it. "I can read Shakespeare as well as anyone now."

A crack of thunder resounded beyond the canvas curtain, but Olivia barely heard it. She was moving toward Quinn, then sitting down beside him, close enough for him to see the gold flecks in her dark brown eyes.

"I'm not crying," she told him, speaking in soft contrast to the violent raindrops that were bombarding the tent.

A bronzed fingertip lightly wiped a tear off the crest of her cheek. "Then what is this?"

She shrugged her shoulders because everything she wanted to say to Quinn included the word love, and he wasn't ready to hear that, at least not yet. She started to speak, but he stilled her words with a now damp fingertip placed gently against her lips. Their eyes locked, and she found herself absorbed by the shape and hues and textures of his face, the dark thickness of his eyelashes, the beard stubble that darkened his lower jaw.

Sitting with him, while the rain drenched the outside world, it was easy to remember all the intimate details of his body and the way he had used it to please her. She knew how gentle his hands could be, and how arousing. She'd felt the power of his desire and the contentment that had come afterward. He'd changed her life in ways he couldn't imagine, and the change was irreversible. She could never go back. Love couldn't be undone once it was felt. Her heart clutched with fear that she might fail in proving to him that love was real, that what she felt for him was right and meant to be.

They were so close that Quinn could see the pulse beating just above the unbuttoned collar of her Victorian blouse. Tension tugged at his body as the wind whistled around the tent, the only sound in the night. His nostrils flared as he inhaled the female scent of her. He thought of how easy it would be to pull her into his arms and love her just one more time. All he had to do was kiss her and she'd yield. The passion between them was too easily ignited. He could have her now, but he knew she'd regret it afterward, when she woke up and realized that nothing had changed. He'd still be a diamond jackal, a man who thrived on danger, and she'd still be a pretty English lady who believed in romance and dreams come true. He'd still be a hellion from the East End who hadn't learned to write his own name until a week before his sixteenth birthday, and she'd still be a former governess, an educated woman who read poetry before she retired for the night.

"You'd better get some sleep," he said, the words strained because he didn't want to say them. He should have gone into one of the other tents, but he hadn't wanted to leave her alone during the storm. For some foolish reason, he couldn't get out of the habit of taking care of her.

"Thank you," she whispered, smiling faintly.

"For what?"

"For talking to me," she told him. Then before he realized what she was doing, she leaned close and kissed him. It was a sweet good-night kiss, the kind a wife of many years might give her husband, casual but heartfelt.

His hands clenched into fists to keep from pulling her back as she made her way to the blanket on the opposite side of the tent. Curiously, the simple kiss she'd given him made him burn more hotly for her than it should. He turned his head away and stretched out again, listening to her fuss with the blanket, spreading it out until there wasn't a wrinkle to be found. The rustle of a starched petticoat followed. She was lying down now, but not next to him, not close enough for him to keep her warm.

Quinn told himself it was for the best. He understood, even if she didn't, that they were taking a risk every time they got close to each other. There was still no guarantee that she wasn't already carrying his child, and he didn't have the slightest idea how he'd react if she told him that she was going to have a baby. He sure as hell wouldn't let her waltz out of his life if she was pregnant, but that was a bridge he'd cross if and when he came to it. In the meantime, there wasn't much he could do but what he was doing, getting her and her diamond to Cape Town as fast as he could. After that, he'd go back to doing what he did best, living one day at a time.

Lying quietly on her own side of the tent, Olivia was shaken by the experiences that had molded Quinn's life. She could only imagine the life he'd led as a child, the insecurity and day-to-day calamities of living in London's poorest neighborhood. She'd heard stories about how children in the East End lived, and how so many of them died from sickness and neglect. She closed her eyes tight against the image of an undernourished little boy with bright blue eyes stealing food from a vendor's cart. Despite the fact that that little boy was now a grown man, strong and independent and financially secure, she couldn't help but grieve for him. He'd missed so much of what life had to offer: love and laughter and the good times that could only be shared with family, all the things Olivia longed to share with him.

The storm continued. Rain slashed at the tent, wind howled across the open African plain, and the thirsty ground soaked up the water until there was so much of it the earth couldn't keep up with the heavens and tiny rivulets of water raced down the hillside.

Inside the tent, dry and passably comfortable, Olivia fell into a fitful sleep. The dawn chirping of birds, sheltered in the rain-soaked branches of nearby trees, joined with another sound. Olivia moaned, then turned onto her side, drowsily thinking the thunder sounded strange. Her mind was still trying to explain the unusual noise when Quinn covered her from head to toe. A bullet ripped through the canvas above their heads.

Someone was shooting at them!

Eighteen

Olivia didn't waste her breathing asking who or why. Quinn was a diamond jackal on his way from the richest mine in South Africa to Cape Town. Whoever was shooting at them in the predawn darkness had to be after diamonds.

Quinn cursed low and long as another bullet ripped through the tent.

Silently, Olivia swallowed her fear. There wasn't much else she could do. Quinn was lying on top of her again, protecting her with his own body.

"Send out the woman. I'm not interested in hurting her."

Olivia's eyes went wide as she recognized the voice.

The sudden tightness of Quinn's body told her he'd recognized the Dutchman's distinct accent as well. He whispered for her not to move so much as a muscle, then rolled to the side, taking his weight off her so he could concentrate on the business at hand. She heard the bolt of the Mauser rifle being slid into place.

Men's voices and the methodical dripping of water off tree branches and canvas drifted into the tent. Olivia heard Echo shouting orders to the men on guard. His commands were answered by more gunfire.

"I'm going outside,'' Quinn whispered, putting his mouth against her ear.

"No,'' Olivia pleaded, keeping her voice just as low.

"Don't worry, butterfly,'' he said, brushing his lips over her temple. "I'm better at this than the Dutchman. I always have been.''

The reassurance didn't keep Olivia's stomach from knotting. She turned her head, wanting to see Quinn's face, needing to see that his eyes expressed the same confidence as his voice. He touched his index finger to his mouth, signaling for her to be quiet, then placed it against her lips. She kissed it, then forced a smile to her face. She didn't want Quinn to be so preoccupied with her that he didn't take care of himself.

"Stay here until I come back for you,'' he told her.

"It's Van Mier,'' she whispered. "He wants you dead.''

"Wanting something and getting it are two different things,'' Quinn breathed against her mouth. Then he was kissing her, quick and hard.

When he moved away, Olivia felt the loss of his body's warmth and immediately began to shiver. She took a slow, careful breath, praying that Quinn was as good as his reputation. Common sense told her that Van Mier wasn't courageous enough to face Quinn and six other men alone. He probably had twice that many men with him.

A deeply controlled vengeance raced through Quinn's body as he made his way toward the tent that had housed Echo and two other men during the stormy night. Crawling on his belly, he vowed that the Dutchman's duplicity would end here and now, on a koppie in the wild bush country he boasted of knowing so well. Quinn was going to put an end to the thievery he was certain Van Mier had been dealing in for years. He suspected that the Dutchman had masterminded several diamond robberies, including the one that had cost Zaruara his life. The thought of Olivia's fate if Van Mier got his hands on her was enough to make Quinn's blood boil. On the surface, the Dutchman gave the appearance of a gentleman, but underneath he was a coldhearted bastard who didn't give a damn about anyone but himself.

"I want the diamonds," the Dutchman called out. His voice echoed through the dim morning air. "And the woman."

Olivia fought the urge to get up and run after Quinn. She lay quietly in the tent, belly down, her head resting on her folded arms while the seconds ticked by as slowly as the night was taking to fade into day. Alone and more frightened than she'd ever been in her entire life, she regretted that she hadn't told Quinn that she loved him. What if she never got the chance?

Long, heartwrenching minutes went by before another shot sliced through the silence. It was followed by a painful grunting sound, then dull silence again.

"That's one less murdering thief to worry about," she heard Quinn shout. "You're not going to get what you came for, Van Mier."

"Don't bet on it," came the reply.

"I'm betting the hyenas are going to make a meal out of you," Quinn countered angrily.

There was more shooting and more grunts of pain as bullets found their mark.

Olivia took a shaky breath as the tent flap slid open. She could make out the image of a man, crawling low to the ground. A big hand came up, signaling that she needn't be frightened. It was Echo. "Missy John all right?"

"Yes. What about Quinn?"

"No worry about Quinn," Echo told her. "He make Dutchman sorry for all this trouble."

"We could give him the diamond," she suggested. "Maybe he'll go away."

"He be too dead to go anywhere," Echo stated with conviction, then stretched out on the ground where Quinn had lain a few minutes earlier. "I stay close. Missy John no worry."

Olivia couldn't help but worry. Quinn was out there. The koppie didn't offer much in the way of shelter or concealment. Once the sun was up, he'd be easy to see. So would the rest of the men.

Without warning Echo's revolver exploded, making Olivia's ears ring. The acid smell of sulfur filled the tent as the body of a man slumped lifelessly against the wet canvas, making it sag to the point of toppling over. One of Echo's bare feet kicked out, pushing the dead weight away. The dull thud of the body hitting the ground made Olivia flinch.

Quinn was positioned a few yards south of the tent, his rifle fully loaded and ready. The heat of anger that had spiked his initial reaction to Van Mier had faded into simple patience. His hunter instincts had taken over, blocking out everything else. Like a lion waiting for a gazelle to wander away from the herd, Quinn waited for the Dutchman to get careless.

Dawn slipped over the bush in a silent wash of color. The outline of grass, trees, and scrub bushes emerged out of the darkness. Another shot, this one to Quinn's right, brought his head around. He saw Amura's white teeth flash a smile as another one of Van Mier's men hit the ground.

Soon, Quinn thought. *The Dutchman isn't a patient man.*

Dawn was barely more than a handful of golden rays when Quinn aimed his rifle and fired. It wasn't the Dutchman, but it was one less murdering diamond thief. The squatty native fell face forward over a thorn bush. The hole in his chest seeped blood, but his heart had stopped pumping the second a bullet had hit it dead center.

Impatient himself, but a hell of a lot smarter than the dishonest man, Quinn made his way around the perimeter of the camp. His bare toes dug into the rain-soaked ground as he pushed his body forward. His naked chest was rubbed raw by the time he stopped near the base of the sour plum tree. The tainted odor of rotting fruit filled his nostrils.

"I'm going to cut off your ears, Quinn, then I'm going to sell them to a Khoisan tribesman for a good-luck charm," Van Mier shouted out. "This is the last time you'll ever cross the karoo."

Quinn didn't say a word. He raised the rifle and fired. Van Mier hugged the ground as the branch in front of him exploded into splitters. Quinn pulled back the bolt of the Mauser and forced another round into the chamber. Once again, the jackal watched and waited.

Olivia counted the shots, praying with the echo of each fired bullet that Quinn wasn't hurt. Echo was still beside her. Nothing about the big native moved but his eyes. He studied the canvas wall of the tent, his revolver reloaded and readied for the slightest sign that one of Van Mier's men was close enough to do her any harm. No human shadows darkened the canvas. All was quiet.

Silently Quinn inched his way closer to the stand of scrub bushes, the only thing big enough to hide a full-grown man. He was almost there when he saw the Dutchman, crouched like an animal in the thicket. His blond hair was plastered to his skull, dripping wet, just like his clothes. *That's how he managed to sneak up on us,* Quinn thought. *He walked all night.*

Van Mier saw him a second later. He fired, putting a

bullet into the ground a few inches from Quinn's head. Mud splattered as the bullet buried itself into the damp ground. The Dutchman's voice ripped through the tawny dawn, ordering his men to forget about the woman and kill anything that moved. Quinn pitched his weight to the left, then rolled. The sound of a rifle bolt pushing another cartridge into the chamber told him to keep rolling. Van Mier had the advantage of being on his feet. He could aim and fire better than a man spinning downhill.

Quinn avoided another bullet before he rolled to a stop. He flipped over and instinctively aimed the Mauser. There was a groan, then a crashing sound as the Dutchman's body gave a violent jerk, then fell face forward onto the muddy ground. The two men who were hiding in the thicket with him stood up and fired. One aimed his weapon at Quinn. The other opened fire on the camp.

Olivia screamed as the world exploded with the staccato crackle of gunfire. Bullets sprayed the tent. Echo flinched, then cursed. She looked over her shoulder to see bright red blood flowing from a wound in his leg.

"You're hurt," she cried out.

"No move," Echo grunted, unable to disguise the pain in his voice.

The gunfire had stopped, but Olivia had no way of knowing which side had been victorious. Blood was seeping from Echo's wound; the bullet had ripped a path through skin and muscle, but it had missed the bone.

A noise from outside brought the wounded native up and around. His ebony eyes were glazed with pain. Sweat dotted his forehead as he aimed his weapon at the approaching sound. Olivia drew in a breath and held it as the flap of the tent was peeled back. Tears born in fear turned to joy as Quinn came into view. Her beloved diamond jackal was covered with mud, but he was alive.

Without realizing that she'd moved, Olivia found herself in Quinn's arms. Her hands stroked every inch of him she could reach, reassuring herself that he was uninjured. All she felt was hard, lean muscle. The fear that had had her trembling moments before vanished, driven away by the strength of Quinn's arms. She buried her face in the curve of his neck and listened to the soft echo of his pulse beat. A deep breath brought the scent of earth and rain and man into her nostrils. Quinn was alive and well and holding her in his arms.

When she could speak without crying, Olivia looked at him. Blood seeped slowly from several shallow cuts on his chest and shoulders. She pulled a hankie out of her pocket and pressed it against the worst of the abrasions.

The concern in Olivia's eyes and the gentle pressure of her hand was Quinn's undoing. He caught one of her silent tears on his fingertip and wiped it away, then took the handkerchief from her and used it to catch even more tears. No one had ever cried for him before. Not even his mother.

A chill ran through Quinn's body. He didn't want to hurt Olivia any more than he already had, and he would, if he gave in to the raw need coursing through his body. He wasn't the kind of man she deserved. All he had to offer her was passion. He hesitated, then combed his free hand through the silken tangles of her hair. When her eyes focused on him again, he managed a smile. "It's just a few scratches."

"You could have been killed!" She looked deep into his eyes, hoping to see something beneath their sapphire surface, something besides the shadows of rage and betrayal the Dutchman had brought with him into the bush, but all she could see was the surety of a man who accepted the dangers of life along with the joys.

"It's what I do," Quinn told her all too calmly. His arms

dropped to his sides, freeing her from the embrace. He'd just given her the answer to all her unasked questions.

His job went hand in hand with putting himself at risk. It was why he didn't allow himself to love or be loved. But more importantly, it was his chosen profession. How many times had he done exactly what he'd done this morning? How many thieves had he outsmarted? How many bullets had he cheated? Not all of them, Olivia knew. She'd seen the scars that proved he wasn't invincible.

Her nails bit into the palms of her clenched hands as she fought the urge to confess just how much she'd come to love this man. *Not now. Too much has happened today. He needs time to calm down, and I need time to think straight. But soon. One way or the other, I can't keep these feelings locked inside me. Telling him I love him can't be any worse than carrying it around unsaid. Unless I'm wrong, and he doesn't love me in return.*

Quinn looked at Olivia's trembling bottom lip and pale face and wanted to comfort her the way she needed to be comforted. He wanted to take her away from the camp, away from the smell of blood and death, and make love to her. He wanted to hold her close to his body and feel the warmth of her breath against his skin. He wanted so much, but not as much as she did. Marriage was too high of a price to pay.

"Help Echo," he told her. "I'll see if anyone else is hurt."

"What about Van Mier?"

"What about him?" Quinn's voice turned as cold as a grave.

Instead of wasting her time asking if the Dutchman was alive, Olivia turned away and ripped off a strip of her petticoat. She gave it to Echo to hold against the wound while she found her satchel. Before Quinn left the tent, she said,

"I didn't tell anyone about the diamond. How did Van Mier find out?"

"He didn't," Quinn told her. "He assumed that I was carrying for De Beers. I usually am when I head for Cape Town." He gave her a quick smile. "Don't worry, butterfly, you aren't to blame."

Olivia smiled, finding some relief in the fact that *her* diamond wasn't the reason Quinn had spent the morning dodging bullets.

While Olivia tended Echo's injury, Quinn counted bodies. Van Mier had had seven men with him, less than Quinn had expected to find. He scouted around the camp and found tracks where another two men had gotten smart and run away. Normally, he'd track them down, but he couldn't spare the time. He had one goal now, getting Olivia across the karoo as quickly as possible. He wouldn't rest until she was at the farm, where he was sure she'd be safe.

Olivia sat in the ox cart, next to Echo, watching the land with anxious eyes. It had been a week since Van Mier had attacked their camp and died for his efforts, but she was far from forgetting the event. There was no forgetting the coldness of Quinn's eyes when he'd ordered his men to break camp as soon as Echo's wound had been bandaged, or the hardness of his voice when he'd informed her that there would be no graves dug for the Dutchman and his cohorts.

"We can't leave them like this," she'd insisted, grimacing as she looked at one of the dead raiders. He was still lying face down in the dirt. "It isn't Christian."

"It's better than they deserve." Quinn's biting reply had ended the argument. "The hyenas and vultures can pick their bones. The devil already has their souls."

He'd picked her up then and deposited her in the wagon next to Echo. They could make better time, Quinn insisted. He'd been pushing forward ever since, stopping only when it was absolutely necessary, breaking camp early in the morning and using every minute of daylight to travel. His determination to make the return trip as fast as possible had gained them several days. One more week and they'd be at the farm.

There hadn't been any more questions.

The mystery that had once surrounded Quinn was gone. Olivia had seen him at his best and at his worst. She'd seen him for what he was, an uncompromising man who lived his life by a set of simple rules, an honest man who expected honesty in return. He could also be a violent man, but only when he had no choice.

She knew Quinn was keeping his distance because he thought that was all she saw, the violence and the uncertainty that came with his profession. Olivia longed to tell him how wrong he was, but he refused to give them so much as a minute alone. Little did he know that his actions had broadened, not narrowed, her opinion of him. She wanted to tell him that he was everything she could ever want, but he was back to being stubborn again, so she had to bide her time.

Once they reached the farm, she'd find a way to make him listen.

Nineteen

"See that she's fed, bathed, and put straight to bed," Quinn instructed Jerulla.

They'd just arrived at the farm. The evening air was warm and humid and thick with the scent of orchids. Olivia scowled at Quinn from behind his back. "I'm not a child," she said as she climbed down from the ox cart. "Stop treating me like one."

Jerulla smiled and said something only Quinn and Echo could understand. One man laughed while the other frowned and skewered Olivia with dark blue eyes. "We're all tired and hungry."

"I didn't hear you telling Jerulla to tuck anyone else into bed," Olivia retorted, grateful that they'd finally reached the farm and what she knew was the end of her patience. Quinn had been nothing but protectively solicitous and coldly polite for the last two weeks. His concern for her safety was flattering, but enough was enough.

Every day since the attack she had thought of nothing but the final question she would put to Quinn as soon as the opportunity presented itself. He'd managed to keep her at a distance for the last two weeks, but no longer. She wasn't getting into another ox cart or onto another train until she had the answer.

She looked at him, but her attention was diverted when the front door opened and Sidney Falk exited the house.

"Quinn wired me to meet him here," Sidney told her before she had a chance to ask. "He didn't say why, but then he never does."

"If anyone can keep a secret, it's Quinn," Olivia replied, looking directly at the man in question. "I gave him a diamond, which I haven't seen since. Nor do I have any idea where he's hiding it."

"A diamond!"

"I'll explain everything once I've had a whiskey," Quinn said, ushering the surprised solicitor back into the house. "It's been a long trip."

Jerulla took charge of Echo while Olivia, Quinn, and Sidney filed into the front room. As much as Olivia coveted a meal and a hot bath, she wasn't going to let Quinn do all the explaining. It was *her* diamond.

"What happened?" Sidney asked the moment Olivia was seated comfortably on the sofa and two whiskeys had been poured. Jerulla would bring tea as soon as the kettle boiled. "I can see that Echo is limping. Were you attacked?"

"Van Mier," Quinn said disgustedly. "The sonofabitch."

Seemingly unsurprised that the Dutchman had had a hand in their trouble, Sidney listened while Quinn told him that Olivia had inherited more than a boardinghouse from her uncle. Once the solicitor's initial curiosity had been satisfied, he leaned back in his chair and smiled. "A diamond. May I see it?"

Wordlessly, Quinn retrieved the Mauser rifle from the gun rack where he'd placed it when they'd first come into the room. He sat down in a chair, then rested the rifle between his legs with the tip of the barrel resting on the floor. Olivia watched in silent amazement as he pulled a small knife out of his pocket and began removing the buttplate. Once the metal casing was separated from the rifle's wooden stock, Quinn turned the weapon right side up and gave it a firm shake. A small leather pouch, concealed inside the hollowed-out rifle stock, dropped into his open palm.

Olivia laughed. "Of all the places to hide a diamond."

"It's as good as any," Quinn replied matter-of-factly. He tossed the diamond, pouch and all, into Sidney's waiting hands. "It's a good twenty carats."

The solicitor agreed with Quinn once the stone was revealed. He held it up to the lantern light, studying the diamond's clarity and size. Olivia didn't give the jewel more than a cursory glance. She was too busy studying the man who had risked his life to bring it all the way from Kimberley.

Quinn was sitting, leaning back in the chair, with his feet outstretched and crossed at the ankles. For the first time in weeks, he seemed relaxed. If Sidney had been looking at her instead of the diamond, he would have seen that Olivia's emotions were about to betray her. She couldn't look at Quinn without thinking about how much she loved him. He looked dangerous in his scuffed boots and wrinkled bush jacket. His skin was tanned to a deep golden bronze, his lower jaw shadowed by two days' worth of beard. He was totally masculine, more man than she had ever dreamed of finding.

Letting her see where he'd hidden the diamond was a telling sign, or at least Olivia wanted to believe that it was. Quinn trusted her more than he was willing to admit. Now, if she could just get him to trust his own heart.

"Sidney will take you and the diamond to Cape Town," Quinn said to her, exposing the plan he'd reasoned out after the attack. "No one will be suspicious once we put out the word that your father is ill and you're returning to England. I'll follow in a couple of days to handle the brokers. Once the diamond is sold, Sidney can arrange to have the funds transferred to a bank in England."

Olivia was too tired to tell Quinn that his well-laid plan was going to backfire. Let the man think he had it all figured out.

"Will you be returning to England?" Sidney asked.

Olivia looked down at her lap. "Everyone seems to think so," she replied, then yawned. "Excuse me," she said apologetically. "I'm more exhausted than I thought."

"I can well imagine," Sidney said, coming to his feet. He returned the diamond to Quinn's keeping, then offered Olivia his hand she rose from the sofa. "We can talk in the morning."

She turned to look at Quinn, but his back was to her as he refilled his whiskey glass. "Please tell Jerulla to bring the tea to my room," Olivia said, giving Sidney a weary smile. She didn't bother telling Quinn good night, but she could feel his eyes following her down the hallway.

When she was in the room where she'd slept the first time she'd visited the farm, Olivia leaned against the closed door and thought about all the things that had happened since the night a tiny bush rat had frightened her. Quinn was probably thinking along the same lines, but in his mind they had come full circle. Well, he was in for a surprise. She wasn't going to be pushed out of his life.

Jerulla joined her a short time later, bringing a steamy cup of tea to ease Olivia's exhausted emotions. While Olivia brushed her hair and prepared to take a long, luxurious bath, the two women talked.

"You will return to England?" Jerulla asked as she smoothed the wrinkles from Olivia's blue robe.

"You've been listening to Quinn." She let out a frustrated sigh, then turned to face the younger woman. "I don't want to go back to England. I want to stay in South Africa. Right here, on this farm. I . . . I love Quinn."

"I know."

"Does it show that badly?"

Jerulla laughed softly. "Only to another woman."

Thankful that someone finally understood, Olivia sat down on the edge of the bed. "Quinn doesn't want to be loved. Sometimes, I think he's afraid to be loved. Imagine that, a man like him, afraid of anything. And he's so god-awful stubborn," she said, letting out more of her frustrations. "He thinks I deserve a life of leisure. He wants to send me back to England, to meet some nice gentleman and be happy. But I won't find happiness there," she insisted. "I can't be happy without Quinn."

Jerulla gave her a rueful smile. "Then don't go."

The thick-chested ox was being yoked to the cart as Quinn stepped outside. It had been three days since he'd brought Olivia to the farm. Three days that had passed with the speed of three years. His patience was wearing thin. Hell, everything about him was on the edge. He'd used up every ounce of discipline the East End and South Africa had ever taught him just keeping his hands off Olivia.

Sunlight streamed along the surface of the land in golden waves that reminded him of her honey-brown hair. The sound of her voice coming from inside the house was enough to make him stomp down off the porch and head for the sheep pens. He didn't want to watch her trunks being loaded, and he sure as hell didn't want to put her on the train.

But what choice did he have? She wasn't pregnant. The disappointment he'd felt when he'd asked and been told that there wasn't any reason for him to be concerned still had him feeling as guilty as hell.

He leaned against the pen railing and watched two black-nosed lambs playing. His eyes followed their lively movements, but his mind was on the woman in the house. Pain drifted across his face at the thought of not being able to say goodbye to Olivia the way he wanted to say goodbye. There was so much that needed to be said, but the words evaded him.

Closing his eyes, he lowered his head in regret. Once, the very idea of caring too much for a woman would have sent him running in the opposite direction. But he wasn't running now. He was standing still, raw on the inside, unable to think straight, unable to do anything but wish things could be different.

The sound of Echo's voice brought Quinn around. He dropped the cheroot he'd lit but hadn't smoked, and ground the glowing tip out with the heel of his boot. By the time he reached the house, the cart was loaded. Sidney was standing on the porch, dressed for travel. So was Echo.

"Where's Olivia?" he asked. The Calvinia Express was one of the few trains in South Africa that ran on time.

Neither Echo or Sidney had an answer.

Quinn went inside, thinking he'd find her in the kitchen, saying goodbye to Jerulla and Montagu, but she wasn't there. He hesitated outside the closed door of her room, then raised his hand and knocked. No one answered.

He called out her name.

Nothing.

He followed the hallway to the rear of the house. Olivia had taken a liking to the small back porch with its wicker chairs and flowerpots. All he found was a forgotten book of poetry and the wide-brimmed straw hat she'd worn the day before, when she'd helped Jerulla tend the vegetable garden.

"Olivia!"

Still no answer.

Where in the hell was she?

He stopped at her bedroom door again. This time, Quinn turned the knob, calling out her name as he opened it. She was standing in front of the window.

"It's time to go," he said, hating each and every word.

Olivia's heart beat wildly within her chest as he hesitated just inside the door, his hand still resting on the brass doorknob. Panic rose inside her for a moment, then subsided. She'd been waiting for days, knowing what she would say when they finally faced each other would be the most important words she'd ever speak. She fingered the high, tight lace at the collar of her blouse, then smiled in spite of the storm going on inside her.

"I have one last question," she told him.

Quinn grimanced, then frowned. "We don't have time for games anymore," he said gruffly. "If you don't leave now, you'll miss the evening train."

"We have time," she countered, taking a step away from the window.

The length of the room separated them, but she could see the emotion in his eyes. Their gaze branded like fire, making her even more uncertain.

Looking at her, Quinn could see the determination on her face. A shaft of sunshine emphasized the golden hues of her hair and the brown depth of her beautiful eyes. He released the doorknob, but made no move to enter the room.

"One last question, one final answer," Olivia said. She tucked one hand into the pocket of her traveling skirt to rub her fingers over the tiny wooden lion that had brought her all the things she'd dreamed of up to now. If only she could have this man, she'd have everything.

"I'd rather have one last kiss," Quinn said, knowing he was a fool for even asking. If he got his hands on Olivia right now, he wasn't sure he could let go.

"Do you love me?"

The words hung in the air between them. Heard but unanswered for so long Olivia felt her heart begin to crumble. Quinn looked at her, then at the window behind her, then at anything and everything in the room. Seconds ticked by, but she refused to budge until he looked her straight in the eye and got it said, one way or the other.

"Do you love me?" She repeated more forcefully this time.

When he still didn't answer, she took a step toward him. "I love you," she declared. He started to speak, but she held up her hand, stilling his reply. "It isn't infatuation, or misguided passion, or any of the other things you'd prefer to call it because it eases your conscience to think that my heart could still be given to another man. It's love, Quinn. Pure and fine and the most wonderful thing I've ever felt. Now, I need to know if you love me."

He'd never said the words to anyone. Love was sweet and gentle. What he felt for Olivia was fire and a stormy kind of passion that robbed him of sleep. Whatever emotions he associated with her tied him up in knots. They turned the moments without her into a pure, living hell. But love?

Olivia knew from the tortured look on his face that Quinn was fighting the biggest battle of his life with himself. She couldn't let his stubborn side win. If anyone had ever needed to be loved, it was this man with all his insecurities and strengths.

She moved to where he was standing. He sucked in his breath and held it. Her hand reached out to touch him. He took a step back. She followed, smiling as her fingertips brushed the underside of his jaw. He stiffened, then stood as still as stone.

"Do you love me?"

"I want you," he said in a choked voice.

"How much?" she urged him on. "Enough to admit that you don't want me to leave? Enough to give up your legendary profession and begin a new life? Enough to give me your name and your children?"

"I don't know anything but jackaling," Quinn said, feeling trapped even though his back was to an open door.

Olivia moved away to stand in front of the window again. The expression on her face was one he'd seen before, in the hotel that first night in Cape Town, and each and every day that she'd trekked across the bush with him.

"I'm not leaving until you tell me," she said as arrogantly as a queen handing down a royal decree. "Echo thinks you love me. Jerulla thinks you love me. Even Sidney realizes that you have some affection for me, although he warned me that I'd have a difficult time getting you to admit it." She took a quiet, deep breath. "I love you," she confessed again. "I don't want to go to Cape Town. I don't care about the diamond, or how much money it will bring. I don't want to go back to England, although it would be nice to have my family visit us here. I think my father might one day understand just how much I love this country, and how much his brother loved it. That was my real inheritance," Olivia said, suddenly needing to tell Quinn all the things she'd felt for so long. "I think Uncle Benjamin kept the diamond hidden at first because he wanted me to experience South Africa. He wanted me to feel the same way he felt about it, the way you feel about it. He wanted me to love the land, and I do. But not as much as I love you."

"I want to stay here with you," she said bravely. "We

can raise orange trees and sheep and babies and have all the things I know you want. You think you're different than other men, but you're not, Quinn. You need a family, a wife who loves you to distraction, and a house full of children who will keep you feeling young no matter how gray your hair grows.''

They faced each other, Olivia taking another deep breath, Quinn unable to breathe at all. She'd said her peace, now it was his turn.

''I am what I am. I don't know anything about being a husband or a father. I live on challenges and danger and all the things you expect me to give up in the name of love.''

''If you love me, you won't be giving up anything. You'll have everything you'll ever need. I'll see to it.''

He moved then, as quick as the fierce lions he admired from a distance. The arms that had been denied for so long wrapped around her. His mouth twisted angrily over hers, stopping whatever words she might have said. Their mouths sealed in a desperate kiss. Powerful hands held her at the waist, as he pushed the hard, aching bulge inside his trousers against her, forcing her to feel his desire through layers of starched broadcloth and stiff petticoats.

His kiss, his body, spoke a message of need so strong, Olivia felt faint. Tearing her lips away, she pressed her face against the hard plane of his chest. ''Answer the question, Quinn.''

He took a ragged breath but said nothing. His hands moved from her waist, slowly downward. They cradled her hips, then moved around to her bottom, to cup her backside and move her more tightly against his arousal.

She kissed him, pressing her lips to the cloth of his shirt, just over his heart.

Quinn groaned, but he still didn't answer her question.

Before she could ask him again, he kicked the door closed,

then carried her to the bed. His mouth sealed hers shut as he followed her down onto the mattress. His hands caressed her face, then her body, pushing clothing out of his way as they moved. The tiny pearl buttons on her blouse were ripped from their anchorage. Crisp linen and starched lace gave way to the desperate search for warm skin. His palms slid inside the hastily unbuttoned garments, touching more and more of her.

"God, you feel so good," he groaned, as he buried his face in the valley between her breasts. When he tugged at a bared nipple, she arched her back.

"Do you love me?"

Once again the question went unanswered.

His mouth moved to her other breast, kissing and sucking and making her body twist and turn from the need he could arouse so easily. He pushed himself up on his knees and looked down at her, lying wantonly on the bed with the sunshine from the window flowing over her skin. Her nipples were hard and wet from his lusty attention.

Olivia searched his face, seeing the need and the desire, knowing if she looked closely enough she'd see the love he was trying so desperately to deny. He continued to stare at her as her hands moved to the front of his shirt. She touched the buttons, slowly, deliberately teasing him as she began to unfasten them. Once his shirt was undone, she pulled it free of his trousers, her eyes sparkling as he made a deep grunting sound of male satisfaction.

Another glide of her hands pushed the shirt off his shoulders and down his arms. He tugged it free, not caring where it went as he tossed it aside and came down on top of her. Bare breasts met a thickly haired chest.

"I'm going to miss the train," Olivia breathed out, thrilled at how wonderful it felt to have Quinn this close again.

"There's another train tomorrow," he said as his hands

moved to the buttons on the waistband of her skirt. They came undone with the same tormenting ease she'd used to take off his shirt.

She rolled away from him as his hand moved to raise her hem. Before he could untangle himself from her lacy petticoat, she was up and off the bed, glaring at him. "Answer the question," she demanded.

She was naked from the waist up, her hair falling over her shoulders in long tangled waves that covered the pink-kissed nipples of her breasts. Her eyes silently pleaded for him to say the words. It was the challenge he needed, the thrill of the fight that always made his heart pump and his blood run hot. But it had never flowed as hotly as it was flowing now. This woman, this prim and proper governess from Portsmouth, had somehow learned all his best-kept secrets. She understood that he loved Africa all the way to his soul, the same way he loved her. The words erupted in his mind, like a flash flood, bathing him in the sweet knowledge that he was loved in return.

"You already know the answer," he said, following the rise and fall of Olivia's bare breasts with his gaze. God, she was the most beautiful thing he'd ever seen. All fire and honey, as wild as the land he loved so much, and just as stubborn, maybe more.

"Do I?" she argued.

"Come here," Quinn said. He was so damn hard he couldn't think straight. "The last thing I want to do is talk."

She yanked at the hem of her skirt to keep from stumbling over it as she stepped beyond his reach, but she made no move to right her clothing. Her hands moved to her hips, to rest there as if she was willing to stand in the middle of the room, half-naked, for as long as it took to get the words out of him.

She purposely remained aloof, just beyond his reach.

"You're going to have to talk if you want to do anything else," she informed him, sounding thoroughly put out by his attitude.

He smiled, his blue eyes tempestuous as he came off the bed after her. She moved away; he advanced, stalking her with skills learned from years of living in a wild, untamed country. "We can talk later," he said, enjoying the game now as much as she was. "I want you naked and under me. You want it, too, butterfly. If you didn't, you wouldn't be standing there."

"I don't want to seduce you," she defended herself. "I want you to answer one simple question." She pierced him with a determined gaze as he reached out to grab her. She escaped to the other side of the room, keeping the bed between them. "It's just one word, Quinn. Yes or no. A simple answer to a simple question."

There was nothing simple about anything Quinn was feeling. He was trembling with desire, with need, with feelings he'd been trying to explain for weeks. Feelings he'd fought and lost. A faint smile came to his lips. His voice softened to a husky whisper. "They're only words, butterfly."

Olivia laughed. She'd said almost the exact same thing to him once. "They may be just words, Mr. Quinlan, but I'll have them said before you put another hand on me."

In all truth, she didn't need to hear the words to know that Quinn loved her. She could see the answer in his eyes, burning as strongly as the need that was still apparent in his body. But the game had come too far to stop now, and they both knew it. They were enjoying it too much. Her pulse was racing, her skin felt feverish, and there was a dewy anticipation between her legs. If Quinn didn't hurry up and catch her, she'd be doing the stalking.

"He loves me, he loves me not," she mused out loud

as she pretended to pluck petals from an imaginary daisy. "Which is it?" she asked, lifting her eyes.

"God Almighty," Quinn raged as he dove against the bed and jerked her off her feet. They tumbled down onto the mattress, all arms and legs and laughter. He anchored her to the bed, as her arms twined around his neck. He moved against her, his hips once again circling, pressing, withdrawing, then returning in the sensual game he played so well. "You're going to make me say it, aren't you?"

"Loud enough for everyone in South Africa to hear," she teased, loving him more at that moment than she'd thought humanly possible. "It isn't every day that a simple woman brings a legendary diamond jackal to his knees. I want my just reward."

"You're going to get it," Quinn said with a throaty chuckle.

With her face cradled in the open palms of his callused hands, he leaned down and kissed her. She felt him shudder and knew he was postponing the inevitable, lengthening the anticipation, the wanting, for as long as he could. Her body began to tingle as he turned the kiss into a silent confession of love. His tongue dipped and teased, tasted and aroused, while his hands stripped away as much of her clothing as he could reach without breaking the kiss.

He pulled away again. Off came her shoes. With agonizing slowness his hands swept up, underneath her single petticoat to where her garters waited. They came off, as well, but not as quickly as her shoes.

"You're not getting out of this room," he said gruffly. "Not until I'm satisfied, and I'm far from being satisfied, butterfly."

She stretched lazily, rubbing herself against his hot hands, loving the game more and more. She didn't stop stretching, and he didn't stop caressing her until she was completely naked. He was so good at this sort of thing, teasing her into doing things no lady would think of doing. But she wasn't a lady anymore. She was Quinn's woman, and if the insufferable man ever got around to asking, she'd be his wife.

"I'm not easy to satisfy, either," she challenged. "Answer the question."

There were no words as he reached for the buttons on his trousers. He stood up just long enough to kick off his shoes, then slowly, seductively remove the last of his clothing. When he was standing beside the bed, as naked as she was, he smiled. "What question?"

She laughed. "You're trying my patience, Mr. Quinlan."

"We'll talk later," he said teasingly. He had loved her before, but this time his heart joined his body. His hands caressed, bringing more pleasure than she'd ever felt. His mouth teased and tormented, his breath hot against her skin, his fingers touching and probing gently. "You want me."

"Yes," Olivia admitted, wishing he'd answer her so they could get on with things. "I love you."

"How much?" he asked as he moved up her body. He threaded his fingers through her hair and pushed suggestively against her. "Tell me, butterfly. Tell me again and again."

"I've already told you," she reminded him. "It's your turn."

"My turn to kiss you," he said, brushing his mouth ever so lightly across her parted lips. "Or my turn to do this?" His hand moved between her legs again, making her shiver from the inside out. He wedged a knee between her silky thighs, opening them.

"Yes, or no, Quinn?"

"Yes," he whispered as he entered her, driving deep with one sure thrust.

Olivia's eyes fluttered close. "I want all the words," she

said. "I want you to say them now. Now and every day of our lives."

"Every day and every night," Quinn promised. He kissed away the tears that escaped from her closed eyes. His body moved deep and strong, giving and taking, loving and being loved until he thought he'd die from the pleasure. "I love you," he said as the ecstasy took him. "I love you."

The room grew quiet once the passion had turned into contentment. Olivia nestled against Quinn's body. The sun was still streaming through the window. Echo and Sidney were still waiting on the porch. The Calvinia Express was still running on schedule.

Lost to the love that had suddenly erupted into his life, Quinn smiled and touched a finger to Olivia's well-kissed mouth. "I suppose I could plant a new grove. I like oranges almost as much as whiskey and women."

She pinched him. "And I suppose I could use the money from the sale of the diamond to build a big house, on a koppie that overlooks the grove. I want a large front porch, where I can sit and watch the sunsets. I love South African sunsets. Almost as much as I love a stubborn diamond jackal," she added. She braced herself up on one elbow and looked down at Quinn. "We're going to have such a wonderful life."

"South Africa isn't paradise," he cautioned her. "It's got some hard times ahead of it."

"Life will always have its hard times," she told him. "But it has good times, too. We'll take each day as it comes. As long as we love each other, nothing else matters."

"You're sure, then?" he asked, finding it hard to believe that his life was changing so suddenly.

"Yes, I'm sure," she told him, seeing the insecurities surface again. "I'm going to spend the rest of my life making you happy," she informed him. "And you're going to do the same for me.'' She smiled then. ''Shall we invite Sidney to stay for the wedding? If it hadn't been for him we would never have met. He can give the bride away.''

''What wedding?'' Quinn teased as he rolled to his side, giving her bare bottom a playful swat on his way around. ''Love and marriage. That's a lot to ask from a man.''

She bashed him with a pillow, laughing all the while. ''You most certainly will marry me, Mr. Quinlan. I'm a lady, after all, who expects all the amenities of a loving courtship. I want flowers and candies and a formal proposal.''

Quinn groaned, then rolled again, putting her under him. ''You're persistent.''

''And you love me,'' she said teasingly. ''Say it again.''

''I've already said it a dozen times.''

''One more time,'' she insisted, as her hands moved in a worshipping caress that said she wasn't going to be satisfied by words alone.

Quinn sat up and roared out loud enough to wake the dead, ''I love you!''

He flopped back against the pillows as though the words had exhausted him.

Echo heard them and laughed, then told the men to unhitch the ox and put the cart away. Jerulla heard the unabashed declaration and smiled, satisfied that Olivia had taken her advice and wouldn't be leaving after all. Sidney heard it and shook his head, amazed that a woman could make such a difference in a man's life.

Olivia laughed to let some of the happiness out. She cried along with the laughter, then touched the round scar on Quinn's chest where he'd been shot. Her fingers trailed upward, to the stubborn line of his jaw, before moving on to the softer texture of his mouth. ''I came to South Africa thinking I could make dreams come true.''

"Have you?" Quinn asked, his voice low, his eyes shining brighter than any diamond.

"Oh, yes," she said, then kissed him lightly. "I can't imagine being happier than I am at this very moment. Who would have thought . . ." Her words drifted into nothingness as he kissed her in return.

"Who would have thought," Quinn echoed softly against her mouth. "Who would have thought that love could feel this good?"

"Does it feel good?" She burrowed against him, resting her hand over his heart.

"Better than good."

Then preferring action to words, Quinn proved just how good love could be.

Be sure to look for HE SAID YES,
in a sexy new series by Patricia Waddell,
set against a Victorian-era gentleman's club,
available wherever books are sold in July 2003!

The Queen of Romance

Cassie Edwards